The Black Art of Killing

The Black Art of Killing

MATTHEW HALL

MICHAEL JOSEPH
an imprint of
PENGUIN BOOKS

MICHAEL JOSEPH

UK | USA | Canada | Ireland | Australia
India | New Zealand | South Africa

Michael Joseph is part of the Penguin Random House group of companies
whose addresses can be found at global.penguinrandomhouse.com

First published by Michael Joseph, 2020

001

Set in 13.5/16 pt Garamond MT Std
Typeset by Jouve (UK), Milton Keynes
Printed and bound in Great Britain by Clays Ltd, Elcograf S.p.A.

A CIP catalogue record for this book is available from the British Library

HARDBACK ISBN: 978–0–718–18739–2
OM PAPERBACK ISBN: 978–0–718–18740–8

www.greenpenguin.co.uk

Penguin Random House is committed to a
sustainable future for our business, our readers
and our planet. This book is made from Forest
Stewardship Council® certified paper.

In memory of Andy Black. A true friend and the first to call me a writer. We still miss you.

I

'No one thinks about death. Any that do are weeded out at selection. It's a job. One that ends up with bodies lying about. But if you're Special Forces material you don't see a corpse, just an absence of threat. Mission accomplished. Someone has to do it. Move on.'

This conversation, the one and only that Major Leo Black had ever had with a psychiatrist, or anyone for that matter, on the subject of his attitude to mortality and killing, had taken place five years earlier. He had agreed to it under sufferance and at the insistence of his diminutive commanding officer, Colonel Freddy Towers, after Black's announcement that following twenty-two years of active service he was leaving the Regiment.

'What the hell brought this on?' Towers had yelled across the desk in his inimitable voice that could rise from measured baritone to screaming soprano the instant he faced contradiction.

'I couldn't tell you, Freddy. It just seems like the right time.'

Towers' jaw had hung slack as he looked at him with an expression that combined incomprehension with a sense of immeasurable betrayal. 'You need your bloody head examined.'

The psych was a top man, a distinguished professor conducting his private practice from sleek modern rooms in Harley Street. He had apparently published a paper proposing that the psychological make-up, even the genetics and brain chemistry, of Special Forces personnel was different to that of the general population. Despite this, his questioning struck Black as touchingly naive.

'When you say "bodies", do you draw a distinction between those of enemy combatants and those, say, of women and children?'

'A threat's a threat. Collateral damage is regrettable but inevitable. That's not to imply an absence of human feeling, but during operations different rules are in play. There is only the objective and the requirement not to be captured or killed. There is no room for emotion any more than there is in the operating theatre.'

'Have you experienced flashbacks? Episodes of anxiety? Insomnia?'

'No,' Black answered truthfully. He had always slept well.

'Was there a period of depression, low mood or lack of physical energy that preceded your decision to leave?'

Black thought carefully about his answer. There had been a change, but not of the debilitating kind the professor was suggesting. He was no doubt angling for a hint that Black had been carrying an invisible, ever-increasing burden that had finally broken him, yet the truth was quite different. 'It was more a sense that there was nothing left in it for me, that I needed new purpose.'

'I understand you want to go back to university. You intend to study for a PhD in military history?'

'That's correct.'

'Because?'

'The nature and purpose of war have always interested me.'

His inquisitor seemed suspicious. He stroked his immaculately tended beard. 'Tell me about the feeling of there being "nothing left in it" for you.'

Black sensed the professor circling around to the same false assumption that had informed his entire line of questioning – that even for a man with his record combat somehow ate away at the soul like acid on tooth enamel, until the raw nerve was exposed. How to explain to him that there was no greater peace than that experienced in the heat of battle; that life reduced to the simple binary of kill or be killed was close to what he imagined a religious experience might be; that in the moment of gravest danger every contradiction of the human psyche harmonized into a single clear note? That combat was a beautiful thing, which, nevertheless, could eventually lose its lustre.

'A number of months ago I was part of a detachment pursuing a target in eastern Pakistan. Unfortunately, our intelligence assets proved unreliable. We were ambushed. I was separated from my team and detained for a number of days by officers of the Pakistan security service, the ISS. I was tortured, beaten, deprived of sleep. They even cut off one of my fingers.' He held up his left hand. The ring finger had been severed beneath the first knuckle. 'But my abiding thought throughout was that compared with me, they were amateurs. If I were to detain you, a threat to cut off your finger would probably be sufficient to get you talking. A credible threat to do the same or worse to your wife would certainly be effective. But to make *me* talk, *a professional*, you'd have to start butchering far more sensitive parts of my anatomy. And with serious intent.'

'May I ask how it ended?'

'I wouldn't like to spoil your lunch.'

'If you wouldn't mind. It may be relevant.'

'Very well. I feigned a breakdown. My two interrogators released my handcuffs so that I could write a statement. I put their eyes out with a ballpoint pen, then ruptured both their windpipes before snapping their necks. One of them had a sidearm. I relieved him of it and there followed a lively period of confusion during which I managed to extract myself from what turned out to be a moderately well-fortified compound on the outskirts of Quetta.'

'How many people did you kill, Leo?'

Black thought for a moment. 'Thirty or so. To the best of my recollection.'

'And you managed this alone?'

'I received assistance from colleagues in due course. Thankfully they had been looking for me and weren't far away.'

The professor nodded. A faint and nervous smile curled the corners of his mouth. 'Forgive me, but this does all sound a little fantastical.'

'Could you or I fly an airliner? Or play a violin concerto? Both are incomprehensible feats to the amateur.' The professor fell silent and shifted in his seat. 'You seem anxious. Are you worried I might lose my mind, leap up from my chair and kill you?' Before he received an answer, Leo said, 'Does the brain surgeon drill into the skull of his fellow commuters?'

'No, but –'

'There are no "buts". If you'll forgive me, that's the whole point – it is just a job like any other. It requires aptitude and practice, but it is only a job, not an affliction.' Black turned his gaze out of the window and felt the urge to be out in the clear autumn afternoon. 'I'm forty-five years old. I've exhausted all the possibilities the army has to offer. Is it unreasonable for me to think there might be more to life than dodging bullets and killing people?'

'No . . . indeed.'

'Thank you.'

And there, their conversation ended.

Later that afternoon Leo Black had emailed his letter of resignation to Freddy Towers and sent another short message to

Sergeant Ryan Finn, the man who for fifteen years had been closer to him than a brother. During operations across four continents they had survived more close calls and saved each other's lives on more occasions than they cared to remember. Finn took three days to reply and did so with his customary abruptness: *Best of luck, you bastard. See you around.*

Time had passed and they never did arrange to meet. Busy lives and a mutual aversion to sentimental reunions had got in the way. Black had now made it to fifty with few regrets, but of those he had, neglecting his best friend and comrade was the one that troubled him the most. And as his guilt mounted so did the subconscious sense that circumstances would one day force them back together again.

What he couldn't have guessed was that it was to happen in the worst possible way.

The runway of Paris–Le Bourget Airport shimmered like molten glass in the heat of the June afternoon. A Gulfstream G450 descended from a cloudless sky, landed softly as a kiss and taxied to a spot on the tarmac where two vehicles stood side by side, their engines idling to keep their waiting drivers cool. The first was a black Mercedes sedan with diplomatic plates. The second was a small white Renault out of which stepped a young officer of the Police aux Frontières.

A door opened outwards from the rear of the aircraft's hull, revealing a set of four inverted steps on its inner face. Three passengers disembarked. At their head was a dark-haired woman in her late thirties with an air of confidence that could only have been possessed by an American. She was followed by two tall athletic men of indeterminate nationality. All three were dressed in business suits and carried identical dark navy holdalls bearing government insignia and the words *Sac Diplomatique*. The police officer glanced at their passports, issued them with permits allowing them to exit the airport and swiftly departed.

The driver of the Mercedes took care of their luggage, which felt heavy and cumbersome as he stowed it in the boot, like equipment for a mountaineering expedition. He returned to his seat behind the wheel and found the woman sitting alongside him. There was no doubt she was the senior of the three.

'Rue Christophe Colomb?'

'*Oui, merci,*' she answered in chilly, though perfectly accented French.

These were the only words she spoke throughout the forty-minute drive to their destination, an apartment building a short distance from the Avenue George V in central Paris. The two men also remained silent. When, from time to time, the driver glanced at them in his mirror, he noticed their eyes scanning the traffic with a level of unblinking concentration that was scarcely human. Their behaviour bore little resemblance to that of the diplomats he was accustomed to driving and they gave him a bad feeling in the pit of his gut.

Immediately after he had dropped them off, he felt an urge to call at a car wash in Saint-Denis where he paid twenty-five euros for the full *Valet Magnifique*. But even after the crew of shirtless Somalis had done their work, the smell of those three still lingered like a dead rat under the floorboards.

3

It was at moments like these that Ryan Finn missed wading through a jungle swamp with his finger cocked on the trigger of a C8 Carbine or leaping from the back of a Hercules at 20,000 feet. Standing like a shop-window dummy in the corner of a Paris hotel ballroom watching other people drink was his idea of purgatory. The young woman he was employed to protect was making matters worse by doing her best to disown him. Throughout the three days of the annual conference of the International Association of Nanotechnology, Dr Sarah Bellman had behaved like a spoiled child, making no secret of resenting his presence. The recent disappearance of one of her senior colleagues from Oxford University's Department of Biomechanical Engineering seemed not to trouble her. Dr Bellman lived in a world all of her own.

Precisely why anyone would wish to harm a twenty-nine-year-old scientific prodigy was not something the civil servant who had engaged Finn through the agency had chosen to explain. Having sat through long, tedious hours of lectures in the Académie des Sciences over the past three days, he had begun to get an inkling. Dr Bellman and her colleagues were making things that were small – very small – chiefly for medical purposes. Earlier that afternoon she had given the keynote presentation. Although most of the technical jargon went over his head, Finn had caught the gist: she had built microscopic containers out of woven strands of DNA complete with lids that could be opened and closed using beams of ultraviolet light. These tiny boxes, thousands of which could stand side by side on a pinhead, could deliver drugs to any cell in the body. She had cured brain tumours in rats without surgery and was about to start work on humans. Even to a layman like Finn, it was clear that it was the sort of breakthrough that would make someone obscene amounts of money.

From his position near the entrance Finn watched his charge standing in the centre of the room shaking hands and accepting the compliments like a princess in a receiving line. With her black hair framing her pretty face and a scarlet cocktail dress hugging a slender, girlish frame, she looked closer to nineteen than twenty-nine. Among those vying for a moment in her presence he identified several corporate types, whose sharp suits and sober alertness singled them out from the relaxing scientists. They moved like hawks through a flock of unsuspecting doves, pressing their business cards into the hands of any they hoped might earn their companies a dollar.

Sebastian Pirot, the conference's head of security, stepped away from the group of organizing committee members he had been chatting with and joined Finn. A smile of faintly mocking sympathy creased the scar that ran diagonally from his left ear almost to the tip of his chin.

'I can see this work bores you, Mr Finn.'

'I've had worse.'

Pirot glanced across at Bellman with a mixture of admiration and lust that caused Finn's hackles to rise.

'Some of the guys and I are meeting for a drink later. Would you care to join us?' Pirot said.

'Thanks, but I'm on permanent duty. I don't get to clock off.'

'Too bad. Oh well, next time you're in Paris. We can swap old war stories.'

Finn maintained a straight face that masked his surprise. He didn't recall having told Pirot that he had been a soldier.

'We've met before; I'm sure of it,' Pirot said. 'It's been preying on my mind. Now I remember. November 2005. Jalalabad.'

Jalalabad. Not a name Finn would easily forget. A rare joint mission between American, British and French Special Forces to neutralize a Taliban stronghold in mountains to the north-east of the city. It had been a bloodbath. Hand-to-hand combat with Saudi-trained Arab mercenaries equipped with British weapons. The sort of operation that left Finn confused as to who was fighting whom and for what.

Finn neither confirmed nor denied his presence in Afghanistan. Like all good former members of the Regiment, he was assiduous in keeping details of his service secret, even from his wife. Nevertheless, he allowed his gaze to linger on Pirot as he tried to recollect his distinctive face with its high jutting cheekbones and strangely empty basalt-grey eyes. A glimmer of memory surfaced: a group of French paratroopers from the 13th Dragoons clustered in a corner of the briefing tent, quiet and intense compared with the boisterous Americans of Delta Force.

'Not good memories, I expect,' Pirot said, 'but at least the two of us survived.' He offered his hand. *'Au revoir*, then, Mr Finn. Next time.'

Finn closed his fist around Pirot's. They shook like comrades.

Pirot turned and left the room. Finn followed him with his gaze as another half-forgotten memory surfaced: a French Dragoon plunging his bayonet between the shoulders of a kneeling, blindfolded prisoner.

Finn blinked, banishing the image, and turned his attention back to Dr Bellman. She had moved away from her admirers to a far corner of the room where she was now talking to a smiling young woman whose cascade of auburn hair tumbled down her back. They took fresh glasses of champagne from a waiter manoeuvring expertly through the room with a silver tray balanced on delicate fingertips. Her companion said something that made them both rock with laughter. Finn checked his watch. It was still only nine p.m. He feared it would be a long night.

Dr Bellman and her new friend remained wrapped up in each other's company for the following hour. The more they drank, the more they laughed and the more they flirted. Finn felt like a voyeur. He couldn't wait for the evening to be over. Then, at last, the crowd began to thin and one by one the waiters retreated. The stragglers drifted out of the ballroom and across the Hotel George V's brilliant marble foyer into the bar.

Eventually, his charge and her new friend drained their glasses and made their way to the ladies' room. Finn grabbed the chance to pay a visit of his own. In the quiet resplendence of the gentlemen's cloakroom he splashed his face with cool water and dried it with a soft white towel. He was tired. His feet and back ached. The skin beneath his eyes was sagging. Just a few more hours and he would be on board the Eurostar and on his way back to Kathleen and the kids. He glanced briefly at the middle-aged face staring back at him from the mirror and wondered whether its hunger had finally gone. Perhaps the moment had arrived – time to think about leading a quiet life in his home town?

Still mulling this not unpleasant thought, he made his way back out to the lobby and waited for Bellman to reappear. A minute passed. Then another. He stepped over to the doorway of the bar and glanced inside. There were only a few remaining patrons in the room and no sign of Dr Bellman.

Reluctant to force his way into the ladies', he brought out his phone and called up the tracker app that connected with the transmitter disguised as a brooch that he had insisted she wear at all times.

The app took infuriating moments to load and synchronize. Finn cursed under his breath as he waited for the wheel on his screen to cease spinning. Finally, a distance reading and a direction arrow appeared. She was, according to the screen, fifteen feet away at ten o'clock to his current position. He lifted his gaze to the spot in the centre of the lobby. It was occupied by a circular marble-topped table decked with an elaborate floral display. Finn felt his heart pound against his ribs as he moved quickly towards it. He spotted the brooch lying beneath the foliage. He retrieved it and crossed immediately to the reception desk.

'Excuse me. Did you notice a woman in a red dress pass through here in the last few minutes?'

The receptionist, who resembled a Dior model, appeared puzzled. *'Monsieur?'*

'Dr Sarah Bellman. Black hair. Red dress.' He produced his security tag. 'I'm looking after her.'

She glanced at it and shrugged. 'I'm not sure. I was on the phone.'

'She was in this lobby just now.' He was met with a blank expression. 'Forget it, I need to see the CCTV playback.'

'CC–?'

'The security monitors.'

'I'll call the night manager.' She picked up the phone and unhurriedly tapped in an internal number.

Finn's patience snapped. He vaulted the counter and ignoring the receptionist's cry of alarm slammed through the door behind the desk into the corridor beyond. He moved along it, trying several doors in turn, all of which opened on to deserted offices. He arrived at a fourth signed SÉCURITÉ.

He burst in, surprising a dozing security guard. The musclebound hulk with a neck as thick as his skull objected noisily as Finn flashed his ID, dropped into a seat and took over the controls beneath a bank of monitors.

Finn stared at the keyboard, unable to make head or tail of it. 'How do you work this thing?'

The guard hauled himself to his feet and growled something in French. Finn ignored him and scanned the monitors for any sign of Bellman. He felt a heavy fist close round his shoulder.

'You can help out or fuck off,' Finn said, glancing over his shoulder.

The guard's other hand reached for the telescopic baton attached to his belt.

Finn responded instinctively, firing out a backfist that crushed the soft cartilage in his nose, provoking a roar of pain.

'What is going on?' A slightly built man with a neat moustache arrived with the receptionist in tow. He looked aghast at the guard, who was now dripping blood on to the carpet through fat, stubby fingers spread across his face.

'Show me how to operate this,' Finn demanded, recognizing him as the night manager. 'I need to rewind. My client's gone missing from the lobby. Dr Bellman. One of the delegates.'

The manager's expression changed from one of anger to alarm. He issued hurried instructions to the receptionist to take the guard out and get him cleaned up, then came alongside Finn and nervously tapped the keyboard. A badge on his lapel gave his name as Christian Deschamps.

'The lobby. Go back through the last ten minutes,' Finn ordered. 'I'm looking for a young woman in a red dress.'

Deschamps did as requested. The monitor covering the lobby began to spool backwards at four times normal speed.

'Faster,' Finn demanded.

'Of course.' Deschamps wiped his perspiring forehead with the back of his hand. The image accelerated.

'There. Stop. Go forward.'

Finn stared hard at the screen. Dr Bellman and her new friend entered the ladies' room followed closely by Finn, who went through the adjacent door. They emerged seconds later, giggling like schoolgirls and made for the lifts. While passing the table, Bellman casually reached out a hand as if to deposit something small beneath the fronds of overhanging ferns – the brooch, no doubt. As they stepped through the opening doors into the lift, they kissed, laughed, then kissed again.

The manager glanced across at Finn. 'Maybe not so serious?'

Finn grunted. 'Find out where they went.'

The cameras picked them up again as they emerged on the third floor and walked hand in hand along the corridor. They went into a room at the far end: number 348. Finn grabbed the phone on the desk and dialled the room on an internal line. It rang four times before connecting to voice-mail. He tried again with the same result.

'The phone can be muted to prevent disturbance,' Deschamps offered.

'Get me her details.'

Deschamps hesitated.

'Tell me who the fuck she is.'

Deschamps flinched. 'Very well. But we have to go to reception.' He hurried out through the door.

Finn followed him to the front desk where the bookings system revealed that Dr Bellman's companion was checked in under the name of Ms Carla Forenzi. She was a US national aged thirty and listed as a delegate to the conference representing MIT's Department of Brain and Cognitive Sciences. Her home address was an apartment in Cambridge, Massachusetts. Finn photographed the screen with his phone and thanked the manager for his trouble.

'I am not the one who was hurt,' Deschamps said.

'Buy him a drink on me.'

Finn let himself out through the gate at the end of the desk and made his way up to the third floor.

'Miss Bellman?' There was no answer. He knocked again on the door of 348, this time more loudly. 'Miss Bellman, I need to know that you are all right. If you don't reply, I'll be forced to let myself in.'

Silence. He pressed his ear to the varnished oak. There were no sounds of movement from inside. No sounds of any sort.

He was left with no choice. The protocols were strict and his duty to ensure her safety at all times was written into his contract. If he were to breach it, he risked losing his fee. A trip downstairs and back again to fetch a spare key card would take vital minutes and so was out of the question. He took a step back, drew the Beretta from the concealed holster beneath his left shoulder, flipped off the safety and aimed his right heel at the edge of the door several inches beneath the lock. It was a motion that during eight tours of Iraq had become second nature. The frame splintered along its length and the door burst open. Finn raised his pistol in a dual hand grip and moved inside.

The lights were on, the bed still made, the large sash window wide open and the floor-length net curtains flapping in the warm breeze. Finn's eyes flicked left through the open door to the bathroom. Empty. He scanned the room: no luggage or possessions. On the carpet at the side of the bed was a single red stiletto: Bellman's.

15

Only vaguely aware of the alarmed voices of other guests who had emerged into the corridor behind him, Finn moved to the window and tugged back the curtain to reveal two dangling climbing ropes secured somewhere on the floors above. He glanced out over the sill and saw that they descended into a narrow pedestrian alleyway that led along the side of the building towards a wider service alley that ran along its rear. He heard sounds of a scuffle and muffled female cries coming from around the corner.

Finn holstered his pistol, reached for the nearest rope, pulled it towards him and stepped over it. He fed it around his right hip and across his left shoulder. Gripping it at head height with his left hand and below and to the side of him with his right, he climbed backwards out of the window and abseiled fifty feet to the ground in the space of four seconds, pushing off the wall with his feet only twice.

The instant he touched the ground, two masked figures emerged from the shadows, both clutching Bowie knives. The long blades glinted in the flickering light cast by a solitary streetlamp. Finn knew at once that they had been waiting for him. He reached for his pistol, but saw an explosion of stars as a blunt object wielded by a third, unseen assailant clubbed into the back of his skull. The impact sent him sprawling face first on to the cobbles. Rendered momentarily insensible, reflex took over. He rolled several times and reached again for his weapon. He heard the sound of metal on bone and lost all sensation in his right hand as a steel blade drove through his upper arm. Finn flailed with his left fist, connecting with the cheekbone of the man who had stabbed him, but even as he did so, a second blade thrust between his ribs.

He tasted blood rising in his throat and heard air sucking through the puncture wound in his right lung, but continued to hurl his fists at the three attackers crowding over him.

There was no more pain, only blind, demonic fury as he tried to swat them. He would crush their skulls with his bare hands.

Their blows rained in, but as far as Finn was concerned they seemed to bounce off his impenetrable hide. He felt invincible, then suddenly electrified. His limbs coursed with liquid fire and he screamed like a wild man into the night.

4

The lamps in the small basement laboratory would take a full five minutes to rise from complete darkness to light. This was intended to mimic sunrise at the equator. Dr Lars Holst's intrusion at four a.m. had brought dawn two hours early, thus disturbing the natural rhythm of the room's inhabitants. Roused from the deepest cycle of sleep the five rhesus macaque monkeys, three male, two female, blinked awake, tired and confused. There was none of the usual immediate clamour to be fed as they yawned and stretched and rose stiffly to their feet.

Holst deliberately kept his back to them as he hurriedly set up his equipment. In the still murky light the mind was prone to perceive their miniature features as unnervingly human. He retrieved the steel ball from a cupboard, set it on an insulated frame in the corner of an empty cage on the central workbench and connected it to the power supply. Next, he fetched a container of chopped fruit from the refrigerator and emptied it into the hopper of the remotely controlled feeder positioned to the side of the ball. The smell of their favourite treat raised the macaques from their torpor. Miniature hands reached out through the bars of the other cage accompanied by a chorus of hungry and demanding grunts and squeals.

'OK, OK. Hold on a moment,' Holst said, with the same tone of affectionate impatience he used with his own young children back in London.

They refused to quieten.

Doing his best to ignore them, Holst fetched a camera and mini tripod from the zip pocket of his case and experimented with several angles before finding the one that gave the most comprehensive view of the cage. Now came the difficult part. Which of the macaques would perform best? He didn't have time to repeat the experiment more than once or twice. He had arranged to meet with Drecker at five a.m. and his flight out of Copenhagen Airport was at six forty-five. He would have commenced the procedure earlier, except that never having tested it on an animal that was less than fully rested, he couldn't rule out the possibility that a tired brain might carry a slight but nevertheless unacceptable risk of failure.

Willie, Merle, Dolly, June and Johnny. Holst had ill-advisedly named the macaques after his favourite country music singers, and over the course of three years had naturally attributed characteristics of his sentimental heroes to each of them. Willie was the quiet one, Merle was given to dark moods, Dolly was the extrovert, and June and Johnny were in love. If only he had stuck to M_1, F_1, M_2, et cetera, it would have made this moment so much easier.

He fetched another container of fruit and pushed it through the one-way steel flap into their cage. He watched them jostle as they selected their favourite morsels. Dolly, as always, grabbed a piece of apple in each hand. Merle and Willie disappeared to opposite corners of the cage to eat their slices of banana, leaving June and Johnny crouched side by side sucking on quartered oranges. To any observer other than Holst or the two lab technicians who assisted in his work, the macaques would have appeared entirely normal. Indeed, there was nothing in their behaviour – aside, perhaps, from their elevated capacity for concentration – that would have given any hint as to the nature of the therapy they had undergone.

Holst's first instinct was to select Willie or Merle. Being a rigorous scientist, he then questioned his motives and found them wanting. His choice, he suspected, was being influenced by the relative levels of affection he felt for each creature rather than by their ability to prove his concept. It would make little difference to Drecker and her associates which he chose, but he realized now that he needed concrete assurance of his technique as much, if not more, than they did. He needed to know that his years of work had not been in vain. In the early stages it had been Johnny who had been most difficult to train. Just like human beings, monkeys exhibited different traits. Some were wary, some adventurous, some compliant, others stubborn. Johnny had been the most innately cautious and obstinate and seemingly the most conscious of his own safety. On reflection, this made him the obvious choice. If it worked with Johnny, it would surely work with all of them.

'Sorry, June,' Holst heard himself saying as he pulled on a pair of thick leather gauntlets.

He opened the door of the cage and fished Johnny out, pinning his arms to his sides.

Johnny hissed and scrabbled at the air with his feet, objecting to being separated from his breakfast.

'There's plenty more in here, my boy. More than you can eat.' Holst nudged the main cage closed with his elbow and transferred the complaining monkey to the far smaller cage on the bench.

Johnny made a circuit of the floor as if searching for an escape route, then, resigned to his confinement, stood dejectedly, looking across at his companions, who ignored him, focused solely on their food.

Holst removed the gauntlets and set the camera to record. He was ready.

From a drawer beneath the bench he brought out a small remote-control unit and selected level one of twelve. He pressed the activate button and a short electronic bleep alerted Johnny to the start of the experiment. His head jerked round to face the steel ball, his eyes suddenly wide and alert. After no more than a second he took two steps across the cage and gingerly reached out with an extended finger to touch its reflective surface. His arm jerked sharply backwards with the force of the electric shock it administered. He squawked and ran a circuit of the cage, but within moments had taken up position again in front of the ball.

'Don't you want your banana?' Holst said, half expecting the monkey to understand.

Seemingly in response to Holst's prompt, Johnny noticed the slice of fruit sitting at the bottom of the chute and reached for it. He ate it distractedly, his gaze never leaving the ball.

Holst selected level three. The bleep sounded a second time. Johnny flicked out a hand. This time the increased voltage caused his whole body to spasm. Johnny jumped up and down and screeched, then grabbed the bars and shook them violently.

'Johnny? Johnny, fruit?'

The segment of orange that had appeared at the foot of the chute remained untouched. This meant that the dopamine coursing through the monkey's brain was already outweighing any pleasure he might have derived from eating it.

Holst selected level six.

The bleep brought Johnny straight back to the ball, which he slapped almost casually with his palm. The force of the shock threw him off his feet. He lay on his side, twitching and shaking as if suffering a seizure, but after several seconds was upright again. He stood quivering in the centre of the cage, fixated on the metal sphere.

Holst had never taken Johnny beyond level eight. There was a balance to be struck. If he progressed by gradual increments there was a danger that his subject's dopamine receptors would become flooded and that he would descend into a temporary catatonic state, which was not the conclusion he was aiming for. He plumped for level ten.

The monkey approached the ball and reached out a trembling hand. The violent impact hurled him to the far side of the cage. Johnny lay in the corner trembling and jerking. Holst thought for a moment that he had misjudged and would have to start again with another subject, but after a short while Johnny's nervous system began to recover. Now the macaque's usually expressive face was set in a dull stare. The eyes were empty. The brain too flooded with pleasure to comprehend or receive any stimulus other than the one it craved.

Johnny hauled himself to his feet at the sound of the bleep and staggered drunkenly towards the sphere. Holst had selected level twelve. He glanced away as his subject received a shock of 2,000 milliamperes, double that which he had just received.

The bitter smell of singed fur reached Holst's nostrils. He looked back and saw the monkey lying motionless, the right arm scorched as far as the shoulder. There were burns, too, on both feet where they had been in contact with the metal floor.

Holst switched off the power supply to the equipment, reached a stethoscope from a drawer and for the benefit of the camera confirmed the time of death as 4.18 a.m.

As he had hoped, the experiment had been an unqualified success. His fleeting sadness at Johnny's passing was quickly superseded by his excitement at the implications of the result. He was going to be a wealthy man. Buoyed by this thought, he took the dead monkey from the cage and carried it across the lab to the incinerator with no trace of remorse. What was life, after all, if not a commodity like any other that could be bought, sold, squandered, relished or, in this case, invested for the good of others?

Willie, Merle, Dolly and June continued to munch their fruit in silence.

Dawn was breaking. Holst hurried from the university building trundling his carry-on suitcase and climbed into the waiting taxi. He instructed the driver to take him to Kongens Nytorv, the large square a short walk from the rendezvous point he had arranged with Drecker. During the ten-minute journey through deserted streets Holst felt as if he were floating between two realities. One was that in which he had lived for the last five years: dividing his working week between London and Copenhagen while frantically trying to keep up with the demands of two faculties, the complexities of overseeing students in two cities and the needs of his young and all too often neglected family; the other was the exhilarating life to come. He taunted himself with the thought that if some disaster were to befall him in the next few minutes it would all be for nothing. The entirety of his work and any prospect of his wife and children profiting from it would die with him. All of his data and the details of his methodology were stored in a series of secure cloud accounts to which only he knew the complex passwords of which there existed no written records. Keeping all of this to himself presented a huge danger, but at the frontiers of science, until the grand moment of unveiling, secrecy was critical. It was simply the risk he had to take.

Throughout his career Holst had sustained himself with the fantasy of one day announcing a world-changing discovery that would bring the acclamation of his peers. His introduction to Drecker, nearly two years ago to the day, had changed everything. The prospect of prizes and professorships had paled in comparison with the promise of money. It was a calculation most scientists never had the privilege to make, hence their hollow claims to be unconcerned with material wealth. Holst knew that there wasn't a single man or woman among his colleagues who didn't resent receiving only a paltry salary while relative dunces prospered. Dunces like an old school friend, Bo, who had once joked to him that the millions he had made in finance were nothing to do with brilliance but merely an accident of environment. If he had worked on a market stall, he liked to joke, he would have come home with pockets stuffed full with carrots and potatoes, but he worked in a bank so got to gorge himself with cash. Bo's smug laughter had filled Holst with bitterness, jealousy and self-loathing.

Then Drecker had found him. The moment Holst had smelled money, real money, he had known that no amount of academic prestige could compete. Prestige didn't buy luxurious homes or portfolios of investments, or afford the time in which to exercise and keep his middle-aged body from bloating and sagging. Prestige didn't even allow for the purchase of a decent watch or a tailored suit from one of the smart boutiques that lined the street along which the taxi was now passing. He had always felt there was something seriously wrong with a world in which a man of his intelligence was forced to live like a pauper. Now was his moment to remedy the injustice.

Holst emerged from the taxi into a fresh breeze blowing in from the sea. He paid the driver in cash and completed the final few hundred yards to his destination on foot. Drecker had requested they meet outside the Skuespilhuset, a muted, modern, distinctively Danish structure that stood at the corner of the Nyhavn dock and the broad expanse of the harbour. The approach to the theatre, once a bustling quay crammed with fishing boats and cargo vessels, was now a cobbled promenade with uninterrupted views across the still water to the lights of Christianshavn on the far side. As he strolled, Holst recalled with a smile of amusement how over-whelmed he had been by the vastness of this city on his first visit from his small home town in Jutland. Twenty-five years later he no longer regarded it as a metropolis but as an agree-able, comfortably provincial town far removed from the centre of things. A place of which he remained fond, but which, without doubt, he had long outgrown.

Drecker was already waiting at the entrance to the sloping boardwalk leading to the theatre's waterfront terrace. She was dressed, as always, in a dark, close-fitting suit and was carrying a slim attaché case.

'Good morning, Dr Holst.' She smiled pleasantly as he approached.

'Good morning. I'm sorry we had to meet at such an inconvenient hour.'

'No problem. How did it go?' As usual, she seemed eager to dispense with small talk.

'Entirely as anticipated. A complete success.' He reached into the pocket of his crumpled summer-weight jacket and brought out a memory card in a transparent bag. 'I filmed the procedure less than an hour ago.' He handed it to her. 'As soon as the fifteen million dollars appears in my Cayman account I'll email all the passcodes to the technical papers. As I hope I've made plain from the outset, I remain willing to help or advise in any way.' He was aware of a new note of confidence in his voice. He felt like a rich man should. 'I plan to stay in my current posts until the end of the year, but after that I'll be happy to place myself at your exclusive disposal – to head up a team or whatever you wish. Subject to terms, of course.'

As he spoke, Holst became aware of a large black car approaching along the road that ran along the side of the promenade. At first he paid it scant attention, assuming it would turn left into Kvæsthusgade, but it passed the junction and continued towards them, slowing to little more than walking pace.

'We assumed as much,' Drecker replied. 'So my colleagues and I have discussed the matter and decided to make you a very attractive proposition based on some of our previous discussions.'

'You have? You want to create a dedicated facility?' Holst's excitement was tempered by the steady approach of the car. He now assumed it was Drecker's transport, but why wasn't it waiting when he arrived? Behind the bluish glare of the halogen headlights he made out the silhouettes of a driver and passenger.

'We would like to talk with you somewhere more comfortable. Now would be a good time.'

'I'm afraid I have to leave for the airport.'

The car came to a stop a short distance away. The passenger, a tall man with an olive complexion, climbed out and stood in readiness to receive them.

'Please, Dr Holst. It's most important.' She gestured towards the vehicle.

'I can't. It's too late for me to change my arrangements – I've classes to teach in London today.'

'Do we have an agreement or not, Doctor?' she said sharply, dropping all pretence at cordiality.

'We have a contract of sale for my intellectual property –' he pleaded, his voice losing all its authority.

'But your work alone is not sufficient for our purposes, Dr

Holst. It's only part of the equation, which is why we need to talk about what happens next.'

'I beg your pardon? I'm sorry, Ms Drecker, but if you're trying to renegotiate terms I'm afraid it's out of the question.'

Drecker reached into her jacket and brought out a pistol, sleek and black, which she levelled at his chest. Holst tasted bile in his throat. The strength bled from his limbs. His legs quivered and threatened to collapse beneath him.

Now he understood the reason she had chosen this isolated spot for their meeting.

'You can't kill me. You'll have nothing if you do,' he protested feebly.

'Please, Dr Holst. Do as I ask and get in the car. I don't want to have to hurt you.'

5

The allotted hour was over, but the first-year students in the history faculty's lecture hall showed no sign of leaving. Dr Leo Black did his best to referee the spiky debate that had erupted following his presentation on President Truman's decision to drop the atom bomb.

'He called them *animals*. He dismissed the whole population as sub-human in order to justify himself. It was the leaders who were the criminals, not the ordinary people, not the women and children. Any leader who claims to be civilized has an absolute duty to do everything in his power to avoid killing innocent civilians. Truman did the opposite.' The young woman in the front row spoke with arresting passion. Helen Mount was never shy of voicing her opinions both in class and in the columns of *Cherwell*, the university's most prestigious student newspaper. She had earned a reputation as a political radical and fierce opponent of anything that smacked of injustice. 'If he wanted to prove that fighting on was futile, why not drop a bomb somewhere uninhabited? Why not show the Japanese High Command what it could do and give them the option of surrender? He had other options, but he didn't take them. He went straight in and destroyed a whole city. If that isn't a war crime, I don't know what is.'

'Powerful point,' Black said. 'Does anyone want to come back on that?'

No one took up the offer. Most of the students present were wary of challenging Helen in any debate in which she held strong opinions. The usual outcome was humiliation.

'Well, if you're all agreed –'

'I don't agree with that.' The voice came from a seat in the back row of the hall. It belonged to a young man Black couldn't recall having seen before. He was seated alone with empty seats either side of him. The left half of his face was hidden behind a curtain of blond fringe. 'The US only had two bombs ready at the time and Truman needed to make them count. Nobody likes what happened, but it didn't kill many more than the fire-bombing of Tokyo. You can call it a crime as much as you like, but it would have been a far bigger crime not to have used it. Millions might have died, not just thousands.'

'I'm saying he had a duty to take all reasonable steps,' Helen shot back. 'Unless we act according to humanitarian principals, we're not even worthy of being called human.'

'So it's just the procedure you object to, is it? Let's say he did try dropping one as a warning but the Japanese had fought on regardless. Would bombing Hiroshima have been justified then? The innocent women and children would have been killed just the same.'

'It would have been better.'

'For whom . . .? Him? It would have been far worse for the hundreds being killed every day the war kept going.'

'That's purely hypothetical. We don't know what would have happened. The point is, he pressed the button while he still had alternatives.'

'OK. What if he had ignored the committee advising him to drop it and decided it was a step too far – that no civilized human being could wreak that much destruction in one go?'

'He would have been perfectly justified.'

'So you would have preferred him to send in thousands of conscripted American troops even though the final body count would have been far higher?'

Helen hesitated.

The young man pressed his advantage. 'It's a simple choice – troops or bomb? Which one is morally preferable?'

'I don't believe that there can ever be a moral use of an immoral weapon,' Helen said. She sat back and crossed her arms defiantly across her chest.

Heads around the hall nodded in agreement. Helen smiled, sensing that she had neatly summed up the mood of her fellow students.

Unfazed, her opponent countered, 'That's irrational. You can tolerate the idea of spreading the blood of millions of civilians across the hands of thousands of soldiers, but you can't stomach the idea of fewer deaths being caused by just one man. Luckily for us, Truman was able to make the cold calculation: kill thousands to save millions. Squeamishness like yours amounts to a death wish.'

'That's ridiculous,' Helen snapped back. 'Trying your best to avoid unnecessary violence is about valuing life and *not* wanting to cause death.'

'You're living in a fool's paradise,' the young man said. 'History proves time after time that if you want to stay alive, it's kill or be killed. It's just a fact. If you truly value life you'd better be ready to rub the enemy out as fast as possible.'

'Now you're being childish.'

'The world's uglier than you want to believe. You're the one who's being naive.'

His response prompted a ripple of laughter.

'All right, I think we'd better leave it there,' Black said, sensing that constructive debate was coming to an end. 'Next week we'll explore General MacArthur's reconstruction of Japan and consider the obligations of the victor.'

Helen slammed her file shut, thrust it into her bag and marched out of the door ahead of the crowd, annoyed at not having scored an emphatic victory and even more infuriated at having been laughed at. Black gathered his lecture notes into his battered canvas satchel feeling a measure of sympathy for her. He admired Helen's youthful idealism. For a man who knew what it was to have plumbed the depths of cynicism only to sink even lower, teaching students brimming with desire to build a better future was like being cleansed. Optimism like hers gave him fresh hope each day.

He made his way to the exit. The young man with the fringe hurried down the hall steps and came after him.

'Can I ask you something, Dr Black?'

'Fire away.'

'Sam Wright, by the way – I'm actually a PP student – Physics and Philosophy. A friend of mine tipped me off that you were worth listening to.'

'I'm glad someone thinks so. What's your question?'

'Truman said men make history, not the other way around. Do you believe that? I mean, isn't he the most obvious example of a man swept along by history you can think of? He's a small-town guy from Missouri who's appointed vice president as a compromise candidate, but then Roosevelt dies and leaves him with the gravest decision that's ever been made. It's like he was destined for it.'

'It's a tempting thought, but, no, I think I'm with Truman. I can't see how the idea of destiny does anything to help us analyse or understand events, which is what we're trying to do, after all. I'd have to put destiny in the category of attractive but fanciful concepts.'

Sam mulled this for a moment. 'I heard you spent a long time in the army.'

'A very long time.' There had been no point in keeping it a secret from the students. A simple internet search would have revealed Black to be one of the oldest junior lecturers in the university, having been awarded his PhD only a year before at the age of forty-nine. But of the intervening quarter-century between his graduating in history and returning to his old college, there would have been no mention. If he hadn't filled in the gap himself, rumour and gossip would soon have done it for him.

'So why do you think you survived? Was it because you made good decisions or did you walk away from situations you shouldn't have?'

Black considered the purpose of the question, wondering where Sam was trying to lead him. 'A bit of both, I suppose.'

'But you still don't believe in destiny? Or put it another way – what if the young Hitler had died of his wounds in the trenches, or the young Churchill had been run through with a spear during his cavalry charge in the Sudan, what then?'

'I'm not a great fan of alternative histories. Isn't the point to learn from past experience in the hope of informing future decisions?'

'With respect, I would argue that's outmoded thinking.'

'I see.' Black tried not to feel affronted. Unlike army officers, academics were meant to welcome contradiction as a spur to new ideas, even when it came from a nineteen-year-old undergraduate. 'In what respect exactly?'

'Think of quantum physics –'

'Physics?'

'Yes. If you fire particles at two slits in a piece of card it turns out they don't just travel in a straight line and hit the wall behind. Some of them travel through both slits, perhaps thousands, even millions of times. According to the maths, they could have taken every possible route to arrive at their destination and might even have been in several places at once. That's mind-blowing, right? Almost inconceivable. But so is the fact that despite the randomness of their journey, they still have an ultimate destination which they all reach. They couldn't buck their destiny.'

'I like it. Clever,' Black said, trying to be generous. 'But as far as I know, there's a practical use for quantum theory. It's a theoretical model that explains previously inexplicable phenomena. What does your destiny model do for history?'

'It gives ultimate meaning. Events unfold only because they're heading towards an inevitable conclusion.'

'Which means that we're nothing more than puppets at the whim of some greater force?'

'Nothing whimsical about it. There are many eminent physicists who truly believe we're just complex robots operating according to a program. I'm not saying I like it or wish it wasn't so. Not many accepted quantum theory or even relativity until they were proved to be true. Maybe one day we'll learn how to rewrite the program ourselves? Maybe that's our ultimate destiny?'

They exited through the main doors of the faculty into bright sunlight.

'Well, it's a fun theory, though I'm not sure it would score you many marks in finals.'

'Watch this space. Give it ten years, I bet you it'll be mainstream. Great lecture by the way. Five stars. I'll be back.' Sam smiled and hurried on down the steps.

The digital generation. They felt free to rate everything. Black tried to imagine how his old tutor, Godfrey Lane, would have reacted to being marked out of five by his students. It didn't bear thinking about.

Black made his way along the path through the small garden that stood in front of the history faculty. On the far side of the railings the pavements of George Street were busy with students and tourists from around the globe. A group of Hungarian musicians was playing a wild reel straight from the market squares of medieval Budapest. Black was struck, as he so often was, by the extraordinary collision of so many times, places and ideas in this one small spot in the middle of England. There was something in its vibrant chaos that seemed to strike a chord with Sam's outlandish theory of predetermination: Black couldn't deny that on occasions he did feel as if all the tangled threads of his own complex and violent history had been winding their way here all along. To this oasis. The embodiment of all that he had fought to protect.

He stepped out into the throng and headed back towards his college. Much as he had come to feel at home in the university, his position within it was precarious. For the past year he had been a college tutor without tenure, earning a wage that barely covered his food and lodging. He wouldn't see his army pension until he was sixty-five and nearly all of his savings, such as they were, had been swallowed up financing three years of study for his doctorate. He had applied for a junior research fellowship, but the decision, which wouldn't be made until early September, lay with the existing college fellows, a body of men and women intensely protective of their reputation as world-class scholars. Most were avowedly liberal (though hardly liberal in the sense of being tolerant of opinions other than their own) whose politics came with an instinctive suspicion of people like him. It would take a small miracle for them to admit a fifty-year-old former soldier into their gilded circle and Black met few of their criteria. He had no body of published work and, as yet, no academic reputation to speak of. All he had to offer was an insider's insight into the workings of the international military machine and an ambition to put that knowledge to use.

The unavoidable fact was that Black had only one realistic shot at being accepted. His twenty-two years of experience in the Special Air Service had earned him an invitation to present a paper at an international symposium at West Point Military Academy in late August. If he could make a favourable impression on the audience of generals, diplomats and strategists with his controversial thesis, he stood a chance. He merely had to convince them that nearly every conflict he had been involved with had been a disaster and that all military interventions that couldn't be avoided should be carried out only with a minimum of arrogance and a maximum cultural understanding. *'Just discard your entire approach over the last twenty years, ladies and gentlemen; admit you were wrong and start again.'*

No one could accuse him of making life easy for himself. They would expect him to be a man of war eager to promote the idea that problem nations could be brought to heel by their billion-dollar hardware and their populations forced to submission and compliance by highly trained soldiers of just the kind he had been. Peace through superior firepower. Instead they would get a man who had come to believe that surrendering to the instinct to violence was the route to perpetual and unresolved conflict. If that's what they wanted, so be it, but he was determined to show them there was another way. A way that meant trying to stand in your enemy's shoes before you even fired a shot. A way that treated violence as the very last resort. If he could change his way of thinking so profoundly, so, he would argue, could they. Each time Black imagined himself at the West Point lectern, all he could picture was row upon row of startled and indignant faces. Sometimes the daydream would end with him being shut down and humiliated in mid flow by some convenient technical fault, but in more optimistic moments he fantasized that his persuasive analysis would bring the assembled company to its feet in rapturous applause, his triumph culminating in a slew of offers to become a trusted advisor to governments and NGOs around the world.

Then he would come back to earth. If he was well received, the most he could realistically hope for was a fellowship. It would mean a modest but steady wage, lend him the credibility to have his articles published in the respected journals and, crucially, the chance to have his doctorate published as a book. If he was going to change the world, it would be a long, tough slog, and he would have to earn every ounce of respect.

And if West Point proved a failure and the fellows rejected him, it wouldn't mark the end of the world. He had a small, slightly dilapidated cottage on the slopes of the Black Mountains in the Welsh borders to retreat to, and sufficient tools in his shed and strength in his arms to scrape a living as a jobbing builder while he worked out what to do next. It was a strange crossroads at which to find himself at this late stage of his career, but after the life he had lived, he was grateful to have reached it at all.

Black emerged from Gloucester Green on to Worcester Street, dodged between passing bicycles and headed for the unassuming doorway set in the plain eighteenth-century façade of Worcester College. The inauspicious exterior hid one of the best-kept secrets in Oxford. He crossed the threshold and entered the cool shade of the cloister, its stone flags polished and foot-worn by a centuries-long procession of scholars. Framed between its supporting columns was a view over the sunken quadrangle, its rectangular lawn mown in diagonal chequerboard stripes. Beyond the elegantly crumbling sandstone wall at the quad's far end was the Provost's garden, whose borders were informal riots of lavender, hollyhocks and peonies, and further on still were the gently stirring trees bordering the college lake. The soft and fleeting beauty of the

English summer was the thing he had missed most while on operations in the baking desert or the steamy gloom beneath the jungle canopy. He paused to impress it on his mind.

'Idling, Leo? That's not like you.'

Black turned to see Karen Peters emerge from the porters' lodge clutching a pile of mail. Karen was a gifted plant biologist, a junior fellow and one of the few members of the Senior Common Room he could count as a friend. Dressed in jeans, pumps and baggy T-shirt with sunglasses balanced on her forehead, at first glance she could have been mistaken for a student. Only the faint lines at the corners of her dark green eyes gave any clue to the trauma of her previous three months. Days before she and her husband were about to conclude the purchase of their first home, he had left her for a twenty-three-year-old PhD student, taking all their savings with him. Aged thirty-four and after five years of marriage, Karen had found herself penniless, homeless and broken-hearted. Her lawyer had advised that even if she were to recover the £40,000 he had stolen from her, the legal costs would leave them both bankrupt. As a tutor in contract and family law, her husband had no doubt been aware of this fact.

Despite these disasters and being reduced to living in two poky rooms in a graduate accommodation block, Karen somehow managed to keep smiling. Fortunately, her cheating husband had been only one of two loves in her life. The other was her work: she was trying to save the dying forests of Canada and Siberia from the ravages of climate change.

'You caught me,' Black said. 'I'm always a sucker for this view.'

'How's the paper coming along?'

'I've planned it, more or less. Starting to rough it out.'

'So what you really mean is that you haven't actually written anything yet?'

'I'm aiming to get a first draft down over the weekend. Hunker down till it's done.'

'Well, if you need another pair of eyes – not that I'm any sort of expert in your field.'

'Thanks, as long as you're not too hard on me – my confidence is easily knocked.' He smiled. Karen smiled back, but Black sensed more than a desire to make harmless small talk beneath the cheerful front. 'How are things?' he asked.

'OK.' She shrugged as if to say she was managing fine, but her eyes told a different story.

Black took his cue. 'Fancy a quick stroll?'

She nodded gratefully.

He led off down the flight of stone steps that connected the cloister to the sunken quad below. At its foot they turned right and wandered side by side along the gravel path that bordered the grass.

'What's happened now?' Black asked.

'Just another letter from Joel's lawyers. I really shouldn't be bothering you with it.'

'It's no trouble. What do they say?'

She glanced away as if she were too embarrassed to share it, but the pressure had built to the point where she couldn't help herself. 'They're claiming the money was all his, that I was emotionally abusive, impossible to live with, that I was determined to frustrate his career . . . it just goes on and on. And there was me believing we were happily married. I know rationally that it's all just lies designed to wear me down, but when you read something like that from someone you loved, you really do start to doubt your own sanity. You can't help it. You start to wonder whether you really were that person . . . Does that sound nuts?'

'It sounds perfectly natural. If it's any comfort, in my limited experience of other people's divorces, his behaviour has been pretty much typical. And the guiltier the deserter, the dirtier they fight. He won't keep it up, though – six-month rule.'

'Tell me.'

'The time it takes for sanity to return. Relative sanity, anyway. Anger fades like the first flush of passion – so I'm told.'

'Maybe I should just let it go and forget about the money. I can't even afford to pay the lawyers' bills I've already got.'

'Anyone would be upset, but you've got to try not to react. If he's being this aggressive, it probably means he's frightened, which gives you the advantage. He'll have told the new girl all sorts of lies about what a bad person you were, but the chances are his conscience will get to him in the end and he'll come back with an offer.'

Karen nodded. She seemed to want to believe him, but something was nagging at her.

'You say conscience, but . . . it only happened a couple of times . . . when we argued, he scared me. It was like there was a dark side to him that I tried to pretend wasn't there.'

'Did he ever hit you?'

She shook her head.

'Threaten you?'

'No . . . not explicitly.'

'Then I shouldn't worry. It'll work out. It nearly always does.'

They arrived at the far corner of the quad and stopped at the foot of another set of stone steps where they would go their separate ways. Black gave her a reassuring pat on the shoulder. 'This time next year it'll all be a memory. I promise you.'

She nodded, her eyes brightening a little. 'You are coming to the Provost's drinks tonight?'

'I'll try.' Black kept the fact he had entirely forgotten about the occasion to himself.

'You've got to do better than that, Leo. If you want that fellowship, you have to be seen. You've got to make yourself part of the furniture, show them your human side. Tell them a few jokes. Soften them up a bit.'

'I've never been much good at cocktail parties.'

'That makes two of us.' The warm breeze scattered her thick brown hair across her cheek. She pushed it away. 'You are very popular, you know – I keep hearing students saying how great your seminars and lectures are. I'm going to make sure the Provost knows it, too. It counts for a lot.'

Black was touched. 'Thanks. I appreciate it.'

'Yes, well – it's not pure altruism. For one thing I need someone I can talk to around here who isn't on the spectrum.' She smiled. 'No excuses. See you later.'

Playfully waving an admonishing finger, she set off up the steps.

Black stared after her for a moment, then continued on his way. Karen was right about the need to ingratiate himself more with the masters of his fate. Her concern for him was touching. He wondered what he had done to deserve it.

He made his way to a far corner of the quad to the last in the row of a terrace of medieval cottages. From the outside his college accommodation looked charming: a centuries-old oak door set back in a weathered stone porch with roses growing around the lead-lattice window. But the reason it was assigned to a junior tutor became apparent the moment you stepped inside. The interior had remained largely unchanged from its last overhaul in the early 1960s. Apart from the laptop on the heavy Victorian desk, the study room, which took up most of the downstairs floor, looked and smelled exactly as it had done when Black had first ventured across the threshold nearly thirty years before. Then it had been occupied by his former tutor, a small, curt man who wore the same tweed jacket every day of the year and chain-smoked unfiltered Woodbines or, when he had been lucky on the horses, slim Panatela cigars. Though he had been dead for nearly fifteen years, Godfrey Lane's presence still lingered in the pair of sagging Chesterfield sofas, the oil painting of the heavy cavalry at Waterloo above the gas fire, and the now threadbare rug his father had hauled back on a troop ship from Alexandria at the end of the Desert War. For an historian the rooms were perfect: the ancient plumbing and frigid temperatures from November through to March a constant reminder of the deprivations of the past.

Black went through to the kitchen at the back, made himself a cup of strong tea and returned to his desk. He had three clear hours before he was expected to be on parade on the Provost's lawn. More than enough time to crack the critical opening paragraphs of his paper.

Resisting the urge to prevaricate, he hurriedly typed out the words that had been forming in the back of his mind throughout the day:

> In the early years of this century I met with Afghan men in a village we had just liberated from the Taliban. They were illiterate, had never heard of President Bush or Osama Bin Laden, were unaware of the destruction of New York's twin towers and considered us hostile invaders. The British, I soon learned, had not been forgiven for their last occupation of their country in the 1870s. The consciousness of these men stretched little further than the walls of their valley. Their minds had been formed by a mixture of tradition, folklore

and the local version of Islam. The Koran teaches that the world is 4,000 years old and that is what they believed. Ignorant of science or even of the very idea of intellectual discourse, there was virtually no mechanism by which I could communicate with them except in the most basic terms.

The British and other occupying armies were, however, expected to win hearts and minds and to convert these tribal peoples into enthusiastic democrats who would discard 1,500-year-old habits, liberate their women and embrace the rule of law.

Who set those impossible tasks? Our politicians. Politicians needing votes and results. Politicians who could no sooner enter the mind of an Afghan tribesman than those of our prehistoric ancestors.

This is the truth on the ground. And only when we acknowledge the truth can we address it and find answers. Ladies and gentlemen, I am a soldier who as a result of long and regretful experience has largely ceased to believe in the ability of war to deliver peace.

Black paused to assess his progress. As an opening salvo it was certainly bold; but, on reflection, its tone was closer to that of a magazine article than learned argument. Arresting as it was, it wouldn't do. There was too much of *him* in it. He couldn't afford to be dismissed as a mere peddler of anecdotes before he had even begun. He tried again with a more impersonal, academic approach:

Conventional paradigms governing military interventions intended to oust elements hostile to native civilian populations have operated according to a number of a priori assumptions. These principally concern the willingness of newly liberated citizens to engage constructively with their liberators in the implementation of social and political policies deemed by those same liberators to be universally desirable.

He paused, imagining eyelids in the audience beginning to droop. There had to be a middle way.

The telephone rang, interrupting his train of thought. He reached for a receiver old enough to be connected by a knotted spiral of cable.

'Hello?'

'Is that Major Black?'

It was a woman's voice, shaky and tearful.

'Yes.' He had an idea that it was one he should recognize but he couldn't immediately put a name to it.

'Sorry to call you out of the blue like this.' He sensed she was about to deliver bad news. 'It's Kathleen. Kathleen Finn. Ryan's wife.'

Kathleen. Of course. Black felt his chest tighten.

She seemed unable to speak.

'What's happened?'

'He's working in Paris, as a bodyguard. He was meant to come home today . . . I just had a call from the British Embassy . . . They want me to go over and identify . . .' She trailed off into sobs, unable to finish her sentence.

Black heard the sound of excited children in the background. The Finns had three, still all quite young as he recalled.

'There's a body and they've asked you to identify it, is that it?' He heard himself speak as a soldier, clipped and emotionless.

'Yes –'

'Then I'll go. You stay with the kids,' Black said without a moment's pause. 'Give me the number of the person who called you and your email address. I'll make contact and instruct him to route all communication through me. I'll send you information as I receive it. I'm going to give you my mobile number, too – you can call me any time. Have you got a pen, Kathleen?'

She fought back tears and whispered a 'yes'.

Black dictated his number and made her read it back to him, then took down the number of an Embassy official named Simon Johnson and all of Kathleen's contact details, both of them finding reassurance in the practicality of the task.

'Have you anyone to keep you company while you're waiting?' Black asked. 'I shan't be there until tomorrow morning.'

'I can call my sister.'

'Do that. It's best not to be alone. I'll be in touch the moment I've anything to report.'

There was a brief, awkward pause in which Black might have brought the conversation to a close, except that it felt somehow incomplete. He and Finn had worked side by side for twenty years. They had been closer than brothers and saved each other's skins more times than he could recall. This was never meant to have happened. Finn was the one with family, Black the man whom scarcely anyone outside the Regiment would have come to mourn.

'I'm sorry, Kathleen,' Black said. 'We haven't been in touch for a long time. We should have been. It's my fault.'

'It was as much his as yours,' she said. 'He was always so busy, you know. He did mean to get in touch.'

'Me, too,' Black said.

They lapsed into another painful silence. Black put them out of their misery. 'Goodbye, Kathleen.'

'Goodbye. Thank you.'

He set down the phone and immediately picked it up again. He dialled the Paris number and got through to Simon

44

Johnson, who sounded no older than a schoolboy. Black explained that he had been Finn's commanding officer and arranged to come in Kathleen's place. Johnson wasn't certain the French police would accept the identification of a non-family member, but Black explained that in all likelihood he had spent more time in Finn's close company and knew more about his habits than his wife. That seemed to satisfy the young official. They arranged to meet at the mortuary the following lunchtime.

Before he rang off, Black asked the question Johnson seemed to have been avoiding during their exchange: 'Are you able to tell me how Mr Finn – if that is who he is – came by his death?'

'It appears he was stabbed. Repeatedly. I'm afraid that's all I know.'

'I see . . . Thank you.'

Black put down the phone and walked over to the window. He stared out over the quad, feeling his sinews tighten and cold anger pulse through his veins.

Finn of all people. A man who had once fought his way out of a crazed Iraqi mob with his bare hands.

Death.

Black had wondered when it would next come to tap him on the shoulder.

6

Holst regained consciousness face down on a cool, hard surface. His limbs were numb. He was blindfolded, bound hand and foot, and a cloth gag pulled so hard against the corners of his mouth that his cheeks felt as if they might tear apart. Despite this excruciating pain he felt heavy and drugged and too lacking in energy to do anything other than draw each breath through his congested nostrils. At first the only sound he could hear was that of the blood coursing through his ears to the jumpy rhythm of his heart. Then he became aware of a vibration, the low hum of engines and the stifled, pathetic sobs of a woman somewhere close by.

There was no prospect of moving or of making an intelligible sound. He was helpless. Trapped. It occurred to him that he might indeed be dead. Images that had not visited his mind since Sunday-school classes began to revolve as if on a carousel behind his eyes. Angels, demons, a shadowy figure of Christ and a serpent's head as large as a man's with black-green eyes. He fought the urge to vomit, fearing that he would choke. Then a sudden sensation like the ground giving way beneath him distracted his attention. The motion repeated itself and he realized that he was on board an aircraft and that pressure was building against his eardrums. They were descending towards the ground.

He was alive.

Time passed – how much, he wasn't sure – and the sobbing continued. He wanted to kick out and stop it. Then came the whir of electric motors and the familiar sound of landing gear lowering and locking into position. He summoned an image of his wife, Laura, and their son and daughter aged ten and eight. For precious moments they seemed to smile at him before fading and distorting and joining the procession of grotesques thrown up from the most fearful depths of his mind. He heard himself groan like a man on his death bed and felt overcome with self-pity. What had he done to deserve this? Why him? All he had done was work like a slave to push back the frontiers of knowledge.

The aircraft touched down, bounced once, then came quickly to a halt. Even in his trussed-up condition Holst was aware that it was a small plane, a light jet of some sort. A door opened. Two sets of heavy footsteps approached and stopped close to his head. Thick hands grabbed him under the shoulders and hoisted him to his feet. The restraints were removed from his ankles. Behind him, he heard the woman whimper in alarm.

'*Allons-y.*' Let's go.

Holst's legs felt like planks of wood attached to his body. His captor half carried, half dragged him several feet, then hauled him down a flight of steps into hot, humid, cloying air that pulsed with the sound of cicadas.

Several voices shouted at each other in French. The words sounded like orders. Military instructions. Holst felt trickles of sweat run down his back and forehead. The heat was intense, like nothing he had experienced before. They walked across a stretch of tarmac towards the sound of another engine, loud and crude compared with the plane he had just left.

'*Escalier. Quatre.*' Four stairs.

They went up, Holst going first, gingerly seeking each tread with the toe of his shoe before committing his weight.

They entered a confined space that smelled of fuel oil and hot vinyl. He was placed in a seat. Seconds later he heard the woman being brought in after him. Now she was weeping and moaning and he heard Drecker's voice shouting at her in English to shut up. She didn't. There was a sharp slap, a wounded cry of pain, then finally her whimpering stopped. Several more people followed them in, a door slammed, there was a roar of engines and the accelerating thud-thud-thud overhead told him that they were in a helicopter. He felt the machine lift from the ground, rock from side to side, tilt slightly, then move forward with a jerk.

The flight was hot, noisy and to the best of Holst's estimation took less than half an hour. He guessed they were in the tropics. Somewhere in Africa perhaps? Probably one of the former French colonies: Ivory Coast or Senegal. But why here? Susan Drecker was an American who worked, at least as far as he knew, for a wealthy entrepreneur based in Silicon Valley. A man whose identity she had kept secret and who wanted to acquire the results of his precious research for commercial purposes. Coupled with the right nanotechnologies, Holst's discoveries about the reward centres of the brain had the power to manipulate human behaviour in ways that hitherto had been inconceivable.

Could it be that Drecker had been lying all along? That she was nothing to do with business but a government agent who had become aware of the horrendous danger his work posed if its fruits were to fall into the wrong hands? The feeling of nausea returned. His life's work for nothing. He was going to be interrogated, asked to spill every last detail and terrorized into spending what remained of his career in undoing what he had done. He had heard dark and crazy rumours of such things happening before, of scientists who

48

had created technologies so radical and threatening to the established order that they were strangled at birth.

His fear and anguish gave way to raging anger. *Fuck these people. Fuck them to hell.*

The engines changed pitch. The helicopter tilted, tipping him forward against his seat belt, then came in to land.

7

Black's remained one of the few unsmiling faces in the second-class Eurostar carriage as the featureless plains of northern France gave way to the outskirts of Paris. All around him weekending couples strained for their first glimpse of the Eiffel Tower above the city's skyline, but his gaze remained focused inwards. The image that replayed repeatedly in his mind was of a victorious Finn crazily firing his carbine into the night sky from the deck of a British cargo ship they had recaptured from al-Shabaab fanatics. It had been one of their more audacious ops. Their team of six arrived by Apache, fast-roped down to the vessel and spent the next three hours eliminating twenty-three battle-hardened fighters for whom surrender was not an option. Finn had accounted for nearly a dozen of them. He had been fearless that night, as if imbued with some supernatural power. He had pursued the last of them into the bowels of the engine room, fighting hand to hand against hot clanking metal. Finn took no joy in killing – for him, like Black, it was simply a job that he happened to do well – and relished being alive like no one else.

Five hundred rounds offered to the stars, whooping with delight.

A scene from another life.

Kathleen's call had been more than a shock. It had been a convulsion that unleashed a torrent of memories, some good, some ugly, that had hit him with the force of a tidal wave. Black had made his excuses to Karen and the Provost and spent the evening walking on Boars Hill in the countryside

50

to the west of Oxford. Mile after mile alone with his thoughts and never seeming to tire. Then a few sleepless hours staring at the cracked distemper on his bedroom ceiling before rising before dawn to catch the London train. The procession of images hadn't stopped.

His reaction puzzled and troubled him. He and Finn had accepted the possibility of death without question. Over the course of their long careers they had lost friends and colleagues too numerous to mention. A day hadn't passed without the thought that the next mission could be the last. Far from being a horror, it had given life a thrilling edge: a soldier exists on a plane elevated above those who take the arrival of the next week, the next month, for granted.

It was all the more odd, then, that Black should find himself feeling as if he had been hollowed out. Disturbed on some level he couldn't yet reach or comprehend. It was as if all the silt that had settled over the previous five years had been violently agitated, leaving him swimming in dark and ominous waters.

He glanced out of the window to see the last traces of greenery vanish and the city close in around them. The train sped through the netherworld of graffiti-daubed cuttings, somehow invisible from the streets above, that several minutes later terminated in the strange magnificence of the Gare du Nord. Black stepped out on to the platform to be greeted by the unmistakable smell of Paris. He had noticed over the years that ancient cities each carry their own distinctive odour, while those of modern glass and concrete smell of little more than traffic fumes. Paris and London both smelled of their earth and brick, and of centuries of habitation. There was a sharply bitter note in central London air that evoked something of its imperial indifference and isolation. In Paris, even amidst its perfumeries and patisseries, there was, to the English nose at least, always the vaguest hint of effluent. A city whose atmosphere, like one great human exhalation, expressed the common condition in all its baseness and splendour.

With a little over an hour to kill before his noon appointment Black wandered through the nearby streets and found a small café in which he drank a large espresso while standing at a zinc-topped bar, attempting to decode a discarded copy of *Le Parisien*. Paris wasn't a happy city, he gleaned. There had been another violent disturbance in one of the poorer suburbs and a police officer had been shot. Racial tensions were running high and politicians of all stripes were using the situation to make hay. No one quite knew what to do with the country's millions of poor immigrants who stood little chance of becoming French in the way that many French understood the meaning of the word. According to some of the more hysterical voices quoted, the city was like a citadel under siege. Black reflected that not much had changed. Paris's troubled history had been regularly punctuated by periods of threat, occupation or revolution, and after each disaster something dogged and determinedly truthful in its character had invariably re-emerged to restore it.

He left the waitress a generous tip – she had kind eyes above her melancholy smile – and made his way to the Métro station.

His journey took him south under the Seine to Chevaleret in the 13th arrondissement. His destination was the Pitié-Salpêtrière Hospital, which turned out to be a large complex of buildings covering several blocks. When, finally, he found his way to its central point, he discovered that in common with most hospitals he had had cause to visit in similar circumstances, there were signs to every department except the mortuary. He wandered fruitlessly for a while before stopping a pale young woman he assumed to be a junior doctor and attempting to ask directions in fractured French. She listened patiently before sending him in the right direction in perfect English.

The mortuary was located in an anonymous wing set apart from the main building and surrounded by an area of well-tended grass. Black arrived at its entrance with eight minutes to spare to find Simon Johnson already waiting. As Black had surmised from their brief phone call, he was a new recruit, twenty-four or -five at the most. Despite his youth, he had already been firmly pressed into the Foreign Office mould: his thin fair hair neatly parted, regulation dark suit and tie, black brogues polished to a parade-ground shine.

'Major Black?'

'Yes. You must be Simon. Pleased to meet you.'

Black offered his hand, sensing Johnson's relief at his friendly, business-like tone.

'I'm only sorry it's in such unfortunate circumstances.' He shifted awkwardly from one foot to another. 'Commandant Valcroix is waiting for us inside. There's an investigation under way, of course, but I should warn you he won't be very forthcoming. The case has already been assigned to a *juge d'instruction* who's directing the inquiry.'

'A judge? Already?'

'It's the way they do things here. It feels rather alien to us, but it seems to work.' He glanced towards the door. 'Shall we?'

Black nodded, readying himself for what he hoped would be a brief ordeal.

The mortuary was on the basement level. Black followed Johnson down two flights of steps to a subterranean corridor whose gloss-painted walls were scuffed along their length at waist height from the constant passage of trolleys bearing bodies from the hospital's wards and operating theatres. They arrived at a secure door. Johnson pressed the video intercom.

After a short exchange with an officious attendant the door buzzed open. They entered another corridor identical to the one they had just passed through, except that parked against the left-hand wall were more than half a dozen gurneys bearing corpses draped with pale blue hospital sheets.

A bow-backed, sallow-faced man somewhere in his fifties appeared from a small waiting room to their left. An olive-green jacket hung off his angular shoulders and flapped around his insubstantial body.

'Mr Johnson?' He mistakenly directed the question at Black.

'*Non*,' Johnson corrected him. '*C'est Major Black.*'

'Ah. My apologies. Commandant Henri Valcroix, Police Nationale.' He looked them both up and down with intense, unblinking eyes, which lent him a presence that more than compensated for his lack of bulk. 'You have a passport, yes?'

'Of course.'

Black produced the document and, for good measure, his driving licence. While Valcroix scrutinized both, Johnson felt obliged to rehearse the fact that Black had been Finn's close colleague and commanding officer for the larger part of two decades.

'And you were in the Special Forces, Major?' Valcroix asked.

'I was an infantryman,' Black replied.

'Of the famous SAS?'

Johnson cast Black an anxious glance. 'Obviously there's no secret that Sergeant Finn was a special serviceman. But even though he is no longer serving, Major Black is still bound by strict obligations of confidentiality.'

Valcroix grunted and handed back Black's papers. 'You know why Mr Finn was in Paris?'

'Only the little his wife could tell me. We haven't spoken for some time.'

'He was working as a bodyguard. To a young British scientist. Female. Attending a conference. Do you undertake such work, Major?'

'No. I'm an academic. Or trying to be.'

Valcroix raised an eyebrow. 'You teach? Where? In a university?'

'Yes.'

'May I ask which one?'

'Oxford.'

Valcroix nodded, seemingly startled by this fact. 'The young woman, too.'

'It's a big institution. May I ask who she is?'

Valcroix avoided the question. 'Let us see if it is indeed Mr Finn. Please.' He gestured them to follow.

A pair of swing doors at the far end of the corridor led into a tiled area. Three of the four walls were lined with refrigerated body-storage units. An overpowering smell of disinfectant barely masked the underlying stench of chilled, decomposed flesh. An attendant, who gave every impression of having far more pressing matters to attend to, was standing by impatiently. Valcroix glanced to Black, who nodded his readiness.

Black was no stranger to dead bodies, but he nevertheless felt a fist-sized knot form beneath his diaphragm as the technician slid open a drawer on the lowest tier.

The corpse was wrapped in an envelope of gleaming white polythene. The technician pulled back the flap revealing the head, shoulders and torso of a large, well-built man. The face was white as if moulded from candle wax. Black's impression was of a cruel and unflattering facsimile of Finn, but his gaze lingered on the facial features only briefly. His eyes were quickly drawn to the dozen or so very obvious stab wounds to the chest and the deep lacerations criss-crossing the arms and shoulders. Any traces of blood had been washed away after the autopsy, but the livid bruises surrounding each wound spoke of the force with which the knives had been driven through skin, muscle and bone. Finn's furious attempts to defend himself were evident from multiple gashes to his arms both above and beneath his elbows.

Black's eyes flicked to Valcroix, who gestured the technician to pull the plastic back further. He opened both flaps out fully, revealing more stab wounds to the abdomen and sides and a pattern of vicious overlapping bruises that suggested he had been kicked repeatedly. There was worse: the fingers and thumbs of the newly revealed hands had been sliced off. Every one. What remained of them had been gathered in a clear polythene bag that rested between Finn's thighs.

'Are you able to confirm Mr Finn's identity?' Commandant Valcroix asked.

Black nodded, lifting his eyes to the detective's impassive face. He noticed that Johnson had turned away, unable to look any longer.

'It was clearly a vicious attack,' Valcroix said, gesturing the technician to slide the drawer back in.

'It would have taken at least three men,' Black said.

'The fingers —' Valcroix let the words hang like a question.

'A lot of mutilation takes place in combat. More than you might imagine. Especially among irregulars.'

'Combat? Why would that be relevant?'

'No common thugs could have done this to Finn. This had to be the work of professionals.'

Valcroix nodded, as if his suspicions had been confirmed.

'What happened to the young woman?' Black asked.

'She is missing. We presume she was abducted.'

'May I ask from where?'

'The Hotel George V. But I'm afraid that is all I can tell you at present, Major. Procedure. You understand.'

'Of course.'

'Mr Johnson, I am sure, will inform his next of kin. I will do my best with the judge – cause of death is very clear. We hope to release the body next week.'

'Thank you,' Johnson said, wiping cold beads of sweat from his lip.

'Good day to you both,' Valcroix said, dismissing them. 'If you'll excuse me, I have a few more formalities to attend to.'

Johnson remained silent as they exited the building. Black half expected him to vomit, but the young official managed to regain his composure and after a few deep breaths the blood returned to his face.

'I do apologize, Major –'

'No need,' Black said, almost as relieved as his companion to taste fresh air.

'The police warned me that he had met a violent end, but I had no idea –'

'I don't suppose you have any more information about who Finn was working for?' Black said, keen to change the subject.

Johnson hesitated long enough for Black to conclude that he did, but that he had been told to keep his mouth shut.

'Is it sensitive?' Black pressed.

'I believe it may have been a government contract,' Johnson confessed. 'I really don't know any more than that. The French authorities will investigate thoroughly, I'm sure.'

'He was employed by the Security Services to protect a British scientist?'

'If I could tell you any more –'

'I understand,' Black said, sparing him the trouble of repeating himself. 'And there's no need for you to call Finn's wife. It'll be better coming from me.'

'Thank you.'

They shook hands once more.

Black turned to go.

'Just one thing, if I may,' Johnson said.

Black looked back.

Johnson swallowed. 'The business with the fingers. What does it suggest to you?'

'In this case . . . ?' He dismissed the possibility of prolonged torture. Finn's injuries were consistent with a far more sudden and explosively violent encounter. 'I've got an outlandish idea.'

'Which is?'

'Agincourt. The French chopped the fingers off captured British bowmen. These things stick in soldiers' minds.'

Johnson looked baffled, as if Black had taken leave of his senses. 'Soldiers?'

'As I told the commandant – this wasn't the work of amateurs.'

'So . . . a sign of some sort?'

'Or a mark of revenge. Finn went down fighting. He'll have done a lot of damage on the way.'

'I see,' Johnson said. 'Well, I suppose things will become clearer in due course.'

'Let's hope so.'

They parted company at the hospital gate. Black declined the offer of a lift in Johnson's taxi and instead made his way back to the Métro. Passing along the quiet suburban street he was aware of the sky seeming to darken and of ugly and violent impulses stirring somewhere in the primitive depths of his being. He paused at the station entrance and told himself to be rational, to trust the police and go directly back to the Gare du Nord. No good could come from acting out of anger, no matter how righteous.

Then he thought of Finn – not merely killed but slaughtered. And of Kathleen and her children, and of the faceless official who would in due course arrive on her doorstep. He would make sympathetic noises over tea and biscuits but tell her nothing at all about why her husband was cut to pieces during a routine job for Her Majesty's Government.

Later, Black would remember this moment as the one that changed everything.

8

The bare facts. That's all a dead soldier's family ever wanted. Just to know where, when and how. Black's instinct already told him that the circumstances of Finn's death were not of the kind that governments liked to publicize, even to close relatives. And in this case there were two governments involved, each, no doubt, with their own pressing reasons to keep the truth to themselves. Black was only too aware of the number of suspicious deaths that even on British soil go entirely unreported or investigated – he had been personally responsible for a number of them. He had also seen how the blanket of secrecy that covered the disappearance of war criminals, terrorist assassins and spies was readily extended to shroud the occasional accidents that befell their executioners. Kathleen Finn deserved better. Black was determined to return home with something to answer the endless questions that would otherwise haunt her day and night.

The journey north-west to the George V Métro station involved two changes and eighteen stops but it passed in what seemed like seconds, as if Black had entered that trance-like state that overcomes late-night drivers who arrive at their destination with no recollection of how they got there.

He emerged from the Métro into the cacophony of the Avenue des Champs-Élysées. Cars, scooters and buses jockeyed crazily with one another on the broad boulevard leading to the Arc de Triomphe. He turned right on to the Avenue George V and took a seat on a public bench close enough to a crowded tourist café to connect his phone to its

Wi-Fi. He searched for any reports of the abduction of a British scientist in Paris and the murder of her bodyguard. There were none, which immediately made him suspect that the *juge d'instruction* had ordered a news blackout and that in response to a request in the UK a minister had issued a D-notice requesting media silence. In Britain such steps were only taken in cases involving perceived threats to national security.

A search on recent scientific gatherings in Paris, however, instantly bore fruit. Within seconds he had ascertained that the International Association of Nanotechnology had held its annual conference at the Académie des Sciences during the previous week. Helpfully, a copy of the programme was posted on the association's website. He scanned through it and found two speakers from Oxford: one male computer scientist and a female biomechanical engineer, Dr Sarah Bellman. Her presentation was entitled *Developments in Nanoscale DNA-Based Delivery Mechanisms*. It was clearly cutting edge, but far outside Black's sphere of knowledge. The last item on the itinerary was the closing reception, which had been held at the Four Seasons George V Hotel the previous Thursday evening.

Black made an educated guess that such a gathering of intellectual capital would have required protection by a professional security company of the sort that employed so many of his former colleagues. With a little luck, if he could find out which it was, he might discover a friendly ex-soldier prepared to share a few confidences. He looked up the contact details for the association and saw that they were based in California, seven time zones behind. The chances of the office being manned at six on a Saturday were slim, but there was no harm trying. He tapped the phone number highlighted on his screen. After a short pause there followed several rings before a voicemail message started to play. Black was about to ring off when the message was interrupted by a female voice.

'Hello. This is Maria at the IANT. How may I help you?'

'Good morning,' Black said. 'I wasn't expecting to find anyone home.'

'The phone calls usually start about now. We're a global association. What can I do for you today, sir?'

'You'll be aware of an unfortunate incident at the Paris conference last week.' He paused. She didn't respond. 'The man who died was a close colleague of mine. I have some important information that I'd like to pass to the conference's head of security. I wondered if you might have contact details.'

'Right . . . umm –'

'I imagine it was a local firm in Paris.'

'I'm sorry. I'm afraid this is way above my pay grade. Can I take your name and number and get someone more senior to call you back?'

'It's extremely urgent. Could you put me in contact with whoever might have that information?'

'You mean now?'

'Yes, please. My name is Major Leo Black. I was Ryan Finn's commanding officer – he was the man who was killed.'

He had flustered her. He could hear the tension in her voice as she tapped on a keyboard. 'The problem is . . . my boss, Dr Goldberg, he and his colleagues are on their way back at the moment. I believe their flight's due in later this morning.'

'There must be an email trail. Can you not try searching "security"? I don't want to compromise you, but it's critical I make contact immediately. All I need is the name of the company – I can take it from there.'

Another pause. He sensed her weighing the consequences of denying his request.

'OK. It's Major Leo Black, right?'

'Correct. I also happen to teach at Oxford University. I suppose that makes Dr Bellman a colleague of sorts.'

'Oh –'

He heard her hurriedly searching his name. He knew precisely what she would be looking at: his profile on the history faculty's website. A benign academic. Smiling and innocuous.

'I'm sorry to hurry you –'

'It's OK. I think I found it . . . Yes, here we are. The company is called ICPS and our contact's name is Mr Sebastian Pirot.'

'Based in Paris?'

'The address on my screen is in San Diego.'

'Do you have a number for Mr Pirot?'

'I think so . . . Yes, here it is. Can I read it out to you?'

'Go ahead.'

Black jotted the number for a French mobile phone on to the corner of his return train ticket, thanked Maria for her help and dialled it. After a single ring he was greeted with a generic voicemail message. He left his name and asked Pirot to call him as soon as possible.

He switched back to the web browser and searched ICPS. International Close Protection Services had a website with high production values but with very little information beyond a list of key services, including the provision of ex-military bodyguards and security for high-end events. The contacts section contained an enquiry form and the number for a San Diego landline. No names. No email address. He tried the number and got through to a message inviting him to leave his details with the promise that a representative would get back to him shortly. He did so, though with no expectation of being called back during the weekend.

A final search on *Sebastian Pirot* returned a number of

results, but none relating to a French security executive. It was frustrating but not surprising. Security was one of the few remaining professions whose practitioners valued their anonymity.

Accepting that his search for Pirot had come to a temporary dead end, Black made his way south along the Avenue George V towards the hotel, sticking to the shade of the plane trees that punctuated the pavement at regular intervals. After a short distance he found himself among the shopfronts of the avenue's many plush boutiques and became aware that he had left the tourists behind. He was now in the heart of wealthy Paris, where the shoppers looked as if they had come straight from the pages of a magazine and the stone façades of the buildings gleamed in the afternoon sun. Surrounded by such opulence it was impossible not to feel like an interloper.

After a further quarter of a mile Black approached the entrance of the George V as a large, sleek Mercedes drew up. He hung back as two doormen stepped out from under a canopy to meet the occupants: a portly middle-aged man in sunglasses and his much younger and very beautiful female companion. She moved gracefully in her four-inch heels, poised and erect, gently swaying her hips on each carefully placed step. Trailing in her perfumed wake, Black followed them inside, barely noticed by the two accompanying doormen hungry for a tip.

Black came through the entrance to find himself in a marbled reception hall filled with the smell of freshly cut flowers. While the wealthy couple was shepherded to the desk, he made his way unobtrusively in the opposite direction.

There were only a handful of patrons scattered among the tables in the elaborately decorated wood-panelled room, all of them deeply immersed in each other's company. Black took a seat on one of the high stools at the bar, behind which a steward with a shiny bald pate was polishing champagne glasses with a virgin-white napkin.

'*Monsieur?*'

'Bloody Mary, *s'il vous plaît.*'

'Of course.' The steward smiled politely.

He set his glass aside, dropped ice into a shaker, tipped in a large measure of Beluga vodka and a little less tomato juice. Black caught his own reflection in the mirror behind the bar and realized why he might have given the appearance of being in need of a strong drink. His sleepless night and the morning's ordeal had left him looking haggard. Deep lines creased the corners of his eyes and his face was covered with a dark shadow of greying stubble.

The steward rolled the mixture just enough to combine the contents without letting the tomato juice lose its viscosity, then decanted it into a tall glass with the practised finesse of a Monte Carlo croupier.

'*Santé, Monsieur.*'

Black took a large and appreciative mouthful, the vodka gently burning his throat and warming his stomach. 'Very good.'

The steward nodded in gratitude and returned to his polishing.

Black sat in silence for a minute or two, working his way steadily down the glass and wondering whether to tap the steward for information or to take his chances getting an interview with the hotel manager. He decided on the former. Barmen were used to talking and easier to bribe.

'You probably saw my friend last week,' Black said. 'He was the bodyguard – the Englishman.'

'Oh . . . yes.' The steward's eyes instinctively swept the room as if scanning for eavesdroppers.

'We were in the army together. Fifteen years. I'm in Paris to identify his body.'

'I'm sorry to hear that, *Monsieur*. We spoke once or twice. He seemed like a gentleman.' He reached a fresh napkin from under the counter.

Black observed the tension in his shoulders, a sudden stiffness in his movements. No doubt he and the other staff had been placed under strict instructions not to say a word on the matter. Murders and kidnaps weren't good for business.

'I don't mean to embarrass you; I'd just like to know where it happened – so I can tell his wife.'

'I know very little, *Monsieur*.' He cast an anxious glance towards the door as if hoping some superior might come to his rescue.

'You must know where it took place. The hotel will have been filled with police. People can't have been talking about anything else.'

'You should speak to the manager, *Monsieur*. Shall I call him for you?'

Black drained the last of his drink and set the empty tumbler on the bar. 'I'd rather you just told me where he was murdered so I can pay my respects.' He fixed the barman with a level gaze. 'Surely that's not very much to ask.'

Pricks of sweat formed on his naked scalp. 'I understand something occurred in a room on the third floor. A woman was kidnapped, lowered to the ground by ropes. Your friend's body, it was found in an alleyway at the back of the hotel.' He gave a nervous shrug. 'That's all I know, *Monsieur*. You have my word.'

'I'm much obliged,' Black said. He brought out his wallet. '*L'addition, s'il vous plaît*.'

'*Très bien, Monsieur. Vingt-six euros, s'il vous plaît*.'

Black gave him a fifty and told him to keep the change.

Black took the stairs to the third floor. Long experience had left him with an ingrained aversion to lifts, which in a tight situation were as good as a coffin.

He arrived on the third floor and looked both ways along the long, carpeted corridor. Aside from a chambermaid's cart off to his right there was no sign of life. He headed left, checking the doors and walls at the rear of the building for any telltale signs of police activity, reasoning that if forensics officers were anything like soldiers, they were certain to have left their clumsy mark on the George V's pristine decoration. Finding none, he turned around and went back in the opposite direction. He reached the maid's cart and found what he was looking for. The door to the right of the room she was cleaning was smeared with greasy fingerprints. On closer inspection he noticed that the vertical left-hand section of the frame was brand new, its mahogany finish a shade darker than the rest of the frame. The door itself might even have been a replacement, the fingerprints those of the carpenters who would have hung it immediately after the police had finished their work.

He tried the handle.

Locked.

Black stepped back and glanced through the open doorway into the next room. The maid was in the bathroom to the left of the short passageway that led on to the bedroom. He could see some personal effects and a suitcase sitting on the stand at the foot of the bed.

He knocked sharply, startling her.

'*Excusez-moi, madame. Police anglaise. Deux minutes?*'

He stepped inside without waiting to be invited, proceeded into the bedroom and made for the set of tall French windows. He opened them and stepped outside on to a small balcony protected by a waist-high iron railing. There was no view to speak of except the rear of the buildings opposite. Three floors below was a pedestrian alley leading to a narrow service road, wide enough for delivery vans and the rubbish truck to pass through with little space to spare. There was a faint smell of chlorine as if the whole area beneath him had been recently sluiced down. The barman had mentioned ropes. He glanced up; there were identical balconies on the floors above. Ropes could easily have been rigged to allow a quick descent to the ground.

'*Monsieur?*'

Black turned to see two large, thick-set figures dressed in dark suits entering the bedroom. They gestured to the maid to leave. She hurried out into the corridor. Both were in their twenties and the taller of the two had a bruise that spread outwards from the bridge of his broad, flat nose beneath both eyes. Badges on their breast pockets identified them as SÉCURITÉ.

'Good afternoon.' Black affected a smile. 'I didn't mean to cause a problem. I'm a friend of the man who was killed. I was just leaving.'

He took a step forward. The two security guards barred his way, crowding the space between the end of the bed and the wardrobe.

The shorter of the two spoke: 'Wait here, please.'

Black looked from one to the other. 'Wait? For what?'

'Police.' He pointed towards a chair at the side of the French doors.

'The police? I merely wanted to see where it happened.'

They stared at him with impassive faces, their outsize shoulders straining the seams of their jackets.

'What offence do you say I've committed?'

No answer.

Black persisted with his reasonable tone. 'Perhaps you

68

might tell me where I can find Sebastian Pirot? I presume you dealt with him during the conference last week.'

Dead eyes looked back at him. Black sensed they were relishing the moment. A real-life intruder and a foreigner to boot. He tried to remain calm and decided to let them justify their wages by having the satisfaction of seeing him have to explain himself to a gendarme, but then a single word, '*Sit*' – spat rather than spoken – tripped a switch in his brain.

The effect was both physical and psychological and bypassed all rational faculties. A burst of adrenalin coursed through his veins. The two men in front of him seemed to diminish in size. They became ridiculous, clumsy, comic-book figures.

'Kindly step aside, gentlemen.'

'Sit.' Shorty stepped in front of his colleague and crossed his thick arms across his barrel chest.

A beginner's error.

Black lunged forward and pushed the man's crossed wrists hard against his sternum. As he stumbled backwards against his colleague, Black aimed a kick into his exposed groin. Clutching his crotch, the security guard collapsed, winded, on to the carpet. The bigger man had now regained his balance and was filling the width of the short passageway, barring Black's way to the door. He squared up, fists cocked in front of his face like a trained boxer. Only the fear in his eyes gave him away as an amateur. Black feinted, causing him to unleash with a straight right. Black slipped left, hooked his right arm inside the oncoming fist and drove the heel of his left palm into his biceps, causing him to swivel and slam forehead first into the wall, but not before his shoulder was wrenched from its socket. As he went down, clutching an arm that now hung uselessly from the middle of his ribs to below his knee, he made a sound like the dying groan of a slaughtered ox.

Black stepped over his prone body, wrenched the solid

brass handle from the door and tossed it out into the now empty corridor. He pulled the door closed behind him, locking the two injured men inside. Then he made his way to the stairs.

Moments later, Black emerged into the lobby where business continued as normal. Descending the hotel's carpeted front steps, he exchanged nods with the doormen and climbed into a taxi.

'*La Gare du Nord, s'il vous plaît.*'

9

A metal gate clanged shut behind them.

'*Arrêtez.*' Stop.

He winced at the harshness of the light and immediately shut his eyes tight. Holst felt the same rough hands cut through the cable ties binding his wrists in front of his body and remove his blindfold, daring only to open his eyes slowly, by tiny degrees, as his pupils contracted.

They were in a room painted white in a single-storey building that carried the breeze-block-and-cement smell of recent construction. There were sturdy, gleaming steel bars at the window. Several figures came into focus: Susan Drecker and a tall, unnaturally thin man, both dressed in military fatigues, stood opposite; next to them stood a middle-aged man of Middle Eastern appearance dressed in a blue short-sleeved civilian shirt.

Holst glanced to his right and saw a young woman with dark matted hair, also blinking painfully into the light. To his left were two men dressed in matching khaki shorts and T-shirts, one aged thirty or so, the other closer to sixty. Both wore glasses and had the soft features and shapeless limbs of professional men. Holst knew instantly and by instinct that both they and the young woman were fellow scientists.

The older man spoke. 'Sarah? Are you all right?'

'She's fine. Shut up.' The rebuke, spoken in a pronounced Afrikaans accent, came from the skeletal figure alongside Drecker. He gestured to someone standing behind them. Two large Hispanic-looking men dressed in similar lightweight military clothing stepped away from the group of four scientists and took up position either side of the prison-style gate that acted as a secure inner door to the building. Beyond it was a further solid door to the outside. Holst noticed the absence of any insignia or markings on their uniforms.

'Dr Holst, Dr Bellman, I'm Colonel Brennan. You both know Captain Drecker, but allow me to introduce our colleague and Director of Scientific Operations, Dr Ammal Razia.'

The man in the blue shirt gave a solemn nod of greeting. 'We apologize for the manner of your transportation and for the basic nature of your accommodation. Unfortunately, all our quarters are similarly lacking in creature comforts at the present time. This facility is new and very much a work in progress. We hope to make our conditions considerably more comfortable over the coming months. Our priority has been equipping our laboratories.' His voice was cultured, his tone apologetic and his accent suggested an English education.

'What are you doing? Where are we?' the young woman to Holst's right demanded in a tone that bordered on the hysterical.

Brennan silenced her with a look and a sideways glance to the two uniformed guards at the gate.

The older man to Holst's left held up his hands as if urging her to stay calm and listen.

'You have been brought here to work together,' Brennan said. 'Regrettably, this was the only viable method to stay ahead of the competition. Each of you is a leader in your field and fighting to stay ahead of the pack, and each of you has agreed to sell your research to our mutual employer for substantial sums of money. So before you object too vociferously to your circumstances, I would urge you to consider the wider picture. The sooner this project is completed, the sooner you will get paid and go home. If you had been entirely trustworthy counterparts in our negotiations, none of this may have been necessary, but –' he gave a thin, philosophical smile – 'we're all of us only human.'

Holst noticed an exchange of glances between Bellman and the older man, as if both were equally surprised and appalled by the other.

'Yes,' Drecker interjected, addressing her remarks to him, 'I'm afraid your protégée turned out to be as mercenary as you, Professor Kennedy. Even more so, as a matter of fact.' She smiled in a way that Holst remembered from several of their discussions concerning his remuneration. It was as if she were revelling in a feeling of moral superiority at having exposed their hypocritical greed.

Brennan gestured to Dr Razia to take the floor. He stepped forward and addressed the new arrivals as matter-of-factly as if they had come of their own free will.

'Allow me to make some introductions. Dr Bellman and Professor Kennedy are close colleagues at Oxford, of course, but aside from that I suspect you may be strangers to each other. Let us start with Dr Angelos Sphyris.' He nodded to the slight young man to Holst's left. 'Dr Sphyris is a computer scientist turned neuromorphologist based in Cambridge, who is well on the way to mapping the one hundred billion neurons in the human brain with the aid of artificial intelligence. This remarkable AI has proved almost infallibly accurate in predicting the function of each new neural circuit it identifies. Dr Alec Kennedy is one of the foremost pioneers of nano-engineering and has created minute particles capable of releasing heat in response to microwave frequencies. These particles stimulate activity in the cells to which they attach. His colleague, Dr Sarah Bellman, has developed an ingenious mechanism capable of delivering a payload of such particles to any cell in the body. Lastly, Dr Lars Holst. His work has focused on the reward and aversion centres of the brain and initially it is these you will be concentrating on.

'Our considerable investment is being committed in the belief that together you will combine your knowledge to create a technology capable of numerous applications, which we will discuss in due course. But first things first. We must show the new arrivals to their accommodation, and later we will begin work on ordering the necessary equipment and supplies for your laboratories.' Razia paused and gave an almost kindly smile. 'It may please you to know that here you won't find yourselves bound by the usual ethical constraints. You may experiment at will on primates and, if necessary, on human subjects. I suggest you start to factor that into your thinking.' He spread his palms as if in a gesture of goodwill. 'I very much look forward to working with you.'

'Two hours' rest,' Drecker said. 'Then we get to work.'

She turned to the gate with Brennan and Razia.

'That's it? We don't get to ask any questions?' The defiant challenge came from Dr Bellman.

'What do you want to know?' Drecker said with forced patience.

'What if we choose not to cooperate?'

'The time to ask that question was before you agreed to sell your soul for eight million dollars, Dr Bellman,' Brennan said. 'No one gets rich without paying the price. Ask anyone who's done it – it's paid in sweat or conscience. Every penny.'

He smiled, his taut skin creasing like a lizard's.

From somewhere deeper in the building Holst heard a macaque screech and shake the bars of its cage.

IO

Black walked at a steady pace across the concourse of the Gare du Nord, aware that his senses remained on full alert. He saw each face, heard every footstep, registered colours, smells and the tiniest flickers of movement, even those from the pigeons roosting on the great iron beams of the station's vaulted roof. The violent encounter in the hotel room had flung him straight back into the vivid hyper-reality from which he had banished himself nearly five years before. And like a wise, dry alcoholic who had inadvertently taken a drink, he attempted to observe his altered state from one remove. He told himself it was a temporary condition, an aberration forced on him by circumstances beyond his control. Equilibrium and normality would soon return.

The shift in consciousness was seductive, nonetheless. Along with ultra-acuity came a sense of invulnerability and physical prowess; he felt like a leopard walking among sheep. Supreme self-confidence is what the army had termed it. It was present in the smile of a psychopath and in the eyes of a paratrooper during the moments before a drop. It was the quality capable of being expressed by a small percentage of human beings who, in life-threatening circumstances, are able to harness both intellect and aggression to the exclusion of fear. All Special Service personnel possessed it, and it was both their blessing and their curse.

With no conscious effort, he picked out the numerous armed police officers moving among the bustling crowds as clearly as if they were dressed in high-vis jackets. The names of their weapons sprang unprompted from dormant recesses of his memory: the St Étienne M12SD submachine gun, the Mousqueton AMD select-fire carbine and the Sig Sauer P2022 handguns holstered at their waists. His eyes scanned the human tide for plain-clothes detectives, each tell-tale signal firing like a point of light: female, late twenties, athletic build, no luggage; male, forties, shaved head, sunglasses; a second male, thirty, touching a hidden receiver in his right ear. The station was crawling with them, but none gave him a second glance. They were hunting for lone-wolf killers and their darkest fear: another gang of marauding home-grown jihadis. A suited Englishman faded as surely into the background as chewing gum into the pavement. He passed through the ticket barrier and passport control without hindrance and made it to the platform.

Only once the train had cleared the Parisian suburbs and was heading towards the north coast at 200 miles per hour did Black feel himself begin to unwind. He closed his eyes and in a deliberate attempt to limit the stimulus to his brain, felt his right forearm resting heavily on his thigh. He turned his focus inwards and tried to hear only the steady rhythm of his heart. Two years of cognitive behavioural therapy had achieved less than a long weekend retreat in a Yorkshire monastery, where an elderly Cistercian monk had imparted the simple techniques that had guided him through a lifetime of inward contemplation.

Black's body relaxed but his brain stubbornly refused to quieten. An image of Finn's mutilated corpse, photographic in detail, refused to leave him. Resisting the urge to force his attention elsewhere, he followed the monk's stern counsel never to shrink 'but always to look Satan in the eye' and confronted the picture of his dead comrade. Against the gentle, rocking rhythm of the carriage, he took in every detail: the waxy skin drawn across the cheekbones, the bruised and punctured muscles of his chest, the fading tattoos criss-crossed with defensive wounds on his thick forearms and the bloody stubs of fingers.

By slow and painful degrees the raw horror receded and with it the fury and blind urges to revenge it had provoked. In their place came the numb sensation of shock and disbelief that accompanies sudden and unexpected loss. A bitter residue of anger still remained, but cool and rational thoughts returned to hold it in check. Satisfied that he had regained as much balance as he was able, he opened his eyes to be greeted by the patchwork fields of the Kent countryside.

He glanced at his watch: more than ninety minutes had passed. He sank back into his seat and glanced at the nearby passengers, smiling, talking and tapping on their phones. He envied their lives lived in a single and predictable reality. Until the incident at the George V he had convinced himself that he had left his past behind and rejoined them. He slowly exhaled and silently prayed that it would never happen again.

The train pulled into St Pancras station. Black disembarked and merged once more into a shifting sea of travellers, unaware that his reassuring sense of anonymity was an illusion. The concealed cameras of the UK Border Force picked out his face and logged his presence. Once detected, he was unerringly followed by other unseen electronic eyes that would track him through the London Underground to Paddington station, watch him drink a large whisky at the bar, and follow him on to the nine p.m. train to Oxford. Microseconds after it was gathered, the surveillance footage was processed by software that analysed the minutiae of his body language and facial expressions, piecing them together to form a more accurate appraisal of his mental state than any he could have articulated himself.

The man watching the results on his computer screen was heartened by what he saw. It had cost him much of his diminishing supply of goodwill to keep the French from detaining Major Leo Black following his unfortunate fracas, and he badly needed a return on his investment.

11

Holst lay awake on a thin mattress in a locked room that in most respects was distinguished from a prison cell only by the presence of an air-conditioning unit.

Such spartan conditions were, he supposed, designed to concentrate minds. It was effective. He could think of nothing except the need to complete their project as soon as possible and being released to enjoy the fruits of his labours.

Bellman, though, seemed incapable of resigning herself to their situation. For the past two hours her persistent sobbing had leaked mournfully through the thin wall that separated them, denying him any possibility of sleep. From his room on the far side of hers Holst could hear Kennedy pleading with her to remain calm. He was having no luck. She was like a stubborn child, somehow convinced that if she made herself wretched enough her suffering would end. He suppressed the desire to yell at her to shut up and think of the money, knowing that it would only make her worse.

Through a thick fog of tiredness Holst tried to reconcile himself to their situation. He resigned himself to the fact that he would have no opportunity to communicate with the outside world and would be confined for months, if not longer. It was a grim prospect. He tried not to think too hard about how his wife would be reacting or what she would tell their children. On the upside, if Brennan and Drecker and whoever they were working for held good to their contract, he and his family could look forward to a comfortable future. This was the hope he had to cling to. If he were forced to organize a similar project, he would be tempted to follow similar methods. Secrecy and speed were paramount. There had been many occasions during the past century when governments eager to develop and exploit nascent technologies had bribed, cajoled or deliberately sequestered scientists to the service of the state. The competition to develop the atom bomb, the cracking of wartime codes and the race to put men into space had all been organized with military methods and efficiency. In the age of global business the state had simply been replaced by a different kind of rapacious and self-serving entity.

He heard footsteps in the corridor. Doors were unlocked: Bellman's first, then his. One of the two guards yelled in at him. '*Allez, debout!*' Get up!

He dragged himself to his feet and rolled his stiff neck around his shoulders. More orders were shouted in French, instructing them to return to the room at the end of the corridor. He made his way along the narrow tiled passageway and joined Kennedy and Sphyris who were already seated at a table with Brennan and Drecker. Each of them had a laptop computer. Two more were waiting for him and Bellman.

Brennan directed Holst to a seat between the other scientists. 'Dr Razia will join us shortly.'

'*Lèves-toi!*' The angry command came from the entrance to Bellman's room. She was evidently refusing to cooperate.

Holst glanced along the length of the corridor and saw the two guards standing in her doorway.

'Excuse me.' Drecker got up from her chair and made her way towards them.

'Professor Kennedy and Dr Sphyris have already received much of their inventory as you'll see when we show you the labs,' Brennan said to Holst, ignoring the distraction. 'What-ever else they require will be ordered in collaboration with you and Dr Bellman. The company is prepared to offer you an unlimited budget – within reason – so please feel free to order all that you need.' He nodded to the laptop. 'This is your machine. For obvious reasons there's no internet con-nection, but you'll find catalogues from all the major suppliers in the documents folder.'

There was a short, terrified scream from Sarah Bellman's room followed by the sounds of a brief and one-sided strug-gle. Moments later, the two guards reappeared bringing her with them. She was dressed only in her underwear and was sobbing inconsolably. They manhandled her back along the corridor, her bare feet only grazing the floor. Drecker fol-lowed behind barking instructions in French.

Holst, Sphyris and Kennedy watched, paralysed and help-less to intervene, as the two guards forced the young woman face first against the closed steel gate inside the entrance to the building. They spread her arms and handcuffed her wrists to the bars above her head.

Drecker drew a pistol from the holster attached to her belt and touched it to Bellman's left temple.

'A simple choice, Dr Bellman – cooperate or save us the expense of dealing with you. There are others in your field more than capable of replicating your work.'

Finally, Bellman fell silent.

'She's more trouble than she's worth,' Brennan said cas-ually. 'Get rid of her.'

'No!' Bellman's desperate cry echoed off the bare walls.

Drecker pressed the barrel of the gun against her skull.

Holst looked away as she squeezed the trigger.

There was a harmless click.

Holst glanced back to see that Bellman had collapsed at the knees and fallen into a dead faint, leaving her body hanging by the wrists. Her legs were fouled and urine had pooled at her feet. The sight turned his stomach. She reminded him of one of his dead experimental animals.

12

The Land Rover Defender sounded every one of its twenty-five years as it coughed reluctantly into life, belching a cloud of soot-laden diesel fumes. The grumbling engine, turning over for the first time in a month, continued to complain as Black manoeuvred out of the cramped college car park and headed north through Jericho. The gentrified terraced houses were still and silent early on a Sunday morning. The odd dog walker and a stick-limbed young woman running with the determination of the lonely and obsessed provided the only signs of life in the empty streets. After two miles he reached the edge of the city and headed west on the A40 towards Gloucester.

Jaded by a second night of fitful sleep, Black wound down the windows and let the cool morning air rush in. Despite his best efforts, during the few hours he had forced himself to lie in bed, he had been haunted by images of Finn and tormented by endless rehearsals of the words he would use to describe what he had seen to Kathleen later that morning. He had visited the newly bereaved widows of men under his command many times, but it had always been in his official capacity and with his emotions, such as they were, locked tightly away. Without the shield of uniform and weighed down with guilt at having neglected his oldest friend, Black was left with what he supposed were the normal human reactions to such an event: unfamiliar feelings of grief and remorse that refused to be reasoned with.

He rumbled on past Witney to Burford where the patchwork fields of Oxfordshire gave way to the broader expanses of the Cotswolds. The early mist had evaporated and beneath a clear and brilliant sky the drystone walls were the colour of honey and the air sweet with the scent of freshly mown hay. He recalled the many times he had driven this road with Finn en route from RAF Brize Norton to regimental HQ at Credenhill. Returning from a stretch in the Middle East or Africa the British countryside had always been balm to the soul. Its softness and fecundity seemed to nurture human life as keenly as the landscapes of other countries challenged it. Finn had been lyrical on the subject – beneath the bluff exterior, the Celt in him nursed a romantic streak – and they had both agreed that the further west they travelled the more at ease they felt, never feeling quite at peace until they had reached the more sparsely populated county of Hereford-shire where the Welsh hills rose up against the horizon. This border country, where lowland woods and pastures merged into untamed upland, was the perfect home for returning soldiers: the junction of civilization and wilderness.

Shortly after nine, Black descended the long sweep of the Callow, the hillside that led down into the valley in which the small city of Hereford straddled a long straight stretch of the River Wye. He made his way by memory to Finn's home, a modest semi-detached in an unassuming neighbourhood south of the river. Finn and Kathleen had moved here when they married twelve years before. Their plan had always been to stay until they could afford a place in the country with a few acres of land and a barn for Finn to turn into a carpentry workshop. Black speculated that with Finn having spent a few years working private contracts, they couldn't have been far from turning the dream to reality. He squeezed the Land Rover into a space behind a builder's van and made his way up a short path to the Finns' home.

Kathleen's anxious face appeared from behind the partially

drawn curtains in the sitting room. Seeing Black, she closed her eyes, then vanished again before appearing at the door.

'Leo. Hi.'

'Kathleen.'

'Thank you, I –' The words stopped in her throat. She swallowed her emotion. 'Come in.'

He followed her through the narrow hallway past a row of pegs stuffed with children's coats and into a kitchen that led on to a conservatory. The three kids were outside bouncing on a large trampoline that took up most of the small square of lawn behind the house. Kathleen went straight to the kettle and filled it from the tap, her hands trembling.

'They've grown. How old are they now?' Black asked, trying his best to make small talk.

'Josh is ten, Meg's eight and Sarah-Jane's coming up for six.' Kathleen set the kettle on its base and turned to face him, tears pooling in her vivid blue eyes. Her slender face was milk-white, her hair jet black. She was still the same beautiful Irish girl Finn had fallen in love with after spending years swearing he wasn't the marrying sort.

'Six . . . She was still a toddler last time I was here. How about you? Still nursing?'

'Part-time,' she answered quietly, wiping her cheek with the heel of her palm. 'I've taken some time off. You?'

'Same college in Oxford – for the moment, at least. I'm hoping they'll give me a permanent position come September, but I'm not banking on it.'

'I thought you'd settled there.'

'They make you jump through a lot of hoops. Nothing's guaranteed. Not being twenty-five any more doesn't help.' He smiled. 'Why don't you sit down? I'll make the coffee.' He reached the jar down from the shelf. 'Go on.'

Kathleen nodded gratefully and went to sit at the small

table. Black took mugs from the cupboard above the sink and fetched milk from the fridge, giving her a moment to gather herself. The kitchen was cluttered, but in an orderly, homely way. A large noticeboard covering much of the upper portion of one wall was smothered in pictures the kids had drawn along with postcards and photographs Finn had sent back from his recent work trips around Europe and the Middle East. Tucked away in a bottom corner, partially obscured by one of Sarah-Jane's efforts, was a photograph of Black and Finn sitting on the bonnet of a desert patrol vehicle parked high up on a ridge in Helmand. They were both smoking fat Cuban cigars. He remembered the day clearly: six of them had parachuted in at night to take out a Taliban mortar position and had met nearly fifty of them up there. Sometimes HQ back at Bastion had devised missions just to prove they could achieve the impossible. It had been a game: who could be the most audacious, the British SAS or US Delta Force?

Black brought over the coffee as Kathleen dabbed away the last of her tears with a tissue, turning her face from the windows so as not to let the children see her crying.

'Thank you.' She glanced at him guiltily. 'I haven't told them yet. I couldn't. Not until –' Her eyes searched his, as if holding out the faintest possibility of hope. Seeing none, her gaze dipped to the table. Her voice sank to almost a whisper. 'My sister's coming later. Flying in from Dublin.'

'It was him, Kathleen,' Black said. 'I'm sorry. There's no doubt. I saw his body, and the Embassy official had his papers.'

She nodded, her jaw clenching tightly. She looked up and squared her narrow shoulders. The truth was easier to face than uncertainty. The truth could be confronted head-on. She was a nurse who had married a special serviceman; she had lived with the reality of death and had been braced for a phone call or a knock on the door ever since Finn had put a ring on her finger.

'I tried to get him to stop last year,' she said. 'He went out for a six-month contract – security at some mine. He got sick and had to come home after eight weeks. That's when he promised me it would only be safe jobs from then on. A couple more years, he said, then back here for something sensible and a move out of town. That's how it was meant to be.'

She gazed, unfocused, into space.

'Who had he been working for?'

'Several different agencies in London. Bodyguarding mostly. Foreign businessmen coming here or Brits going out to the Middle East. He'd stopped doing Africa and Russia. Said they were too dangerous.'

'And this assignment? Did he talk to you about it before he went?'

'He just said it was four days in Paris. It was through Coulton's – a government contract, he said.' She shrugged and gave a slight shake of her head. 'Some jobs he'd get keyed up for, but this one was just run of the mill. Looking after some woman scientist, wasn't he?'

'Yes.' Black took a sip of coffee, hoping that if he remained calm it would make things easier for her. She would have questions. His answers would be hard for her to hear. 'He was guarding a young biologist who seems to have gone missing. I'm afraid it looks as if he was killed by her abductors while going after them.'

Kathleen's body was rigid, her eyes unblinking.

'What about the Foreign Office?' Black asked. 'Have they given you any details?'

She shook her head. Her eyes cut towards him. 'Tell me, Leo. I need to know. It's not like I haven't been ready for it all these years.'

He nodded and gave what he hoped was a reassuring smile.

'His charge was professionally abducted from a third-floor room at the back of the hotel. It seems she was lowered to the ground by ropes. I don't know the exact time frame, but it looks as if Ryan forced open the door of the room and abseiled down after them. He was overpowered on the ground. Stabbed. Many times.'

Kathleen didn't flinch but absorbed the information without a flicker. She had retreated inside a hard shell. The one that had carried her through years of nursing and being married to a man who had spent half of his adult life in one war zone or another.

'Why kill him? What for? If they'd got the woman, why not drive off?'

'I can't say. It's possible there was a reason – some politics or tit for tat I know nothing about – or perhaps he was just unlucky.'

'I have to *know*, Leo. I've got three kids who are going to grow up wanting to know why their dad had to die.'

'There'll be a coroner's inquest –'

She gave a dismissive shake of her head. 'How many of those ever get to the truth? I know the widows, Leo. This town's full of women who'll go to their graves without answers. It's not fair.'

Black met her uncompromising gaze and felt himself backed into a corner from which he knew there was no escape. Finn had found a true match for himself in Kathleen. Beneath her disarming exterior she was a force of nature.

'I'll try speaking to the official from the Foreign Office – see if I can squeeze anything more out of him. I've also got the name of the conference's head of security.'

Kathleen glanced away. She knew as well as Black did that the chances of anyone who had signed the Official Secrets Act offering anything more than the sketchiest details were close to zero. Her shoulders rose and fell as she took a slow, deep breath. Black had seen enough already to know she wasn't a woman to break down and wail. She'd stay strong and guard her children like a lioness.

'What about money?' Black said gently. 'Was he insured?'

'We'll be all right,' she said dismissively, her mind still on the questions that might never be answered.

Black sat in helpless silence. There was nothing more he could offer, not without making promises he was in no position to make. They both looked out of the window at the children crashing and tumbling on the trampoline with innocent exuberance. The ten-year-old, Josh, was already unnaturally strong with broad shoulders and the makings of a thick, muscular torso like his father's. He picked up both his younger sisters at once before collapsing into a heap of laughing, intertwined bodies.

'Ryan envied you,' Kathleen said at last, 'finding another life to move on to.'

'I should have been in touch.'

'So should he. He kept meaning to phone you, but if he wasn't working he was busy here. The moment never seemed right.'

She was trying to make him feel better. Black knew the truth: Finn had thought his friend and former CO had turned his back on him. How else could he have interpreted the years of silence? He had no way of knowing that Black had felt too embarrassed to call until he could tell him that his efforts had actually turned into something from which he could earn a living. That his silence had been down to pride.

'If there's anything I can do? If you need help with the arrangements?'

'I'll cope.'

Black felt an urge to reach out and squeeze her hand, to offer some small physical gesture of sympathy, but even as he had the thought Kathleen seemed to flinch away and retreat further into herself. It wasn't comfort she wanted. It was answers he couldn't give.

'You know where I am, Kathleen. You can call any time.'

'Thank you. And for going to Paris. I appreciate it.'

They exchanged glances, and after a further awkward silence both stood up from the table at once, tacitly agreeing that their meeting was at an end.

'He was a good man,' Black said, the words coming out woodenly. 'The best soldier I ever knew.'

There was a loud wail from the garden. The kids had clashed heads and Sarah-Jane was scrambling, sobbing from the trampoline.

'You see to her. I can let myself out,' Black said, and left Kathleen to comfort a crying child who was still expecting her father to come home.

Stepping around the collection of children's shoes inside the front door, Black felt Finn's looming presence in the hallway behind him. He imagined him giving that look he would throw him when they found themselves in a tight spot. The one that said, *'Is that all you've got, you soft bastard?'*

13

The visit to Finn's home left Black with an overpowering urge to escape to the hills. Ditching his plans to head straight back to Oxford, he headed west. After a brief stop for groceries and whisky, he continued along twisting back roads and lanes through villages whose names had long ago become signposts to his sanctuary: Clehonger, Kingstone, Vowchurch, Michaelchurch, and finally up the hill to Craswall – more a hamlet than a village – where the air became cooler and keener and the tended fields gave way to windswept hills.

The lane narrowed and dog-legged up a steepening gradient. Thick grass grew in the middle of the crumbling tarmac, which became steadily looser and more potholed before merging into a rough dirt track that crossed over a cattle grid before splitting in two. The left fork led up to an old stone byre used by the local farmer for lambing and shearing. Black turned right. The track wound through a copse of hawthorn and emerged on the far side as no more than a pair of wheel ruts that took him over a short, steep rise and down into a sheltered dell. There the 500-year-old stone cottage named Ty Argel, Welsh for 'Secret House', stood on a small area of flat pasture next to a stream. To the side of the building were two ancient apple trees and a stone shed. Behind it, the bracken-covered hillside rose steeply towards the upper slopes of the Black Mountains.

Black drew up in the long grass that had overwhelmed his parking spot, jumped down from the cab and breathed in deeply. He grabbed his bags of provisions and lugged them up the sloping dirt path to the front door.

Ty Argel was less a house than a glorified cabin built from flat slabs of stone dug from the hillside by sixteenth-century shepherds. When he had bought it, there had been two small dark rooms downstairs and two above, a wooden outhouse and a pump at the back door fed by the stream. Over the course of three summers and with occasional help from Finn, Black had spent his leave gutting it back to four bare walls, one of which then collapsed, requiring him to rebuild it from the ground up. The heavy oak front door opened into a single stone-flagged room with a small rustic kitchen at one end and a sitting area arranged around a wood stove at the other. An open staircase led up to a mezzanine big enough to accommodate his bed and a small bathroom. The power line stopped at the farm half a mile away, so the lights were powered by an array of solar panels on the roof and water heated by the stove.

No TV. No internet. An occasional phone signal but only when the sky was clear, which wasn't often. If Black was in need of entertainment he had his history books and vinyl record collection and there was always the endless distraction of an old cottage to keep weathertight. A small puddle of water inside the front door confirmed that the patch-up job he had done on the roof two years before needed redoing – properly this time. He'd get to it when his paper was written. Slipping unconsciously into the routine he repeated each time he returned, he checked the power levels on the solar battery pack, opened the stopcocks, switched on the pump that filled the water tank from the borehole, then fetched wood from the log store. Twenty minutes later he was trimming a red-hot stove that was warming the lime-washed walls and bringing his coffee to the boil.

Lunch was a hunk of bread, cheese and cold meat, which he ate outside in the shade of the apple trees. He had built the table at which he sat from an ash that had once stood by the stream until a summer storm had brought it down. Finn had helped him plank it up on an old diesel-powered saw bench he had bought at a farm sale. It had been a long day of sweat and cursing. Finn had accused him of being a mad hermit and yelled at him to move to a proper house and get himself a wife. Black had never cared much for indulging nostalgic memories, but his old friend had worked his way into the grain of this place. Everywhere he looked, there were more reminders: he had helped him set the lintel over the back door and rebuild the stonework above it as high as the roof. The date inscribed in the cement beneath the apex of the gable was in Finn's hand. Of the two of them, and to Black's lasting frustration, Finn had been by far the better builder, untrained, but with natural ability like that possessed by men who knew engines without ever having opened a manual.

Eventually, the procession of unprompted recollections grew too much and Black tried to banish them from his mind, reminding himself that sentimentality was the very opposite of what had bound him and Finn together. Yes, they had been firm friends away from their work but they had gone about their military tasks with cold, rational detachment. They had been professional soldiers who had accepted the risks. Death was always a possibility, but both had known that it was most likely to come about as the result of poor judgement or lack of planning, with bad luck trailing a distant second. If Finn had made a mistake in Paris, it was a great pity, but not a tragedy. Tragedies happened to the innocent. There was nothing innocent about Finn.

Enough.

Impatient with his mind's restless churning and disconcerted by the unfamiliar feelings they were stirring, Black tossed his crumbs to the sparrows, changed into his walking boots and set off up the hill, determined to keep going until his thoughts became his own.

His muscles complained loudly as he pushed on up to the ridge and continued across the level summit to the trig point at the top of the Twmpa. He paused a while to rest and take in the fifty-mile view across mid-Wales: a thousand shades of green rippling with shadows cast by a restless sky. Buffeted by the wind, he followed the ridge south for six miles, then, as dark clouds moved in from the west, descended towards the valley bottom before making his way back northwards, following the narrow trails cut through the heather and bilberry by sheep and wild ponies.

The storm broke when he was still an hour from home. He picked up to a jog, abandoned the paths and took the shortest route across open country. Chest heaving, he slipped and scrambled over wet, tussocky grass to the accompaniment of thunder claps that ricocheted off the mountainsides with the drama of exploding shells. The clouds grew lower still, shrouding the landscape in mist. Without map or compass he was forced to navigate by memory and instinct. He had lost his touch: having made his way back over the ridge, rather than hit the stream he had planned to follow to his front door, he found himself chest-high in bracken. Wet to the bone and with no chance of retracing his steps, he bushwhacked downhill before eventually emerging in familiar territory, though well off course.

Feeling every one of the twelve miles he had covered in his aching legs, Black stepped gratefully out of his sodden clothes and into a hot shower. The sensation of the near-scalding water needling his flesh was close to bliss. His body and mind slowly unwound in tandem, the accumulated tension of the previous forty-eight hours yielding to a pleasantly leaden sensation.

Heavy and relaxed, he dressed in jeans and an old plaid shirt and drifted downstairs to reward himself with a large whisky in front of the fire.

Here's to you, old friend. So long.

He raised his glass in a silent toast and drank.

14

Black woke abruptly in his armchair, convinced for a moment that someone had stabbed a finger in his chest. He glanced around the room. He was alone, of course. Coming fully to his senses, he noticed that it was dark outside and that the fire had reduced to a glowing heap of embers. He leaned forward to fetch a log from the basket and checked his watch. Ten thirty. He had been asleep for nearly two hours. No wonder he felt groggy. He sank back into his chair and stretched his aching feet out towards the warmth, far too comfortable to drag himself up to bed. Staring into the flames licking the glass of the stove, he thought idly that there could be far worse fates than making a quiet life here if his hopes of an academic career came to nothing. Perhaps, after all, his destiny was to be no more or less significant than the men who came to this empty hillside and built Ty Argel all those centuries ago.

Black reached for the whisky bottle to pour himself a nightcap. As he did so, a flicker of light caught his eye. He turned his gaze to the uncovered window but saw nothing. Dismissing it as a trick of the imagination, he settled to his drink. Moments later there was another, this time accompanied by footsteps on the path. Black stood up from his chair as three loud knocks sounded on the door.

'Hello? Anybody home?'

It was a voice he hadn't heard in five years.

'Leo? It's Freddy. I come in peace.'

Black hesitated before moving to the door and lifting the cast-iron latch. He opened it to reveal the smiling, compact figure of his former CO, Colonel Freddy Towers. All five feet five of him, exuding the same inexhaustible energy that had earned him the nickname 'Fireballs'. He was a little older and greyer, but the lights in his eyes shone as furiously as ever.

'Dear God, Leo. When Kathleen said you were out in the sticks I didn't know she meant halfway up a bloody mountain.' He stepped inside and wiped his muddy brogue boots on the mat. 'Had to leave the car down at the farm. Thankfully, the old boy stopped me going any further before I sank it in a bog.'

'Hello, Freddy,' Black said, slipping naturally into the same overly patient tone he had used to pacify his former superior for over two decades.

Patience had been necessary because Towers had perfected the art of self-parody to the point where the intricate complexities of his true self – of which Black had caught only occasional glimpses, invariably in eruptions of uncontrolled rage – were almost unreachable. The only way to deal with him was to play along. He hid his sharp, astute intellect and unrelenting ruthlessness behind an eccentric, clubbable persona modelled, no doubt, on the gin-soaked masters at his public school and the senior guards officers who had impressed themselves on his young mind. It was both an act and a shield and also a compensation for being the shortest officer in the mess, but it had made him a leader. And one who had been universally feared.

'Still, you always were a bit of an odd one.' Towers made for the stove, critically scouring the inside of the cottage as he removed his battered waxed jacket. 'Very you. Could do with a woman's touch. No progress on that front, I suppose.'

Black ignored the remark. 'Would you like a drink?'

'Not something you brewed yourself, is it?'

'Whisky. Blended, I'm afraid.'

'That'll do.' He stood warming himself while Black fetched another tumbler. 'You wouldn't believe it was bloody June. It must be close to freezing out there.'

Black returned to find Towers settling into the second armchair. He had always had an unnatural ability to make himself instantly and comfortably at home, whether in jungle camp, Iraqi desert or a suite in the Ritz Carlton.

'Rotten luck, eh?' Towers said without further explanation.

'Something like that.' Black poured large measures into each of their glasses. He had a feeling they would need it.

'Cheers.' Towers threw back most of his drink in a single mouthful and exhaled deeply. 'That hit the spot. Getting soft in my old age – too used to city living.' He gave the short dismissive laugh he had always used to make everything seem a joke, even the prospect of parachuting into a hornets' nest behind enemy lines. 'Oxford treating you well? Up for a fellowship, I heard.'

'Junior research fellowship,' Black corrected. 'All being well.'

'How do you rate your chances?' He didn't wait for an answer. 'Contending with a bunch of dewy-eyed lefties, I suppose. Sooner have some silver-tongued mufti at high table than an old soldier. Think tolerance is the answer to everything, that sort –' the laugh again – 'until some lunatic has a knife to their throats. Oh well, I suppose the deluded are as entitled to their freedom as much as the rest of us.'

Black was reminded of another of Towers' persistent habits: frequent unprompted homilies on the folly of the thinking classes.

The colonel fell silent for a moment and stared into his glass. 'Poor Finn. No way to go. Not for a man like him.'

Black nodded in agreement.

More silence. Towers' face creased and twitched as he wrestled with evidently troubling thoughts.

Black waited and sipped his whisky, sensing that he was about to learn the reason for this unannounced visit.

'You know, Leo,' Towers said abruptly, 'there really is no ill feeling, not on my part. None at all. I still haven't a clue why you walked when you did, drove myself crazy thinking about it, if I'm honest – wondered if it was my fault – but there we are. You had your reasons, I'm sure, and I . . . well, I want you to know I respect them.'

So that was it. Unlikely as it seemed, Towers had travelled through the night to bury the hatchet. Or perhaps even to seek absolution for all the times he had sent him and Finn to almost certain death. Was it actually possible that he had harboured a grain of compassion for his men, after all?

'Thanks,' Black said, failing to disguise the note of surprise in his voice. 'If it makes you feel any better, you weren't the reason, Freddy. I think I'd had enough, that's all.'

'I believe *a psychopathic game of whack-a-mole*, were your precise words.'

'In the heat of argument.'

'*In ira verum.*'

'Do you really want to have this discussion?'

'It would be nice to know, Leo – whether you really do think it was all a waste of time? Isn't that the line you've been peddling?'

'I don't . . . I just think that we didn't learn the lessons. I don't want to see another generation repeat the same mistakes.'

'Ha! So you're an *idealist*!' He exclaimed the word triumphantly, as if it explained everything. 'You hid that well . . . Not the worst trait, I suppose. Within limits.'

Black refused to rise. Long experience had taught him that once Towers felt he had a willing debating partner he'd happily keep the discussion going till dawn.

Towers tossed back the rest of his whisky and held his glass out for more. 'Just a drop, if you wouldn't mind.'

Black poured him three good inches.

'Bit of a shock, if I'm honest,' Towers said, changing the subject yet again. 'Finn and I stayed in touch, met up in town now and then. Got the feeling he rather missed you.'

'He could have called.'

'Perhaps he wasn't sure what sort of reception he'd get?'

'I'd have been glad to speak to him. He should have known that.'

Towers fixed Black with an intense, questioning gaze, his steel-rimmed glasses perched on a nose battered flat across its bridge during his years as army lightweight champion. 'Do you mean that honestly, Leo?'

'Of course. I didn't disown my old life; I just wanted to have another.'

Towers nodded. 'Well, that's good to know. Because we were close, weren't we – the three of us? Saw more of you two than I ever did my family. Claire and I separated, by the way. Well, she left is the truth – virtually the day after I retired from the Regiment.'

'Sorry to hear that.'

'Probably for the best. At least the kids had grown up. If she wants a lonely old age in Norfolk, it's up to her.' He gave a grunt, then a wistful look came over his face, and for a passing moment Black was seized with dread at the thought that he had come to him for solace. His fears proved unfounded. 'Actually, I've been a good deal happier. Got myself another job. Did you hear?'

'I'm afraid I've been out of the loop.'

'Had a tap on the shoulder about six months after I left. The Cabinet Office asked me to run a little operation out of the Ministry of Defence.'

'The MOD? I thought you despised those people? *Limp-dicked desk jockeys* was one of your kinder descriptions.'

'Sounds like flattery coming from me.' He smiled. 'No, I haven't sunk quite that low, I'm a PC – private contractor. Interesting work, actually. Fallen on my feet. Beats grubbing around for some private security outfit.'

Black tried to resist the unspoken invitation to pry further, but curiosity got the better of him. 'Are you allowed to tell me more?'

Towers looked at him over his glasses as if weighing whether he could trust him. He took another gulp of whisky. 'I suppose I'm meant to be a sort of spy-catcher, though I haven't caught many yet. Not in the sense of having enough evidence to bring them to justice, but we've weeded out a few bad apples.'

'Isn't that the Security Service's territory?'

'Ah, well – there's the thing. It's a job that arose out of something else entirely. When I left the Regiment I was offered a berth in the MOD with a brief to identify emerging technologies with defence applications. It was a lot of fun going out to meet young scientists pushing at the boundaries. I was making good progress, building up contacts, generating a steady flow of intel which I passed on to a team at MI5, and then we started leaking.'

Black felt his hand begin to tighten involuntarily around his glass.

'Several of our most sensitive technologies – all ones which I had identified – were stolen and popped up in the US and China. And in the last six months we've had four leading researchers disappear.' The lightness left his voice. 'Dr Sarah Bellman was the third. Her senior colleague, Professor Alec Kennedy, went missing two months ago and a young computer scientist shortly before that. The morning after Bellman was taken another of ours went missing – from Copen-hagen. A neuropathologist named Holst.'

In a few short sentences any sense of contentment Black had managed to regain during his retreat to Ty Argel bled away.

'After the second went missing I fully expected to be shown the door, but the opposite happened. My brief was expanded – to detecting the source of the leaks. There are wheels within wheels, but strictly in confidence I can't help wondering if the powers that be knew they were leaking before I was put in post. It would make sense, I suppose.' He nodded, as if banishing any lingering doubts. 'Yes, the task I'm now faced with is rather more up my alley.'

'Sarah Bellman was one of your contacts?'

'Correct,' Towers said with a note of regret. 'One of my most promising.'

'So it was you who employed Finn to look after Bellman?'

'I did recommend him to the relevant party, yes. Thought he'd do a good job.'

'Have you told Kathleen?'

'I can't see that it would help.'

'You've been to see her – she's beside herself. She'd like to know why he died, Freddy.'

'I'm sure she would.'

'It's not as if he died in uniform. He was a civilian.'

'Of course. And I would like nothing better than to be able to tell her . . . I'm not sure what you think of me, Leo, but you have to believe me when I say this grieves me deeply. I was almost as close to Finn as you were.'

Black met his gaze and saw a side to Freddy Towers he had never seen before; he had the pained eyes of a man with a troubled conscience.

'And you came here to tell me this why exactly?'

'Because I thought you needed to know.'

The half-truth. Another of Towers' specialities. Black glanced away and shook his head. He had a bad feeling.

'I know you went to the George V, Leo. And it wasn't exactly easy persuading the French not to bang you in a cell for the weekend.'

'You had me followed?'

'Purely for your own safety.'

'How –?'

'The Foreign Office called me for a reference,' Towers said, anticipating his question.

Black felt a surge of anger rise in his chest. 'Whatever it is you've come here for, Freddy, I want no part of it.'

Towers drained his glass and thoughtfully wiped his lips. 'I guessed that's what you'd say. Fair enough. I shan't beg. I'll leave you to it. Sorry to disturb your evening.' He pushed up from his chair, reached for his coat and rooted around in its pockets. He retrieved a business card and handed it across with one hand while continuing to rummage with the other. 'In case you need to get in touch.'

Black glanced at the Bayswater address, wondering how he could make his position any clearer without marching him out of the door.

Towers found the second item he was looking for and brought it out: an army-issue Glock 17 pistol. The seventeen signifying the number of rounds held in a full magazine.

'Better safe than sorry.'

He tossed it on to Black's lap. Black laid it on the arm of his chair, straining to hold his temper.

'It may interest you to know that some forensic results came through this morning. They found traces of blood from three separate assailants on Finn's body. Two male, one female. The conference's head of security, Sebastian Pirot, has vanished from his apartment and as far as we can ascertain he was operating under a false identity. I'm not sure who I'm dealing with yet, Leo, but I would hate to feel responsible for another accident.'

Black tossed the gun back to him. 'Thank you for your concern. But if you're looking for someone to find Pirot, I'm sure you have better options than a middle-aged historian.'

Towers nodded with an expression that seemed to accept that he'd come on a fool's errand. He pulled on his coat and slipped the gun back into a side pocket. He crossed to the door, where he paused. 'Dr Sarah Bellman was honey-trapped – by a woman. We're only sixty per cent sure, but we think the CCTV stills are a match with a twenty-eight-year-old CIA agent named Linda Courteney. Our friends across the pond tell us she went missing presumed killed in Libya over a year ago. It's all very strange.' He lifted the latch and stepped out into the night.

Leo reached for the bottle, tipped out what remained and swallowed it in a single mouthful. As he stared into the silence, a gentle rocking sound caused him to look round. Hanging from a nail on the back of the door was the Glock.

Towers followed the small oval of light cast by his torch along the rutted track leaving Ty Argel and the man he had once considered the bravest and most resourceful soldier in the British Army to his illusion of solitude. Credenhill had been good enough to keep eyes on Black while he was in their neck of the woods. Spaced out in the darkness beyond the cottage there would be two young troopers in full camouflage keeping watch. Their night-vision goggles would light up the scene as if to daylight and state-of-the-art listening equipment would convey the tiniest sounds from within to their earpieces and thumb-sized digital recorders. Towers wanted every detail down to the last curse word, belch and toilet flush.

It was only in the detail that you could truly own a man.

15

After her initial reluctance to cooperate Dr Bellman had adapted to her new circumstances just as Dr Razia had hoped. Long experience had taught him that in terms of basic human psychology, brilliant intellectuals were no different to common labourers: they were brought to heel best by a combination of carrot and stick. Or rather, stick then carrot. Rough handling followed by several days of deprivation had broken the young woman's spirit to the extent that she had become grateful even for small acts of kindness such as a fresh bar of soap or a clean set of clothes. Only once she was rendered into this state of cooperative dependency did Razia take her to his office and bring up details of a Panamanian account in her name containing $4 million. The offer of the access codes and an additional $4 million on successful completion of the project to Razia's satisfaction had a positively miraculous effect. She and Holst had begun work immediately and had since scarcely left the laboratory.

Even after it had been explained to her in minute detail, not once had Dr Bellman questioned the morality of their task. Having been confronted with a simple choice between continued suffering and self-interest there had been no contest. The percentage of human beings prepared to tolerate moderate discomfort, let alone lay down their lives for the benefit of others was vanishingly small. Dr Bellman and her colleagues did not, thankfully, number among them.

Razia, too, had begun his professional life as a young idealist troubled by the ethics of the work he was required by his government to undertake. But under the tutelage of his superiors he had gained an insight shared by all the greatest scientists: in the pursuit of knowledge human morals are of no relevance. If the scientist is to strive for the facts alone, nothing must be allowed to cloud the judgement. On the occasions this proved difficult, he would remind himself of the bees in his father's orange groves. These marvels of nature cared only for the survival and prosperity of their species. Those that ceased to be productive were immediately culled by the others. The individual was of value only insofar as it contributed to the good of the whole. Nature dictated these rules with an honesty and clarity that put prevaricating human beings to shame. Had we acted with the determination of our insect cousins we would by now be bringing into the world human beings only of the highest genetic quality who would enjoy long, healthy and useful lives. Human beings wise enough to act only in accordance with the common good.

With this in mind Razia ran his eye along the row of thirty or so volunteers, each of whom had been promised the princely sum of $100 if chosen to assist in his work and began to isolate the healthiest physical specimens. He passed up and down the line three times, pausing to check teeth, nails and the brightness of the eyes of those that caught his attention. Finally, he narrowed his selection to six: three male, three female, ranging from a slightly built young woman of twenty or so to a stocky man in his forties.

His subjects greeted their selection with grateful smiles and went willingly with the guards who led them across the compound to their new quarters while the unhappy rejects shuffled away across the hard-baked dirt, casting jealous glances at their departing co-workers. Razia could have told them that they needn't be disappointed as there would be several further opportunities to assist in the coming weeks, but there was a point at which justified deception became gratuitous cruelty. As a man of science, that was a line he was not prepared to cross.

Satisfied that he had the raw materials he needed, Razia lit a cigarette and headed over to the mess hall in search of breakfast. He had a long and taxing day ahead.

16

Black emerged from the college seminar room into the warm late afternoon. Two hours of discussion over whether the appeasers of the 1930s were responsible for the atrocities of the Nazis had turned into a furious debate over the threat posed by modern-day Saudi Arabia and Iran. Unusually, the two-wrongs-don't-make-a-right faction had been matched in number by the interventionists, one of whom was the son of a famously hawkish US admiral. Policing the dog fight had done little for the whisky-induced headache that had dogged him since his five a.m. start from Ty Argel, but it had been a spur to get back to his paper: belief in the peace-giving powers of high explosives was, it seemed, still alive and well among tomorrow's leaders.

Hoping a short walk would chase away his lingering hangover, he took the long way back to his rooms around the college lake. It was an Elysian scene: curtains of willow shot through with shafts of sunlight and lilies floating beneath. Groups of students lolled on the grass at the water's edge, subconsciously absorbing a vision of civilized perfection that would remain with them for the rest of their lives. He tried to imagine what Finn would have made of it. *Privileged little dicks don't know they're born*, probably. He'd been raised in a council flat in Belfast at the height of the troubles. And if that wasn't hard enough, his mother was a lapsed Presbyterian and his father an equally lapsed Catholic. Everybody had hated them, even God.

'Ah, Leo.'

Black turned to see the college Provost, Alex Levine, striding after him. A tall, rangy man of fifty-five, who, besides being a world-renowned economist, had once been an international athlete. His all-round brilliance aroused admiration and jealousy in equal measure. He caught up and fell into step.

'I've been hoping to catch you. Karen told me you were called away and couldn't make drinks on Friday.'

'Sorry about that,' Black said. 'An old army colleague died suddenly. Had to lend a hand.'

'She told me. My sympathies.'

Black nodded his appreciation.

Levine let a respectful moment pass before continuing. 'We had a meeting of the Appointments Committee last week – your application was discussed. There's support for you, there really is, but . . . how should I put this? Everybody appreciates that your real-world experience is hugely valuable, quite possibly unique, but we can't disregard the need for a depth of scholarship. I want to back you, Leo – you're a gifted teacher, very popular with the students – as Karen has emphasized on several occasions – but there's no point sugaring the pill, you're going to need a little more to get over the line. I understand you're due to present a paper in the States this summer?'

Black maintained an expression of relaxed imperturbability even as he felt the ground crumbling beneath his feet.

'That's right. Late August.'

'And you plan to publish?'

'I'm hoping for the *Harvard International Review.*'

'Harvard's good. Excellent. That should help a lot.'

Black took this as code for, *If they don't publish, you can forget it.*

Levine stooped forward with a look of earnest concentration. 'Off the record, OK?'

'Of course.'

'I sense a slight feeling among some of the fellows that your appointment might send out a difficult signal – politically.'

'Have they any idea what I'm writing?'

'No. Well, not in any detail, I don't suppose,' Levine confessed. 'Look, I hesitate to say this, Leo, but you've come to this rather odd world of ours rather later in life than most of us – after a few decades you develop sensitive antennae.'

'No, I hear you loud and clear, Provost. If I want a job, I'd better write something to their liking.'

Levine shrugged, as if the suggestion were entirely Black's but perhaps worth a try.

They stopped by the wooden bridge that led to the walled garden surrounding Levine's elegant Georgian lodgings. The inner sanctum reserved for the tiny handful of the most politically adept and ambitious.

'Best of luck, though,' Levine said in a way which, whether he intended it or not, sounded as if he were abandoning him to his fate. He gave an awkward smile and headed off across the water.

A sudden impulse prompted Black to call out after him. 'Be straight with me, Alex; how many do I have to win over?'

Levine stiffened and glanced uncomfortably over his shoulder, his neck reddening in embarrassment above the soft blue collar of his hand-stitched shirt.

Black waited for his answer.

'It's seven to three, roughly,' Levine mumbled. 'But that's just a guess. There was no vote as such.'

'I'm grateful,' Black said, softening. 'And I appreciate I've only got this opportunity because of your support.'

Levine raised a hand in a gesture that was both a wave and a dismissal.

Black watched him cross the bridge and disappear through

the door in the wisteria-clad wall at the far side, wondering at the somersaults he must turn inside his complex mind. He had single-handedly constructed economic policy for several emerging economies and was a vocal champion of the poor and a fierce critic of the international caste of the super-rich. Yet his brothers sat on the boards of two of the world's largest banks and his father had been an Israeli cabinet minister and hero of the Six Day War. Black had never known a man contend so successfully with so many contradictions. But did Levine know the truth of himself or had he merely harnessed his phenomenal intellect to react against a family whose name alone threatened to subsume him?

I *want* to back you, not, I *will*.

Black continued on his way, realizing that the Provost had just set out the terms of his appointment: he needed to be sure Black was cast squarely in his own image before putting his weight behind him. The only version of him he would back was the warmonger who had seen the light and been born again to preach a new gospel. A gospel of peace.

Had he become that man?

An image of a fourteen-year-old boy stepping out from a doorway in a narrow Baghdad alleyway appeared behind his eyes. He pictured the expression on the boy's face in the split second before the bullets from Black's semi-automatic had sliced his slender body in half.

If there had been a moment that had caused him to change direction, that had been it.

He hadn't realized at the time. The killing had been a reflex. One of tens of similar occasions when he had shot first in order to guarantee his survival. He had felt no emotion as he looked down at the boy's bloody remains but he had noticed its absence. The act of taking a life had become mundane. Part of the job.

The West has a weapon far more powerful than any aircraft carrier or infantry battalion: money. Cash. Rich countries breed few terrorists compared with poor ones and possess the resources, if they choose to use them wisely, to all but eradicate the problem of 'home-grown' terrorism. It is simply a question of aiming resources at the tiny proportion of the population in danger of falling under the extremists' spell. But in the developing world the pool of urban, unemployed and disenfranchised young men – those most likely to turn to violence – is vast. Yet the youth of Cairo, Baghdad, Tripoli and Damascus have the same aspirations as that of London, Paris and New York, the same cultural influences, the same material ambitions.

At last the words began to flow. Ideas that for weeks had remained stubbornly fragmented formed into a coherent whole.

The real enemy confronting the West is not one that can be bombed, assassinated or imprisoned. It is, in fact, the very force that built our thriving democracies: the basic human urge for betterment and security that when allowed to flourish leads inevitably to peace, and which, when frustrated, leads with equal inevitability to destruction.

Black's landline rang. He paused briefly from his typing to disconnect it from the socket, then switched off his mobile. Whatever it was could wait.

He missed her call by two minutes.

17

There were days when Karen's work frightened her. A superstitious voice inside her head whispered that no good could come from interfering with nature as profoundly as she was doing. But then the latest data from the Canadian and Siberian forests would arrive. New satellite photographs would reveal tens of thousands of additional acres of dead conifers added to the several million already wiped out by the incessant march of the humble mountain pine beetle. Winters a degree or two warmer meant earlier thaws and later freezes. Genetically programmed to survive six months of sub-zero temperatures rather than the four they were now routinely encountering, the beetles were proliferating. Viewed from the air, the once uniformly green forests of the north were a mottled patchwork of green and brown. In places whole hillsides and entire valleys had been wiped out. A few trees had been discovered to produce sap sufficiently concentrated that the beetles avoided them, but if the current decimation continued, it would take centuries for these few survivors to repopulate the landscape.

Human beings didn't have a few centuries. They had only a few decades at most. If enough forest died, the carbon released into the atmosphere would accelerate global warming to the point at which ice caps would melt and coastal cities and existing nuclear facilities become submerged. Drought and floods, famine and huge movements of refugees would lead inevitably to wars and chaos on a level unimaginable except to the few scientists who spent their waking hours working on myriad ways to prevent it. The terrible irony was that Karen and her colleagues were people who loved and revered nature, but who in order to protect their own species now found themselves compelled to manipulate and even defy it.

The laws of nature dictated the rise and fall of populations as an inevitable consequence of the perpetual competition for survival in a changing environment. Dinosaurs existed for 160 million years but were wiped out within a few seasons by sudden cooling caused by dust thrown up into the atmosphere following a meteorite strike. Jungle turned to tundra. In their changed surroundings the large cold-blooded lizards froze and starved. Only insects, small mammals and a handful of reptiles survived. A mere 200,000 years into their existence, homo sapiens faced a similarly dramatic annihilation, although if it came to pass, it would be one almost entirely of their own making.

Karen rationalized her work by telling herself she was merely engaged in temporary emergency measures. If humankind could be persuaded to behave differently, it too could prosper for millions of years, just as the dinosaurs had. She was the fire brigade, quenching the flames before the edifice collapsed. Once the immediate crisis was over, sanity stood a chance. They could rebuild. And learn.

She had raised her hybrid trees in one of the department's greenhouses sited just beyond the northern fringes of Oxford. The genetically modified lodgepole pines stood over twenty-five feet high but were only four years old. A tree growing from seed in the wild would be little more than waist height at the same age. Karen had achieved this feat by splicing in genes from the fastest-growing varieties and by controlling greenhouse conditions to trick the trees into believing they had passed through an entire annual cycle every three months.

Further genetic modifications caused them to produce a pheromone-imitating compound that attracted the beetles as well as sap that was toxic to them.

What Karen had created were living flypapers with potential to prevent an ecological disaster, but they also posed a risk. How they would interact with naturally occurring species was unknown. There was no telling whether in the medium to long term they would thrive or die. But they were fast becoming a necessity, and that was what truly frightened her: human beings had passed the point at which they could rely on the balance of nature to sustain them. That balance had already tipped and if left unchallenged, nature would dictate that the future belonged to other species. Human survival meant interference on a dramatic scale. Playing God.

And all the while, the world went about its business as if there were no looming disaster. In her very darkest moments Karen wondered if perhaps this was the simple evolutionary test to determine whether humanity had a future. To know of the problem but not to act on it would be absolute proof that the species was defunct. Of no further use to the single project of life: survival.

She checked the thermostat inside the greenhouse entrance one last time and stepped outside into air ten degrees cooler. The sudden change in temperature brought her out in goosebumps. Pulling up the hood of her top, she fished her keys from her jeans pocket and locked the metal door behind her.

The greenhouse was one of three rented by the Department of Plant Sciences on the site of a former commercial nursery. Set among fields and shielded from the surrounding landscape by rows of poplar trees, there was nothing to indicate that it was home to a research facility of such critical importance. Only the twelve-foot-high chain-link fence surrounding the three-acre plot gave any clue to its sensitive purpose.

Karen walked along the short paved path to the rack where she had stowed her bike while mentally rehearsing what she would tell her Canadian colleagues during their conference call later that evening. They were close to getting their government to allow experimental planting in British Columbia but needed assurances Karen couldn't give. She would come under pressure to present her results in a way that played down the risk of unforeseen consequences. Politicians would take a gamble on her trees only if she were prepared to massage the truth to the point of lies and then take responsibility if the worst should happen. It was an absurd situation, but somehow she had to navigate it. *Survival*, she told herself. Ultimately, that was all that mattered.

Her thoughts were interrupted by a sudden movement at the fringes of her vision. She glanced up towards the locked gates some twenty yards ahead of her with the impression that she had briefly seen a figure. But there was no one there. An overhanging branch perhaps, or the shadow of a passing cloud. Imagining things again. She had been anxious and on edge ever since Joel had walked out without warning, apt to startle at the slightest thing. She took a deep breath, leaned down to fetch her helmet from the pannier and felt the irrational sense of being observed intensify. Another nervous glance around the site confirmed that it was deserted. There was no man at the gateway, just a cock pheasant wandering across the farm track on its far side.

She fastened her helmet, climbed on to the bike and made her way over to the high gates. Beyond the wire mesh the verges of the access track were overgrown with nettles and cow parsley. After thirty yards or so it turned sharply right, then continued in a straight line for a third of a mile before it met the lane which connected with the main road into Oxford. The drone of bees from the hedgerows either side merged with the sound of the rustling poplar trees and the hum of distant traffic. At eight p.m. in early June it was still broad daylight.

Karen was all too aware that her anxiety was illogical and that the main cause of her fragile state was the difficult call she had to make to Canada, but that didn't make it any less real. Since he had left, Joel had taken on a sinister aspect in her mind. He was a brooder, a man whose anger was cold and suppressed but occasionally revealed itself in dark, vindictive glances. Part of her harboured a fear that having stolen her money he wasn't beyond intimidating her into giving up her claim on it.

Furious at allowing herself to succumb to such irrational thoughts, she took out her phone and dialled Leo's landline. Of all her friends he had been the most understanding of her fragile state. While others had been full of well-meaning advice and platitudes he had simply accepted her as she was. He had also been a soldier. A man used to facing down danger. His words of encouragement would count for a lot.

The phone rang five times, then connected to voicemail. She tried again with the same result. She scrolled hurriedly back through her contacts and found his mobile number. Her call connected immediately to a message informing her that his phone was switched off. Typical. She guessed that he had probably unplugged the landline, too. He was like a hermit sometimes, never happier than holed up in a darkened room, cut off from the world.

There were other friends she could call, but all those within range were also friends of Joel's. She didn't want him to hear that she had become a nervous wreck. She still had some pride.

Get a hold of yourself!

Karen thrust the phone back into her rucksack, a burst of

anger at her own weakness finally giving her the courage to unlock the heavy padlock on the gates and push her bike on through it. She locked the gates behind her and pedalled off along the track. Picking up speed, she channelled her frustration into exertion, her wheels clattering over the uneven surface. She rounded the corner and caught her first glimpse of the traffic passing to and fro along the road up ahead. She felt suddenly foolish, her cheeks reddening with shame.

The figure stepped out from an overgrown gateway to her left. He was dressed in black, a balaclava rendering him featureless. A jolt of fear like a powerful electric shock shot through Karen's body. She swerved, but there was no room to avoid him. He ran straight at her, sending her and the bike flying into the verge. She flipped over the bars, saw a flash of sky, felt brambles tearing her cheeks and then he was on her. A knee drove into her sternum, pinning her to the ground. A gloved fist struck her hard in the face. A flash of stars briefly wiped out her vision. She couldn't breathe. He punched her again, this time in the jaw. She felt the muscles of her limbs go into spasm. Her brain screamed at them to move but nothing responded.

He grabbed her roughly between the legs, then tore the small rucksack from her back and vanished as quickly as he had appeared.

18

Black spotted her sitting alone in the far corner of the busy accident and emergency department. Her right hand was braced diagonally across her chest in a sling and a thick dressing was taped to her temple. Her head was lolling towards her chest as if she were drifting in and out of sleep. He picked his way towards her, weaving between drunk students, an old man who looked like death and a young woman who smelled of poverty nursing a screaming baby.

'Karen? What happened?'

She blinked and looked up, then smiled with relief as much as her battered face would let her.

'Leo. Thanks. I got the nurse to call the porters' lodge. I couldn't –'

She seemed overwhelmed and confused. Her speech was slurred from a large dose of codeine. She struggled to stand. He took hold of her arm and helped her to her feet.

'Let's get you home.'

He led her between the rows of seats, along the corridor and out to where he had parked his Land Rover. She moved slowly and stiffly and seemed to be injured in several places. There were grass stains on her jeans and scratches along her cheek and neck. The message the college porter had brought to his door shortly after eleven p.m. was simply that Karen had been in an accident and needed collecting from the John Radcliffe Hospital. Black knew that like most people in Oxford she cycled everywhere, and he had assumed that she had had a crash. He waited for her to tell him what happened, but she didn't say a word. He noticed there were bruises on both sides of her face, as if she had received multiple impacts. He struggled to picture how they could have occurred.

Only once he had safely installed her in the passenger seat and fastened her seat belt did he venture a joke.

'So, what did the other guy look like?'

'I don't know. He was wearing a mask.' Silent tears spilled down her cheeks.

Some joke.

'He?'

She spoke falteringly through sobs: 'A man – outside the site at Woodstock . . . jumped out at me . . . pushed me off my bike . . . fractured my wrist . . . I thought he was going to kill me, Leo, then . . .'

'It's all right.'

Karen's breath came in short bursts between sobs.

'Have you told the police?'

She nodded and wiped her eyes. 'They sent a woman to take a statement . . . She asked if it could be domestic. I had to tell them about Joel . . . I don't think it was him. This man was . . . he was like a . . . he was so quick.'

Black tried his best to remain calm. 'Did he say anything?'

She shook her head.

'Was he trying to rob you, or –'

'He took my rucksack . . . My purse and phone were in there.' She swallowed. 'I thought he was going to . . . He must have followed me. How else would he have known I was there?' She looked at him through red, swollen eyes. 'I'm scared, Leo.'

'Don't worry. I'll sleep on your sofa.'

She nodded gratefully.

Black touched her reassuringly on the shoulder. He turned the ignition and started for home.

By the time they arrived back at college Karen was out on her feet, the opiates rendering her into a stupor. Black looped his arm around her waist and supported her full weight as he helped her up the stairs to her rooms on the second floor. She crawled into bed still dressed in her clothes and within moments fell deeply asleep. He closed the door and retreated to the small sitting room that doubled as a study into which she had crammed the few possessions she had salvaged from the ruins of her marriage. A large framed photograph on the wall above her desk showed Karen during a recent field trip to British Columbia hugging a vast cedar tree that must have been thirty feet round. He recalled her stories of the expedition: of how the First Nations people had, over the centuries, harvested planks from the outside of the trunks by tapping in wedges which, aided by the action of the wind, slowly caused pieces of timber to split away. The trees repaired their own wounds and lived on for centuries alongside their human companions. The idea of people living in harmony with their forests had moved her deeply.

She was a botanist whose work, as far as he knew, was purely altruistic. He could think of no possible reason for anyone to hurt her except for purely opportunistic reasons. Muggings were rare but not unknown. A lone woman on a bicycle in an area beyond the scope of any security cameras was an easy target. Only one detail troubled him. She had said 'balaclava'. If her memory was correct, that meant her attacker was more than a mere opportunist. He had planned.

A small paranoid voice sounded in the back of his mind suggesting a connection with the missing scientists. He dismissed it. Karen was a plant biologist. Her work had no defence application that he could conceive of. She had been attacked and robbed in a city that for all its wealth had more than its fair share of poor and desperate vagrants, addicts and street criminals. Such things happened every day.

He sank into the chair beside her desk and found his thoughts drifting back to Finn.

He should never have agreed to go to Paris. Ever since seeing Finn's body he had been stirred by a primitive desire for revenge. He could feel it now. If he knew where to find the man who had attacked Karen, he knew exactly what he would do to him: break his jaw and ensure he never had children. It would be over in seconds. He pictured the limp, groaning body at his feet. He tried to push the image away, to replace the anger with rational thoughts: who was to say what he would be capable of if he were hungry and destitute enough? It didn't work. Since his trip across the Channel something inside him had shifted. The ghost of his old self was haunting the new.

What if whoever killed Finn wants to kill you, too? How many people must there be who would gladly see the two of you dead? How many sons, fathers, brothers and cousins have you killed, Leo?

The more he tried to silence the taunting voice the louder it became until he could think of only one way to silence it. Reluctantly, Black brought out his phone and found, buried at the back of his wallet, a business card. He took them into the bathroom and locked the door behind him.

In the bedroom of his sixth-floor flat in a nondescript block in Lancaster Gate Freddy Towers stirred from the semi-doze which these days so often passed for sleep and reached for the phone ringing on the bedside table. He squinted at the screen and saw that it was the call he had been hoping for. He sat up excitedly and switched on the reading lamp as he answered.

'Leo? Is that you?'

'Yes, Freddy.' He sounded flat and morose. 'A friend of mine has had an accident.'

'A friend? Who?'

'Dr Karen Peters. She's a botanist. She's also a close colleague.'

'What sort of accident?'

'She was attacked and robbed by a masked man. It could be purely coincidental –'

'But you think there's a French connection . . . ? What would be the point of hurting your friend?'

'You tell me, Freddy.'

Towers paused to think. 'No, I can't see any obvious link.'

'It seems premeditated, frankly, the sort of thing I'd do to soften up the genuine target. What I'm getting at, Freddy, is whether there is anything you're not telling me . . . The past . . . My guess is there is.'

'Careful over the phone, Leo. Perhaps we ought to meet? How are you placed tomorrow lunchtime? I can come up if you like. How about the Randolph?'

Black answered with silence.

Towers tried again: 'I can make it tomorrow evening if you're busy. I'll call the local police now if you like, tell them to keep an eye on her for a few days. Karen Peters – is that right?'

'I don't want you coming here. London. I can make lunch tomorrow.'

'Excellent. Army & Navy, then. Shall we say one?'

Black rang off.

Towers lay back on the pillow, feeling hopeful for the first time since he had received the news of Dr Bellman's abduction. If Leo could be prised from his lair, anything was possible.

19

Towers' word with the Oxford police brought a young female detective to Karen's door shortly before seven the next morning. Karen emerged groggy and disorientated from her bedroom to meet her, still dressed in the clothes she had slept in. While Black made coffee for them both in the kitchenette he overheard the detective explaining that her superintendent had decided to offer her the option of a twenty-four-hour personal protection officer while they attempted to trace her attacker. It was a purely precautionary measure, she assured her, but in light of the fact that two scientists employed by the university had gone missing in recent months it might be a wise one. Karen hesitated then declined, opting instead to take up the offer of a portable panic button.

Black felt both guilty and duplicitous as she was prompted into discussing the intimate details of her break-up with Joel. The detective noted every word on a laptop and promised they would speak to him. The only salve to Black's conscience was the thought of Karen's thieving ex-husband having police officers arrive at his door, preferably when his young girlfriend was at home.

Thirty minutes later the interview was over and the detective was on her way. She left Karen with her business card, a leaflet advertising the services of Victim Support and a promise that her case would be treated as a priority.

'She seems competent,' Karen said, as if trying to reassure herself.

'Yes,' Black said, feeling even more guilty as he watched

her tugging anxiously at the cuff of her sweater. 'Would you like me to stay a while?'

'No, I'll be fine. Look, I'm so sorry to have imposed on you. I can't have been thinking straight last night.'

'It was no trouble.'

'Thank you.' She gave a grateful smile and pushed the hair back from her face.

Black noticed the scattering of delicate freckles on her cheeks and the fullness of her lips. 'Call me any time. I'll try to remember to keep my phone on.' He smiled.

She smiled back and briefly met his gaze before quickly glancing away as if embarrassed.

What was the appropriate gesture – a handshake, a kiss on the cheek? As Black tried to decide the moment for anything that might have felt natural or spontaneous passed, leaving him no option but to make do with an awkward wave as he stepped towards the door. 'Goodbye, then.'

'Bye, Leo.'

Making his way down the stairs he couldn't help but feel that something had changed between them. Until the previous evening they had been professional colleagues on friendly, polite terms, but they had woken up as more than that. As what, though? Were they *close* friends now? Confidants? The way Karen had looked straight into his eyes had felt like an invitation to cross a boundary but tempted as Black was his instinct was to remain at arm's length. His relationships with women had been few, unhappy and a long time in the past. He had learned to live without love or sex and it had brought a kind of peace. Romantic feelings, he had long ago decided, were a complication he could live without.

But try as he might to put her out of his mind, Karen's presence lingered and refused to leave.

*

Black showered, changed, grabbed breakfast and taught an early tutorial before catching one of the many buses that shuttled between Oxford and London day and night. Ninety minutes later he disembarked at Marble Arch and set off across Hyde Park hoping that a walk would give him an appetite for the doubtless heavy lunch that awaited him.

The warm weather had brought out the crowds and with them all the fantastic contradictions that only London seemed able to contain. Large clusters of black-clad Middle Eastern mothers were enjoying picnics on the grass with their children while nearby several young white women were sunbathing in bikinis. Skateboarders, a party of orthodox Jews, rich Saudis in flowing robes and Roma beggars mingled amidst the drifts of Chinese and American tourists. Differences insurmountable elsewhere seemed to have been overcome in this corner of the capital that had somehow managed to become neutral territory.

At Hyde Park Corner he crossed beneath the Wellington Arch and headed along Constitution Hill, caught up in the excitement of the sightseers heading towards Buckingham Palace. The pink tarmac, the great Union Jacks draped from pristine white flagpoles and the sentries dressed in their red tunics and bearskin hats combined to create a spectacle of glorious and benevolent permanence at the heart of a turbulent world. He supposed the crowds gathered here in the belief that behind the palace walls lay some magical secret, Her Majesty a benign semi-deity who stood in stunning contrast to all that was base and venal in human nature.

Leaving the throng behind he continued along the Mall before cutting through Marlborough Road to Pall Mall, the home of London's most exclusive clubs. Black had never understood the appeal of retreating into a recreation of an Edwardian country house to spend hours in the company of others exactly like oneself, but he was the exception among his former colleagues. Part of military life was being 'the right sort', or, in other words, behaving with impeccable manners, while at the same time being prepared – if senior ranks were in sufficiently boisterous mood – to drink to oblivion and humiliate oneself in a bout of broomstick jousting. Black had played his part but often through gritted teeth. He had little time for the childish rituals of British establishment men. The club, the officers' mess, the draughty boarding school seemed to him all to be extensions of each other.

The doorman in top hat and tailcoat greeted him warmly. It had been half a decade since Black had crossed the threshold of the Army & Navy (known to its members as 'The Rag'), but he was received as if it were yesterday. To his astonishment the old retainer at the desk remembered his name and had ticked it off the list of expected visitors even before he had reached the mahogany counter, where he was politely informed that Colonel Towers was waiting for him in the Coffee Room. Black ascended the sweeping staircase hung with oil paintings of imperial generals and recalled the particular brand of deference with which officers of the Special Forces were greeted within these walls. The club's staff had always prided themselves on knowing who they were and liked to display their knowledge through subtle displays of exaggerated discretion.

The Coffee Room was, in fact, the club's restaurant. Tradition dictated that while a room's function may change, its name must not, hence the club's bar was still the 'Smoking Room' and always would be. Panelled in light oak and decorated with more life-size portraits of long-dead men of valour, the Coffee Room was alive with the sounds of clinking cutlery and middle-aged male chatter. He found Freddy Towers already seated at his favourite corner table, a white napkin tucked unselfconsciously into his shirt collar.

'Leo, there you are. I was beginning to wonder.' He gestured to a tumbler sitting at the centre of Black's place setting. 'Got you a straightener.'

Black checked his watch as he drew up a seat. It was barely three minutes past one. Towers had lost none of his old obsession for punctuality.

'I was enjoying the stroll through the park.' He took a sip from a gin strong enough to fell a carthorse.

'How's your friend? Did the police contact her?'

'Yes. Thank you.'

'Good. Think I'll have the beef. They've an exquisite little Pinot that'll wash it down nicely. Join me?'

Leaving him no choice, Towers nodded to a waiter and an evidently prearranged order was placed. Moments later a sommelier appeared and filled their glasses with a clear, delicate red that slid across the palate with dangerous ease.

'Tell me about Ms Peters,' Towers said. 'Just a friend, or something more?'

'Just a friend.' Black nudged the gin aside in favour of the wine. 'And a colleague. One of the few who thinks I deserve a fellowship.'

Towers gave a thoughtful nod. 'Do you think she was targeted deliberately – a payback of some sort for your adventure in Paris?'

'Do you know something, Freddy?'

'After your call yesterday I had another – from Kathleen Finn. Her eldest girl was assaulted on the way to school. A man passed her on the street and stubbed out a cigarette on her scalp. By itself it could be considered a coincidence . . .'

'What did the police say?'

'Not a lot. Pretty young blonde girl. Just the sort that unhinged predators target.'

Black felt his sinews tighten. He thought of Megan's

carefree laughter the day he had visited the family home. The innocence of the three children who had yet to learn their father wouldn't be coming home.

'I suppose the point would be to make a show of strength. They now have four of our scientists and, I suspect, a number of our Security Service personnel on their payroll. It's the act of an entity that wants us to know that it has a long reach – inspired by the Russians and their adventures in Wiltshire no doubt.'

'What kind of entity? A state?'

'Possibly, but it's not my first instinct.'

'What then? A terrorist organization?'

'More likely to be a commercial enterprise.'

'What makes you say that?'

Towers took a thoughtful sip from his glass. 'Have you researched the names of the missing I gave you?'

'I've already told you, it's not my battle.'

'You wanted to know if there was anything I hadn't told you. Are you interested or not?'

Black gave a reluctant nod.

'Dr Bellman and Professor Kennedy work in the same department. He has created some fairly exceptional nano-particles for medical applications and she has developed the delivery mechanism. You do know what nanoparticles are?'

'Vaguely.'

'They're microscopic machines. In this case they heat up when exposed to certain frequencies. Delivered to the right cells in the brain they can activate neural circuits. The possibilities are endless. Until recently the problem was how to get them to their destination. Dr Bellman solved it. Through some incredibly skilful micro-engineering she has developed a basket-like structure made of woven strands of DNA that carry the payload of particles to any given destination. It's a really quite astonishing achievement.'

Black changed his mind about abandoning his gin and reached for the glass. He sensed that Freddy was embarking on a lecture.

'Dr Andy Sphyris is the computer genius I mentioned – the second one they abducted. Anglo-Greek. He works for a biotech start-up in Cambridge that's come up with the closest computerized simulation of the human brain in existence. A three-dimensional road map of billions of neurons and their functions. It's early days, but within a few years they hope to be able to model the effect of any given stimuli – they actually aim to predict the physiological and psychological response. Can you imagine it – knowing how the brain would respond to a chemical or an advertisement? Incredible.' Towers shook his head with an expression of awe. 'Sphyris's unique contri-bution was creating a form of artificial intelligence which maps what they glean from scans and imaging, and the more it learns about how the wiring fits together, the more it's able to fill in the blanks. I'm told that thus far it's predicted with almost ninety-nine per cent certainty what each unmapped area of the brain's function will be. An entirely logical pro-cess, I'm sure, but breathtaking, nonetheless.'

'Nanoparticles and a map of the brain. Where does that take us?'

'To Dr Lars Holst, our fourth hostage. He's a Dane but spends at least half his time working out of Imperial College here in London. Keeps his research animals over in Copen-hagen where he holds a chair in neuropathology. British universities have got a bit squeamish over experimenting on primates – have to say I quite agree. Anyway, Holst's special-ism is addiction. Broadly speaking, his work shows that it's the chemicals in our brain we're addicted to rather than whatever stimulus or substance causes them to release. He hasn't published much in the last five years, but the word among his colleagues is that he's about to lift the curtain on something big. The best information I can get is that he's been working on rewiring the reward centres of the brain to make them fire in response to specific stimuli. It's another science in its infancy, but five years ago he was implanting electrodes into the skulls of rats and training them to substitute one addiction for another. He could take an animal addicted to heroin and switch its dependence to sugar, nicotine, caffeine or whatever he chose.'

Towers paused for breath and another large mouthful of wine. 'As I said, these are the four we know about. If the Americans have lost any of theirs, they're keeping quiet, but that's their way these days – batten down the hatches and admit nothing.' Lecture over, he sat back in his chair. 'What do you think?'

'About what?'

'Come on, Leo. You must be as fascinated by all this as I am. An outfit going to all the trouble and expense of corrupting British agents and placing itself at the cutting edge of neuroscience. And here's the kicker: the one thing these four had in common was that they were all assets that I had spent months cultivating. Over the last two years I must have submitted detailed reports on the work of over a hundred researchers and fed them into the system. The system leaked and out of all of that number these are the four that have vanished.'

He waited for Black's response.

Black, for his part, was wrestling with the fact that his offer to identify Finn's body had, he was sure, caused two innocent and vulnerable people to be violently assaulted. He reached for his tumbler and swallowed the remaining dregs of his gin.

'All I need to know, Freddy, is how much danger whoever you're dealing with poses to Karen and Finn's family.'

'Honestly? You have as much idea as I do.'

'What if the man who assaulted the child also attacked Karen? You can't move in this country without being caught on camera.'

'Resources, Leo. They're spread thin. We've three thousand Islamic extremists and almost as many other assorted lunatics to keep tabs on. And in this instance, the usual channels can't necessarily be trusted. Which, I suppose, makes *me* the resource.' Towers looked him in the eye with a level of sincerity that was as unnerving as it was uncharacteristic. 'And, of course, whoever might be good and trustworthy enough to help me.'

The waiter arrived with their lunch, affording Black a brief reprieve while Towers turned his attention to his tender steak and a second glass of Pinot. The food was precisely as Black remembered: simple, well cooked and comforting, just the way Towers and his fellow members liked it.

Towers ate like a man who had been starved for a week. His pent-up nervous energy channelled into an almost obscene concentration on his plate. Several minutes passed during which Black wondered if he had forgotten that he wasn't alone. It had been a running joke in the mess: Towers ate as intensely as he worked, argued, fought or schemed. Only when he had dispatched his last roast potato did he return to conversation, picking up the threads as if he had dropped them only seconds before.

'Neuroscience wasn't high on my list of the most vulnerable technologies, if I'm honest. Bit niche. Some future applications perhaps – planes piloted by pilot's brainwaves, that sort of thing – but not much of current interest. It was meeting Sphyris that first piqued my interest. I met him at a conference. He was talking about the possibility of decoding and reprogramming the human brain as if it were just around the corner. It conjured the prospect of fearless soldiers or, worse still, terrorists. He mentioned Holst. They'd collaborated a few years back when Holst was still working with needles and catheters to inject drugs through minute holes in the skull, but, well . . .' He paused and scratched distractedly at a gravy spot on the starched linen tablecloth. 'I think we have to fear that things have moved on rather a lot.'

Towers cocked his head thoughtfully to one side. 'I've thought long and hard about it and this is about the best I can come up with: there's Holst with the knowledge of how to change behaviour through altering brain chemistry, Bellman and Kennedy who have developed the mechanical means of achieving it, and Sphyris who models and predicts the outcomes. You would only put the four of them together if you were interested in changing people's thoughts, perhaps even without them realizing that it's happened. I can see why a state would be interested, but a commercial outfit would stand to gain a lot more with the entire world as its market. Whatever way you look at it, it doesn't take much imagination to realize that the motives can't be good.'

Black continued to eat, trying hard to maintain his pretence of indifference.

'I have to admit, it's all taken me rather by surprise.' Towers shared the last of the wine between their glasses. 'All the while I've been fretting about jihadis and rogue regimes getting hold of biological weapons the most sinister enemy has had its sights on something else entirely. I don't suppose you're shocked. You were always fond of telling me that we were always fighting the last war.'

Black felt a strange and disquieting sensation creep through his body. Mild enough to shrug off, but a portent nonetheless.

'Who is it, Leo? That's the question.'

Towers held him in a piercing gaze that demanded an answer.

Black felt himself weaken. His natural curiosity, fuelled by cold rage at the events of the previous day combined to undermine his defences.

Towers sensed the moment the tide turned in his favour and seized it. 'We need to know. And quickly. A Special Purposes Committee has been formed under the auspices of the Cabinet Office. The Permanent Secretary is chairing it and reporting directly to the PM. The other members are the Chair of the Joint Intelligence Committee, the Director, Special Forces, the PS to the Ministry of Defence and yours truly. We can't trust the Security Services on this one; we've no idea how far the rot's penetrated. We hope not to the top but we can't take the risk. I've taken the liberty of mentioning your name and it was approved unanimously. There's a fee, of course.'

Black stared at him across the table.

Towers pressed on. 'I've isolated six MI5 officers who could credibly have had access to my reports and two with pressing motives to take the enemy's coin. One of them's a gambler living far beyond his means and the other's a family man with a sick wife at home who banked several significant sums in the last three months.' His eyes quickly circled the room before settling again on Black. He lowered his voice. 'We'd like you to interrogate them.'

Black's face remained expressionless.

'I know none of this is ideal, but the stakes are too high to follow normal protocols. This has to be done off the record. Deniably. We need guaranteed answers and you're the only man I trust thoroughly enough to get them, Leo. Anyone else would be second best. This is a situation that calls for excellence.'

Black remained silent.

'A day's work with minimal prep. A one-off. Twenty-five thousand pounds. Look at you, Leo – I recognize that suit from twenty years ago. These waiters are earning more than you are.'

Temptation tugged. Black resisted. 'I'm not that man any more, Freddy. Even if I wanted to be.'

He stood up from the table and made his way out of the dining room, leaving his wine undrunk.

Towers tugged his napkin from his collar and tossed it angrily on to the tablecloth.

20

The figure who emerged from the belly of the helicopter with his entourage of four young executives was not an impressive physical specimen – five feet six, balding with soft fleshy features. The kind of man who was chauffeured from one air-conditioned space to another, seldom seeing daylight. Nevertheless, he carried himself with the poise and certainty only possessed by the supremely self-assured. Carl Mathis had every reason to be confident. He was a self-made billionaire by the time of his fortieth birthday and had added over twenty billion more in the intervening fifteen years. He had made his money gambling on the next big thing, on technical innovations that he believed would sweep the world. From personal computers to personalized medicine, he had been right on the money every time.

Mathis had acquired Sabre Systèmes de Défence Internationale, as it was then called, from its French founder, Colonel Auguste Daladier, only four years before. He had since anglicized the company's name and diversified its work in ways which even that short time ago would have seemed unimaginable. While Daladier continued to run the conventional arm of its business providing the services of highly trained mercenary forces, he had moved Mitch Brennan and Susan Drecker sideways to head up a new venture. In a skilful move for which he still congratulated himself, Mathis had based their operations deep in the South American jungle alongside another of his successful businesses. It had been a perfect fit. They weren't yet in profit but their operational success had surpassed all expectations. If he had needed any confirmation of what he already knew to be true, the last few years had delivered it: money offered with a smile and the promise of more to come had proved able to buy almost anything or anyone.

Government agents of all stripes had proved particularly easy to corrupt. Salary men and women with no chance of ever attaining fame or fortune in their pedestrian careers could seldom resist the allure of easy cash. Scientists' egos made them only slightly harder nuts to crack. Often they had spent years convincing themselves that status and recognition were what they valued most, but once the smell of dollar bills had filled their nostrils such ideals invariably dissolved. Given another year, no doubt the four scientists they had been forced to bring here against their will would have co-operated willingly, but Mathis couldn't wait that long. His business plan required them to break even during the next twelve months and he had come for an update on progress.

Brennan and Drecker met their visitors at the edge of the landing area and led them the short distance through the tropical heat to the meeting room situated in the compound's administration block. There they arranged the party around the large conference table in the welcome cool, Mathis flanked by his team of energetic young executives at one end and Brennan and Drecker at the other.

After a minute or two of polite chitchat to break the ice, Brennan proceeded to deliver an update on progress. 'I am pleased to report that we have now successfully assembled our core team and aim to have an established proof of concept within three months.'

'Let me ask you up front, Mr Brennan,' Mathis interrupted in his soft Californian lilt, 'Do we have the full cooperation of our team? Do they like the deals we've offered them?'

'Yes, we now have their full cooperation,' Brennan said. 'After some initial resistance the financial packages have all been agreed and signed. They have begun the process of collaboration. Within a fortnight our laboratories will be fully equipped with everything that they need to get us to the next stage.'

'A human trial?'

'Yes, sir. The aim is to replicate Dr Holst's experimental findings with a human subject but using Professor Kennedy and Dr Bellman's delivery system. Their nanoparticles will be transported to the target areas of the brain and activated by frequencies to which they will have been programmed to respond.'

'How are these frequencies transmitted?' The question came from a woman Brennan guessed to be no more than twenty-five seated to Mathis's left.

'They could come from any number of sources, but in this instance a mobile phone,' Brennan said. 'The signal can be disguised in a sound or video file that causes the emission of something you might describe as the auditory equivalent of a barcode. The particles activate, deliver heat to the neurons to which they're attached, causing them to fire and trigger the desired response.'

'Initially the responses will be binary – positive or negative,' Drecker interjected, 'creating an attraction or aversion to a given stimulus.'

'How confident are we of success?' Mathis asked.

'Each link in the chain has already been proved,' Brennan said. 'The only difficulty is putting them together. Fortunately, that's a technical rather than a theoretical challenge.'

'How do we propose getting the particles into the body in a real-world situation?'

Drecker took the lead. 'There are several options. The

particles can be inhaled, consumed by mouth, and they're even small enough to be absorbed through the skin. For product association the latter is the obvious choice. For example, you unwrap your smartphone, swipe the screen and particles are taken in through the pores ready to be activated the moment you switch it on.'

Mathis exchanged glances with his team, then addressed himself to Brennan and Drecker. 'This is all very exciting and precisely the kind of outcome my investment was designed to achieve, but since we've started work my team and I have been thinking more deeply about appropriate applications.'

'Sir?' Brennan said.

'I'm a businessman, Mr Brennan. I never set out to be anything else. But by accident more than design I think I can say that over the last thirty years I've done more to improve the overall human condition than any politician. The problem with politicians is that they have many interests and progress is only one of them. The technology we are developing here has untold potential for good and also for evil. We consider it too powerful for broad commercial application or for licensing to governments, no matter how benign. We would like to reserve it exclusively for ourselves.'

There was a further exchange of glances between Mathis and his team.

'For example,' Mathis continued, 'my mining operations on this site are critical to the scaling-up of my battery and super-conductor business. The president here knows it and he knows that his country is sitting on some of the largest deposits of exactly the natural resources we're going to need to fuel the post-carbon economy – the coltan, the rare earth metals, ninety-eight per cent of which are still to be exploited. He's sweetness and light for the moment, but in future I strongly suspect he may be tempted to hold me to ransom.

Likewise, there are many politicians in the US, in the pockets of one lobby or another, who could cause me and the public I serve considerable inconvenience.' He folded his hands on the desk in front of him. 'I see this technology as a way of buying loyalty and influence. Loyalty to the aims of my wider business among those with the potential to stand in its way.' He looked first Drecker then Brennan in the eye. 'I want that as your objective. Do you think you can fulfil it?'

'Of course, sir,' Brennan said. 'If I may say so, I consider it a very wise strategy.'

Less than an hour later Mathis and his retinue concluded their meeting and a helicopter took off for the airstrip forty miles to the west where their Learjet was waiting for them. They would be back in their Silicon Valley offices by evening. Brennan and Drecker stood side by side watching the Super Puma rise up from the ground, dip its nose and head out across the jungle canopy.

'What do you think?' Brennan said.

'I think we keep playing the loyal servants,' Drecker said.

Brennan nodded. They had an understanding.

21

Kathleen Finn had wanted a quiet funeral service for family
and close friends. A week to the day after his lunch with
Towers, Black found himself among the modest gathering of
mourners in St Martin's, the regimental church that stood on
the busy Ross Road, less than half a mile from Finn's home
and close to the Regiment's former HQ on the southern outskirts of Hereford. Like most things associated with the
Regiment, the church was low-key and unobtrusive: a Victorian construction most wouldn't give a second glance. An
appropriate last resting place for the country's most secretive
warriors.

The congregation was spread across half a dozen rows of
pews. Kathleen, dressed in black, sat at the front with her
sister and brother-in-law and their respective broods of restless, upset children. Finn's relations were few: an elderly aunt
and uncle and a distant cousin or two. He had been an only
child and both parents were long since dead. A coffin draped
in a Union Jack flag sat in the centre of the nave. There were
only a handful of men in uniform present – junior officers
appointed to the Regiment since Black had left – but there
was no sign of Towers. A dozen or so men from A Squadron,
all now retired from active service, sat grouped together several rows ahead of Black. He had never been told what had
been said about him after his sudden departure, but from
their cursory nods and muted greetings he sensed suspicion.

The priest, a cheerful character with a full and ruddy face,
delivered a eulogy that painted Finn as a quiet, sober family

man who having served his country had settled to a workaday existence. There were elements of truth to the story but no hint of the real life he had lived. The blood, the stink, the fear, the exploded brains or the crunch of bayonets through ribs. Finn had out-fought and out-killed all of them. The guts he had spilled would fill a slurry pit. That was the truth, but the truth of combat was seldom spoken of, not even between soldiers. People preferred to enjoy their peace and liberty without reference to its origin, just as they preferred not to dwell on the realities of the slaughterhouse while eating their lunch. The priest, Black thought as his mind wandered over these things, was a man who clearly enjoyed a good lunch.

Black had lost count of the number of funerals he had attended in this place, all of them for men cut down in their prime. The white walls and plain windows seemed somehow to sharpen the divide between life and death more acutely than the worn stone and stained glass of medieval churches in which the living and the dead seemed somehow to unite in the sepulchral gloom. As the service moved through the penultimate hymn to closing prayers his sense of loss grew sharper. It was a new and disconcerting experience, as if he had been stripped of the outer layers that used to shield him from the emotions that afflicted other people. As the priest approached the coffin and recited, 'Go forth, Christian soul, from this world,' he felt a lump form in his throat.

He fought back against the sensation, dismayed at himself.

But Black wasn't the only battled-hardened soldier who had been touched by the proceedings. The clique of former troopers and NCOs who had eyed him suspiciously before the Service tacitly accepted him into their circle as they gathered in the graveyard for the interment, bowing their heads in solemn silence. Kathleen and the children sobbed as the coffin was lowered jerkily into the ground and hit the earth below with a muffled thud. A young captain in crisp uniform placed a hand on her shoulder and looked briefly across the grave to the men who had served alongside Finn, several of whom, including Black, owed their lives to him. No words were needed. The message passed between the former comrades as clearly as if the RSM had bellowed it. *There but for the grace of God.*

Black was standing alone at the bar in the tired function room of the nearby pub when Kathleen appeared from amidst the chatting mourners. Her eyes were still red and swollen. 'Aren't you going to talk to the men? I know they'd like to say hello to you.'

'Of course.' He felt a stab of guilt and as if he had offended her. The truth was that he had needed a few drinks inside him before launching into reminiscences. 'How are the children?'

She shrugged. 'Up and down.'

'I spoke to Freddy Towers. He mentioned Megan –'

'People make you sick,' Kathleen shot back. 'And the police are useless. I know what Ryan would have done. She'll be all right.' She glanced away, then turned sharply back towards him. 'I had a visit from someone at the Foreign Office. They said I may never know why it happened – not if there's national security involved. The coroner said he can't do anything until the French police have closed their case. It could be months, or longer.'

'You know I'll do what I can, Kathleen.'

'Why the bodyguard? If they'd already got away with the woman he was looking after, why wait for him? And if they wanted to make sure he wasn't going to come after them, why not *shoot* him? It doesn't make sense.' She swallowed, determined not to spill any more tears. 'He'd talk to me, Leo. Tell me things he wasn't meant to. I've learned enough over the years to know there's more to this.' She looked at him with eyes that seemed to cut through his mask of feigned ignorance. 'What do you think . . . ? In my shoes would you let it go?'

Black met her gaze, seeing the strength and resilience that would have made her a match for Finn. She would survive, but he was certain she would never rest until she knew. He tried to find words that wouldn't leave him a hostage to fortune but she beat him to it, as if sensing his weakness.

'Thank you for coming, anyway. You'll stay in touch?'

'Of course.'

She managed a smile of sorts and nodded towards the group he'd been avoiding. 'They're all good blokes. Ryan only stuck with mates he could trust.' She touched his arm and went back to the relatives minding her children.

Black drained his pint, ordered another from the bar and ventured towards some of those he had stood among at the graveside. The faces were older, most of them now well into their forties, but their names came rushing back to him: Corporal Robbie Hines, Sergeant Con Tyler, Troopers Dave Blunt and Jed Salter and Lance Corporal Dan Hart. Helped by the alcohol, Black greeted them with a warm hello and without further comment was absorbed naturally into their conversation.

The talk among the old soldiers was mostly of friends and colleagues, who, like them, had made the difficult transition out of the army. Most had found themselves niches in the world of private security and close protection, but others they mentioned had taken up regular trades. The Special Forces, it seemed, turned out a healthy crop of plumbers and electricians. Some hadn't had it so easy and had turned to drink or worse. A couple had found religion. A former corporal had joined a Buddhist commune in Cornwall and a trooper Black had known from a boy was training for the priesthood. Listening to their stories, he was struck by how mild and unassuming these men were compared with the preening and neurotic academics he now called colleagues. Every last one possessed an aura of calm self-containment that bordered on the monk-like. With the singular exception of Freddy Towers, there had been no place for big egos or attention-seekers in the Regiment.

They ordered another round of drinks and were joined by two younger men who introduced themselves as Chris Riley and Ed Fallon, both of them serving troopers who had worked with Finn during his last years in uniform, much of which were spent in Syria and Yemen. Riley was a stocky Yorkshireman with a mischievous smile and a glint in his eye. Fallon was a taller quiet type with the wiry frame and quiet intensity of a mountaineer. Just the kind of combination Finn would have selected to make up a small team for operations in the desert.

Riley ventured the fact that the three of them had spent a lot of time on obbos and sab missions behind enemy lines, the kind of work that tests nerves and friendships to their limits. 'Finny was a good boss, though I'll not miss sharing a dugout with him.'

His joke raised a laugh from all of them. One of the joys of covert observation was sharing the same hole for days on end, urinating into bottles and defecating into plastic bags. There were some men who could be civilized about it and those like Finn who coped with the squalor by revelling in it.

'He only spoke well of you, sir,' Riley said to Black. 'Said you went back fifteen years.'

'Felt like thirty,' Black said, raising another laugh. 'He was there the day I joined and still there when I left. Thought he'd outlive us all.'

There was a brief, respectful silence.

'Finn said he had you down for the big time.' The comment came from Riley. 'Thought you could go all the way to general. He could never understand why you left.'

The question was innocent enough but caused all eyes to turn on Black. It occurred to him that he had never formulated a truthful answer. He had left on impulse, not for a thought-out reason. The words that came out of his mouth were entirely new to him.

'If you'd asked me five years ago I'm not sure I could have told you, except to say I probably felt there was more to life than the army. Now, well . . . I wonder if underneath it all I wasn't thinking that my luck couldn't hold for ever. All that door kicking we did in Iraq, I should have been under the sod a dozen times. I could have sat behind a desk somewhere, I suppose, but it never appealed.'

'You didn't lose your marbles, then, sir?' The flippant remark came from Robbie Hines, a Geordie with arms like capstans.

Black smiled. 'Is that what they said?'

'And the rest,' Dave Blunt chimed in. 'I heard you'd run off with a ladyboy.'

'That was after I left.'

More laughter. Black felt a weight lift from his shoulders and sensed that he was being greeted back into the fold.

'Kathleen told us you went to Paris, sir,' Hines said quietly, careful not to be overheard by any of Finn's relatives. 'Heard he got cut up pretty bad.'

'I'm afraid so.'

'Do we know who the perp is?'

Black shook his head.

'I'll bet you Towers does.' The speaker was Con Tyler, a squat, shaven-headed man from Staffordshire with still, black eyes. 'Finn was on the phone to me a couple of weeks back saying Towers had got him a job in France. Looking after some scientist.'

'I've spoken to Towers,' Black said. 'He doesn't know.'

'So what's he doing about it?'

Black hesitated. The five men looked at him, all of them assuming that he had inside information.

'Obviously his work was classified. I don't know details, but I do know Towers is on the case.'

'Still mates with Fireballs, are you?'

'Not really, no. He got in touch with me, after Kathleen asked me to go to Paris to identify the body. He's working with the French authorities trying to piece together the evidence.'

'If he needs a crew, he knows who to ask,' Hines said. 'We'd be out there tomorrow.'

The others murmured in agreement.

'I'm sure he knows that,' Black said. 'And I know he feels like the rest of us.'

'It would have been nice of him to show up,' Jed Salter said.

'I understand he's been to pay his respects to Kathleen,' Black said, feeling an inexplicable need to defend Towers' absence.

'Afraid to show his face,' Salter said. 'Might have had some questions to answer.'

Black remained silent, aware that Riley and Fallon, the two in the group still in the thick of their careers, were listening intently.

'He was livid when you left, sir,' Tyler said. 'Didn't have any officers lunatic enough to carry out his crazy fucking orders. Had to start behaving like he cared if we got to go home. Best thing you ever did for us, buggering off.' He laughed, breaking the tension.

'I'm glad some good came of it,' Black said and caught sight of Kathleen glancing over at him as she leaned down to comfort her two girls.

He watched her stroke their hair and kiss their foreheads and knew that he couldn't desert them.

22

Black climbed down from the Land Rover on to the rain-flattened grass at Ty Argel. The earlier storm had passed, the sun had emerged from behind the clouds and the air was filled with the heavy scent of warm, damp vegetation. Now mid-June was approaching the garden was humming with life. A dragonfly hovered in a puddle of light beneath the alder by the stream. Bees flitted between the flowering weeds thriving in what was supposed to be lawn and purple buddleia sprouted from the crevices of the stone walls. This was what he called the golden time. The short span between late June and the penultimate week of August when the evening chill would return and the bracken start to brown at its tips.

Still groggy from the beer he had drunk at the wake, Black made his way up the path, intending to change out of his suit and spend the last hours of daylight peacefully taming his wilderness. Minutes later, dressed in a pair of cut-off jeans and an old T-shirt, he came downstairs to make coffee. He was filling his old stove-top kettle from the tap when he noticed a padded envelope sitting on the small pine dining table beneath the window. Having no recollection of having put it there, his first thought was that Towers must have left it behind the evening he called. He stepped over and saw that beneath it there was a slip of paper headed, *With the compliments of Colonel F. Towers.* Beneath, Towers had written in longhand: *Apologies for the intrusion. Needs must, FT.*

Intrusion.

Black ran his eyes around the cottage for signs of break-in

but there were none. The windows were shut fast and the back door bolted from inside. Whoever had left the package – and it was unlikely to have been Towers himself – would simply have picked the locks. With the right tools it was as easy as using a key. It was a cheap trick. There was no reason Towers couldn't have made a delivery to him in Oxford. This was simply a way of letting him know that he couldn't escape. And in all likelihood if he had used Credenhill boys to run his errand, there would be one of them out in the bracken right now, checking to see that he had collected.

He snatched the package from the table intending to toss it unopened into the stove, but something stopped him – guilt, loyalty, anger – a whole confusion of emotions that made him reach for a kitchen knife and slit it open. He shook the contents on to the worktop: a contactless credit card in the name of 'David Harris', a driving licence bearing his photograph in the same name, and a single folded sheet of paper. He opened it to find the names and London addresses of two men and a pin number for the card. At the foot of the page Towers had written, again in longhand: *Who are they working for?* followed by the initials, *CB*, which, as ever, stood for *carte blanche*.

Black stared out of the window across the garden and saw a pair of crows at the far end of the overgrown lawn tearing at the remains of a dead pigeon. They were cunning and resourceful creatures but pitiless hunters. He had seen them peck the eyes out of sick lambs. Black hated cruelty as much as he hated dishonesty. He had hoped never to inflict any again.

It was a fine ideal.

He opened the cupboard beneath the sink and pulled away the loose panel that shrouded the pipes. Behind it was the Glock. His visitor had added three boxes of ammunition, a bone-handled Bowie knife and a double-sided shoulder holster. Black brought the knife out into the light thinking that he recognized it.

He did. Every nick and scratch.

He hadn't seen it since Helmand. He and Finn had sneaked up on a Taliban sniper in hostile territory and found themselves confronted with six men camped out on a mud roof. Having gunshots ring out wasn't an option that would have ended with them escaping alive. Other men would have urged a quiet retreat. Not Finn. They had waited silently until all but two of them were asleep before vaulting the parapet and silencing all six within seconds.

Black recalled the sensation of hot blood running over his hand and the animal thrill of the assassin. He had never been more alive and less human than on that night.

23

It was noon on Saturday and the hottest day of the year. The air con in the rented Ford transit needed regassing. Even on full power the vents were pumping out air no cooler than the eighty-five degrees outside the closed windows. Sweat trickled down Black's spine, soaking through the short-sleeved shirt he wore beneath a high-vis vest. Several days' growth of thick, dark stubble and a pair of mirrored wrap-around sunglasses served as a basic but effective disguise. He was just another van driver enduring the London traffic.

He was travelling eastwards along Holland Park Avenue in west London, approaching the point at the top of the rise where it merged into Notting Hill Gate. The traffic slowed to a crawl and came to a stop. Roadworks had combined to make this stretch even more tortuous than usual. He took a slug of water from a plastic bottle and fought an overpowering temptation to abort. He hadn't felt fear so physically since his very first missions in Bosnia: parachuting by night deep into Serb-controlled territory to take out artillery positions. Now, like then, the object of his dread was not the dangers that lay ahead but his ability to meet them. He felt trapped in a fallible body unequal to the task.

He crept forward by painful inches until finally he passed the Tube station. His destination was the second turning on the left – Linden Gardens, a leafy circular cul-de-sac which he had already recced twice since Tuesday. The lights up ahead flicked to green and the queue of cars ahead of him began to move. He indicated to make the turn, feeling his heart pounding against the inside of his ribs.

He drove clockwise at walking pace around the Gardens, waiting for the adrenalin surge to pass. Slowly, he felt his body coming back to something approaching equilibrium. The street was quiet, the residents still recovering from their eighty-hour weeks. Five-storey stucco-fronted terraces that had once been crammed with low-rent bedsits were now home to wealthy young bankers and lawyers with no lives of their own but more money than they knew how to spend. The kind too caught up in themselves to take much notice of what was going on outside their front doors. The anonymous van, identical to a million others, passed by unnoticed.

Black's target, thirty-four-year-old Max Quinn, occupied a flat on the third floor of the only modern building in the street: a rectangular 1960s construction with a small garden separating it from the road and a driveway to its left side leading to a car park behind. During his first recce Black had spotted the CCTV cameras covering the car park and was keen not to use it. He was in luck: a midnight-blue Maserati Quattroporte pulled out of a space almost directly outside the block as he approached. It was a tight squeeze that left no room to open the van's rear doors, but in anticipation he had selected a model with an additional door that slid open along its side and which was now facing the pavement.

The block had a secure lobby, the locked door to which could be buzzed open via a video intercom connected to each apartment. Additional security was provided by a porter who occupied a ground-floor flat at the rear of the building. An internet search had produced estate agents' particulars of a recently sold apartment on the first floor that had included the helpful detail that the porter worked weekdays only. This had provided Black with the most obvious route in. He pulled on a navy baseball cap and stuffed a roll of duct tape along with several plastic cable ties into the pockets of his vest. From the passenger seat he picked up a heavy eighteen-inch-square package carefully wrapped in plastic and addressed to *Mr Max Quinn, Flat 8B, Linden House*, along with a clipboard bearing a delivery note for signature.

Black approached the front door of the building and pressed the buzzer for Quinn's flat. There was no answer. He tried a second time, this time for a full five seconds.

A hungover voice crackled over the intercom speaker. 'Yes?'

Holding up the box so that it could be seen by the camera, Black said, 'Courier. I've got a package for Mr Quinn, 8B.'

'Oh, right,' Quinn mumbled. 'Leave it with the porter round the side. He'll take it.' His accent was pure public school – privileged and complacent. Typical MI5. Just like the army, the Service seemed forever doomed to recruit in its own image.

'Sorry, sir. Can't leave this one with a third party; needs your signature. Sender's instructions.'

There was a brief silence, which Black interpreted as the spy's instincts stirring to life. Agents of the Security Services were rigorously trained in the dangers of abduction and assassination, hence their preference for residences such as this one that offered several lines of defence.

'I've got a deliver or return on this, sir. What would you like me to do?' Black said impatiently.

'Who's it from? Does it say?'

Black fumbled with the package and the clipboard and made sure Quinn got a good view of him scanning the delivery note. 'Here we go. Mr Michael Hamden.'

An email exchange with Towers had established that 'Hamden' was the official alias of Quinn's line manager, a fact which would be known only to a small circle inside their department.

'All right. Come on up,' Quinn said with a weary note of resignation. A delivery from the boss on a Saturday morning could only mean unwelcome work.

Black rode up to the third floor in the lift, and as he stepped out on to the carpeted landing he speed-dialled a number he had preset on his phone. It was no more than six paces to Quinn's front door. Quinn opened it on a sturdy security chain. His face was puffy and his body out of shape. He was wearing shorts and a crumpled T-shirt and looked as if he had met the dawn in a West End casino. From somewhere inside the flat a phone started to ring. Quinn glanced over his shoulder with a puzzled expression. Hopefully, he would assume it was his boss letting him know about the delivery.

'There you go, sir,' Black said, passing the clipboard through the narrow gap afforded by the chain. 'Leave it here, shall I?' He nodded to the floor outside the door as Quinn scribbled his signature.

'Yeah, that's fine.' The phone continued to ring behind him. He passed the clipboard out as Black straightened from setting the box down.

'Cheers.' Black smiled and turned back towards the lift, hearing the flat door close behind him.

If Quinn was any sort of professional, he would answer the call before collecting the package. Black reached out his phone and ended it before Quinn could answer. He stopped and stepped back towards the flat, pressed close to the wall. He waited while Quinn called back the mobile phone number that had just attempted to reach him. It would ring four times and deliver a message which Black had recorded using text to speech software. An automated female voice would announce: '*Your package will be delivered by Stephen between 12.05 and 12.15 p.m. today. Thank you.*'

Silent seconds passed. Black heard footsteps approach along the hall and the sound of the catch being pulled back. Repeating a drill he had rehearsed a thousand times before, he stepped in front of the door, drew his right knee up to his chest and stamped heel first with his whole bodyweight, sending a startled Quinn sprawling backwards on to the floor.

'Don't move,' Black said quietly while drawing the Glock from its holster. He levelled it at Quinn's chest and pulled the door closed behind him. 'I'll be asking you some questions today, Mr Quinn, about who you've been associating with. It's going to take a little while to get where we're going, so you'll have time to reconcile yourself to telling the truth. Do you understand?'

Quinn stared up at him with wide frozen eyes, his lips parted in an expression of disbelief.

'On your front, please. Hands behind your back.' Black spoke quietly and matter-of-factly.

Quinn stared at the gun, then did as he was told.

Holstering the Glock, Black crouched, forced his right knee hard into the small of Quinn's back and fastened his wrists behind his tailbone with three cable ties.

'Who sent you?' Quinn said, wincing as Black drew the ties tight.

'Hamden.'

'Am I under arrest?'

'We'll discuss your status later.'

There was a sound of movement from behind a door at the end of the hallway.

'Who's that?'

Quinn didn't answer.

Black pressed a knuckle into the side of his neck, finding the pressure point beneath his ear. Quinn exclaimed in pain.

'Who?'

'A girl.'

'Friend of yours?'

'No.'

'I see.'

Black let him go, snatched the duct tape from his pocket, wound it twice around his ankles and left him trussed on the floor while he went in search of the girl.

He pushed open the bedroom door and entered the darkened interior that smelled of sweat, stale perfume and alcohol. A black dress and underwear hung over a chair. A tangle of sheets lay in the centre of a bed. A young woman with pretty Slavic features was crouching behind it. High cheekbones and ice-blue eyes. She was naked and clutching a phone in front of her bare breasts like a miniature shield.

'Put it down, please.'

She stared back at him like a mistrustful child, refusing to let it go.

'Now.' He gestured for her to place it on the bed.

She remained motionless.

There was no time for games. He stepped towards her. At the same moment she sprang up and scrambled over the bed towards the door. Black shot out a hand and grabbed her slender arm above the elbow. She let out a scream, leaving him no choice but to press his other hand over her mouth and force her on to the mattress. Terrified, she fell silent, let go of the phone and curled, quivering, into a foetal position. He grabbed it from the crumped bedclothes and bent it double between his fists and tossed it aside. Broken shards of glass scattered across the sheets. The girl let out a sob. Battling a wave of revulsion, Black cable-tied her wrists and ankles and taped her mouth with two strips of duct tape. Mute and help-less she looked up at him pleadingly.

'I'm sorry. You won't be here long.' He tugged the sheet out from beneath her and covered her nakedness.

It was the least he could do.

He turned to the wardrobe, slid open the doors and from beneath a neat pile of tailored shirts folded in their laundry wrappers dug out an old hooded sweat top. In among an expensive collection of shoes he found a pair of trainers. He gathered them up and took them through to the hall. As he closed the door, he apologized once again to the girl.

Collateral damage. Ends and means. It never got any easier.

Quinn offered no resistance as Black removed the tape from his ankles, hauled him to his feet and pulled the hoodie over his head. No doubt the young spy had, as intended, con-cluded that a well-spoken middle-class intruder could only be part of some elaborate training exercise. Black was more than happy to encourage the delusion. It would make the shock of what was to come later all the more effective.

They made their way down to the ground floor using the internal fire escape. Quinn remained silent. Hungover and without the use of his arms his full attention was focused on maintaining his balance. Black walked behind him, the hot stale air in the windowless staircase reminding him of so many others down which he had escorted men at gunpoint. If Quinn had even a lingering fear that his detention was genuine, he gave little sign of it. As they crossed the empty lobby, a trace of arrogant self-assurance returned to his pam-pered features. He moved at his own unhurried pace and paused for a moment, making Black wait like an attentive servant as he held the door to the outside open for him.

Black let it pass. He had always believed in treating prisoners with dignity until the moment at which that was no longer possible.

They left the building and approached the van. 'You'll be travelling in the back, I'm afraid. You may find it a little warm. Can't be helped.'

Black opened the locks with a click of the key fob, waited for a Filipina nanny pushing a toddler in a buggy to pass, then climbed into the back with Quinn, before sliding the door nearly closed again.

'On your knees, please.'

Quinn sighed, tiring of the game. The first sign of resistance.

'I won't ask you again.'

Quinn turned his back to the boarded side of the van and slid down to the floor in a seated position.

'I said knees.'

'What difference does it make?'

'Please do as I say, Mr Quinn.'

'Or what? Are you going to kill me?' He glanced up with a cocky, mocking smile.

Black kicked him sharply in the side of his left thigh. Quinn convulsed with the sudden shock of the pain, gasping through gritted teeth. Working quickly and without emotion, Black hauled him, still grimacing, on to his front, grabbed the roll of duct tape from his waistcoat pocket, pulled his head back from the floor and wrapped tape twice around his neck and jaw, covering his mouth. Quinn writhed and kicked out as panic took hold. Black let go of his head, thrust a knee into the back of his thighs, caught hold of his thrashing ankles and bound them tightly together.

Quinn's breath came in short, terrified bursts. Defenceless and unable to move or breathe through his mouth, he would feel like a drowning man. Black took a length of nylon tow rope from a small holdall in which he had stowed his few necessary pieces of equipment and secured Quinn's legs to one of the metal anchors welded to the van's internal struts.

'Try to relax.'

Quinn looked round at him with wide, desperate eyes that seemed to be fast approaching the edge of consciousness. He had succumbed to panic and in all likelihood would hyperventilate to the point of passing out for a short while. He would then wake and the cycle would repeat itself several more times before his body's supplies of adrenalin were finally exhausted. Each time, it would feel like dying all over again.

Black felt a fleeting measure of pity, which was quickly displaced by a mental image of Finn's mutilated body. Forty stab wounds in marble-white skin. He reached back into the holdall and brought out one of two cotton laundry bags he had bought from a homeware stall in Oxford's covered market. One was printed with sunflowers, the other with poppies. He pulled the sunflowers over Quinn's head and secured the drawstring behind his neck. He looked faintly ridiculous but it saved Black having to look at his face.

Quinn's breathing became even more frantic. Patches of bitter-smelling perspiration appeared through his clothes. It wouldn't be long now. Black waited, crouching on his haunches, watching his prisoner's lungs work faster and faster until they weren't so much inhaling and exhaling, as vibrating multiple times each second. Then, at last, he took one deep, desperate gasp of air before his body tensed, became rigid and fell slack. Black leaned forward and listened. He was still breathing, slowly but steadily, his body's life-support system gradually resetting the balance of gases in his blood.

He was a young man. He'd live.

Black stepped out on to the pavement, slid the door closed and made his way around to the cab. The street was still empty. No one had seen their neighbour abducted in broad daylight, and even if they had, he suspected that most would simply have looked the other way. Every rich man for himself. He climbed behind the wheel, brought out his phone and sent an encrypted text to Towers instructing him to send someone to come and see to the girl. 'And maybe pay her something for her trouble?' he added as a postscript. He felt sorry for her.

He started the engine and headed west for his next pick-up.

So far so good. He had surprised himself.

Four years without practice and he hadn't lost his touch.

24

Freddy Towers' briefing notes described Elliot Clayton as thirty-five years old, six feet two inches tall and of muscular build. His English father and American mother were both retired college professors. He had studied history and politics at Cambridge and completed a PhD on the evolution of modern terrorism at Princeton where he had continued his passions for rugby and boxing. His tap on the shoulder had come from the British consul in New York during a summer internship. Genuine Anglo-Americans able to pass themselves off as a native on both sides of the Atlantic were a surprisingly rare breed, it seemed. Rarer still were those of high intelligence who weren't intent on a strictly mercenary career. Clayton had been sufficiently flattered by the approach to lend his intellectual gifts to the British Security Services. This alone had been enough to raise Towers' suspicions. *What sort of man gives up the chance of riches to work for HM Government?* he had added in longhand. *Must have a kink.* 'Kink', in Towers' parlance, could mean anything from a preference for suede shoes to an extreme sexual fetish.

Black kept an open mind. A career in MI5 presented an intellectual challenge and for a man living in the shadow of successful if not wealthy parents, it had the advantage of placing him beyond the inevitable comparisons: a spy's life was secret, even from his loved ones. Of the two suspects he suspected Clayton the least. But all this remained speculation. Before he could begin to form a judgement, there was the small matter of apprehending him.

Black turned left off the Uxbridge Road on the border between Acton and Ealing, drove a short distance along Hillcrest Road and turned right into Whitehall Gardens. A little over 100 yards long, it was lined on both sides by well-kept Edwardian terraced houses. The German estate cars and SUVs parked outside them were those of well-heeled professional families. He passed a middle-aged woman clipping the hedge in her front garden and a window cleaner at work on the opposite side of the road. As he had anticipated, anonymity was not an option. Further along, two labourers were loading furniture into a small removal van which filled the width of the carriageway. When making his getaway, he would have to reverse out.

Sited almost directly halfway along the road, Clayton's house had no distinguishing features aside from a bunch of pink helium balloons emblazoned with *Happy Birthday* tied to the cast-iron gate. A woman in her thirties emerged from the front door carrying a baby in a sling. She walked along the pavement in his direction, smiling and stroking the baby's cheek. Black stared at the balloons and thought of the innocent children inside. For a moment he was tempted to back up and drive away. Then he reminded himself that unlike Finn, Elliot Clayton would be returned to his family. It was not a question of morality. There was a job to be done.

He had given himself two options and decided on the second. Clayton's car, a black Toyota Prius, was parked three spaces along from the house. Black slowed as he came alongside it and steered in tight. The front nearside corner of the van connected with the Toyota's mirror and tore it from its moorings. He came to a stop, turned the wheel a little further to the left and nosed the van's front corner gently into the Toyota's off-side wheel arch, denting it. He checked his mirror. The gardener was still clipping her hedge and the

window cleaner scrubbing an upstairs window with a telescopic pole. Black reversed a touch, then pulled forward so
that the side door of his van was positioned alongside the
small gap between the Toyota and the Audi parked in front
of it. He reached into the glovebox and brought out a
preloaded syringe, ran through his mental calculation once
more and decided to lose five mils. It was a fine line between
knocking a man out and killing him. Better to err on the side
of caution.

The front door was opened by an attractive but unhealth-
ily thin woman wearing a red bandana to cover what Black
assumed would be a hairless skull. According to Towers'
briefing notes, Helen Clayton was a clinical psychologist
who for three years had been suffering with leukaemia.
Shortly before her diagnosis, she had left her hospital job
to set up in private practice. It had proved a costly move.
Due to her ill health she was able to work only part-time and
without her regular salary the family had fallen into debt.
The unexplained recent deposits in Clayton's personal account
were, it seemed, all that stood between them and losing their
heavily mortgaged home.

Black greeted her with a smile. 'Sorry to trouble you,
ma'am. A neighbour said that black Toyota is yours. I'm
afraid I've given it a bit of a scrape with my van. A kid ran out
into the road.'

The squeals of excited six-year-old girls travelled along
the hall from the kitchen at the back of the house.

'Oh –' Helen Clayton brought a slender hand to the stark
line of her jaw. Wide brown eyes glanced anxiously towards
her car.

'It's not too bad. I'm sure my insurance will cover it. We
ought to exchange details. I do apologize – I'm spoiling your
party.'

His contrite tone disarmed her. She gave a sigh and shrugged. 'These things happen. Hold on, I'll get my husband.'

She pushed the door almost closed and disappeared along the tiled hallway.

Black returned to the van, slid the side door open a little and reached a pocket-sized notebook and pen from the hold-all. He glanced right to check on Quinn, who was lying on his back near the rear doors. All was well: he could hear him breathing. He pulled the door back across and tore a sheet from the notebook on which late the previous evening he had written details of a fictitious insurance policy.

He turned to see Elliot Clayton approaching. A tall, square-shouldered figure with receding temples and the hint of a paunch beneath a New York Jets T-shirt. A once fit young man turning the corner into middle-age. He gave Black a reproachful look, playful but semi-serious as he surveyed the damage.

'So sorry about this,' Black said. 'A lad ran straight out in front of me. Lucky I was going slowly. Your name and address is all they'll need. I'll get on to it straight away.' He handed Clayton the piece of paper and the notebook and pen.

Clayton gave a philosophical shrug, evidently in no mood for recriminations. 'It's my wife's car, actually.' He pocketed Black's details and wrote down his own on a blank page.

'Daddy, hurry up! We're waiting for you.'

Black glanced over his shoulder to see a young girl standing by the gate, her face painted to resemble a panda's.

'Won't be a moment, sweetie. Go on inside.'

'Now, Daddy! We need you for our game.'

The girl stamped her foot, refusing to move. Clayton dashed off the last line of his address. Black looked from one to the other. Time slowed as he weighed his options. But there was only one. Clayton handed back the notebook and at the same moment Black reached into his waistcoat pocket with his right hand.

'Sorry, again. Enjoy the party.'

Clayton turned. Black brought out the syringe and thrust the three-inch needle through the fabric of Clayton's jeans into the top of his buttock, forcing the plunger down hard with his thumb. Sodium thiopental would take seconds to work. Seconds in which Clayton could have put a lot of distance between himself and the van. Black was ready. As the big man wheeled round, eyes wide in alarm, Black slammed his right elbow into his solar plexus and snapped the back of his fist into Clayton's jaw, at the same time driving his knee upwards between his legs.

Clayton gasped and doubled over, blood spilling from a split lip.

Black glanced over and saw the girl's frightened, bewildered expression. She turned and ran back into the house, calling for her mother. Clayton's knees collapsed beneath him. Black threw open the van door, hooked his hands under his shoulders and hauled him inside. He was a dead, unwieldy weight. It took all of Black's strength to drag him over the sill and roll him on to the floor. There was no time to tie him up. Black turned him over, laying him face down and jumped out on to the tarmac as Helen Clayton emerged from her front door.

'What's going on?'

Black ran around the front of the vehicle to the driver's door.

'Where is he?' Her voice rose to a pitch of hysteria. 'What have you done with my husband?'

Black jumped behind the wheel, hit the locks, fired the ignition and jammed the stick into reverse. Helen Clayton's tormented face appeared at the passenger window. She pounded the glass with her fist.

'What have you done with him?'

Black stamped on the throttle, using his mirrors to reverse. Helen Clayton clung on to the outside handle of the door, yelling at him to stop.

Stupid woman. Let go.

She held on as if her life depended on it. He sped up, jerking the wheel sharply left and right. There was a thud and a scream as the sudden movement threw her clear and hurled her emaciated body across the bonnet of a parked car. He continued on to the junction at the end of the street, braked hard and eased backwards around the corner. As he stopped and shifted into first, he looked left to see the woman who had been trimming her hedge running towards the crumpled figure lying at the edge of the road.

More collateral damage.

He hoped that was the end of it.

Black drove for half a mile at a steady pace, then pulled over and fetched a pair of number plates from the passenger footwell. With steady fingers he peeled the protective film from the adhesive pads he had earlier attached to each corner. Less than thirty seconds later they were fixed in place and he was on his way. He headed west towards the junction with the North Circular Road. Shortly before the turn, a police car with lights flashing and siren blaring careered towards him between the opposing lanes of traffic. Black tightened his grip on the wheel, expecting trouble. It whipped past and continued on. He watched it disappear from view in his side mirror and tried to wipe the image of Helen Clayton's terrified face from his mind. But it remained stubbornly imprinted. Like a reflection on glass.

25

The abandoned cement works were on the site of an exhausted quarry a thirty-minute drive north of Oxford. Towers had suggested it as a suitable venue for the interrogation and had assured Black that he wouldn't be disturbed. Black had taken him at his word.

The entrance to the narrow access road was unsigned and almost invisible between encroaching verges. Black left the A road and turned on to it. He continued for a third of a mile over crumbling tarmac as far as a set of locked plate-metal gates at the entrance to the redundant site. Here he turned right along a rough service track that ran along the outside of a perimeter fence. He had recced on foot two evenings before and been pleased at how overgrown the track had become. The hedge separating it from the neighbouring fields hadn't been cut in several years and in places springy overhanging boughs extended from one side to the other. He nursed the van along, branches scraping noisily along its side and knee-high weeds dragging at the undercarriage.

After a further quarter of a mile he arrived outside a smaller set of wire-mesh gates smothered with bindweed and bramble where he pulled up. He climbed out to fetch a pair of bolt cutters and check on his passengers. The sound of the door sliding open caused them both to flinch. It was a good sign: they were alert. He studied them for a short while, like animals in a cage. Their breathing accelerated as they sensed danger. They also stank. Fear did that to people – it had a rank quality all of its own. He hoped he could make quick work of it.

Black drew the door closed again, stamped down the brambles and placed the blades of the bolt cutters around a link in the short length of hardened steel chain holding the gates together. Bracing one of the thirty-inch handles against his body, he pulled the other towards him. The blades bit but the power of his arms alone wasn't sufficient. It was always the most trivial problems that threatened to foul things up. Cursing the delay, he retrieved the remainder of the tow rope from the holdall.

He tied one end of the rope to the upright of the gate six feet from the ground and employing a series of simple climbing knots and loops created a crude pulley system that allowed him to double his bodyweight in order to force the arms of the cutters together.

The stubborn link snapped with a satisfying clink.

He moved the blades to the other side of the link and repeated the process. The broken chain fell away.

He was in.

Black parked the van behind a crumbling brick wall and climbed out to take in the strange surroundings. The scene resembled those in photographs he had seen of the post-Chernobyl ghost town of Pripyat. It was hard to imagine that he was within minutes of commuter villages and the prosperous market town of Kidlington. The crude concrete mixing tower in which imported minerals had been combined with crushed limestone from the nearby abandoned quarry was sprouting grass and weeds from its many cracks and fissures. The several surrounding acres that had once been the factory yard had been broken up by successive winters and was slowly reverting to scrub. Rectangular ponds that had played some part in the industrial process were filled with thick, matted algae and cast in semi-shadow by dense clouds of circling midges. The impression of desolation was completed by the decaying hulk of a tipper lorry sitting on flat, perished tyres.

Black stepped through the empty doorway to the deserted building and entered an area roughly fifty feet long and thirty wide. The floor was strewn with rubble and broken glass. Where once there had been a steel staircase leading to several upper floors, rusting stubs of ground-off metal protruded from the walls. In the centre of the room were the remains of the three-storey-high mixing mechanism which had been fed at each level with different materials brought in from the outside by conveyor belts. He approached the circular guard rail surrounding it and peered down through the foot-wide gap between the edge of the floor and the mixer's cylindrical body. A glint of natural light partially illuminated an even lower level at which the finished cement must have emerged. Curious, he went to investigate further.

The ground sloped downwards from the front to the rear of the tower, where Black found an open doorway at the entrance to a passageway some ten feet wide. Running along the length of its left-hand side was an open-topped horizontal chute made of galvanized steel that sat on a raised concrete plinth. In the centre of the chute was a rusting auger whose corkscrew motion would have pushed the finished cement from the base of the mixing mechanism outside to waiting delivery lorries.

He stepped inside. The air was damp and musty, the walls spotted with mildew. It was exactly what he needed.

Liberals and humanitarians (the HRBs, or Human Rights Brigade, as Freddy Towers had always referred to them) had long claimed that physical torture was no more effective at extracting information from a prisoner than polite questioning across a desk. To a certain extent it was true, but only up to a point. To be successful hands-off interrogation required time in which to build rapport and resources with which to offer incentives: friendship and reward were a persuasive combination. But the hard fact was that when searching for a ticking bomb or a sleeper cell about to spring into action, bonhomie and offers of used banknotes were of little use. Quick results called for brutal methods.

It was nearly three o'clock in the afternoon when he brought first Quinn, then Clayton, into the tunnel beneath the mixing tower at gunpoint. Keeping their hoods on, he spread their hands and feet wide apart and tied them by lengths of rope to the rusty auger. He lifted their hoods above their mouths but not their eyes, removed the duct tape and allowed them each a sip of water. Clayton drank calmly and silently. Quinn gasped and spluttered, then groaned in protest as Black replaced the tape and pulled the hoods back down.

Then he left them, closing the door behind him so that they were confined in total darkness. Standing bent over and spread-eagled with legs, backs and shoulders aching, even the most hardened terrorists would invariably crack within four hours. Only those intent on becoming martyrs tended to last longer. Such cases provided a different order of challenge: they would have to taste death, then life, then death, then life again before they decided which they preferred. Black had no fear of either Quinn or Clayton wishing to be a martyr.

He waited in the cab of the van listening to the radio and watching swallows swoop through the clouds of flies above the stagnant ponds. A pair of rabbits emerged and grazed on clumps of scrub growing out of the decaying yard. Life was determined to continue its normal course. Life had no guilt or conscience. These were strictly human afflictions.

Shortly after five p.m. Black re-entered the tunnel, bringing a pair of industrial ear defenders – the last unused item in his holdall. He placed them over Clayton's hooded head. At first glance the big man appeared to be holding up well. His hands were braced firmly against the auger, shoulders solid. Then Black noticed the tremor in his legs. The screaming muscles would be near the end of their resources and beginning to cramp. Before long, they would give way beneath him, but even so, without the ability to stretch them out, neither the pain nor the cramps would stop. He left Clayton to cook and turned his attention to Quinn.

The younger man's legs had already collapsed. He was slumped forward with his head resting uncomfortably on the auger and most of his bodyweight supported by his chest where it crossed the lip of the chute. His breathing was fitful, his body trembling and his clothes soaked with urine. Suppressing his disgust at the sight, Black lifted the hood as far as his nose, removed the duct tape from his mouth and pulled the hood down again. Quinn gulped in air with such force that the cotton laundry bag clung to the contours of his face.

'I don't want you to suffer a moment's more discomfort than you have to, Mr Quinn,' Black said evenly. 'You should already have gathered that this is most definitely not a training exercise. You are being interrogated over your involvement in the recent disappearance of four British scientists. You will have become familiar with their research during the course of your work. You should also be under no illusions about the lengths to which I am prepared to go to ascertain the truth. Do you understand?'

Quinn gave a jerky nod.

'Are you familiar with the work of Dr Sarah Bellman?'

No reaction.

'Mr Quinn?'

The prisoner's head twitched. An attempt at another nod, perhaps. His breathing was wheezy and laboured.

'I will release you unharmed, Mr Quinn, and, indeed, if you prove sufficiently helpful, you may even escape prosecution, but in order for that to happen I need you to tell me who you have been passing information to and for what purpose. Do I make myself clear?'

Quinn's body convulsed like a landed fish. Then, suddenly, he stood upright, his shoulders thrusting backwards as if in a desperate effort to drag air into his lungs.

Responding on instinct, Black unfastened the hood and ripped it from Quinn's head. The sight that met him was horrible. The young man's eyes bulged from their sockets and his lips were blue. Black had seen this several times before among prisoners in Iraq – an attack of nervous asthma brought on by the stress of prolonged confinement. Quinn's efforts to draw oxygen through his restricted airways were proving futile. Black quickly untied his hands. Quinn's body slumped, forcing Black to catch him. He lowered him to the ground, untied one ankle and laid him out on the dusty floor.

Quinn's eyes were glazing over and he was no longer fighting for breath. Black placed his circled thumbs and forefingers over his open mouth and attempted CPR. The air filled Quinn's mouth but penetrated no further. His constricted lungs refused to inflate. Black tried again and again, but the airway was closed tight shut. He switched to chest compressions, pounding Quinn's sternum with the flats of his hands, hoping that by some miracle his nervous system could be rebooted at the point of death.

Five minutes and several hundred compressions later, Black paused to wipe away the sweat dripping into his eyes and noticed a solitary fly land on Quinn's lower lip. It paused, as if to assure itself that all signs of life had departed, then crawled inside his open mouth.

Black stared at the corpse, scarcely able to comprehend. One minute the prisoner had been alive and complaining and the next he was dead.

He had done what he had hoped never to do again.

He had killed a man.

Crouched over the lifeless body he waited for something to happen. It occurred to him that his mind might implode under the weight of his conscience. But it remained clear and strangely absent of emotion. Dust circled in the shaft of light coming from the doorway and outside the birds continued to sing.

Black rose to his feet in a strange state of almost peaceful detachment, rolled his stiff neck from side to side and turned his attention to Clayton. He pulled off the ear defenders and hood. Clayton winced and blinked as his eyes adjusted to the light. His clammy face was blue with stubble and his thinning hair plastered to his skull. He was weak, dehydrated and quite probably in more pain than he had ever known.

'I'm afraid your colleague didn't make it. Asthma.'

Clayton followed Black's gaze to the body lying eight feet to his right. Black watched his eyes widen in alarm.

'I take it you would like to see your family again, Mr Clayton?'

Clayton's gaze remained fixed on Quinn's lifeless form.

He was good. Black guessed that he was still in sufficient possession of his faculties to be able to calculate that being the only one left alive, he was unlikely to suffer the same fate. And this in turn would give him hope and strength to resist, or at any rate, prolong his ordeal.

Black was in no mood for waiting. 'Excuse me, Mr Clayton.'

He walked over to Quinn's body, untied the remaining rope attaching it to the auger, then hoisted it over his shoulder.

Adjusting to the heavy weight, he made his way slowly to the door and leaving it open so that Clayton could follow his progress, carried it outside. He made it as far as the first pond and heaved it over the edge. He stepped back and watched it sink slowly beneath the thick layer of green sludge. A few residual bubbles rose to the surface and then the dense mat of algae closed in again.

The demonstration was effective.

Black returned to find Clayton suspended from his bound wrists, his knees tantalizing inches from the ground. His face was a picture of unbearable pain. Still Black was aware of a disconcerting absence of pity or sympathy. He regarded his prisoner with the same clinical curiosity with which a surgeon might appraise an anaesthetized patient.

'In a moment I'm going to remove the tape from your mouth, Mr Clayton, and if you wish for it to remain off, you will give me the name of the person to whom you have been passing information in exchange for payment. Will you do that for me?'

Clayton clamped his eyes tight shut and nodded.

'And when I have that name I will let you sit and you can give me your full statement. Only when I have that statement will I return you to your family. If you choose not to cooperate, you will be joining Mr Quinn. Do I have your assurance that you will cooperate?'

Another nod. His eyes were pleading and pathetic. He was broken.

Black took hold of the tape and gently peeled it away from his mouth. Clayton's head lolled backwards as he gasped in relief.

Black closed his hands around Clayton's throat and applied the slightest pressure to his Adam's apple. 'Your contact's name.'

He felt Clayton tense, the sinews protruding from his neck. The last show of resistance.

'Drecker,' he whispered. 'Susan Drecker.'

A woman. *Droplets of blood from three assailants, two male, one female.* Towers' report of Finn's post-mortem had included the surprising fact that one of Finn's killers was female.

'Nationality?'

'American . . . I think.'

'You're not sure?'

'No . . . But she sounds American.'

'And who does she work for?'

'I don't know.'

'Don't play games with me, Mr Clayton.'

'A company . . . That's all I know.'

'She works for a corporation, not a state? You're sure about that?'

'Yes.'

'And how much has she paid you?'

Clayton swallowed. A sign that Black had hit a nerve. 'One hundred thousand dollars.'

Tears spilled down Clayton's cheeks. It made a pathetic sight. The tears of a man whose life, once so full of promise, had come to nothing. He hadn't even been well paid for his treachery.

Black released the bonds from his wrists and let him slump to the floor, allowing him a moment to recover himself before they started on the statement.

'Shall we begin?'

26

Freddy Towers glanced up from the hand-written statement. 'You instructed him to return to work as normal on Monday and await further instructions?'

'I did.'

'What sort of shape was he in?'

'No visible trauma. He'll live.'

Towers nodded and continued to scour the two sheets of paper for anything he had missed.

Black had released his surviving captive in a street close to his home only forty-five minutes before, yet already the day's events had taken on a surreal quality like something he had dreamed rather than acted out. They were sitting in the living room that doubled as a study in Towers' Lancaster Gate flat. The decor was contemporary and the furniture comfortable, but the plain magnolia walls were absent of pictures. The only clue as to the personality of the apartment's inhabitant were the titles of the books in the small bookcase – political memoirs, military biographies and a few light novels. It reminded Black of a government safe house and suggested to him that Towers had another home elsewhere.

Towers looked up thoughtfully. 'Drink?'

'No, thank you.' He planned to drive back to Oxford and knew that one drink would lead to two, then more.

'Pity about Quinn. Now he's gone, they'll suspect we're on to them.'

'Why not use Clayton to feed in a cover story? He can tell Drecker he's been posted abroad. Covert ops.'

'We'll come up with something,' Towers grunted, his mind already moving on. 'I can't believe Clayton was prepared to sell intelligence knowing so little about the buyer. If we're to believe his story, she could have been anyone.'

'Put yourself in his shoes. Sick wife, two young children, on his uppers. Meets an attractive woman at a conference, caves in to lust then faces the choice between selling secrets and destroying his marriage at the worst possible moment.'

'All brains and no judgement.'

'Like so many we've known.'

Towers raised his eyebrows in weary acknowledgement.

The banality of Clayton's account was what made it so credible. Almost exactly a year before, he had been attending a weekend gathering of international cyber security experts at Edinburgh University. An attractive woman in her late thirties, who gave her name as Susan Drecker, seduced him at a party, assuring him that she was married to a colonel in the US Army and was interested only in a one-night stand. She told him she was a vice president of a major security contractor but didn't specify which one. Clayton had half suspected that, like him, she was a government agent sent to listen to impenetrable presentations and had gravitated towards a kindred spirit. Five weeks later he had been holidaying with his family and American relations in Cape Cod. He was stepping out of South Wellfleet General Store having taken his children to buy ice cream, when Drecker climbed out of an SUV and handed him an envelope containing a flash drive. Along with video footage of their antics in a hotel room it contained photographs of his wife and children going about their daily lives. There was a phone number for him to ring. He called later that day and Drecker issued her first demand for information. Over the following eleven months he had met with her five times, handing over a total of forty files. On each occasion he had been paid $20,000 by bank transfer. Among the files had been details of two of the four missing scientists. Clayton had been unable to say where they had gone or who had taken them, insisting that Drecker had told him nothing. He had been so easily duped that Black believed him.

'Maybe he is as stupid as all that,' Towers said. 'It's easy to forget how bloody feeble some of these young agents are. Promoted to sensitive positions with virtually no field experience whatever.' He sighed and sipped diluted single malt from a cheap tumbler. 'Doesn't bode well for the rest of '5. Doesn't bode well at all. They're a shambles.'

He lapsed into gloomy meditation.

Black was tired. He was eager for the meeting to be over and for Towers' assurance that his obligations were at an end. He wanted to wipe today from his memory and lose himself in writing his paper.

'What do you make of this woman, Drecker?' Towers asked.

'I'd have said CIA but for the way they murdered Finn. It was a bit messy for them.'

'It may have been a feint.'

Black shook his head.

'What makes you so sure?'

'We're still friends, Freddy. Despite everything. The politicians might fall out and insult each other but as far as I can see we continue to cooperate from top to bottom.'

Towers appeared reluctantly to concede. Several decades of butting heads with American allies had left him with a level of mistrust which Black had always considered close to irrational. He suspected that the truth was that Towers had always been jealous of the US's superior resources and the swagger that naturally accompanied them. On joint operations British officers were invariably forced to play second fiddle.

'There was a woman's blood on Finn's body. What do you make of that?'

'There's no reason to suppose it's Drecker's,' Black answered.

'Suppose that it was and she's not CIA. The pool of suspects narrows rather, doesn't it? We're talking ex-military or ex-CIA now working for an outfit with plenty of money and reach, not to mention ambition. And if you are such an outfit, who are you going to hire – only the best and most ruthless, surely? Now the pool is even smaller – a tiny group of highly mercenary, battled-hardened female operatives of American origin. In Britain we would struggle to produce even one candidate to fit that profile. I'm sure even the Americans wouldn't have more than half a dozen.'

Black felt the stirring of a memory. An exchange of fire in an Iraqi street during the chaotic free-for-all of 2005. Saddam was gone and every neighbourhood had seemed to spawn its own militia.

Towers' antennae twitched. 'What are you thinking?'

'It's probably nothing.'

'Try me –'

'April '05. Baghdad. We had a tip-off that members of the Mahdi Army were going to rob a bank in downtown Baghdad. I led a detachment and threw up a roadblock to catch them. Finn was there.'

Towers nodded, trying to isolate the engagement from a thousand others over which he had presided that year.

'They came, but it wasn't the Mahdis. It was a group of Western irregulars with more weapons than Delta Force. Eight of them, in two armoured pick-ups with heavy machine guns and RPGs.'

'Rings a bell. Rogue security contractors, weren't they? Moonlighting meatheads from Bush's friends in Blackwater.'

'Probably, though we could never confirm it. They got away and the Americans claimed the bodies of the two we shot. One of the fighters in the lead truck was a woman in her twenties. She was in the passenger seat with a Hechler and Koch. The only time I've faced a fully armed female combatant.'

'You didn't shoot her?'

'Didn't get a chance. We were outgunned and scattered.'

Towers considered this for a moment, got to his feet and stepped out on to the balcony that overlooked a small garden at the rear of the block. Black remained in his armchair, uncomfortably aware that Towers was out there *thinking*.

'I ought to be going, Freddy,' Black said after several minutes had passed. 'I'm sure you and your people will track her down.' He stood up and shook the stiffness from his limbs. 'I don't like to press the point, but when can I expect payment?'

He was met with silence. A brood. Always an ominous sign.

'And what would you like me to tell Kathleen Finn? I'll have to speak to her soon. She wants answers.'

Still no reply. Black sighed impatiently and glanced through the doors to see Towers staring intently into space, the wisps of grey hair on his balding crown waving gently in the breeze.

'Freddy?'

'Hmm?' His head shifted slightly but he didn't look round. 'Oh, yes. Tuesday. You can expect it Tuesday.'

Black waited for some acknowledgement or word of thanks for his work. None came.

'Goodbye, then.' Black headed for the door.

'I don't have *people*, Leo. That's what I'm for. *People* can't be trusted. I cleaned up Quinn's flat myself.' Towers' disembodied voice travelled through from the balcony. 'The girl was fine, by the way. Poor thing was terrified.'

Black exited the sitting room into the hall.

'I'd appreciate your help, Leo. We need to find Drecker. The Committee will want it done quickly.'

Black reached the front door and hesitated, fighting the urge to turn around. Then, in a flash of realization, he pictured himself as a dog that had learned to sit, stay and attack on his master's command.

'They're mocking us. We've become weak. The timber's so worm-eaten it's about to crumble away. How many times did I say this day would come?'

'There must be others, Freddy. I've had my fill of killing.' He let himself out.

Towers heard the sound of the door closing and felt the cool breeze playing over his face. He would have preferred a compliant Black, but there were still ways to achieve it. He would give him a little time to recover, then confront him with the inevitable.

27

Dr Razia greeted Drecker and Brennan at the entrance to the experimental facility with an uncharacteristic smile.

'Making progress?' Brennan asked.

'Excellent, thank you,' Razia replied. 'All four subjects that emerged successfully from the surgical process have proved highly responsive.'

Together with Dr Holst, he had established a test bed in a separate building from the main laboratories and was excited by the speed of their progress. Having assessed the members of his team in the days after their arrival, he had swiftly concluded that he and Holst were most suited to conducting the live experiments while Bellman, Kennedy and Sphyris were able to function best when allowed to remain in their intellectual bubbles, insulated from the practical applications of their work. The human mind was astoundingly capable of organizing itself into convenient compartments and only rare and exceptional individuals could tolerate the larger picture. He was undoubtedly one of them, and so, he was pleased to say, was his new colleague.

He led them across the tiled floor to where Holst was standing at a long raised bench sited next to a window glazed with one-way glass. Beyond it was a small area occupying the far portion of the single-storey building in which a young woman dressed in a plain surgical gown was seated at a desk hungrily eating a lunchtime meal of rice, beans and steak. The only clue to her recent procedure was a small shaved area on the left side of her scalp. Aside from her plate, the only other object on the desk was a shiny, steel hemisphere the size of a golf ball set in a disk of insulated ceramic material attached to the desk's surface.

'Dr Holst's methods have proved extremely sound. He has worked hard to perfect them,' Razia continued. 'I have been more than impressed.'

Holst responded with a modest smile. 'The procedure is well established, as Ms Drecker knows.'

Drecker's expression remained chilly and aloof. 'How soon until we can combine your work with Bellman and Kennedy's?'

'That depends entirely on the speed of their progress,' Holst answered. 'Their work is delicate, but we hope to conduct a live test within weeks.'

'We are paying you to work fast,' Drecker said. 'We have customers waiting. The sooner we can close deals, the sooner we can all get out of here and move on.'

'Nobody will delay a moment more than necessary,' Razia said, thinking of the wife and children he hadn't seen in nearly eight months. 'Everything we have achieved so far assures me we are on track for huge success. Allow us to demonstrate.'

He nodded to Holst.

Taking his cue, Holst adjusted the voltage on the control unit sitting on the desk. 'Twelve volts. Equivalent to the shock you might receive from a car battery.' He pressed a switch which caused the object on the desk in front of the young woman to pulse with a green LED glow.

Her hand hovered midway between her plate and her mouth as her attention switched away from her food and fixed on the half-round ball. Her hesitation was only momentary, however. She reached out with her free hand and gingerly touched its surface with her fingertips. The muscles of her arm spasmed as the current coursed through her, causing her to drop her fork but there was no hint of pain in her expression, only one of intense and instantaneous pleasure. She sat back in her chair, her shoulders relaxing and her eyes drooping as the dopamine coursed through her veins.

'Looked like she enjoyed that,' Brennan said with a leer that Razia found distasteful.

'The next stage is to programme a response to more subtle stimuli,' Razia said. 'We will expose the subject to an image while causing the implant to emit a far lower charge. The result should be a highly positive association rather than this extreme level of nervous arousal.' He looked to Drecker and smiled. 'Perhaps you would like some input into what images we choose?'

Refusing to engage, Drecker's face remained fixed in a frown as she stared through the glass at the young woman whose eyes were slowly coming back into focus like those of an addict coming down from a trip. 'Is this the first time you have experimented on a human subject, Dr Holst?'

'I must confess it is,' Holst said.

'Do you find it difficult?' The question came from Brennan.

Holst hesitated. 'I can't pretend it's not challenging.'

There was a moment of silence. The young woman had picked up her fork and was continuing to eat her meal.

'Would the maximum voltage you can administer prove fatal?' Drecker asked.

'Yes . . . it would.'

Dr Razia shifted uneasily from one foot to the other. He knew what was coming. Sadly, it was a necessary part of the process for one new to this kind of work. His only regret was that it was the girl who would be the subject. A sentimental part of him had already grown rather fond of her.

'Would you care to demonstrate?'

Holst appeared shocked. He looked to Razia for help.

Razia lowered his eyes to the floor. 'Do as you are requested please, Dr Holst.'

Razia glanced up and caught a glimpse of the young woman's bright, innocent eyes and full lips, then averted his eyes as Holst reached for the control unit with unsteady fingers. The pulsing light appeared for the second time.

This time there was no hesitation. The subject moved to stroke the sphere as she might have done a baby's head. The laboratory lights flickered as she was thrown off her chair by the force of the shock, her body coming to rest lifelessly in the far corner of the room.

Drecker watched with fascination as thin wisps of smoke curled up from seemingly randomly arranged patches of scorched flesh along her arm and across her face and neck.

Razia looked up to see Holst staring at the uneaten plate of food on the far side of the glass. He was impressed by what he saw. His colleague had not crumpled as some did, rather he could see that his intellect had triumphed over emotion. He truly was one of the rare breed for whom ends could justify the ugliest of means. A kindred spirit, indeed.

'I think we can count that a success,' Brennan said. He turned back to the door with Drecker. 'I'll send in a couple of men to help clear up the mess.'

28

'MacArthur's plan to reconstruct Japan with vertical rather than horizontal ambitions was, most historians agree, a resounding success. The energy once poured into militarism and aggression was channelled into industry and inventiveness. The same can be said of Germany – from a broken, bombed-out nation to one of the most stable and successful in the world. But this was no accident. It happened by dint of huge effort. America poured money, food and resources into both countries. The British public endured food rationing well into the 1950s to ensure that Germans, the very people who had been killing them only a few years before, didn't starve.

'Now compare the success of this approach with our abject failures in the post-conflict zones of the twenty-first century. Think about it. No plan, little investment and certainly no question that in victory we might make painful sacrifices at home for the benefit of the defeated . . .'

Black had expected his nine o'clock lecture the following Monday morning to have attracted only a handful of the keenest students, especially given that it was the final week of term, but to his astonishment nearly every seat in the hall was taken. The presence of such a large crowd was both flattering and disconcerting. He could see young minds being opened to new ideas in front of his eyes but after his experience of the previous week he felt like a fraud. He was preaching peace, but in the knowledge that the only thing that stood between peace and conflict were people like him. People whose humanity could be switched off and on at will.

His inward struggle seemed only to spur him on. The forty minutes of his presentation seemed to pass in moments. He concluded with a flourish: 'If you truly are fighting in the interests of peace, you must know that peace is not secure until every building is rebuilt and every crater filled; until every life lost is compensated for and until hope exceeds despair. These are huge and costly obligations, and unless a leader can convince his or her people that they are worth meeting, he or she can hope for nothing more than chaos and ultimate defeat.'

He had borrowed these closing lines from a section of his partially written paper and was gratified to be met with a burst of applause. He could only hope that he would receive a similar reception at West Point. He took a sip of water from the glass on the lectern and invited questions.

Helen Mount was first to put her hand in the air. 'How much of this Western generosity to the Japanese and Germans do you put down to guilt, Dr Black?'

'None. Of course, the Allied soldiers were horrified by what they saw on the ground – Dresden, Berlin, Hiroshima, all of which we've discussed – but there's no doubting where they felt responsibility lay.'

'There were plenty who didn't see the need to carpet-bomb Dresden,' Helen countered. 'Freeman Dyson, the physicist who was working in Bomber Command, said there was no moral justification for it whatsoever.'

'Don't forget that this was a war for survival,' Black said, 'like nothing you've ever experienced, and only twenty years after the last. Part of the thinking was, *We are going to destroy you so absolutely and emphatically, using the very weapons with which you tried to destroy us, that you will never even think of repeating this horror again.* The corollary was: *We will also rebuild you and enable you to live in peace and prosperity. You may have forced us to descend to the level of animals, but we refuse to remain there and we will also give you every opportunity to elevate yourselves to where you belong.'*

'OK, but isn't your argument a way of justifying more colonial wars? Aren't you saying it would be fine to invade and kill hundreds of thousands of people as long as we're prepared to pay for the clean-up? How about taking far greater risks for peace? I mean, talking and talking and talking and locating the new potential leaders and doing *everything humanly possible* to enable the change to come from within a hostile country.'

'So you find the idea of destabilizing a country more acceptable than invading it? Sometimes the results can be worse.'

'I'm talking about a fundamental change of attitude – projecting peace, not threats of violence.'

'And against enemies who refuse to talk?'

'The more peaceful we are, the less threat we pose and the less violence will be directed at us. That has to be right.'

Black felt the sympathy in the room shift away from him. Helen had found a position her fellow students found more attractive than his model of carefully modulated aggression. They were young. It was only right that they gravitated to ideals rather than practical reality.

Then a lone dissenting voice spoke up. It belonged to Sam Wright, the young man with the fringe who had collared Black after his Hiroshima lecture. 'How much more peaceful could we have been towards Germany in 1939?'

'That was different. I'm talking about now,' Helen responded.

'Fine. Let's talk about now,' Sam said. 'Bottom line, we're still human beings, still biological organisms programmed to preserve our gene pool, at the expense of others if necessary. The laws of nature dictate that we'll develop strategies to ensure our survival. At the end of the Second World War it was cash-bombing the Germans and Japanese into swapping imperial ambitions for capitalism. It worked. Success. The last thing the communists wanted was capitalism, so to deal with them we armed ourselves with nukes. Great. That did the trick for fifty-six years. Then, suddenly, up pops a new enemy that takes us down from the inside with hijacked planes, rented trucks and ideology that spreads through the veins of society like a virus. They have no leaders to negotiate with and no demands with which we can possibly contemplate compromise. Faced with that, all your peaceful instincts are useless. We're back to the elementals again: we've got to start killing people to save ourselves, only they're much harder to find and even harder to predict. And who, exactly, are you asking us to be generous to when this particular war is over? Saudi Arabia? Qatar – the richest per capita country on the planet? Would a few extra dollars persuade them to turn off the funding pipe? Would it hell.'

There was an astonished silence. It was as if Sam had uttered an unspeakable heresy but at the same time hit on an unavoidable truth.

He hadn't finished. 'You know what? Sometimes I'm almost grateful to the jihadis for giving us the chance to remind ourselves what's required. We all want to live in a society where you can have seminars on the appropriate gender-neutral pronouns, but that doesn't free us from the need to have to kill the people who threaten it. And there is no way to sugar that pill. My only worry is that we're being so slow to act, so reluctant to stoop to their level, that we'll have lost this war before we even accept that it's started.'

Black found himself momentarily unsettled by Sam's blunt and stark analysis. The words of a young student were easy to imagine as those of a politician of the future. In this case a bleaker future than he cared to contemplate.

'Helen?'

Black could see her make a conscious effort to contain her indignation. It was a good sign. She was maturing fast. She delivered her answer calmly. 'I think we should always act from the highest moral principles. And I think we should work much harder to articulate precisely what they are. Mac-Arthur's plan was needed to repair a lot of damage that shouldn't have been done in the first place. In the Second World War, in Vietnam, in Iraq and Afghanistan, we allowed ourselves to sink *too* low. We should act with as little violence as possible. And we need a world forum on Islamic terrorism. *Them and us* isn't good enough any more. On one level we're all *us*. We just have to work harder to find that level.'

There it was: the voice of hope. Her answer prompted nods and murmurs of approval.

Sam graciously declined to come back at her.

Equilibrium was restored.

Another hand went up. It belonged to Sadiq Nizamani, a second year at Christ Church College and a nephew of Pakistan's foreign minister. 'I think both speakers are in part correct. The civilized conscience and the instinct for survival will always be in tension. You have said many times this year, Dr Black, that the progress of mankind must be towards non-violent resolution of differences, but while we strive for this ideal we have to cope with those who do not share it. Regrettably, peace is maintained through a *measure* of violence. But to enlarge on my friend's point —' he nodded to Helen seated two rows in front of him — '*as little violence as possible* — I consider that an insufficient principle. A sufficient principle might be *as little violence as possible to secure the triumph of my ideals.* If your ideal is to secure the future of a *free* society, then significant violence may be required. If it is merely to secure the future of a *democratic* society, which may in due course choose to abandon its freedoms, less violence may be required. These are fine distinctions but in reality may prove the difference between winning and losing.'

As Black listened, he felt the superior force of Sadiq's intellect. Minds like his that coolly got straight to the nub were rare. Black looked to Helen, 'Do you agree? Or do you think that exercising the greatest degree of restraint might set an example that others will inevitably follow?'

'I believe that people in power should never stop saying how determined they are that violence is the very last resort.'

'So, ultimately, I suppose we can all agree that the answer lies in the power of argument,' Black said, drawing proceedings to a close. 'Discussions like this one are taking place around the cabinet tables of the world. Probably, the very best we can hope to do is to examine every option as carefully as we are able, informed but not handcuffed by history.' He glanced at the clock. Time was nearly up. 'OK, I think we'll call it a day. And thank you all for your contributions. It's been illuminating. Genuinely.'

He reached down to gather up his notes and students began to rise from their seats.

A voice called out above the rising babble of conversation. 'Is it true you were involved with renditions to Guantánamo, Dr Black? Were they the result of careful discussion around the cabinet table?'

Black glanced up and saw that the speaker was a slightly built young man in the second row. The chatter in the hall died away. Black sensed the anticipation as all eyes turned in his direction. It dawned on him that the impertinent question must have been asked as an end-of-term stunt. The students had been gossiping about him. But who or what had started it? Had someone been digging into his past?

'I'm curious to know why you ask that,' Black answered, stalling for time.

'You were a major in the SAS, weren't you? And all throughout the period during which the SAS were busy capturing and illegally rendering people.'

'No, I wasn't,' Black lied. He had no choice. 'And even if I were, I would hardly be able to admit it. As you probably know, all members of the Special Forces are bound by the Official Secrets Act. Discussing any past operations would be a crime.'

'So what was your regiment?'

Black saw students bringing out their phones ready to Google his answer.

'I understand your curiosity, but I'm here to teach history, not to answer questions about my past career. Enjoy your summer. See you next term, I hope.'

The young man exchanged a look with his neighbour, who gave him a nudge, urging him not to push it any further. 'Fair enough.'

The tension broke, leaving a deflated atmosphere of anticlimax. Black turned his back to the room and pretended to busy himself while he waited for the hall to clear. He could hear the gossip continuing as the last of them made their way out and filed away along the corridor.

Only when he was sure that he was alone did Black turn to face the empty room. The question had rattled him. He realized that somehow he had managed to convince himself that he could draw a veil over the details of his past. Suddenly, the very idea seemed preposterous. Another product of his compartmentalized mind. And if his students had started making assumptions about him, his colleagues would naturally be doing the same. He was probably already an object of their morbid fascination. *How many have you killed? What does it feel like? Can you sleep at night or are you haunted by their ghosts?* Those were the questions everybody wanted to ask but didn't dare to.

He could live with their curiosity but he would never be constrained by it. He would show them. He would study and write until his eyes bled if that's what it took.

He refused to be dismissed as nothing more than an old soldier who had stooped to the depths because someone had to. He was a man with ideas. And ideas had the power to change the world.

29

The only sounds were the gentle ticking of a clock, the quiet turning of pages and the occasional shuffle of feet over the polished floor. Black sat at a sloping desk in a corner of the Codrington Library – in his opinion Oxford's most magnificent – in the same spot where for nearly 300 years generations of scholars had come to formulate ideas that would shape history. Paid for by the legacy of a notorious slave owner who had given his name to it, 'the Cod', as it was affectionately known, was designed in the early 1700s by the architectural genius Nicholas Hawksmoor in the style of the ancient Greeks. Here the best and the worst of Western civilization were combined in a single building that seemed to possess an almost unearthly power to concentrate the mind.

Black had come from teaching a late-morning tutorial to spend the afternoon in the Cod's cathedral calm, researching Victorian thinking on the balance between military and soft power. It was a curious fact that in the middle of the nineteenth-century Britain had presided over the largest empire in history, yet maintained the smallest standing army of all the major European nations. The vital element to the country's success seemed to have been self-belief combined with an unswerving religious conviction that the project of civilization was divinely ordained. In other words, the Victorians had gloried in an almost complete absence of cynicism. In the second half of the twentieth-century America had taken over this mantle, similarly turbo-charged by a belief in its superior technology and moral righteousness. As soon as that nation, too, began to doubt its own motives, the religious absolutists of the Middle East were sucked in to fill the vacuum.

His afternoon's reading confirmed beyond doubt what he had instinctively concluded years before in the blood-soaked sands of Iraq: ideas were indeed more powerful than armies. And this concealed a yet deeper truth: the human need for a guiding principle was a constant, like the force of gravity. Every man and woman alive believed in something, even in the negative sense of rejecting established dogma. It was these negative ideas that worried him most. A society that was busy destroying its own shibboleths, even in pursuit of higher values, was dangerously weakened. Victorian history stood as testament to the fact: British self-confidence had started to wane from the moment Darwin relegated the once all-powerful God to the status of a competing theory. The system of belief that had driven men across storm-tossed seas and into the depths of Africa was holed beneath the waterline by the force of a mere scientific observation. By the end of the First World War the country felt godforsaken and spent. By the end of the second Britain owed its survival entirely to the USA, a country yet to be contaminated with the disease of self-doubt.

Black looked up from his desk at the life-size marble statue of William Codrington himself, which stood grandly and commandingly in the centre of the room. He was set high on a plinth and dressed in Roman costume, a scroll clasped in his right hand. He was certainly not a man who had lacked confidence, which was to his credit, Black supposed, but he was still a man who had seen his slaves clapped in irons and whipped for minor misdemeanours. A man who embodied all the contradictions that still plague us: we thrive at the actual and theoretical expense of others. How to get beyond that? How to invite everybody to the party? What kind of idea has the power to disarm both the despots and the lone fanatics of the world? It would take far greater minds than his to frame it, but he could think of two conditions it would have to fulfil: it would have to promise dignity and it would have to involve sharing the spoils.

He picked up his pen and began to write.

What is within our power and what is outside it?

We cannot persuade hostile nations, cultures and individuals to our way of thinking overnight but we can offer the security and resources within which change can occur. Above all, we have to be ambitious and universal in our vision, not ad hoc, not piecemeal, inconsistent, or, worst of all, devious. We have to act and to talk as if we have a plan for the next 100 years. History tells us that only with such grandeur of purpose can we hope to win the hearts and minds set against us. Only with such grandeur of purpose can we hope to square our actions with our consciences. And if we act outside conscience, we do our enemies' work for them.

He read his words over again, unsure if they were worthy of a public airing or if they were no more than empty rhetoric. He decided he liked them, even if they were a little flowery. He had spent his adult life fighting wars that no one in authority had ever justified to him except in the most technical terms of immediate threats and objectives. He had never been *inspired*. No general or prime minister had ever convinced him he was risking his neck for a high and glorious purpose. And if you couldn't even convince your own side, what chance had you of convincing an enemy?

His phone buzzed silently in his inside jacket pocket. He brought it out to find a text from Karen: *You'd better show up tonight! I am NOT facing that lot alone. K :)*

Damn. The Provost's invitation to high table had conveniently slipped his mind. He glanced at his watch. It was evening already. The afternoon had vanished. Inwardly groaning at the prospect of dinner with the fellows, he had to remind himself that he was running out of chances to ingratiate himself. No matter how warm his reception at West Point, he needed at least a few of them on board.

Reluctantly returning Edward Shepherd Creasy's *Imperial and Colonial Institutions of the Britannic Empire* to the shelves, Black resolved to face the ordeal at his charming best, but in truth he would have preferred to negotiate with smiling warlords while a dozen men aimed Kalashnikovs at his back.

'There you are. I thought you were going to bail on me again.' Karen was waiting for him in the cloister, wearing a long black academic gown over a dark blue dress and matching heels. She had tied up her hair, exposing a pale, graceful neck.

'Sorry. You needn't have waited for me. I thought you'd be up in the SCR with the others.'

She shrugged, too embarrassed to confess that she hadn't felt able to face pre-dinner drinks alone.

'Shall we?' He nodded towards the staircase at the far end of the cloister that led up to the Senior Common Room.

'There's no point now. It's nearly time. I can't stand sherry, anyway.'

'Fine.' Black smiled. He couldn't help stealing another glance at Karen. He could hardly recall having seen her in anything other than jeans or Lycra. He was glad to see that her damaged arm was now wrapped only with a tight crêpe bandage and that the shine had returned to her eyes. Nevertheless, the sense of guilt that he might be the cause of her suffering gnawed at his conscience like a dirty, unspeakable secret.

'Don't say it.' She gave him a playful look. 'Admittedly this dress hasn't left the cupboard all year, but at least I fit into it.'

'I was going to say you look very elegant.'

'That must be a first. Shame about this.'

She held up her bandaged arm and smiled.

Their eyes met, a spark passing between them that caught Black by surprise. For a fleeting moment he felt as if they might fall naturally into a kiss. He sensed her moving fractionally towards him but in his surprise he stiffened and clammed up, then groped awkwardly for something to say. 'Any word from the police?'

'No.' There was the merest trace of disappointment in her voice. 'The best they can come up with is that it was a one-off. Some lunatic wanting to pay for his fix. At least we've got security cameras out at the greenhouses now.' She was anxious to change the subject. 'Anyway, how have you been? I didn't see you at the weekend. Did you run away to the country again?'

'Yes,' Black lied. 'Spur of the moment. I thought it might help me think.'

'I'd like to see it some time. I love the hills.'

'You're welcome – if you don't mind slumming it. It's a bit rough and ready.'

'I grew up on a council estate in Sheffield. Most places feel like luxury.'

She laughed. And, as she did so, Black noticed her eyes flittingly anxiously, as if she were still on the alert for lurking attackers.

The college clock struck the half hour. It was seven thirty. A group of late-coming students dressed in undergraduate gowns ran up the steps from the quad and through the large doors to the dining hall. Shortly afterwards, the sound of well-lubricated voices travelled through the open doorway to the Senior Common Room staircase. A dozen or so of their colleagues and a handful of invited guests emerged, flush-faced. Black and Karen crossed the flagstones to join them, exchanging polite greetings as they waited for the Provost to lead them into dinner.

The ritual hadn't altered since Black's undergraduate days and had probably gone largely unchanged during the three centuries since the college's foundation. The students, seated at three long tables perpendicular to the door, rose from their benches and stood in respectful silence as the Provost led the procession to the high table at the far end. The senior party arranged themselves behind their chairs and dipped their heads while one of the undergraduate scholars read the Latin grace from a lectern. Christ Church used a version of the same text, but Worcester prided itself on using the full and unexpurgated form. It was the most elaborate grace in Oxford and Black knew it by heart:

Nos miseri homines et egeni, pro cibis quos nobis ad corporis . . .

On and on it went for a full paragraph until the young woman reading paused, and in unison, the assembled company intoned the *Amen*. There was a scraping of chairs and the evening began.

Black had taken care to position himself directly opposite Karen to afford her maximum cover. It was an immutable law that the higher the collective IQ at the table, the greater the probability of being cornered by either a bore or a lecher. Karen had mixed luck: to her left was Claire Symes, a young, earnest but rather humourless fellow in law and to her right was Professor Silvio Belladini, a renowned political philosopher with an extravagant mane of white hair. His recent nomination for his discipline's highest honour, the Kyoto Prize, had done nothing to diminish his already swollen ego. Sitting to Black's right was Dr Gina Marlowe, an unassuming but fiercely intelligent immunologist, and to his left Dr Mike Callaghan, one of the country's foremost modern historians and a self-proclaimed post-modernist. Professor Alex Levine, the Provost, sat at the head of the table, two to the right of Black. As the winner of multiple prizes and already widely tipped for a Nobel, his authority was undisputed.

To Black's relief their pre-dinner drinks had left his colleagues in good humour. Conversation over the starter of smoked Argyll salmon drifted good-naturedly around several uncontentious subjects before Levine told the story of his ill-fated attempt to purchase a small Umbrian vineyard the previous summer. At the eleventh hour his Italian lawyer had suffered a fit of conscience and forewarned him of the informal 'taxes' he would have to pay to the local mafia, who were the de facto government in the area.

Belladini laughed uproariously. 'I am afraid old habits die hard in my homeland. But these local clansmen are perfectly pleasant when you get to know them. Tell me, how many times have you settled down to a bottle of fine wine and some pleasant conversation with a British taxman?'

Levine conceded that he may have been too timid in backing out of the deal but that some cultural differences were just too daunting to navigate.

Callaghan picked up the thread and launched into several amusing anecdotes of growing up in a Northern Ireland border village governed by an unholy alliance of bumbling priests, cattle smugglers and the IRA. Black observed the shocked reactions Callaghan's stories provoked from Claire Symes with amusement. Born in the early 1990s, it was almost beyond her comprehension that armed banditry was still flourishing on United Kingdom soil during her lifetime.

'They actually gave shelter to terrorists? How did these priests justify their actions to themselves?'

'Well, that would have required a period of sober reflection, and I don't think I ever saw Father Dominic in that condition.' Callaghan crossed himself with an expression of mock piety. 'God rest him.'

They all laughed, except for Claire, who seemed appalled by their reaction.

'I don't think it's particularly funny either,' Karen said in an effort at solidarity.

Black gave her an appreciative smile between the arms of a silver candelabra.

Talk veered off on to the college's latest fundraising efforts and a discussion on the morality of accepting a large donation from a minor Saudi prince to endow scholarships for students from the Middle East. The mood took a serious turn as they navigated a delicate topic strewn with potential bear traps. No one dared risk a monosyllable that might be misconstrued. Black ventured his opinion that any initiative that promoted the exchange of ideas with the Islamic world was to be applauded as long as the emphasis was on *exchange*. Anything was an improvement on mutual ignorance. His comment received general approval. It was his first substantial contribution to the conversation and he counted it a success. Gina Marlowe, who had remained virtually silent until that moment, added her view that there was no antidote to religious fundamentalism of any kind quite as effective as the empirical scientific method: the students in her laboratory witnessed the evolution of bacteria occurring from week to week.

There was a murmur of approval. Black kept his thoughts to himself: that for all their post-imperial guilt everyone at the table, even Callaghan, believed as fervently in the export of Western critical thinking as their Victorian forebears had in spreading Christianity.

Waitresses in white aprons appeared to clear away their starters and replace them with the main event: gigot of lamb accompanied by Chateau Grand-Puy-Lacoste 1986. Karen had requested the vegetarian option: a dish consisting mostly of cauliflower and broccoli, the sight of which made Black's stomach ache. Nevertheless, he admired her restraint. He took a mouthful of the lamb. It melted on the tongue. The wine was soft and complex. They were decadent pleasures, but after years in the field subsisting on army rations, he relished them.

As glasses were refilled, the gregarious Belladini became the natural leader of the conversation and regaled them with an account of his recent fortnight spent as a guest lecturer in Beijing University.

'I was appointed not one but three official "assistants"!' he exclaimed. 'One surly young man who made not the slightest attempt to disguise the fact that he was a government agent and two women as beautiful as porcelain dolls.' He smiled apologetically at Karen and Claire. 'I think it was quite deliberate on my hosts' part. They are not beyond playing the old tricks, but, I assure you, I behaved impeccably. These three attended every lecture, not seeking to censor me – quite the reverse, they nodded along attentively, but I also saw them observing the students for signs of subversion. They were effective. Very effective. All my questioners took a critical stance: Why is the West so tolerant of political chaos? Do our warring politicians take no blame for the hedonism and neurosis of our younger generations? Do our endless elections not frustrate our governments' ability to be productive? I longed for one of them to ask me something frivolous or irreverent like my Oxford students – the other day one young undergraduate asked me whether I had ever been to one of Berlusconi's bunga bunga parties. Ha! If only! The Chinese would never dare. The thought wouldn't enter their heads. They are so unnervingly *reverential*.'

'Did you suspect your audience had been forewarned?' Levine asked.

'Possibly, but I also sensed a genuine commitment. Theirs is a goal-orientated society. Beneath all the fizz of consumerism its fundamentals are still deeply rooted in a sort of deferential feudalism the communists have adapted and exploited to the full.'

'You don't detect the stirrings of individualism?' Callaghan asked. 'Surely the internet is changing the culture profoundly? The kids must at least be looking at porn for goodness' sake.'

'Technology is stimulating desires, material and carnal, no doubt. But fomenting a desire for democracy? For earthquakes? No, I don't think so. My impression is that the underlying consciousness of the population remains the same. It seeks to preserve itself in all its vastness. And the mind of a people is attracted to the most efficient method of survival, don't you think?'

'That depends what you mean by *a people*,' Claire Symes said. 'There are plenty of Chinese minorities hungry for democracy: the Tibetans for a start.'

'One of my students from Pakistan made an interesting point today,' Black interjected. 'Democracy and freedom are very different things. A repressive state can offer protection that majority rule certainly won't. Look at the exodus of Christians from Iraq. Democracy hasn't done much for them.'

'And that's an argument for what, precisely – propping up repressive regimes?'

'A more graduated approach perhaps.' Black became aware that the others had fallen into expectant silence. Karen met his eyes. She had sensed it, too. This is what they had been waiting for, a glimpse of just who and what this former military man was. Suddenly self-conscious, Black chose his words carefully, aware of the heat beneath his tightening collar. 'My approach, partly based on personal experience, is that repressive regimes exist for a reason. They're containing pressure of some sort. Release it too quickly and you'll get an explosion which the supposed beneficiaries of your intervention won't thank you for. You have to proceed with maximum historical and cultural understanding. If you want to sell democracy to another Iraq, you have to make it an irresistible proposition. If the population don't know they want something, then, by definition, they don't want it.'

There was another silence as his words were digested. Black and Karen exchanged a glance. He felt as if he were being subjected to a pre-planned audition.

Belladini smiled, rolling the stem of his glass between thumb and forefinger. 'If you'll pardon me for saying so, Dr Black, it sounds as if you may have experienced a Damascene moment at some point.'

'No particular moment. Just an accumulation of observations.'

'But there came a time when you chose to leave the military. The Special Air Service, wasn't it?'

'I'd always hankered after returning to my studies. The time seemed right,' Black said, avoiding the latter part of the question.

'And we happened to have run out of wars to fight,' Callaghan said. 'Although I expect your former colleagues have since found plenty to occupy them elsewhere.'

Black sensed the vultures circling. At the corner of his vision he spotted Levine lower his gaze to his empty plate.

'Yes, I'd had my fill of conflict,' Black said, hearing a note of defiance enter his voice. 'Although I'm under no illusions – while there is such a thing as freedom, there will be a continual struggle to preserve it.'

'A violent struggle? Perpetual war?' Belladini challenged.

'Some violence, yes. Contained. Localized. Specific. War is something bigger. I hope we've learned to avoid it except in the most parlous circumstances.'

'And the legality of this localized violence – does it worry you?'

The question came from Claire Symes. Black knew what was coming next. The rumours. They had reached his colleagues, just as he had expected. He resolved to remain calm. 'Holding ourselves to the highest standards is imperative. If we fail in that, we have no authority whatsoever.'

'But you have personally been involved in illegal covert operations. Or at least, that's what you are accused of?' she pressed.

There it was. The bomb they had all been waiting to drop. Delivered – no doubt by arrangement – by the most junior of their number. Claire had drawn the short straw.

'Really? I'm not aware of any such accusations.'

'There was an article on the *Cherwell* website this afternoon,' Gina Marlowe chimed in. 'Haven't you seen it? I'm sure it's been picked up by the nationals by now.'

'No,' Black answered honestly.

He glanced across at Karen. It seemed to be news to her, too.

'May I ask what's been said?'

'A Libyan named Yusuf Ali Mahmoud has cited "a former British officer, now an Oxford University lecturer" as one of his abductors,' Claire Symes said. 'He claims that in 2007 he was kidnapped in Tripoli and rendered to Guantánamo by British Special Forces.'

'I confess, I've never heard of Mr Mahmoud. It sounds as

if someone's stirring up mischief. I suppose it would be surprising in the current climate if someone like me didn't go unchallenged.'

'I should deal with it sooner rather than later, if I were you, Leo,' Levine said, inserting himself carefully into the conversation. 'At least they've had the good sense not to name you. I'm sure the college lawyers can assist.'

'Thank you for bringing it to my attention.' Black took a mouthful of wine and was grateful to see that his hand was steady.

'Well, is there any truth in the accusations? Were you involved in rendering to Guantánamo?' Claire Symes was on the warpath.

'Shouldn't we let Leo deal with it?' Karen said, coming to Black's defence. 'I can't see it's any of our business.'

'Let's not mince words, shall we?' Belladini spoke over them, emboldened by his third glass of Lacoste. 'Leo, we will shortly be discussing your application for fellowship. We will need this matter resolved as a matter of urgency. You understand. The college and all of our reputations are at stake.'

'Rest assured, I shouldn't like to stain your reputation, Silvio.' Black could have planted a fist between his plucked eyebrows and sent him sprawling, bloody-nosed, in a shower of crockery, but instead he delivered an emollient smile. 'But you had better lock your door tonight or I might just sneak in and abduct you.'

There was a chill silence, then Belladini's suntanned face erupted into a delighted smile. He tossed his white mane and guffawed.

30

'Leo, I had no idea —'

'It's fine. Honestly.'

Black placed a reassuring hand on Karen's arm as they moved towards the dining hall's exit. He had left the others to finish their coffee and port and Karen had excused herself to come after him.

'What will you do?'

'Talk to the MOD. They're pretty efficient at dealing with these things. It's nothing to get excited about.'

They stepped out into the late evening. Standing against the sinking sun, the trees in the Provost's garden looked as if they were alight.

'You know, you're not a bad liar.'

'Is that a compliment?'

'Don't change the subject. Is someone trying to sabotage your career?'

'Possibly. Good luck to them – it wouldn't take much. Perhaps I should be flattered by the attention?'

'I really don't understand you, Leo.'

He smiled. 'Well, that makes two of us. How about a turn around the lake? I feel like I need to blow off some steam.'

He led the way.

They walked through the cloister in silence, both of them processing the many barbed layers of subtext buried in the dinner table conversation.

'I don't know how you managed to sit it out,' Karen said

eventually. 'I never knew Claire could be so *waspish*. And Silvio – what a self-important bore.'

'At least he's got a sense of humour.'

'I could have hit him. All that nonsense about reputation.'

They headed down the steps to the quad and made their way through the covered passageway that connected it to the gardens beyond.

'He's right, of course,' Black said. 'I am trying to break into the most thin-skinned profession in the world. Imagine the trouble it would cause him if he approved my appointment and the story stood up. *Philosopher approves war criminal.* He'd never be invited to a symposium again.'

They emerged from dark into the fading light and made their way across the wide expanse of lawn towards the lake. Some undergraduates were having a raucous party in an upstairs room. The sounds of high-spirited voices and loud music travelled out over the grounds from their open windows.

'I don't think I'll ever understand them,' Karen said. 'I've been here for six years and I still can't get my head around the politics of this place.'

'You're a scientist. You're judged by your results. Us poor dolts in the humanities have nothing to offer except our ideas. Ideas that can go out of fashion as fast as you can say metaphysical deconstructionism.'

'You lost me.'

'I believe it's one of Silvio's specialisms.'

'It is? You're going to think I'm a complete philistine, but I don't actually know what he does.'

'He looks at ways of comprehending the world. Centuries ago, the priests told us what to believe and that was enough. Now we've decided we know better, we need new tools for understanding. Philosophers search for them, usually without

209

trying to mention God or anything that might possess a superior intelligence to theirs. That's about it.'

'And what does Silvio say life's all about?'

'From what I've read he seems to believe that the meaning of existence is the search for meaning.'

'Wow. They flew him all the way to China to say that?'

'There was some point to it. The project of life, according to Silvio, is to discover our unique, individual essence. If all we are is another identical leaf on the same tree, we have no independent or worthwhile existence.'

'What my dad would have called *flowery bullshit*.'

'You said it. Not me.'

They arrived at the fringes of the lake and paused to watch a mother duck with her darting, squealing brood of ducklings. Black sensed Karen's mood softening.

'I can't imagine spending every day thinking abstract thoughts,' Karen said.

'You never stand back and wonder why we're all here?'

'I spend a lot of time wondering how we're going to stay now we are here . . . and answering to my imaginary grandchildren for what I did or didn't do about it.' The ducks disappeared into the safety of a reed bed, leaving the surface of the lake perfectly still. Black and Karen moved off along the gravel path. The sounds of the student party were replaced by the soft rustle of willows in the breeze.

'What's your greatest fear?'

'Getting it wrong. Making a mistake that can't be reversed. Intervening in nature is a big thing. I've created the means but I almost feel like I'm not the right person to be making the decisions.'

'Give me the worst case.'

She shrugged, as if reluctant to give voice to her fears.

Black waited, suspecting that he had hit on something that troubled her profoundly.

'That we disrupt the forest eco system beyond repair,' she answered finally. 'Create a species that overtakes all the naturally occurring trees or, worse still, generates even more resilient beetles that destroy even my GM hybrids. There are so many unknowns. And no way to predict.'

'And if you don't plant your trees?'

'Millions of acres of forest will die. Billions more tons of carbon will sail up into the atmosphere. The climate will warm even faster. There'll be storms, hurricanes, floods, deserts will spread, farmland will shrink – you know the kind of thing. It's coming down to a fairly stark choice in our lifetime: we can manage our environment or be consumed by it.'

'Sounds like an easy call to me.'

'There are so many obstacles – government regulators, environmental campaigners. All of them paralysed by fear of the unknown.'

'No one likes to be the first to jump. Sometimes it has to be you.'

'Just head out to the wilderness and play God?'

'If it's the right thing.'

She laughed and shook her head, as if the very idea were insane. They walked on in silence, Black sensing her retreat deep into her own thoughts.

Finally, she said, 'They really don't like the fact you were a soldier, do they? It's not your ideas they're objecting to – they liked them. It's something else. What do they think you're threatening?'

'Their power, I suppose. Places like this are all about creating the ideas that change the world out there. I think I feel like an invader. Someone who's jumped back over the wall.'

'I think you're too real for them. You represent the hard choices that being hidden away in a university saves them from making. The last thing they want to believe is that they owe their cosy lives to people like you.'

Black made no reply. He understood perfectly why some among his colleagues were happy to maintain the illusion that they owed their privilege and security to the power of their thoughts alone. They were idealists. Dreamers. The tender heart of civilization. While men like him were its rough skin.

They arrived at the far end of the lake where the path skirted the college playing fields. The last rays of sun had leaked away and long fingers of shadow were stealing across the turf. A few yards further on they arrived at a parting of the ways, where they stopped: one path led to Karen's building and another would take Black around the remainder of a circle of the college estate to his rooms on the quad.

'Well, goodnight, then,' Black said.

'It's still early. I can make you a coffee, if you like,' Karen said.

She glanced away, then looked back, catching his eye. Black found himself held in her gaze and realized that for the second time that evening he could have leaned forward and kissed her, and that more than that, she was inviting it. It had been so long he had forgotten how to cross the barrier.

He faltered, his tongue feeling wooden in his mouth.

'Thanks. But I probably ought to be going.'

'Fine. If you're sure –'

She knew he wasn't. Black could see her trying to find a way through his buttoned-up exterior and reach to the man inside.

'I've got a pile of stuff this high to read –'

Now there was no way back. Not without humiliation.

'Never mind. Goodnight, then.'

She turned abruptly and walked away without looking back.

He had hurt her feelings. He wanted to call out after her and apologize, but he couldn't find the words. Christ, he was an idiot.

What was his problem?

The battle continued to rage inside him but Karen had already faded out of sight.

Preoccupied with thoughts of how to repair the damage, Black rounded the corner from the quad into the recessed doorway of his cottage where he came face to face with a male figure staring back at him from the darkness.

'Sorry to alarm you, Leo.'

It was Freddy Towers.

Black exhaled and uncurled his fists.

'I need a word. It's urgent,' Towers said without a word of apology. 'There's been a development.'

Black could barely contain his anger. 'Freddy, for God's sake –'

'Five minutes. Please, Leo.'

'You're wasting your time.'

'I'm here to save you from prison. It's not good, Leo. Things have got worse than I thought.'

Towers made himself comfortable on the sofa. Black remained standing, leaning against his desk, anxious to hear what Towers had to say and get rid of him as soon as possible.

'Elliot Clayton called me today. Susan Drecker contacted him this morning. She's in London on Friday and has arranged a rendezvous. I asked him if he thinks this was prompted by events at the weekend. He assures me not. It's been nearly a month since he saw her last.'

'Get to the point, Freddy.'

'I heard about your trouble with the university paper. Or rather it was brought to my attention. The MOD aren't good for much but very little that appears in the press passes them by. I presume you've no idea who the source is?'

'I've a feeling you're about to tell me.'

'It's Drecker, obviously, or whoever she's working for. It's an attempt to shut you down, Leo. Your mistake was in going to Paris and asking too many questions. They've treated it as a provocation.'

'For all I know it was you.'

Towers sighed. His sixty-year-old features were tired and slack as if he had gone several nights without sleep. 'It most certainly wasn't me, Leo. I'm afraid the story leaked from somewhere inside the Security Services but I can't be sure. Just be glad I managed to put the brakes on it before it was picked up by the nationals.'

Black drummed his fingers impatiently against the desk.

'For well over a year now there have been whispers coming out of the Foreign Office that Iraq are ready to sign up to the Statute of Rome and submit to the jurisdiction of the International Criminal Court. Of course, the Americans have never signed and they've put pressure on Iraq to stay outside, too. The last thing they want is for any of their people to be tried in the Hague at the behest of the country they spent thousands of lives liberating. Sadly, our government isn't so protective. There are forces in Iraq that need to be contained, swathes of the population still hungry for a reckoning. What better way for an unstable government to cement its credibility than by having a few British officers put on trial for war crimes?' Towers glanced up at the picture above the mantelpiece as if nostalgic for the days of cannon and cavalry charges, when war was war and soldiers were heroes rather than the hapless pawns of politicians. 'You and I were in the thick of it, Leo. How many hundreds and thousands did we pull in? How many high-value detainees among them? Politicians, lawyers, scientists. Credible, well-educated people not beyond dragging us through the mud if it helps their careers. And do you think our government won't be willing accomplices if it keeps the oil taps turned on?'

'I didn't commit any war crimes, Freddy.'

'Not by your reckoning, perhaps, or by that of any soldier, but that wouldn't stop them.'

'We executed political orders. We detained the leaders of the regime and their most senior servants along with terrorist militias.'

'Since when was obeying orders a defence? And have you forgotten how we used to soften the HVDs up on the way to Camp Cropper? A dig in the ribs here, a broken finger there. Threats against their wives and children. *Purgatory.* Wasn't that what we called it? Under the law that's torture, Leo. You and me, we oversaw it all.' Towers met Black's gaze. 'I agree, it was the worst kind of war and there was no other way to fight it, but you can't say we didn't revel in it. The anarchy. The freedom to run riot. Up every morning determined to haul in more insurgents than the Yanks? Remember those scoreboards where we kept the running totals? Some days I had to save you and Finn from yourselves. You wouldn't stop till you were at the top.'

Black became aware of a strange sensation stealing over his body: a dark, unnerving, thrilling echo of the near euphoria he had felt on those bright mornings setting out in a convoy of APVs bound for the belly of Baghdad. He had been like a surfer riding the crest of a wave. Invincible. Unstoppable. Drunk on the moment and oblivious to the future.

'I was with the Committee this afternoon. They're troubled by you, Leo. On the one hand you're an asset, on the

215

other you're a huge potential liability. And the tone of your academic work isn't making things any easier.'

'The day I'm indicted, you and half the squadron will be, too.'

'It doesn't work that way, Leo. This is politics. Protection will be given, but only to those considered deserving.' He drew an envelope from his jacket pocket and offered it up.

Black took it. It was addressed to him. He opened it and unfolded a letter headed with the Cabinet Office crest. In two short paragraphs it stated that Her Majesty's Government undertook to guarantee him complete protection from prosecution in domestic or international courts for any alleged offence committed while in military service.

Such protection, however, was conditional on his co-operation with Colonel Towers in relation to the matters currently under investigation. It was signed in ink by the Permanent Secretary.

'It took a good deal of negotiation, I can tell you,' Towers said. 'I'm afraid the Committee took full advantage of the situation. My protection is also conditional upon completion of this operation.'

Black lay the letter aside. 'This is absurd, Freddy. There are dozens of men younger and fitter than me you can call on.'

'We have the opportunity to apprehend the woman who was probably one of the three who killed Finn, Leo. You want nothing to do with it? I don't understand.' His voice rose in anger. 'I don't understand what you've become. If men like you fall away in times like these, I don't know what we've got left. Maybe nothing . . . We don't abandon each other, Leo; we're a family.'

Black gave him a weary look.

'Can't you see, Leo? Can't you see what we're up against? I'm dealing with a security service that can scarcely trust anyone who works for it. Do you know why? There's scarcely a soul serving for a cause any longer. Ask a young officer to define the freedom he or she is defending in a few simple words and they go into contortions. It's a mess. For men like you and me, it was God, Queen and country, and that was enough to go to war.' He shook his head in exasperation and cast his eyes around the room. 'Look at you, existing here in these dingy rooms – no one's bought you off. No one could. That makes you virtually unique, Leo. Let me tell you, there is not one of your former colleagues from the officers' mess who hasn't gone chasing gold. Not *one* . . . Could you imagine trading arms in Sudan or guarding some tinpot desert princedom? That's where they all are. Money buys almost anyone in this world. It's terrifying. I need someone I can *trust*.'

He darted up from the sofa and stood upright in the centre of the tattered Persian rug, his diminutive figure barely containing the outrage boiling inside him.

'This is what the end of empires looks like, Leo. When it's all taken for granted and nobody cares any more. The Vandals are in Rome and we have flung open the gates . . . Oh, and they will kill you, by the way. Without a shadow of doubt. Unlike us, these are people with a purpose. It would be quite beneath their dignity not to.'

He strode to the door and slammed it behind him as he left.

Black let the silence consume him. Then picked up the letter and read it again. This time he read between the words and saw its true meaning. Towers was right. It wasn't an offer. It was an order. And from the highest authority.

31

Black stepped past the security desk at the entrance to the British Museum feeling the gentle press of a Glock fitted with a Gemtech suppressor tucked into his waistband against the base of his spine. It was six p.m. on Friday, the building was at peak capacity and the cheerful security guards, busy searching the rucksacks of a party of Spanish students, didn't spare him a second glance. He passed through the entrance hall and into the Great Court disguised in nothing more than a pair of square steel-framed glasses of the sort that rendered a man of any age sexless and invisible. A shapeless linen suit, scuffed suede shoes and a navy raincoat folded over his arm added to the impression of a divorced school-teacher, marooned in midlife, drawn to the museum in the hope of rediscovering the elixir.

The sight of the vast glass roof covering what had once been the museum's two-acre courtyard momentarily silenced the voice in his head urging him to turn around and leave. Its scale and ambition overwhelmed the senses. Here was an inspiration, a vestige of the invincible energy that had created the magnificent buildings it now shel-tered. In its rolling, arcing form, he saw both the sea and sky, and where it funnelled down to meet the roof of the white rotunda in the Great Court's centre the curved shape of gravity itself. From the rotunda's base two opposing staircases spiralled upwards along its outer surface like temple steps, leading to the museum's circular reading room on the upper level. A pillar of knowledge connecting seamlessly to the universe beyond. A spectacle that inspired hope.

You crazy, crazy bastard, Leo. You really have got a head full of shit. Finn's disembodied voice snapped him out of his reverie. It was right, of course. He should have been in Oxford at his desk, writing. This all belonged to his old life, not his present. How *had* he got here? How had he let it get this far?

Towers, that's how. That bloody speech of his had pressed his buttons just like he knew it would.

He lowered his gaze to the crowded concourse and swore to himself that this would be the very last time. This one was for Finn, and for all the times he'd saved him from an early grave. Then they would be square.

'Can you see him, Leo?' Towers' insistent voice came over the tiny receiver hidden inside Black's left ear.

'Not yet.' He moved forward in the direction of the museum's café, where Clayton had arranged to meet with Drecker, and arrived outside the bookshop housed in the open-sided ground floor of the rotunda. He glimpsed through a gap in the crowd and saw the back view of a large man he took to be Clayton, dressed in a grey suit, seated at one of the café tables lined up in the far-right corner. They were arranged canteen style in several long communal rows.

'I've got eyes on him now. He's alone.'

'Well, stay out of sight.'

'Thank you, Freddy. I don't know what I'd do without you.'

'Concentrate.'

Black stifled his response and turned left into the bookshop. He drifted idly among the shelves before positioning himself close to the shop's entrance, where, between the passers-by, he had a sporadic line of sight to Clayton's position. He picked up the nearest book and turned through glossy pages filled with pictures of ancient Egyptian artefacts.

The plan was simple. He would follow Drecker outside the building, apprehend her and place her in a car Towers would be driving along Great Russell Street. If she attempted to run, he would put a bullet through her leg. Towers had arranged a debrief room in the high-security Paddington Green Police Station, which, if required, was a stone's throw from St Mary's Hospital. They had discussed the possibility of involving armed police, but Towers had rejected it on the joint grounds that (a) more bodies meant more chance of a cock-up, and (b) it risked creating a scene that would be captured on a hundred phones. He preferred to be quick and discreet and ruthless only if necessary, which suited Black fine.

The allotted meeting time of six thirty came and went. Black exhausted the statuettes of Horus and Roth and moved on to a book of Canadian First Nations art. He passed the time looking at pictures of totem poles and decorated coffins that were placed high in the trees so that the spirits of the dead could be closer to the heavens. An image of a shamanic mask dating from the 1850s caught his attention – an eerily pale face that looked like that of a corpse. The text described it as a depiction of a white man, and death was indeed what it presaged.

Towers' indignant voice sounded into his ear. 'What the hell's going on? Is there no sign of her?'

'Not yet.'

'What about Clayton?'

'Still there. Relax. How far are you from the museum gates?'

'I can be there in twenty seconds. Fifteen at a push. You do realize she's six minutes late?'

Black glanced up and spotted Clayton looking to his left. Continuing to feign interest in the book, he watched through his peripheral vision as a woman in her late thirties strode towards him. She was dressed in a formal black jacket and skirt. Her equally black hair was short but elegant. She moved with grace and purpose, like a Wall Street lawyer or an ambitious young politician. Something in her appearance – the intensity of her eyes even when seen from a distance, perhaps – chimed with Black's fleeting memory of the female irregular he had encountered all those years ago in Baghdad.

Another figure stood out from the crowd. Several yards behind Drecker, Black spotted a tall, unsmiling man with olive skin and close-cropped hair. He, too, was smartly dressed in a tailored suit and tie. He was tall – six feet four or five – and keeping watch. His alert yet expressionless face was of a kind Black knew well.

'She's here, with company,' Black said into the microphone hidden behind his lapel. 'Male. Thirties. Cuban maybe, or mixed-race Hispanic. Military background.'

'You'll just have to take care of him.'

'In front of a thousand tourists?'

'Never mind them, where's she?'

'Taking a seat next to Clayton. A few words. Not much. Now he's handing her the USB under the table.' He noticed her take it in her right hand. 'There we go. All over. Not even a thank-you for your trouble. She's up now, leading off. Her colleague's following.'

'Stay with them. ETA?'

'Ninety seconds.' He replaced the book on the shelf. Drecker and her companion passed within twenty feet of him heading back towards the entrance. The male was an even tougher-looking proposition close up. Broad-shouldered as well as tall, though with the agile, tapered physique of a boxer rather than the hefty bulk of a weightlifter. Not a man you could bank on putting down easily.

Black stepped out of the bookshop and followed. They had sped up and were now moving at a brisk pace, forcing people to step out of their way. Black felt his focus narrow and his conscious mind gave way to instinct as he shifted from observer to predator. 'They're leaving the building. I'll have to drop him outside.'

'Roger that. Carry on.'

Black remained ten paces behind them, his eyes fixed on the crease at the back of the minder's neck where it met his skull.

They moved through the entrance hall and passed the security desk. Drecker and her companion exited the building one after the other through the same revolving door.

'Stepping outside now. ETA forty seconds.'

'Roger.'

Black emerged into daylight as Drecker arrived at the bottom of the stone steps and headed off across the wide thirty-yard stretch of paving stones that led to the elaborate wrought-iron gates separating the museum's grounds from the street beyond. She brought something out of her pocket – a small handset – and spoke into it as if she were giving an instruction.

'I think she's got a car coming, Freddy. She's calling someone.'

'Let me worry about that.'

Black swept the surrounding area with his eyes. There were numerous scattered clusters of people and lone individuals, some moving, some standing, either taking pictures of the museum's classical façade or simply enjoying the atmosphere. The largest group was gathered by the gates: a tourist party waiting for the stragglers before they went to their bus. It would be impossible to shoot too close to them. He had to make his move either before or after reaching the gates.

It would have to be after. Less distance to drag Drecker into the car. Fewer people to get in the way. He reached round to his waistband with his left hand, brought the silenced

Glock under his jacket and passed it to his right, where it remained hidden beneath the raincoat draped over his wrist.

'I'm hitting them outside the museum grounds,' Black said. 'Twenty seconds.'

'Pulling up now. Your left. Between the first and second plane trees. Just beyond the cab rank.'

Black glanced through the gates and saw the anonymous black Ford crawl past, Towers an indistinct figure behind the wheel.

There were two pedestrian exits to the street, one to the left and one to the right of the gates. Drecker headed left, which was helpful, as the tourist group was bunched towards the right. She had ten yards to cover. The male was six feet behind her, Black ten feet behind him, treading lightly on his crêpe soles. He found the Glock's safety catch with his thumb and released it.

Five more yards. Time slowed to half speed. The minder's neck expanded to twice its width. Three paces until Drecker reached the gate.

Another face. It could have belonged to the minder's twin. A little shorter and thicker through the body but with the same smooth, dark tan. He was standing on the pavement. A lookout or driver. Six yards in front of Black.

'There's a third. Just outside the gate.'

'Deal with him.'

'Sound your horn.'

Towers obliged and leaned on the car horn. The sudden noise caused the new arrival to turn his head and in the same instant Black loosed off a single shot with a sound no louder than a pronounced metallic click.

The round hit the taller man square in the rear of his skull pitching him forward, but not before the eruption of blood and brain through the exit wound in his forehead had struck

Drecker's neck, causing her to glance over her shoulder to see the dead eyes of her minder as he fell to the ground.

She didn't pause to identify the shooter. She sprinted for the gate as the second man turned to see his colleague on the ground and bemused tourists scattering in all directions. He shouted something to Drecker in French. She muscled her way in among a group of fleeing teenagers, denying Black a clear shot.

Black ran with the panicked crowd for the gate. Women were screaming, men yelling. He was no more than eight feet behind his mark but now separated by a mass of bodies trying to force themselves through a gap not wide enough to take them.

He made it out to the street as the second bodyguard and Drecker were disappearing into a Range Rover that had pulled up in the centre of the road. Tinted windows. Toughened glass. A third male behind the wheel.

Black had no option. Amidst the noise and confusion he stepped up to the kerb and loosed off a round into the Range Rover's rear tyre. It bounced off and spun away into space. Bullet-resistant. Military grade.

The car took off with a screech, taking Drecker and her companions with it.

'Hold fire. Back to the car.'

The Range Rover slewed into a side road and disappeared from view.

Black's muscles slackened. He had failed. Careful not to draw attention to himself, he strolled towards the waiting Ford.

Inside the museum gates, the few terrified tourists who had thrown themselves to the ground picked themselves up, recoiling at the sight of a sprawled body with half its skull blown away. No one spoke. Several people reached for their phones and took photographs. Others hurried back to the safety of the building. After only moments pigeons descended and squabbled over the tiny gobs of brain tissue peppering the pavement.

'Bad luck. Can't be helped. My fault for biting off more than you could chew. Didn't count on her coming with tooled-up protection to the British Museum. Probably should have done. She's audacious, all right.' Towers drove as quickly as traffic would allow down Kingsway towards Aldwych. Yet another police car screamed past them at seventy miles per hour, sirens wailing. 'Don't worry about them, they've been told to look out for a different vehicle.'

Black didn't ask for further details. As far as he was concerned, the less he knew about Towers' dark web of connections the better. His principal emotion was one of frustration at having come up short. The soldier in him had had his pride dented. Nevertheless, he couldn't deny that it was strangely intoxicating to be driving through central London gliding above the law, or that the taste of action had stirred something dormant in him back to life. Despite all his better instincts, his blood seemed to vibrate with wicked elation.

'The body will be sent over to Guy's. The pathologist should have it on the slab within the hour,' Towers said.

His phone, sitting in the tray next to the gear stick, buzzed twice.

'Check that for me, would you?'

Black reached for it and glanced at the screen. 'From Clayton.'

'Did he get pictures?'

Black swiped the message open. There was no text, just a short video clip. He played it. The footage was taken from a minute camera disguised in Clayton's wristwatch. Black tilted the phone to get the picture the right way up. Clayton had managed to catch Susan Drecker's face square-on as she approached him. It vanished for several seconds as she took a seat, then reappeared, this time seen from below and mostly in profile.

'Good ones. Face shots. Several angles.'

'Thank God for that. Fancy helping me find out more about her?'

'If she's as good as I think she is, she'll be out of the country within the hour.'

'That's not what I asked, Leo. You'd at least like to know her identity before you head back to Oxford? That's an invitation, by the way, not an order.' Without waiting for an answer he nodded to the glovebox. 'You'll find a flask in there. I could do with a drop myself.'

Black reached inside and brought out a tarnished silver hip flask decorated with the regimental crest. The same one that Towers had passed around so many times in Bosnia, Sierra Leone, Baghdad and Bastion. He flipped the lid and took a slug, the cold metal tingling slightly against his lips. Single malt. Nectar. Like something conjured by an alchemist.

'Thought you'd like it. Craigellachie. Thirty-two years old.' Towers smiled at Black's contented expression. 'Don't hog it, man.'

Black took another drink and passed it over. Towers raised it to his lips and swallowed several large mouthfuls as he navigated the turn into the busy Strand traffic.

'My God, that's good.' He gave an appreciative sigh. 'You know what, Leo – I wasn't sure you still had it in you. But you have, you bastard. Look at you. You look ten years younger.'

Towers was right. He felt alive. From the moment Drecker had appeared he had been like a caged hound released to the scent. He took back the flask and drank some more. The whisky danced down his throat and glowed inside him.

'Yes,' Black said, as Nelson's Column hoved into view, 'I would like to know who the hell she is.'

32

Towers' semi-official operation was limited to a pair of laptops linked by satellite connection to the MOD's intranet. This gave him only limited access to certain secure government databases and none to those held by the Security Services or police. His ability to marshal the resources of the State had, he told Black regretfully, diminished significantly since the Committee had first commissioned him. Government networks were now so closely monitored there was no way of him navigating through them with sufficient secrecy. A particular source of grief was loss of access to the capital's comprehensive network of security cameras and the facial-recognition system that had allowed him to track Black's progress across the city several weeks before. As in the buccaneering days of post-invasion Baghdad, he was supposed to live off his wits.

Stooped over the keyboard at the desk in the corner of his living room, Towers attempted to track down Drecker and her associates with the limited resources open to him. Each request for assistance had to be made on an individual basis and using the cover of his official job inside the MOD. The result was that Towers found himself engaged in a laborious process that required him to work the phone to cajole and persuade myriad gatekeepers to let him share their precious information and resources for contrived reasons.

Towers had begun by trying to positively identify Susan Drecker and sent stills of her face to trusted contacts in both MI5 and the Secret Intelligence Service, otherwise known as

MI6. What should have been a simple matter of running the image through facial-recognition software connected to their respective databases of domestic and foreign subjects of interests turned into a protracted exercise involving calls to officials of ever more senior rank. Meanwhile, he tasked Black with scouring social media for images from the scene outside the British Museum. The few that had appeared online were mostly of the aftermath rather than of the incident itself. A passer-by on the pavement had caught a side-on image of Drecker climbing into the Range Rover and another had caught a similarly vague rear-view image of Black strolling towards Towers' waiting car.

'Typical bloody shambles!' Towers exclaimed, cupping the receiver while he was placed on hold for the third time. 'God knows how the Russians haven't walked all over us. Perhaps they have!'

Finally, clearance was given. The searches were run and within the space of ten minutes, a call came back confirming that Drecker's face was not among the several million stored on any of the government's databases. The margin of error, the junior officer assured him, was less than five per cent.

'Fuck!' Towers slammed down the phone and thumped his fist on the desk. 'Don't know her from Adam. How is that even possible? She must have been through a bloody airport.'

'How are you placed with the Americans?' Black asked. 'Maybe they can put a name to the face.'

Towers hurled himself back in his chair and groaned. 'Bloody Yanks are even worse than us, I swear.'

Black looked up from his screen with a puzzled expression.

'The bureaucracy. Have you ever tried calling the US government? By the time I'd convinced them I was legit we would both have grown old and died.'

'So call in a favour from someone they will listen to.'

Towers looked at him blankly for a moment, then snatched up the receiver and dialled Scotland Yard's Anti-Terrorism Command. He was put through to its Deputy Chief, Eleanor Grant, and switched tone without missing a beat. 'Ah, Eleanor, hello. Freddy Towers here. We met last month at the Home Office. Yes, that's right . . . Look, I know you've got your hands ever so full, but I wonder if you could do me an awfully big favour. There's someone I'm trying to identify, I'd be hugely grateful . . .'

He got his way. The Chief Superintendent was charmed into submission and agreed to put in urgent requests to the NSA, FBI and CIA.

'There's one woman I can always depend on,' Towers said, putting down the phone. 'Good sort. Married to a QC. Went to Cambridge.'

'A *proper* person,' Black said, aping one of Towers' favourite phrases.

'Exactly.' He tapped the desk with his forefinger. 'Manners. Honour. Decency. Where have all those things gone, Leo?'

'To the senior ranks of the Metropolitan Police, evidently.'

Ignoring the quip, Towers leaned over his keyboard and started typing furiously. 'Remind me of the Range Rover's registration again.'

'401 D 894.'

'Diplomatic plates. That's one database they do deign to let me into.' He worked his way through several screens, navigating the government network until he arrived at a secure section of the Driver and Vehicle Licensing Agency. He keyed in the registration and waited impatiently for the result. 'No current match. Discontinued 2015. Previously registered to the government of Tunisia. Well, that gets us precisely bloody nowhere.'

'Traffic cameras?'

'That would involve the Met again. I'd rather avoid that if I could. Things could get complicated.'

'You'd rather risk her getting away? I don't follow.'

'Ideally, it's the rat's nest we want, Leo, not the rat. If the police get to her before we do, she'll never talk.'

Black struggled to keep up with Towers' reasoning. 'You told me this afternoon's op was cleared with the Met, that we were taking her to Paddington Green.'

Towers gave a snort and pushed his glasses up the flattened bridge of his nose. 'It was cleared, certainly.'

'But you were going to take her somewhere else?'

Towers didn't answer.

'I do have lines, Freddy. I always have had. You know that.'

'Then it's a good job she got away, isn't it?' Towers picked up the phone and dialled another number. 'Colonel Towers, Ministry of Defence. Can you patch me through to Mr Khan, please . . . ? Then I'd be grateful if you'd contact him at home; it's most urgent.'

While Towers wrangled with the switchboard at Transport for London, Black contemplated what he might have had in store if they had managed to snatch Drecker. Would he have expected Black to tie her up in some basement flat and torture her? That would be far beyond the pale even in the height of war. If female suspects were to be interrogated, female officers had to be present. He struggled to comprehend what Towers was thinking.

What else was he hiding? Why not just be straight with him?

He pondered darkly on the possibilities while Towers argued his way through to someone able to access the capital's congestion charge database. There were cameras positioned all around the perimeter of the circular zone that covered central London north of the Thames and a sliver of the city to the south. The number plates of every vehicle that entered and left were recorded and the owners charged for the privilege. In true Orwellian style all these movements were duly recorded and saved.

'The Albert Embankment? Really . . . ? Yes, that would be about the time. Any chance you could send me over the picture? Thank you.' He spelled out his government email address as if to an imbecile. Then, call over, he turned to Black. 'They were travelling west south of the river. Virtually went past MI6's front door.'

Black brought up a map on his computer and honed in on the location. 'So they were either planning to turn left and head south or –'

'London heliport. Battersea. Three miles to the west.' He snatched up the phone. 'What's their number?'

Black couldn't help but feel sympathy for the receptionist who answered Towers' next call. He demanded to be put through to the control tower immediately, threatening dire consequences if he was stalled. He succeeded.

'Colonel Freddy Towers, Ministry of Defence, I need your full cooperation, this is a critical matter of national security. We are tracing two suspects involved with a fatal shooting in central London earlier this evening. One Caucasian female, late thirties, one male early thirties, Hispanic or mixed race. We believe they arrived at the heliport approximately seventy-five minutes ago. Our best guess is that they were bound for an airfield outside London . . . I appreciate that . . . Yes, if you would.'

Having secured cooperation, Towers demanded details of all flights that had taken off during the hour after Drecker and her companion's estimated arrival. Two flights fitted the bill. One was bound for Biggin Hill Airport in Kent, the other for RAF Northolt in west London. A call to Biggin Hill revealed that the passengers who had embarked comprised a party of businessmen en route to Inverness.

'Northolt doesn't make a lot of sense,' Towers muttered. 'I know the RAF has opened its runway to civilian aircraft, but it wouldn't be my first choice in her shoes.'

'It's virtually a commercial operation these days,' Black said, skimming over the airfield's website. 'Over thirty private flights a day. Small jets, mostly.'

Towers found details of the station commander in the MOD's internal directory and moments later was speaking to him on his private mobile. Although he didn't know Group Captain Tommy Chandler personally, Chandler knew exactly who Towers was. He had served extensively in Bastion where Freddy 'Fireballs' Towers had a reputation for demanding air transport to obscure corners of Afghanistan at a moment's notice and for screaming blue murder if he didn't get his way.

Knowing better than to offer any resistance, Chandler kept Towers on the line while he called through to the operations manager at Northolt. He came back with the information that only one civilian flight had taken off during the relevant window. There were two passengers on board a Gulfstream G450 bound for Miami, Florida. The aircraft was registered to a private operator whose company address was in Panama City. Their names were Jean-Baptiste Bonheur and Marianne Villiers. They were travelling on diplomatic passports issued in the overseas French Department of French Guiana. The aircraft had been in the air for over an hour, meaning that it would already be well out into the Atlantic. It was possible that Miami was to be a refuelling stop rather than a final destination, but there was no record of the fact.

Towers thanked Chandler for his help, put down the

phone and sat back in his seat. 'Did you catch that?' he said, staring intently into space. 'French Guiana.'

'Yes,' Black said, the unsettling seed of an idea starting to form in his mind.

'What do you make of it?'

'Unexpected,' Black said, keeping his theory to himself. He studied Towers' face and tried to read it. He could see his mind turning, struggling to make connections. Black began to wonder if the doubts that had been forming in his own mind about the nature of Towers' intentions had been entirely groundless. Perhaps beyond a vague plan to capture and interrogate Drecker there was nothing else. Perhaps this was genuinely how off-the-record operations were haphazardly conducted. It was no more or less chaotic than the way they had run things in Baghdad for more than two years. They had made up the objectives of the war as they went along, isolating targets day by day, hour by hour, and begging, borrowing and stealing whatever resources they needed to catch them.

'It can't be the French,' Towers said. 'Surely –'

The telephone rang, interrupting Towers' flow of thought. It was Professor Simon Wilkie from Guy's Hospital. He had completed the post-mortem on Drecker's associate and was in a state of high excitement. He knew Towers would be bursting to come and see what he had found.

33

Once again, Black's curiosity got the better of him. Towers drove, too fast, along the Embankment into the City where, at Moorgate, he turned right over London Bridge. The river sparkled in the late-evening sunlight. Off to their left a vast cruise liner was passing through the raised bascules of Tower Bridge. Ahead of them, the Shard rose like a two-pronged dagger. Black was able to view the modern additions to the central London skyline that had arisen in the new millennium either as hubristically dystopian or as striking parts of a harmonious continuum, depending on his state of mind. Tonight, his feeling was ambivalent. The gleaming glass skyscrapers reached for the clouds but gave no food to the soul. The spirit of the city was still to be found in the grimy bricks and blocks of stone set by human hands.

Towers seemed to read his mind. He nodded towards the Shard, which was now looming over them as they drew closer to Guy's Hospital. 'Looks like Stalin's wet dream. Whoever gave it the OK ought to be shot. Can you imagine having to go to work in something like that? I'd sooner slit my wrists.'

'I doubt the situation would arise, Freddy.'

'Too bloody right.'

He shifted down into third and slammed his foot to the floor, eager to put the building behind them.

Professor Simon Wilkie was a tall, smiling man in his mid-sixties with a contagious, irrepressible energy. Due to the late hour Wilkie was alone in the mortuary and greeted them personally at the door dressed in green surgical scrubs.

'Come in, come in.' He ushered them inside like the genial host of a cocktail party.

'Simon, this is my colleague, Major Leo Black.'

'Delighted to meet you. We're along here.'

He led them through a corridor that smelled of heavily perfumed disinfectant. Black hung back as Wilkie and Towers engaged in animated conversation. The two had a long association: Wilkie had made a specialism of conducting post-mortems on servicemen killed overseas. He and Towers had conducted a lot of business together.

They passed through a set of swing doors into the autopsy room, which was maintained at several degrees cooler than the corridor outside. Wilkie tugged two flexible paper face masks from a dispenser screwed to the wall and handed one each to Towers and Black. 'Just to be on the safe side. I caught TB off a cadaver once. Not a pleasant experience.' He gave a mischievous smile and strolled over to the large stainless-steel dissection table on which the body was laid out.

In the fullest extent of dismemberment it had been turned into a mere object. The torso had been opened from neck to navel and the ribs cut through and spread apart to allow removal of the principal internal organs. These had been weighed and sliced into sections for detailed inspection and were now sitting in a row of kidney dishes on a steel-topped counter at the side of the room. What remained of the face had been peeled backwards over the jagged remnants of the skull, leaving a single eye staring out from its bony socket. The portion of the brain that had not been blown out by the bullet had been removed, exposing the smooth inner surface of the cranium, which was the colour of clotted cream.

'Right, well, there's no question what killed him.' Wilkie

picked up a scalpel to use as a pointer. 'Three entry wounds from nine-millimetre rounds on the right side of the skull and most of the left side missing. He's approximately thirty years of age and seems to have been fit and strong. Not quite an athlete but getting on for one. You asked me to look for any clues to his origins, Freddy – you'll be happy to know I found a number.' He glanced up, smiling with twinkling eyes. 'The most obvious are immediately visible.' He pointed to a healed scar on the outside of the left upper arm. 'This is a previous bullet wound. At least five years old, I'd say. A small arms round. X-ray doesn't show any healed fractures, so we can assume he was lucky and it was just a flesh wound. Now, these are more interesting.' He pointed to the back of the left hand, where there were three circular healed scars. 'There's another on his right hand and one on his right cheek. I'm pretty certain we're looking at leishmaniasis. You might know it as Jericho Buttons.'

Black was all too familiar with the syndrome. He had experienced a minor dose in Libya. 'Ulcers caused by bites from infected sandflies.'

'Not always sandflies. Some jungle insects are vectors, too. These aren't too bad, as they go. Probably had prompt medical attention. But that's the ancient history; the more recent stuff is up here.' He shifted his focus back to the head. 'Chipped and cracked upper-right incisor. The sort of thing you'd get from a punch in the mouth.'

Towers shot Black a glance. They were both sharing the same thought.

'Working on that assumption, I took an X-ray, and, indeed, I found what appears to be a recently healed hairline fracture to the right zygomatic bone.' He pointed his scalpel to the bottom outer edge of the eye socket. 'A blunt force injury consistent with the damaged tooth but not *necessarily* related. Is this useful?'

'Extremely,' Towers said. 'The blood match I asked you to perform?'

'I'll have it tomorrow. Our colleagues in Paris seemed reluctant to exert themselves after office hours. I've yet to receive the three DNA profiles you requested.'

'Bloody typical. I'll put a rocket under them,' Tower promised. 'Any idea of his nationality?'

'He's of mixed race – as you guessed. Partly African or West Indian and partly Hispanic. If I were pushed, I'd say the facial structure suggests South American rather than European.'

'Any idea which part of South America? It's rather a big place.'

'From his body I couldn't tell you. But this might give you some clue.' He reached beneath the table and brought out a hand-held lamp. 'Would you mind turning off the lights, Major?'

Black stepped over to the bank of switches and plunged the room into darkness. Relishing his moment of theatre, Wilkie switched on the ultraviolet lamp, casting a purple glow over the body. 'Step closer.'

They shuffled forward.

Wilkie concentrated the light on the left upper forearm. 'Look carefully, you'll see the outline of a tattoo. It's been lasered, and really rather well – it's quite invisible in normal light.'

Black leaned in further and made out the ghost of a design beneath the outer layers of the smooth, pale-coffee-coloured skin. It appeared indistinct at first, but as he accustomed his eyes it came into focus. The background shape was that of an anchor. Crossed in front of it were what appeared to be a sword or cutlass and a lightning bolt.

'Recognize it?' Wilkie said.

Towers shook his head.

Black had seen it before, a long time ago. In 2003 he had been sent on a covert reconnaissance mission to gather intelligence on the connection between the Chinese Special Forces, the Quantou Budui, and those of Venezuela, which at the time was under the presidency of the arch socialist and antagonist of the West, Hugo Chavez. It had been one of the few assignments in which Towers, caught up in Iraq at the time, had played no part. Operating entirely alone, Black had observed joint exercises deep in the jungle that had revealed a high degree of skill and expertise from both parties. The symbol tattooed on to the dead man's arm was the badge of the Venezuelan naval Special Forces.

'Venezuela? You're sure?' Towers seemed reluctant to accept his word on the matter.

'Certain.' Black was already searching for the symbol on his phone's web browser. There it was. Identical. He showed it to Towers and Wilkie.

'Mystery solved,' Wilkie said.

'Venezuelan . . .' Towers said, as if nonplussed by the idea. He gave a short exclamation of surprise.

Black kept his thoughts to himself.

Still mulling over the implications of this discovery, Towers thanked Wilkie for his swift work and arranged to speak later the following day, when DNA comparisons had been made between the blood spatters recovered from Finn's body and that of the Venezuelan former special serviceman. With a promise of lunch at his club by way of thanks, he bade the professor goodbye.

They had got only as far as the top of the staircase at ground-floor level when Towers' phone rang. The caller was Eleanor Grant. He held her at bay for a moment and gestured Black to follow him through the nearby door into the multi-faith prayer room. They entered a quiet, soothing space containing only a few chairs, some kneelers and prayer mats. Towers switched to speakerphone.

'Sorry about that, Eleanor. Fire away.'

'We've got a positive ID on your suspect.' Grant's confident, purposeful voice betrayed no doubt. 'You've caused quite a stir.'

Black, who until now had spent the evening in a state of unnatural calm, felt his nerves tingle.

'She was on the CIA's files. Her name is Irma Stein. A captain in the US Army Intelligence Corps. She was stationed in Baghdad during late 2004 and early 2005. In February 2005 she went missing going about routine business inside the Green Zone. She was twenty-four at the time. It was presumed she was kidnapped by enemy insurgents but no ransom demands were received and she was never found. She's still officially unaccounted for. The CIA is obviously intrigued to know more.'

'Email me your contact's details and I'll be happy to fill them in,' Towers said. 'Thank you so much. You've been most helpful.'

He rang off and met Black's gaze. 'It *was* her, wasn't it – the woman you engaged in the firefight?'

'Quite possibly,' Black said.

'Intelligence Corps. She must have jumped ship and joined one of our friends in the private sector. She probably had the inside track on some of Saddam's hidden billions.'

'You should let them arrest her at Miami,' Black said. 'Use your information to negotiate access to her interrogation.'

'And have the Americans take the whole thing over? Our science is our national property, Leo. Finn was murdered defending it.'

'I can't see you've any option. Her cover's been blown. If you don't have her picked up now, she'll disappear.'

They remained staring at one another as they had over so many difficult and unpalatable decisions in the past. Neither said a word. They didn't have to. Black knew precisely what Towers was asking him to do and Towers knew with equal certainty what the answer would be.

Black glanced at the clock on the prayer-room wall. It was past ten. It would be midnight before he got back to Oxford. 'I should be going.'

Towers nodded. 'I can give you a lift to the Tube.'

'I think I'll walk. Thanks all the same. Goodnight, Freddy.'

'Goodnight, Leo.'

He let himself out and made his way briskly across the hospital's lobby with Towers' parting words ringing in his ears: 'I'll leave it with you, then. Safe home.'

34

I am not going to bloody Venezuela. The words with which Black had gone to sleep were those with which he woke.

He went resentfully about his morning routine of shave, shower and breakfast of toast and strong coffee. He was at his desk by seven thirty but spent a fruitless thirty minutes staring at a blank page. His mind had been invaded and occupied by thoughts of Irma Stein and her colleagues. It refused to focus on his paper and insisted instead on attempting to order a logical sequence of events that would explain how a young American deserter had ended up, fifteen years later, coordinating the abductions of leading British scientists under the diplomatic cover of French Guiana.

The college clock chimed eight and Black had achieved precisely nothing. In frustration he decided to head out in an attempt to clear his head. The clear, warm weather of the previous week had given way to low cloud and a fine penetrating drizzle. He pulled on boots and a windcheater, strode out of the college, turned left along Walton Street and after half a mile arrived at the open expanse of Port Meadow.

The three hundred acres of open pasture, grazed by the freemen of Oxford since the tenth century, was a precious stretch of wilderness sandwiched between the northern suburbs of the city and the River Thames. Early on a dismal Saturday morning on the first day of the summer vacation, he found himself completely alone. He left the path and set off in the direction of the riverbank. In the near distance a small herd of ponies moved lazily through the mist, grazing the rough grass. Black weaved between them and arrived at the water's edge where he headed north.

He pushed his legs harder, feeling the muscles stretch and the blood course through his veins. As the effort of walking began to absorb his nervous energy, by slow degrees the confusion of competing thoughts began to resolve into separate strands. He was angry at Towers for intruding on his fragile but settled existence; he was beset with doubt over his paper and his professional future, and he was grieving for Finn. And beneath it all he was disturbed by his instincts for violent revenge and enraged that he had let Irma Stein slip through his fingers, not once but twice.

He pushed on another mile, upping his pace until he was almost at a run. He held himself at the same level of exertion all the way to the end of the meadow and back again. Finally, he felt a measure of balance return. Rational thoughts began to gain the upper hand. During the final mile through the Jericho streets he resolved to send Towers an encrypted message containing his theory of who he believed Finn's murderers to be while making clear that his involvement in the operation was now over. They were, he believed, mercenaries who in all likelihood styled themselves as private security contractors. He suspected that this particular concern would have a powerful French element. The big security corporates often had former senior military men at the helm. A retired French general with political connections would be among the few able to secure diplomatic passports for his staff. Perhaps the quid pro quo was the provision of services in some of the many African trouble spots where the French maintained commercial interests in their former colonies.

That much was straightforward. The question of to whom Stein and her superiors were passing scientific intelligence was less obvious and not a problem he could solve. It was, in

Black's opinion, a matter that should be handled at the highest levels, with the involvement of government ministers and as many resources as the Special Forces and a specially vetted team recruited from the Security Services could muster. Much as Towers had always liked to be the rogue operator who succeeded where the big battalions failed, this was no time to go it alone. The enemy was too powerful and the implications of failure too vast.

Black arrived back at the college gates with his thoughts in logical order. He stopped off in the porters' lodge to collect his mail and headed back to his rooms.

'Leo?'

He turned midway across the cloister and saw Karen hurrying towards him. They hadn't spoken since their awkward parting at the beginning of the week. He felt himself tense with embarrassment.

'Karen. Hi.'

She responded with a look of puzzlement.

'Is something wrong?'

'You haven't heard, have you?'

'Heard what?'

She swallowed and pushed the hair back from her face. 'The man who made the allegations against you . . . he's sent a statement in an email. He's copied it to all the fellows and the Provost. It's not good, Leo.'

Karen made coffee in the kitchen while Black sat with his laptop on the sofa reading the email she had forwarded to him. Towers had promised him that the government lawyers had put Mahmoud back in his box. The article that had appeared in *Cherwell* had been removed and no other trace of it was to be found in the three other online newspapers that had picked it up.

The MOD had done its work. Arms had been twisted and

editors threatened. He had been assured that was an end to it. But far from going quietly, Mahmoud had gone back on the offensive, doing damage that Black feared could not be undone.

At the time of his detention in 2007 Yusuf Ali Mahmoud, a senior civil servant in the Libyan Ministry of the Interior, had undoubtedly been part of an al-Qaeda affiliate in Tripoli. Black, Finn and two others had captured then interrogated him over a period of several days before organizing his transport to Iraq, where he was handed to the Americans. Four years later politics intervened and Mahmoud, along with several other prominent figures detained in Libya, were quietly released from Guantánamo in exchange for their cooperation amidst the chaos that had overwhelmed his country after Gaddafi's bloody end. His subsequent career in politics did not go well. The faction of which he had been part was crushed in 2014 and he had sought sanctuary in Lebanon, from where, penniless, he tried to instigate legal actions against the British and US governments, claiming damages for kidnap and illegal detention. All his claims were tossed out.

Not content to have escaped with his life, Mahmoud had clearly set his mind on revenge as a substitute for compensation. He had chosen to aim his fire at Black, whom he saw as the chief agent of his betrayal:

At that time, I had contact with a number of anti-Gaddafi groups in Tripoli. Some were democrats, others were religiously motivated. I myself was chiefly concerned with the removal of the regime and the instatement of a parliament and government that would reflect the range of opinion in my country. In 2006 I had a number of meetings with members of the Libyan Islamic Fighting Group, an organization which in the late 1990s had mounted a failed assassination attempt on Gaddafi, partly funded by Britain's MI6. My intention was to determine whether this group would commit to democracy, in which case they could be considered potential allies.

Upon my illegal arrest in 2007, I was interrogated for several days – I cannot recall exactly how many because I was held in a room without daylight or clocks – about my alleged membership of the LIFG, which my captors were convinced was part of al-Qaeda and participating in the insurgency in Iraq. The bulk of my interrogation was conducted by Major Leo Black of the British Special Air Service, a man whom I have subsequently identified with assistance from a sympathetic party within the British government. At first Major Black behaved in a civil fashion, but as time passed and as I continued to assert that I was not engaged in terrorism and never had been, his treatment of me became steadily more inhuman. I was hooded, deprived of sleep, placed in stress positions for hours at a time, and finally subjected to bouts of temporary suffocation, during which I repeatedly lost consciousness.

Following this near week-long period of torture, Major Black transported me to a location in the desert where he threatened that I would be shot and buried in an unmarked grave unless I provided him with details of LIFG operations and personnel. My continued protests that I did not have this knowledge and that it would not be an easy matter for me to invent false information fell on deaf ears. After several hours of this I was blindfolded and transferred to an aircraft which delivered me to Baghdad Airport, where I was handed to the American military and taken directly to Abu Ghraib prison, where I was held without charge. There I was subjected to further interrogation of the most humiliating and distressing kind for a period of two months before I was eventually flown to Guantánamo Bay . . .

The statement continued in a similar vein for several more pages, outlining his degrading treatment in the American military prison before his eventual release and return to Libya four years later at the behest of the British Secret Intelligence Service. His freedom was granted on condition that he acted as a British agent while he attempted to become part of the newly formed Libyan national government. In a closing salvo Mahmoud wrote:

> It has recently come to my attention that Major Black, a man whom I consider to rank among the many hundreds of war criminals employed by the coalition forces, has secured a position in your esteemed university. I would urge you to consider most carefully the implications of employing an individual who has acted with flagrant disregard for basic human rights, the Geneva Conventions and the commonly accepted standards of international law.

Black looked up from the screen to see Karen standing watching him. He had been so absorbed he hadn't noticed her, or the mug of coffee she had set on the low table to his right.

'Well?'

'Not what you'd call a glowing reference.' His attempt at a joke turned the frigid air even cooler.

'Is it true?'

'You know I can't discuss operational matters.'

'Who am I going to tell, honestly . . . ? Don't you trust me?'

'It's not a question of trust, Karen.' He closed the lid of the laptop and set it aside, trying to resist the temptation to connect the email with Irma Stein and whoever it was she worked for.

'But you're not denying it?'

'I can't even afford to play that game,' Black said. 'Denial and affirmation are two sides of the same coin. We don't do it.'

'*We?* Who the hell are *we?*'

246

'Look, I'm sorry this was sent to you,' Black said, avoiding the question. 'It was good of you to let me know.'

Karen dropped into the swivel chair next to the desk and fixed him with a searching look. 'Leo, do you want a fellowship? Because if you do, you are going to have to give an account of yourself. Do you think Alex or Silvio or Claire will be happy with anything less than a complete explanation of what this is all about? They need to know who you are.'

Black stared back at her, wishing he could tell her the truth – that Mahmoud was a terrorist drenched in the blood of innocent people, that the world would have been far better off without him – but it wasn't an option. If word got out that he had betrayed confidences, he could lose his army pension and expect to be prosecuted. He was caught in the worst possible position: of being not guilty and unable to defend himself.

'Karen, I was a soldier throughout one of the busiest periods in the British Army's history. I served in every major theatre of conflict and more besides . . . All I can do is point to my current work. If you want to know who I am, what I believe, what I'm here for, read what I've written.' He pointed to the small pile of handwritten sheets on his desk.

'I know what you are, Leo. You're not as good at hiding it as you think you are. You're a man who's done bad things and is trying to atone. You've seen the worst and you think there's a better way. I can live with that. People change all the time. I can even live with your keeping secrets, but what I can't cope with is you –' She faltered and bit her lip as if holding back tears.

Black fought an urge to reach out and touch her hand.

'The man who attacked me . . . Tell me he's nothing to do with all this.'

'I can't see why he would be.'

She looked at him with wounded, accusing eyes that saw straight through his lie.

'Because I'm the only friend you've got in this place, Leo. If someone is hell-bent on making sure you don't survive here, I'd say alienating me would be a pretty good part of the plan.'

He tried to find words that would square with his conscience, but they eluded him.

'Well, if you can't reassure me on that, perhaps you could be decent enough to tell me honestly whether I'm in any further danger? And the reason I ask is because I had a call at four o'clock this morning, and another at the same time yesterday. Both silent. I know it could be nothing, but I can't help it, Leo. It scared me.'

She waited while Black tried to weigh the implications of this latest piece of information. His mind kept returning to the Paris hotel room and his momentary loss of temper that sparked the chain of events that had already led to him killing two people. The depths of his hypocrisy disgusted him.

'All right,' Karen said, rising from the chair, 'I'll take this to the police instead. They told me to call them if anything happened.' She marched towards the door.

'Karen. Please.' Black found himself going after her. He caught hold of her arm and spun her round. 'I'm sorry . . . I'll make some calls, make sure you're looked after.'

'Calls to whom?'

'I can't tell you.'

'I liked you, Leo. I trusted you . . .'

Black's fingers loosened from around her arm. His hand dropped to his side.

'I'll give you one last chance – who *are* you?'

'Right at this moment, I'm not entirely sure.'

Her eyes filled with angry, disappointed tears. 'I think it's probably best if we don't speak to each other for the time being.'

She left, slamming the door behind her.

Someone always seemed to be slamming his door.

Hearing her footsteps disappearing along the gravel path, Black realized just how deeply he felt for her. And as with the few times it had happened before he knew that it was already too late.

35

'I'm afraid there's no question of our considering your application while this matter remains unresolved.' Alex Levine turned from the window of his study overlooking the garden surrounding the Provost's lodgings and gave a brief, distant smile of apology. 'I'm sure you can appreciate our position, Leo.'

He was dressed for the weekend: jeans and a black polo shirt that fitted tightly over his flat-fronted torso. Black imagined him rising before dawn to pound the treadmill. He had the body of a man who punished himself, who wouldn't afford himself an inch of slack until he had achieved his ambition. And right now, Black was one of the obstacles in his way.

'I'm not sure I do.'

Levine's eyes widened in surprise.

'Quite apart from the issue of due process, the presumption of innocence, the possible political and even financial motives the sender of this email might possess, there is the other small matter of what exactly this college, this university is for. Is it for the pursuit of knowledge or for the continued reinforcement of some unspoken agenda?'

God, he sounded pompous.

Levine shifted uncomfortably from one foot to another, looking as if he had found himself trapped in the company of a madman.

Black continued, aware that he was fighting for his professional life. 'Let's imagine, for the sake of argument, that everything alleged in that email is true and that the British officer is, in fact, me. Wouldn't that make my knowledge some of the most valuable in the field? Knowledge is knowledge, truth is truth. There's no morality attached to facts. If you are only prepared to consider knowledge that comes from someone sufficiently in tune with your politics or prejudice, you've negated the whole purpose of intellectual endeavour. You've stopped enquiring. And even if through some mangled logic you manage to convince yourself that I am a useful *source* of information but because of my past career not a fit and proper person to *impart* it, you've done it again. Because truth is nothing, Provost, is it, except the power to transform? To turn darkness to light. What better illustration of all that you and this university stand for is there than the difference between me, the man you know, and the man depicted in that email?'

Black's words echoed in the silence. He had stunned himself by the force of his outburst as much as he had Levine.

The muscles of Levine's jaw tightened. He was used to colleagues who played by the rules, who obeyed and enacted the implicit codes without question. Who understood without thinking exactly why a man accused of unethical behaviour could never be accepted into their ranks. Black understood his dilemma perfectly. In a world in which diversity was the ultimate good everybody was categorized and pegged according to their antecedents and associations. There were no means for a person to escape their designations, no mechanism that responded to the spirit of the individual outside the set criteria. There was no room in a modern university for a heretic, reformed or otherwise.

'It's not a matter of principle, Leo; it's one of practicalities. Can you imagine the press?'

'You would prefer that students learned their military history from someone who has never been near a conflict?'

'Now you're being contrary.'

'I'm simply stating the obvious.'

'There's a limit to how far I'm prepared to stick my neck out, Leo, especially when I have absolutely no access to the facts.' He sighed and pressed his long, delicate fingers to his temples. 'Leo, this is nothing personal. I like you. The students like you. I admire your work. I'm prepared to keep the door open, but for the sake of the college's reputation we can't take on a fellow embroiled in this much controversy. I propose you do what you can over the summer to resolve these accusations. You can keep your rooms in college. We'll meet again at the start of September after your address to West Point and reassess the situation. That's the best I can do.'

The two men looked at each other across the room and silently agreed that there was nothing more to be said.

Black rose from his chair and, accepting the Provost's handshake, offered his thanks. He had secured himself a lifeline. A slender one, but it was better than falling into the abyss.

Towers remained incommunicado throughout the morning, failing to answer calls or emails. Only when Black had given up hope and was loading a hastily packed holdall and a cardboard box loaded with books into his Land Rover did his phone finally ring.

'Sorry not to have got back to you earlier. Wanted to work out what the hell was going on.' Towers sounded irritated rather than apologetic but Black let it pass. 'Had a word with the Libya desk in '6 and they're going to send someone along to have a chat with him.'

'A chat?'

'They don't want the embarrassment any more than you do, Leo. All these claims were meant to have gone away years ago. I think Mr Mahmoud might be one of those who thought he didn't get his fair share when the government cheque book came out.'

'But why now?'

'It's possible some unscrupulous lawyers of the kind who trawl for incidents of imaginary wrongs committed by British soldiers put him up to it, or, I fear, it's something by way of an inducement to you to get our job done.'

'Freddy?'

'The Committee wants this dealt with. As quickly as possible.'

Black slammed the tailgate closed and marched to the cab. 'Why should I work for people who treat me like that?'

'If my fears are correct, it strikes me they're people who think exactly as we do, Leo. What better way to stimulate a man to action than to threaten all that's most precious to him? In your case your reputation.'

Along with the one person in his new life that mattered to him.

'Ours is a strange calling, I admit,' Towers said with a trace of wistful regret.

Black remained silent. He climbed on to the hard bench seat behind the wheel and pulled the creaking door shut. His view through the windscreen was of the small apple orchard that bordered the fellows' car park. A gardener was carefully clearing weeds from the base of a recently planted sapling.

'What do you want me to do for you, Leo? I'll try my best to put the lid on it, but you know what the price will be . . . Leo? Are you still there?'

'Yes,' he answered shortly.

'Sorry to change the subject, but you might be interested to know that Stein and her friends slipped the net. Their plane changed course mid-Atlantic and made it to Cayenne, French Guiana. From there they seem to have flown on to Puerto Ayacucho. Had to look it up – a one-horse town in southern Venezuela.'

Black made no comment, afraid of where Towers was heading.

'This you'll find very interesting – what you said in your message was bang on. I looked up the list of private contractors operating out of Baghdad back in '05. There were a dozen or more. Triple Canopy, Vinnell, Blackwater, all the usual suspects, and an outfit called Sabre. Started by a retired French colonel, Auguste Daladier, as far as I can gather. Daladier spent his career in the Foreign Legion, much of it in Africa. It seems he was particularly active in the Democratic Republic of the Congo during the nineties through to '03. According to my man in the Foreign Office, the French took advantage of the civil war and got themselves a bunch of mineral rights in return.'

Black listened. He couldn't help but be intrigued.

'It seems Sabre have stayed in business ever since. Contracts all over the world. All the rough stuff that pays the most – they were first in securing the Libyan oil fields; the French government employed them to counter insurgents in Mali and Chad; they've been busy in northern Nigeria. We suspect they've also been involved in Central and South America, policing the drugs business – the kind of stuff we used to do back in the eighties, knocking out the cartels and seizing their assets. We haven't got a location for Daladier at present, but my money would be on a rather agreeable tropical villa overlooking the southern Caribbean. If he's our man and he's spent the last dozen years recruiting the finest and best to his private army, it still begs the question, what's he doing with our scientists? Is he taking them to order or what?' Towers paused briefly to give Black time to assimilate. 'I thought you might have a theory, Leo.'

'No, I don't,' Black lied.

'Can I tempt you to formulate one? Isn't this right up your alley – modern warfare?'

He glanced right out of the driver's window and saw Silvio Belladini strolling out of one of the college buildings, accompanied by a beautiful young woman who appeared to be hanging on his every word. Seeming to sense his presence, Belladini glanced over, inadvertently caught his eye, then quickly looked away again. He put a hand in the small of the young woman's back and moved her along.

'Freddy, for the last time, I am not going to bloody Venezuela. Enjoy your weekend.'

He switched off the phone, tossed it to the far side of the passenger seat and started the engine. Oxford was starting to feel like a prison. He needed to break loose.

Late afternoon rolled into evening and finally faded to dusk. Black came to a halt for the first time in four hours and looked out from the top of the ridge at a Welsh landscape dissolving in shadow. His lungs burned and his muscles were screaming, but the anger inside refused to subside. He had set out from Ty Argel intending to reason each cause of it away but at some moment during his long tramp across the countryside he had abandoned the effort and accepted that was just how it was, who he was: a man caught in an endless loop of promise and frustration. Doomed by his past.

Then, as if in response to the setting sun, the vengeful rage that had propelled him up hillsides and through valleys seemed to retreat from his extremities to settle in his core, where, slowly, it coalesced into something hard, cold and flint-edged. Like an object he could weigh in his hands.

The cacophony of voices in his head reduced to one. It told him he had been here before. Many times. The dilemmas had been different but the choices the same.

Attack or retreat.

Live or die.

Reluctantly, he chose his path.

With a feeling, if not of peace, of purpose, Black watched the day snuff out and turned for home.

36

Midnight had come and gone. Sarah Bellman was alone in the now well-equipped laboratory, stooped over her computer screen, staring at the latest sequences of DNA code that Sphyris had introduced to his infinitely detailed map of the brain. They belonged to tiny clusters of cells grouped in the ventral tegmental area towards the base of the skull. These were the Holy Grail: the cells that he and Holst had been attempting to isolate and distinguish from those grouped around them. A few short lines expressed in the genetic language that comprised only four letters, C, A, G and T, lent them their uniqueness and held the keys to dopamine production. When mildly stimulated, the cells bearing this section of code brought about a sense of warmth and well-being. When excited more vigorously, they could provoke a high that was more intense and overwhelming than any caused by an intravenous shot of heroin.

Now they had their target, her and Professor Kennedy's task was a purely mechanical one. Over the coming days, with the help of gene-splicing machines that could do in hours what even ten years before had taken teams of technicians months of painstaking manual work, they could set about creating their microscopic containers, woven from strands of DNA, that would deliver charged nanoparticles to exactly the cells, and only the cells, they were targeting.

When she had started her work the objectives had been entirely noble. Her delivery systems would attack cancer cells wherever they lurked without the need for drugs that indiscriminately destroyed everything in their path. She had never for a moment contemplated their destructive capacity.

She heard footsteps outside the door. She turned to see Dr Holst's face framed in the observation pane. He smiled at her and came through.

'Couldn't sleep?' he said, rubbing his tired eyes beneath his reading glasses. 'Me, too. Exciting, isn't it?'

'Very,' Bellman murmured.

Holst wandered towards her, admiring the newly installed banks of equipment. 'This must feel like home from home. Possibly better. It would take me years to persuade the funding committee back home to come up with something like this.' He perched on one of the stools at the workbench at the side of the lab. 'It makes you realize just what can be achieved with enough money and determination.'

Bellman nodded, finding his presence unnerving.

'Forgive me, Sarah, but do I detect some misgivings about our work . . . ? I know none of us chose to be here, but now that we are –'

'I need to know how you got this data.' The words seemed to come out of her mouth without conscious thought. She immediately regretted them and felt her cheeks burning as Holst regarded her with an even more searching gaze.

'You know how we got it, Sarah. I took biopsies. On a purely human level it's not a pleasant task, but for the betterment of mankind . . .'

She felt the urge to hit him. To wipe the look of false sincerity from his fleshy features, but she remained paralysed, too frightened and unsure of herself to do anything but stare at him like a resentful child.

Holst struck his most mollifying and avuncular tone. 'Of course you feel squeamish. We all do. But many of the greatest breakthroughs have the bleakest of beginnings. Wernher von Braun was the Nazis' chief rocket scientist. His creations rained death on London but two and a half decades later put men on the moon. Don't you find that inspiring . . . ? It's as if there is a natural order to these things. Knowledge finds its true purpose in the end. We are just its instruments.'

He eased off his stool and stepped towards her.

He placed a clammy hand on her shoulder.

'Out of this darkness you *are* bringing light into the world, Sarah. Never forget that . . . Goodnight. Don't stay up too late.'

He patted her twice on the arm and made his way out, closing the door quietly behind him.

Bellman sat in silence for a long moment, then lifted her eyes to the screen.

It was code. Letters. That's all it was.

Holst did his work and she did hers.

No one was asking her to hurt anyone.

37

Black pulled up outside Kathleen Finn's house shortly before midnight. The blind twitched at the downstairs window. She peered from behind it and beckoned him over. He stepped out of the Land Rover, stiff and aching from his long walk. He would gladly have delayed his visit until the morning, but Kathleen had wanted to meet while the children were in bed, 'So they don't have to see me crying again.'

She opened the door and let him in, glancing left and right at the darkened houses of her neighbours.

'It's all right. I don't think anyone's seen me,' Black said.

'You don't know what gossip is till you've lived in this street.' She gave a strained smile. 'Hi, Leo.'

'Good to see you.'

The house was still and quiet and immaculately tidy, as if Kathleen had responded to the turmoil of her grief by obsessively ordering every item she possessed. Black noticed that Finn's walking jacket had gone from its peg in the hall along with his boots, which the last time he had visited had still been among the collection of wellingtons and trainers now arranged on wire racks. He followed Kathleen into the neat front room, where the children's toys were stowed out of sight in a stack of newly bought plastic boxes. Every surface was gleaming. He sat on plumped cushions and cast an eye along the framed family pictures carefully arranged along a shelf. There was only one small photograph of Finn – dressed in uniform, looking dignified and dependable. An image for the children to hold on to as other memories faded.

'Can I get you a drink?'

'No, thanks.'

Kathleen perched on the chair opposite. She had tended her appearance as meticulously as she had organized the house. Her nails were polished, her skin was smooth and clear and her black hair had been cut so that it perfectly framed her face. She wore black jeans and a blue cotton top the colour of her eyes. Small, delicate items of silver jewellery completed the impression of a woman determined not to show a chink in her armour.

'You're sure you don't mind me coming here?'

'I asked you to, didn't I?' She straightened her back as if bracing herself. 'What do you want to know?'

Black hesitated, not wanting to distress her any more than he had to, but her defiant posture told him that she was ready for whatever he had to say. 'Something's been on my mind, Kathleen. Probably like you, I can't help thinking about what happened in Paris. Perhaps Ryan was just unlucky, but I'd like to rule out the possibility that whoever did it had a history with him.'

She stared back at him, her expression impassive. 'What kind of history?'

'My best guess is that the perpetrators were also in the security business – the dark end of it. Did you ever get the impression he'd made enemies in that world, or had had some bad experiences?'

'None that he mentioned.'

'Do you have any idea who he'd been working for lately?'

'He kept the contracts in his desk. I've been meaning to clear it out but it's the one thing I haven't been able to face.' Black followed her through to the kitchen diner. In the centre of the room was a door he had assumed led to a pantry, but it opened instead on to a spacious cupboard beneath the stairs.

It was large enough for a desk and chair with shelves above, on which were arranged a number of files containing the household bills and papers.

'He kept all his work papers on this side.' She pointed to the two drawers on the right-hand side of the desk. 'Are you sure you don't want a drink? I bloody need one.'

'I don't suppose you've any whisky?'

'I think there's some in the back of the cupboard. You bought it for Ryan's fortieth. He said it tasted like ditchwater.'

'That would be the fifteen-year-old Bruichladdich. He told me it was the best thing he'd ever tasted.'

'You were an officer. He didn't like to hurt your delicate feelings.' She smiled. 'Straight ditchwater, is it?'

'Please.'

She left Black to the task of sorting through the contents of the drawers. The uppermost of the two was full of the usual accumulated detritus: spent insurance documents, various pieces of official correspondence whose relevance had long since expired and, buried at the bottom of the heap, Finn's official letter of acceptance into the Parachute Regiment, complete with orders to report to Colchester barracks on his nineteenth birthday. Finn had beaten Black into uniform by several years and was already a battle-scarred corporal of twenty-four when Black had first arrived in the old camp at Stirling Lines in Hereford.

The contents of the bottom drawer were more promising. There were letters from various close protection and security companies acknowledging his applications for work, remittances itemizing his fees and a number of standard contracts of engagement. Black glanced through a few. Karen was right – all contained strictly worded confidentiality clauses. They also excluded liability for any injury suffered in the line of duty but gave no detail as to what those duties were to be, instead stating vaguely: *to perform such tasks and duties as the employer has prior to signature of this contract set out orally or in writing.* Clearly the security business wasn't keen on paper trails.

He gave up on the drawers and glanced at the contents of the shelf. Lying on their sides at the end of a row of files were desk diaries for each of the last two years. He picked up last year's and flicked through. The pages were virtually empty, just the odd entry in Finn's surprisingly neat hand, noting meetings with people whom Black supposed were prospective employers: *5 Jan., 19 Russell Square, Kieran Grant . . . 12 March, 35 Mortimer Street, Dan Weirside.*

Kathleen returned with a tumbler half filled with pale amber liquid and a large glass of red wine for herself.

She handed him his drink. 'Any luck?'

'Not a lot. A few names to check.'

'He preferred to keep things in his head. Army habit. How's the whisky?'

Black took a sip of earthy petrol. 'I'll let him off – it's an acquired taste.'

She gave a wry smile and took a mouthful of wine. Almost at once, it relaxed her. Her eyes softened and her tense shoulders dropped. She leaned against the door frame and watched him turn through Finn's diary.

He arrived at a long stretch of blank pages that extended from the previous June through to September.

'Is something wrong?' Kathleen asked.

'Did he have the summer off?'

'No. It was the job I told you about. He went away in July. He was meant to be gone six months but he was back in the September.'

'I remember . . . You said he got ill.'

She nodded.

Black detected something evasive in her manner as if whatever had occurred carried a taint of shame.

'Any idea where the job was?'

'He didn't say exactly, but –'

She stalled. Her eyes briefly glistened with tears. She lifted her chin and regained control of herself. 'He told me it would be a lot of money – a hundred and fifty thousand. I had a bad feeling about it, but I knew he was thinking it might be enough to sell up here and move out to the country like he'd always wanted.'

'A bad feeling because you knew this wasn't an ordinary job?'

She shrugged.

'Was this a mercenary contract, Kathleen?'

'He didn't say so.'

'But that's what you suspected? But thankfully he got ill and came back in one piece.'

She nodded but was still keeping something back. Black could sense it.

'You can tell me, Kathleen. It might help.'

She turned away and moved over to the kitchen table, where she dropped into a chair. Black joined her, pulling up a seat opposite. They drank in silence for a short while before she steeled herself to speak. 'I was worried it was something dangerous or illegal. He swore to me it wasn't, but I always knew when he was lying.'

'Where did he go?'

'Africa is all he would say. Reading between the lines I think it was the DRC. That's where a lot of them go. He mentioned something about training troops to deal with illegal mining. But when they say "training", they mean fighting, don't they?'

'If it's any comfort, it sounds like a regular gig,' Black

said. 'It could have been far worse. How did he come to get ill?'

'It was a tropical fever of some sort. He said that as soon as he'd been sick for more than a few days they sacked him. Didn't get paid a penny. The whole thing was a disaster. I should have stopped him going. As soon as he took that job I knew it was time for him to walk away from it all. I *knew*.' Tears dripped from her eyes and spotted the tabletop. 'The only reason I didn't put my foot down was that I was frightened that he couldn't stop, that he'd be like all those others who end up hitting the bottle or their wives. You won't know what happens to all the regular soldiers when they come out, but I do. You can't turn a man into a killing machine and expect him to walk back into normal life like none of it ever happened. It doesn't work that way.'

She dried her eyes with a tissue.

'For what it's worth it's not everyone, Kathleen. And it's never the guys who lasted as long in the game as he did. Ryan was just unlucky. There's nothing you could have done to make things turn out differently.'

'Maybe.'

'I'm certain of it.'

His words seemed to comfort her. The emotion that had briefly consumed her subsided. 'I suppose I married the stupid bugger with my eyes open. I'm just about young enough to have another life, I suppose . . . Eventually.'

Black couldn't help but admire her strength. Finn would have been proud.

'One last question. Had Ryan always been involved with Freddy Towers since leaving the army or was it a recent thing?'

Another sore point. Kathleen sighed and closed her eyes. 'After he came back he said people weren't prepared to touch him. Someone had put the word out that he was a quitter. He was all set to pack it in when one of the guys from the Regiment told him to give Freddy a bell – said he might be able to pull a few strings for him.'

'And that's how he got the Paris job?'

Kathleen nodded. 'We could have managed . . . I used to tell him it was him I wanted, not a fancy house.'

'It's late. I should let you get to bed,' Black said. He got up from the table and touched Kathleen affectionately on the shoulder. 'Do you mind if I borrow the diaries? I'd like to check out some of the names.'

'Whatever you want.'

He collected them from Finn's desk and turned to go. 'Look after yourself. I'll be in touch.'

'Leo?'

He glanced back. She was still sitting at the table, cradling her empty glass, her back to him.

'You will get to the bottom of this, Leo.'

It wasn't a question. It was an order.

Black drove away from the house and once he had cleared the outskirts of the city, pulled over into a field gateway. By the dim light in the cab of the Land Rover he again checked a diary entry Finn had made on 15 May the previous year: *Mitch Brennan, 1 p.m., The Lanesborough.* He hadn't made a mistake. When he had first seen the name it had hit him like a fist. He had hidden his reaction from Kathleen, but now the memories came cascading back.

The Mitch Brennan he remembered was a newly promoted captain of the Australian Special Air Service Regiment. He had been seconded to Black's squadron in the early days of the occupation of Iraq, between 2003 and 2004. His role had been chiefly to observe and learn as part of a professional exchange programme. But in the maelstrom of Baghdad and the daily missions to kill or capture insurgents who seemed to multiply like maggots on a corpse, Brennan had taken an increasingly active role. Soon he was leading missions of his own and earning a reputation for being a fearless then a vicious and reckless operator. He had been known to hang suspects out of upstairs windows by their ankles then drop them when they failed to talk. Eventually Brennan's behaviour became too much even for Towers, who sent him back to his regiment before his six months was up. Several years later Black had heard a rumour that Brennan had gone missing during a covert operation to track down al-Qaeda militants in Indonesia. He remembered thinking it was a good day for the Australian army.

Missing but not dead.

Black switched off the map light and sat in the darkness contemplating the call he felt compelled to make. He peered up out of the windscreen at an ink-black sky smeared with stars. It had always amused him to think that his eyes were receiving photons emitted at the dawn of the universe at the same time as others only seconds old and every age in between, that a simple tilt of the head raised the vision from the present to the whole of eternity. Most would live their entire lives unaware of this simple fact, but every soldier knew it, whether by book or by instinct.

He drew out his phone, brought it to life and dialled Freddy Towers' number.

Towers answered enthusiastically. 'Leo! I was going to call you. I'm in your neck of the woods. Any chance you could pop by tomorrow?'

'Pop by?'

'To Credenhill.'

'You've had me followed?'

'Let's not quibble, shall we? We've a mission to organize. The Committee has got the all-clear from the Director, Special Forces. I hear you've been talking to Kathleen.' He offered the non sequitur without explanation.

'What of it?' Black answered, concealing both his surprise and indignation.

'Anything I should know?'

'I found a name in his diary. Mitch Brennan. They met in London last May. I think he may have given him a lucrative job in Africa. It didn't work out. Finn left early and didn't collect his pay cheque.'

'*Brennan.* I remember that bastard. Well, well, well.' Towers sounded genuinely delighted. 'Looks like you may be on to something. About time. Midday tomorrow, then? Main gates. They'll be expecting you.'

He rang off, leaving a roaring silence.

Black started the engine, switched on the headlights and pulled away. He glanced in the mirror and caught a glint of moonlight glancing off the car travelling without headlights some fifty yards behind him. Towers had had him tailed. Whether he liked it or not, his life was no longer his own.

Black drove into the dark tunnel of the night resigning himself to one unavoidable fact: wherever he was going, there was killing to be done.

38

Black drew up to the guard post at thirteen minutes past twelve. His lateness was deliberate. The sooner Towers realized he was here on his terms, the better.

What he still thought of as the new SAS camp, even though it had occupied its current home for eighteen years, was a former RAF base three miles outside the city of Hereford. From the outside it was an unassuming collection of 1940s brick buildings enclosed by fences and the obligatory coils of razor wire. It sat on a quiet road on the edge of the village of Credenhill surrounded by fields and wooded hills. All that distinguished it from other military bases was the conspicuous lack of signs at its entrance and the extra armed police officers unobtrusively patrolling its borders. Britain's most secret military installation, the repository of some of the world's most sensitive intelligence, was hidden in plain sight.

Black lowered his window as a young corporal of the Military Provost Guard Service approached.

'Good morning, sir. Would you mind looking this way?'

From the pocket of his camouflaged tunic the soldier produced a hand-held device with which he took a picture of Black's face. Within seconds it had confirmed his identity.

'Good afternoon, Major Black.' The corporal dipped into his pocket and handed over a ready-prepared security pass. 'If you'd like to drive through the gate and park outside Block C, Colonel Towers will be there to meet you.'

'Thank you.'

A barrier lifted. Black drove on through the entrance and into a camp that hadn't visibly changed since his abrupt departure. He turned left and made his way past a row of anonymous buildings surrounded by neatly cut grass. He hadn't known what his reaction would be on returning to the place which for so many years had been the closest thing he had had to a home. Passing the entrance to the officers' mess and then the offices from which he and Towers had meticulously planned so many operations, he felt strangely detached. The old sensations, the excitement and anticipation that had propelled his younger self into action, refused to stir.

Towers burst out of the entrance to Block C as Black parked nose first in a space reserved with a sign: MJR L. BLACK (RETD). He hovered impatiently, radiating nervous energy as Black switched off the engine and climbed out.

'You're late! Come on. Hurry.'

He turned and darted back into the building.

Black glanced up and down the empty roadway expecting to see a familiar face, but all was quiet. Most of the officers and their staff would be at home with their families. The young troopers and NCOs training for ops would be over at the Pontrilas training area ten miles to the south, where the Regiment had its Close Quarter Battle House, more popularly known as the Killing House. There buildings as diverse as the London Iranian Embassy and Baghdad apartment blocks could be simulated for rehearsals so rigorous that, by their end, troopers could have navigated the real thing blindfold.

Pontrilas was also home to the shell of a Boeing 747 in which, during the mid-1990s, Black had learned to take out hijackers without killing passengers. Back then they hadn't planned for dealing with suicidal terrorists. After 2001 it was all they did. The shift had made them more brutal. It was no longer a question of attempting to save every innocent life but merely as many as possible. A numbers game. Every member of the Regiment became an instinctive utilitarian. They were all men who in Truman's shoes would have dropped the bomb. It was one of the many things that set them apart.

With these thoughts still circulating in his head Black followed Towers into the building.

Block C was, like most military buildings, a strictly functional place. Stark corridors with hard, shiny floors, hung with regimental photographs. In Black's time 'C' had been the home of the back-office staff who dealt with kit, basic logistics and finances, and he got the impression little had changed. Like the rest of the camp, the building was virtually deserted. Towers scurried up the stairs to the second floor where he ushered Black into a spacious office that contained little more than a large desk, a computer with an outsize monitor and a number of chairs.

'Blagged this yesterday,' Towers said. 'It's not much, but it'll do for our purposes.' He gestured Black towards the desk. 'The Director has been good enough to grant me access to images from our Carbonite-2 satellite. I think I'm on to something.' He sat at the computer and started working the mouse. 'I know what you're thinking, Leo, but I had to assume you'd come round. This Mitch Brennan connection really starts to unlock things. I got on to the CO over in Perth first thing this morning. He wouldn't quite admit that Brennan had gone AWOL, but he certainly gave me that impression. According to the official record, he went missing presumed dead in 2007. My guess is he made dubious contacts in Africa – the Australians have been all over it in recent years: Nigeria, Kenya, Zimbabwe. Don't buy all the PC bullshit their politicians spout; they're as rapacious as the rest of us.'

'Have you found any record of him since?'

'Not a thing. Which I'm sure is entirely intentional.'

'And Finn didn't mention him?'

'No. I got the impression there was a good deal of injured pride and a fair degree of shame connected with whatever he had been up to, so I didn't press him. If Brennan was in any way involved, I can see why. It also explains why he jumped ship halfway through his contract.'

'You don't believe he was ill?'

'Do you ever recall him having a day sick?'

Black had to admit that he didn't.

'So I think we may be on to something. The Ryan Finn we knew had his red lines. From the little I recall of Brennan he was a thorough-going bastard. Here – something for you to read. Had a friend of mine in the City get one of his analysts to do a bit of digging.' He hit some more keys, causing several pages to spew out of a printer beneath the desk. 'Those are for you. Now where the bloody hell are those pictures?'

Black took the three freshly printed pages to a chair by the window, leaving Towers to wrestle with his computer. The document set out what little was known about the corporate history of Sabre. It had begun life in 2004 as Sabre Systèmes de Défence Internationale SARL, a private company with registered offices in Marseille. The two directors were listed as Colonel Auguste Daladier, formerly of the French Foreign Legion, and Pierre Gaumont, a retired investment banker. The firm offered corporate asset and personal protection services and was known to have operated extensively in Africa and the Middle East, specializing in protecting mining and oil-drilling operations in conflict zones. After two years in business its turnover was north of ten million euros. In 2007 it relocated to Panama, where the law allowed for almost complete corporate secrecy. Daladier and Gaumont's names were replaced on the register of directors by local nominees and thereafter no accounts were made publicly available.

The trail went cold for over a year, but, according to unconfirmed reports that had circulated among commodities traders, in late 2009 Daladier was one of a small number of international businessmen invited by the then Venezuelan president, Hugo Chavez, to a secret summit at which he discussed the potential for exploiting the country's untapped natural resources in the southern Amazonian jungle. 2008 had seen the price of crude oil crash by nearly three hundred per cent, leaving Chavez's economic miracle in tatters. In desperate need of a quick fix Chavez swallowed his pride and prepared to enter into murky deals with the hated capitalists.

Geological surveys had revealed huge potential deposits of gold, diamonds, rare earth metals and coltan. In a separate boxed-out section of the report the author explained that, of all these, coltan was the biggest prize. Columbite-tantalite, coltan for short, is a dull metallic ore, which when refined becomes a heat-resistant powder that can hold a high electrical charge. Critical in the manufacture of miniature circuit boards, coltan is found in virtually every modern electronic device. The proliferation of mobile phones, laptops, games consoles and every conceivable gadget besides has driven demand ever higher. When, in the early 2000s, Sony released its PlayStation 2, global demand for coltan outstripped supply and poured fuel on the flames of civil war in the Democratic Republic of the Congo, where competing factions fought for control of the lucrative illegal coltan mines.

Among the other guests reputed to have attended this gathering was Carl Mathis, a publicity-shy serial entrepreneur who, over a long career, made his billions successfully anticipating the next wave of technological revolution. He had backed personal computers in the early 1980s, mobile phones in the 1990s and biotech in the 2000s. In 2009 rumours circulated that he had liquidated $800 million from across his portfolio. A freelance journalist based in Silicon Valley sold a story to *Inside Business* magazine reporting that Mathis had signed a deal with China's biggest manufacturer of printed circuit boards, guaranteeing their supply of coltan for the next twenty years. A source close to Mathis was quoted as saying that the digital, electrically powered future would create a demand for certain materials, coltan among them, that would outstrip supply by a multiple of at least five. Governments were unprepared for the consequences of such a dire shortage, leaving the field open for smart investors. The article was taken down from the magazine's website within six hours of publication and never made it to the print edition.

As a result of the article, rumours spread through the markets that Mathis had signed a deal with Chavez but no proof of this could be found, and as Mathis owned all of his businesses personally, there were no shareholder prospectuses to mine for information. Nevertheless, the global supply of coltan remained roughly equal to demand, suggesting that new sources of supply had indeed come on stream.

The report ended near the top of the third page. In the space below were two separate items pasted from other documents. The first read:

CARL MATHIS. MALE. DOB 09.07.47 (USA) appears only once in our files.

Item: Station report of Alan Huntley, British Embassy, Caracas, 28.02.13

... agent reports Pres. Chavez received a number of visits in private room at Hospital Militar Dr Carlos Arvelo during the afternoon. Security passes issued to ... Mr Carl J. Mathis (USA) and Col. Auguste Daladier ...

The second item read like dialogue from a bad play and featured Freddy Towers in the lead role. It was a transcript of a phone call he had made only three days before:

FT: Hello, my name is Daniel Riley from Hamilton Bray solicitors, Panama City office. I've an urgent message for Mr Mathis. It concerns my client, his colleague, Colonel Auguste Daladier.

PA: Is he expecting your call, sir?

FT: No, this is an unexpected emergency.

PA: I'm afraid Mr Mathis isn't available at this time.

FT: Please tell him that Colonel Daladier is in Venezuelan military detention and that I am about to have a meeting with President Maduro. Maduro is threatening to nationalize the whole Sabre operation.

PA: Could you please give me your number, sir?

FT: I don't have one. I'm on an extension in the presidential palace in Caracas and they've taken my mobile phone. Please just tell him. I'll hold.

PA: I'll see what I can do, sir.

(Pause – 20 seconds)

CM: Hello? Who am I speaking to? Hello? Hello . . . ? Is anybody there . . . ? Shit.

'Enjoy that?' Towers looked over from behind his monitor and beamed. 'Thought I'd leave him dangling, thinking his eight hundred million had gone down the Swanee. Can you imagine?' He grinned.

'I'm sure it was a lot of fun.'

'It proves Daladier and Mathis got together for a Venezuelan operation. Fat lot of good it did comrade Chavez. He sold out, turned up his toes and the country still went bust. Nearly there with this thing. Won't be a moment. I've got images of what we think is their coltan mine down near the Brazilian border. They've recently added what looks like a military compound.' He returned to his computer.

Black put the document aside. He was prepared to believe that Mathis and Daladier had found each other and that, like many old rich men before him, Mathis had decided on one last spectacular roll of the dice to cement his legacy. What persuaded a man with more money than he could ever use to embark on a reckless South American adventure wasn't a question he could answer. It was no different to asking a soldier why he wasn't working in the safety of a warm insurance office. Human beings did what they felt they had to.

Black glanced around the room as Towers continued to stoop over his keyboard, cursing as he jabbed at the keys. It was a functional military office like any other with no remarkable characteristics except the fact that it had been supplied with a computer connected to the most sensitive images available to the British Armed Forces. Usually, such material was closely guarded by the Intelligence Corps, who would share their precious information with SAS teams only once they had assembled at Pontrilas for their compulsory period of isolation in the days before departing on a mission.

'I don't know what it took to put this together, Freddy, but it's looking rather like an official operation,' Black said.

'Not exactly, Leo. No one likes to be too precise, but we're what the Committee has termed "irregular extraordinary". Cooperation from the Regiment this end but no official cover once we're out in the field – including for the two extra pairs of hands I've negotiated for you.' Responding to Black's look of surprise, he said: 'I couldn't send you alone, Leo. You're the only one I could trust to lead such a mission, but not even you can handle something of this scale alone.'

'And what have these two men been told about me? I'm not sure I'd have agreed to a grey op under the command of a man I've never met.'

'A reputation like yours doesn't take much selling to serving troopers, Leo. They both knew Finn and they've been picked. Received their orders straight from the Director.'

'Back up a minute, Freddy. Let's begin with the objective.'

'In an ideal world the Venezuelan government would simply hand our people back unharmed. But of course we would first have to prove they're there and being held against their will.'

'So this is a reconnaissance mission?'

'Not exactly.'

Black gave a slow nod and waited for further clarification. Insisting on drip-feeding unpalatable information was yet another of Towers' many infuriating habits.

'This is how it looks to me. We can safely assume that Sabre have invested heavily in a highly secretive operation with the blessing of their Venezuelan hosts. We all know the rules of the diplomatic game – if we were to establish the presence of the hostages we could only expect a protracted series of persistent denials, while meanwhile Sabre remove the evidence and shift their operations elsewhere. The Committee has concluded that for all practical purposes we have only one small bite of the cherry.'

Black glanced impatiently at his watch. 'Is this going to take all day? I could be doing something useful, like fixing my roof.'

Towers tapped the tips of his fingers together, his features twitching uncomfortably. 'Much as we feel for the hostages, safeguarding our national security is the principal priority. I'm certain Sabre have turned a number of our agents. I admit we're all speculating on the basis of limited evidence, but on my advice the Committee has concluded that what we're dealing with is a private mercenary army that diversified into the espionage business. Having skilfully succeeded in cornering the market in the commodity of the day, like all ambitious men Mr Mathis needed another challenge. He's made each of his many fortunes anticipating the *next big thing*. What more valuable commodity is there in this globalized world than information? For a relatively small investment his spies were able to go to scientific conferences, meet scientists, seduce a few government agents and, hey presto, they got their hands on some of the hottest intellectual property on the planet. It was too exciting for Mathis to resist. He had to have it by whatever means. He had a ready-made facility in one of the most inaccessible places on earth and decided to turn it into his R & D department. It's the perfectly logical thing to do. Surprisingly commonplace, in fact. It isn't much talked about, but I can tell you for certain, Leo, there are a number of countries in the world more than happy, for a fee, to host the most unethical forms of scientific research. I have concrete evidence that there are biological weapons being developed by Western scientists in laboratories in the Middle East that are the stuff of nightmares.'

Black peered through the fog of Towers' meandering speech and tried to discern its meaning. 'So this is a sabotage mission? You want the facility destroyed.'

'That would be the most desirable outcome.'

'And the four scientists?'

'I'm sure you'll do what you can ... but in the grand scheme of things, I'm afraid they're a lesser consideration.' He turned back to his computer and hit several more keys. 'At last! Come and look at this.'

Black came alongside Towers as he homed in on a satellite map of an area of south-eastern Venezuela, deep in the Amazonian rainforest close to the Brazilian border. One of the most impenetrable areas on the planet, inaccessible by road and navigable only on foot or by canoe. He zoomed in further until the images on the screen were of such high definition they might have been filmed from a low-flying aircraft.

'This area here is the Parima Tapirapecó National Park. The only thing approximating a town for hundreds of miles is this place – Platanal.' He pointed to a cluster of buildings on the banks of a wide river that ran through the dense forest: the Orinoco. 'Our focus of interest is fifty miles or so to the east.' He zoomed in further on what appeared to be a large rectangular clearing in the otherwise unbroken canopy. As the resolution increased, the area revealed itself to be an opencast mine working with a number of buildings positioned in a grid formation at its western end.

'This photograph was taken exactly a month ago,' Towers said. 'Now look at this.' He brought a second image up on screen alongside the first depicting the same area. The date at its foot showed it to be two years old. The difference between them was striking. 'Two years ago a clearing of approximately ten acres appeared. It's hard to see beneath the canopy, but here and there you catch glimpses of a dirt track that you can just about trace all the way back to the airstrip at Platanal. Now look at last month. The clearing has trebled in size. There are mine workings this end and more than half a dozen substantial buildings at the other.' He zoomed in further. They could now make out vehicles – earth movers and a number of pick-up trucks – and grainy clusters of pixels that were distinguishable as workers on the site. 'Look at the roof of this building – three, four, five satellite dishes. You don't need all those to run a mine. It's a communications station. And look at this area on the right – a helipad. And, over here, what looks like a military parade ground.'

'Can we go tighter?'

Towers went to maximum resolution. The helicopter had five rotor blades and the bulky body of a large heavy-lifting machine. They were looking at a machine capable of carrying thirty personnel or a five-ton cargo.

'That would certainly get their coltan to market,' Towers said.

Black scoured the blurred image and picked out the other necessary components of a permanent off-grid base. Besides the six substantial buildings at the heart of the complex, there were large above-ground fuel tanks, a water tower and various smaller buildings necessary to house pumps, generators and maintenance equipment. It was impressive. As sophisticated as any of the similar operations he had come across in far more developed parts of Africa.

'We're sure it's coltan they're mining here?'

'It's sited right in the Orinoco arc, where all the major known deposits are to be found,' Towers said.

Black considered the alternative explanations to this being Sabre's enterprise and by a process of elimination discounted them. No commercial mining company would choose such a remote location with no infrastructure unless they had an ulterior motive. But it was also sufficiently accessible to get personnel in and out. A fifteen-minute helicopter flight got you to the airstrip at Platanal, which was sufficient to land a Gulfstream or even something a little larger. From Platanal it was only a little over 1,000 miles to Cayenne, French Guiana. Two hours' flying time.

'What do you think?' Towers said. 'Can three of you take it out?'

Black looked at the huge swathe of rainforest on the screen and tried to imagine a fifty-mile hike through its midst loaded with ammunition and kit. He had been in his mid-thirties and at his physical peak when he had last undertaken anything comparable.

'I don't feel I've been given much of a choice.'

'You'll be in your element. Think of it as research. The new enemy – private armies in the Amazon. I bet you didn't see this one coming.' Towers laughed, as if it were all a fantastic joke. *He* was certainly in his element. One of the bravest armchair soldiers in the world.

Still smiling to himself, Towers got up from his chair, crossed to the window and looked out towards the open fields that lay beyond the camp. 'It really is a most peculiar world we live in, Leo. The great powers continue to spend trillions on fighters and aircraft carriers, but the real battles are being fought in different realms entirely, against enemies we can't even identify. We're all groping in the dark, not knowing who to trust. Who's for us, who's against us? We don't even understand their motives, if indeed they have any beyond the obvious. I couldn't tell you whose interests Sabre represents and nor could all the spooks in Vauxhall . . . It certainly makes you wonder. Who knows who is in whose pocket in this brave new world?'

He continued to gaze out at the landscape, prolonging his meditation for a long silent moment, then turned abruptly. 'Fancy some lunch? They'll be waiting for us.'

'Who will?'

'The others!'

Black struggled to keep Towers' Jaguar in sight as he drove at high speed along the narrow Herefordshire lanes. If he had met a tractor or a milk tanker, he would have been crushed, but he rode his luck and it held, as it always had. After several miles they arrived in the hamlet of Tillington, which was little more than a cluster of houses set among apple orchards. Towers braked abruptly and pulled over into the car park of the Bell Inn.

He was already waiting impatiently outside his car by the time Black drew up next to him. 'Thought you'd never make it.'

He strode off across the grass towards the beer garden.

Black followed towards an unlikely scene for a meeting with his potential comrades in arms. Couples and family groups were enjoying lunch in the afternoon sun. A play area was busy with excited children. Towers headed for a table at the far end of the lawn beneath a spreading cherry tree, where two men in their mid-thirties, both dressed in shorts and T-shirts, were seated at a table drinking pints of lager.

'Sorry we're late, chaps,' Towers said. 'Leo Black, Sergeant Chris Riley and Lieutenant Ed Fallon. I believe you've already met.'

'Hello again,' Black said as the two men he had first seen at Finn's funeral rose to exchange handshakes. 'What have you done to deserve this?'

'We volunteered,' Riley said. 'We must be off our heads.' He laughed. Fallon, the quieter of the two, gave a faint smile.

'Steaks all round?' Towers asked and was met with nods of approval. 'Another drink, gentlemen? Excellent.' He set off for the bar, not waiting for a reply.

'I don't know what Freddy said to persuade you,' Black

said, taking a seat on the wooden bench and feeling the warmth of the sun on his face. 'If I'd been in your position, I wouldn't have been in any hurry to set out with some has-been I'd not worked with before.'

'That's Fireballs,' Riley said. 'You don't say no to him, do you?'

'Finn talked a lot about you,' Fallon added quietly. 'That helped. We feel like we know you.'

Black smiled and nodded, appreciating the compliment. It was good to know Finn had spoken well of him despite his neglect.

'How much has Freddy told you?'

'Briefed us this morning,' Fallon said, reaching for his glass.

'What do you make of it?'

'Fucking insane,' Riley said, 'but that's what we live for, isn't it?' He grinned broadly and necked the remains of his pint.

And then Black felt it.

The old thrill.

He was going to war.

39

Sarah Bellman watched Professor Kennedy inject the pieces of fruit with a liquid that would carry nanoparticles into the digestive tracts of the four macaques crouching listlessly in their cage. She noticed a tremor in his normally steady hands. His skin had taken on an unhealthy grey pallor as if he were coming down with a fever and he looked a decade older than his sixty-five years. The breezy, permanently cheerful man she had worked alongside for five years was reduced to a silent, brooding ghost of his former self.

She knew the reason why. She was young enough to spend several years in obscurity and later emerge from their ordeal to redefine herself, but this was the end of her mentor's career. What they were about to achieve here in this place would be his legacy: a black stain that would cancel out forty years of pioneering work.

Kennedy dropped the syringe into the trash, lowered himself stiffly on to a chair and gestured for her to continue.

Bellman pulled on a pair of gauntlets, opened the principal cage and reached for one of the two male macaques – the friendliest and most amenable of the four. He clung to her hand like an infant to its mother. Even through the layer of tough fabric that separated them, she felt the warmth of his belly and the rapid beating of his heart as she transferred him to a smaller cage on a bench at the side of the room. She placed him inside, secured the door, then fed several pieces of fruit into the feeding chute. Having been starved for several hours in readiness, he devoured them greedily. Bellman stared, entranced, at his tiny semi-human face and marvelled at the fractional differences in genetic make-up that separated this creature from a human being.

They waited for ten minutes for the nanoparticles to be delivered through the monkey's bloodstream to their target. Sarah attempted to lighten the atmosphere with small talk, but the professor was too deep in thoughts of his own to engage. She wanted to ask him what he was thinking, whether he was as appalled by the perversion of their work as she was, but decided to spare him. He had a wife, three adult children and a clutch of grandchildren to think about. One day soon he would have to answer to them. She guessed that in his silence he was composing his defence or even his confession.

An alarm sounded the end of their wait. If their modelling was correct, the particles would now be attached to the target cells, primed and ready to activate.

Without exchanging a word Bellman and Kennedy went about their tasks. While Kennedy recorded the experiment on a video camera, she produced a small red chew-toy, moulded, for reasons known only to the manufacturer, into the shape of a bear. She poked it through the bars and quickly turned to her computer.

With her finger poised ready to hit the key that would play a short burst of white noise the moment their subject's skin came in contact with the toy, she waited and watched. The monkey approached the unfamiliar object cautiously, searching for signs of life or danger. He studied it for a while and only when he was sure that it posed no immediate threat reached out a tentative finger and prodded.

Bellman hit *play*.

A sound like a burst of static resounded around the room. The codes it contained activated the nanoparticles, stimulating the target cells. The effect was instantaneous. The macaque took a step backwards as if suddenly having to correct his balance, then, without any trace of fear, picked up the toy with both hands. Sarah played the sound a second time, reinforcing the program. The monkey clung to the plastic bear and rolled over on his back, all four of his limbs wrapped around it.

They allowed him to hold on to it for a full minute before Sarah opened the cage door and attempted to prise it away. The macaque screamed and kicked and scrabbled, holding on to its new possession as if his life depended on it. Finally, Sarah used her superior strength to tear it away from him and slammed the cage door shut. The macaque shook the bars and screamed and screamed with wild, staring eyes.

'For God's sake, let him have it,' Kennedy said.

'But surely we need to observe the tailing off —'

'Give it to him. I can't stand the noise.'

Bellman pushed the plastic bear back into the cage. The macaque grabbed it and instantly fell silent, wrapping it once again in a tight embrace. What she observed in the monkey's expression was the closest thing to a state of ecstasy that she had ever seen. Its eyes were closed, its face fixed in an expression of bliss.

This result was both shocking and thrilling and far beyond anything they had anticipated. But as soon as her initial amazement had passed, Bellman was gripped by an overwhelming sense of terror at the possibilities it unlocked.

'What have we done?' she said.

Kennedy replied in a flat monotone. 'We made a monkey like a plastic toy.'

She turned to look at him. There was no need for words — they understood each other perfectly.

Somehow, this had to be stopped.

40

The British Airways Boeing 747 was cruising at 40,000 feet over the mid-Atlantic. After a brief stop at Madrid it was now en route for Caracas. Black settled back into his cattle-class seat and closed his eyes, hoping that the two miniatures of whisky he had downed would be enough to send him to sleep. It was eight hours until touchdown and he knew he could do with all the rest he could get. Across the aisle, Riley and Fallon were already dozing. He envied their ability to shut down at will. As a younger man, he, too, had been able to sleep anywhere, any time. It was part of the make-up of the active soldier. The body adopted the rhythms of a wild animal: it was either hyper-alert or switched off and recharging itself.

The nine days since his first meeting with his new comrades had passed in a blur and produced far from satisfactory results, which was no doubt the reason he couldn't sleep. The office in Credenhill had become the headquarters for their off-the-books operation. Cooped up together for ten hours a day, the four of them had attempted to stitch together a plan that stood an outside chance of success. They had been thwarted at almost every turn.

Their original intention had been to arrange a shipment of arms to the friendly, English-speaking country of Guyana, where they would charter an aircraft from which they would parachute at night into Platanal. Towers pulled all the strings available to him in the Foreign Office, but word came back that Guyana was not prepared to sanction any action that might place it at odds with its South American neighbours. Less still was it prepared to act quickly. It was a small country determined to shake off its colonial past. Jumping when London said jump was no longer something it was prepared to do.

With Guyana's rejection Towers' capital at the Foreign Office was exhausted and he was politely reminded by the Committee that his remit was to operate insofar as he could without assistance from the normal channels. He had licence and a budget, but he was to retreat as far back into the shadows as possible and take care to stay there.

The team had two problems to crack: arms and transport. Caracas was roughly six hundred miles from Platanal across inhospitable country, much of it jungle. The only feasible way in was by air. Chartering a local aircraft from Britain was an impossibility. Venezuela was a bankrupt and unstable state that nevertheless maintained a large intelligence network loyal to the government. No one who was still managing to run a business wanted to risk doing a deal over the phone with an unknown foreigner. They all gave the same reply: come and speak to us in person, and bring cash.

Acquiring arms was an even tougher proposition. Despite the fact that Venezuela was swimming with them – underpaid soldiers and police officers had flooded the black market with weapons which were bought by the criminal gangs that roamed the Caracas slums – the problem was finding a reliable source. Where to begin? Three gringos with a fistful of dollars stood little chance of emerging from the lawless barrios with much more than empty pockets and their lives. If they were lucky.

They had reached a dead end and for a period of twenty-four hours came close to abandoning the mission. Every angle had been exhausted. Then Towers had woken in the middle of the night with the bright idea of playing the enemy at its own game. In typically impulsive fashion, he drove to London before dawn and spent the day touring the city's private security companies in search of someone who could get him a line into the Venezuelan arms trade. By close of business he had a result. A former Scotland Yard commander, now working for a company named Impel that specialized in safeguarding corporate assets in hazardous territories, came up with a trusted contact in Caracas. His man had helped arm British and American personnel assigned to protect Canadian mining executives setting up shop in the city. Impel collected £20,000 for a name and an email address, and Towers had the excuse he had been longing for to book three plane tickets.

In the following days of furious activity Towers had organized three clean passports with assistance and had pored over maps and satellite photographs, plotting routes through the jungle to the last yard. It was all a fine distraction from the principal challenges, which, in his customary way, he had managed to relegate to the level of mere details to be overcome on the ground.

Meanwhile, Black, Riley and Fallon had refreshed their jungle survival skills with help from a resident expert, Sergeant Jimmy 'Sasquatch' Fletcher. In a Nissen hut in Pontrilas, he took them through the techniques they would need to survive alone in the rainforest equipped with nothing more than a knife and a stomach strong enough to hold down a meal of grubs and roots. When Fletcher made them dig for worms and swallow them still alive and squirming, Black was transported back to his earliest days of basic training. The Sasquatch parroted precisely the same words the Company Sergeant Major had barked at new recruits in the early nineties: 'If you puke, I want to see you scoop it up and eat it again!'

Returning to his vomit had seemed an appropriate metaphor while on his hands and knees in a muddy field, trying to stop his lurching stomach from spewing its contents. But Black hadn't puked. He had held it down. Riley and Fallon, though, had both heaved repeatedly.

Black may have had the stronger stomach, but the two younger men had both got the better of him in the ring. Sparring in the gym at Credenhill, Black discovered that while he still had the muscle memory, the whip and snap had gone from his limbs. He was strong enough, but at close quarters his fractionally slower reflexes rendered him clumsy by comparison. The answer, he learned, after collecting several bruised ribs, was to compensate for lack of speed with brutality. If he engaged, it had to be with lethal intent. Feint to the head, heel to the groin, sweep to the ground, boot to the skull. Not pretty, but effective. When they had switched the rules of the game from first man down to kill or be killed, Black had more than held his own.

'You're a proper evil fucker,' Riley had said with grudging admiration, as he picked himself off the canvas for the fifth time, Black's foot having stopped an inch short of his temple.

Black had enjoyed the praise but reminded himself that Riley's choice of words was quite wrong. There was nothing evil in wanting to live more than the other man. Survival was always the main objective. In over two decades of combat it had been his credo and it was why he was still drawing breath.

The intense preparations – the training, planning and anticipation – had been all-consuming, occupying every inch of his mental space except for one small quarter: he hadn't been in touch with Karen since they parted on an angry note. He felt guilty at leaving her alone and ashamed at his necessary lack of communication. And secretly, hardly even daring to admit it to himself, he was frightened that he wouldn't see her again, that he might never have the chance to feel her touch.

The aircraft shuddered as they entered a patch of turbulence. The seat-belt sign illuminated. Black glanced out of the window and saw lightning fork across the night sky. The plane dipped suddenly through a pocket of warm air, causing the hull to shake then thud as firmly as if they had landed on solid ground. A number of passengers exclaimed in alarm. On the seat-back screen in front of him, a graphic of the aircraft's progress showed that they were still two thousand miles from land. As far out over the ocean as it was possible to be. The pilot's smoothly understated voice came over the loudspeakers. He warned them that they would be skirting a storm and that the ride might be a little bumpy for a while. The couple occupying the two seats to Black's right held hands, and in whispered Spanish the wife muttered a prayer.

Black pulled down the blind and finally felt the welcome pull of sleep. With an image of Karen's face playing behind his eyes he let the movement of the plane rock him like a baby.

Black woke, refreshed, to the sound of the undercarriage descending and locking into position. He lifted the blind and looked out to see that they were flying parallel to the Venezuelan coast on their approach to Simón Bolívar International Airport. Large-scale industrial units were spread along the inland plain to the south, and columns of white smoke rose from the chimneys of a power station. The coastal strip resembled that of any other modern country – a product of Chavez's brief oil-fuelled miracle – but only a few miles beyond the wooded mountains with their summits lost in halos of cloud were a reminder that this was a country whose precarious pockets of civilization had only recently been carved from wilderness.

The cabin crew took their seats for landing. Black glanced across the aisle and saw that Riley and Fallon were awake and already in character. Both had their noses buried in tourist guidebooks. To avoid unnecessary complications, and because Venezuela required no visas for British tourists, all three were travelling under their own names with their passports declaring them to be civil servants. They had reservations for accommodation in Cainama National Park and rucksacks filled with hiking equipment to back up their cover story: they were three colleagues from the Birmingham tax office who had come on a charity hike and to visit the world-famous Angel Falls.

Black turned his gaze out of the window and watched the ground come slowly up to meet them. There were palm trees at the airport's margins. Traffic was moving to and fro along the wide approach roads and the whole scene basked in brilliant tropical sun. The murder capital of the world couldn't have looked more inviting.

The plane touched down and taxied to the stand. Minutes later Black, Riley and Fallon were queuing along with the other weary passengers in the line for passport control. In the airport, at least, there was a glossy illusion of normality. The walls were decorated with colourful advertisements for luxury brands and posters depicting the country's famous sites. But despite the atmosphere of friendly welcome there was little sign of genuine tourists among their fellow passengers. Most were locals returning from trips to Europe. Of those that weren't, the majority were business travellers – middle-aged men already checking their phones and calling drivers who would whisk them away to homes in one of the capital's gated and fortified communities.

Black was the first of the three to step up to the passport officer's booth. The poker-faced female official, one of the same breed that exist at border crossings the world over, glanced from Black's tired, unshaven face to the image in the passport, then swept it under a reader. Tense seconds elapsed while the computer digested the information.

'The reason for your visit?' she asked in English.

'My friends and I are going hiking. We hope to see the Angel Falls.'

The official looked at him dubiously, but the computer had come up with no reason not to let him pass.

'Enjoy your trip.'

Black smiled amiably. 'Thank you.' He carried on through to the baggage reclaim.

Fallon followed soon after him. Riley, who had chosen to queue at the alternate booth, presented his passport to an older male officer, who regarded him with a lizard eye.

'You're going to Cainama, eh?'

'That's right.'

The officer nodded. 'Your government advises tourists to avoid our country.'

Riley shrugged. 'We did our research. We thought it was safe enough in the east.'

The officer nodded, keeping his thoughts on the subject to himself. He waved Riley through, but before dealing with the next passenger lifted the phone and dialled the extension number for the desk of the SEBIN, the Bolivian National Intelligence Service.

The call was answered by a bored male voice, thickened by too many cheap cigarettes.

'This is passport control,' the officer said. 'Three English-men just came through claiming to be tourists on their way to the Falls. Male fifty, dark hair; male thirties, light brown hair; male thirties, shaved head. Just a feeling. They're in baggage reclaim.'

'I'll take a look.'

In his windowless office next door to the Customs zone, the SEBIN officer, Luis Romero, lit another Belmont and ran his eye across an array of monitors relaying images from security cameras positioned around the airport. He settled on the feeds from the international baggage reclaim area and spotted the three pale-skinned men. He zoomed in to take a close look at them. Business travellers were invariably impatient and on edge while waiting for their luggage to arrive and tourists to Venezuela were usually nervous, given to checking their passports and patting their wallets zipped inside their clothes. There was nothing twitchy about these three. They joked and chatted like three friends on an adventure would, but they were a touch too calm for Romero's liking. Prospectors working for some international conglomerate perhaps? Usually, they were Americans or Canadians eager to extend their rape of Central America down into the southern landmass – if you were foolhardy enough, Venezuela was a cheap place to do business. British tourists were rare but not unknown, particularly adventurous sorts heading out to the national parks like these claimed to be.

Romero vacillated, then decided to have them followed. If they turned out not to be tourists, perhaps they might be heading to an office in Caracas where he might net some even bigger fish.

Meanwhile, Black, Riley and Fallon passed through Customs and made their way to the car rental desk. The booking had been made online in the local currency, bolivars. Five days' hire of a Toyota Hilux SUV was the equivalent of £1,700. Most of the cost went to insurance. The odds of a rental car being hijacked currently ran at one in two hundred. It was a small miracle that an international company bothered to operate a concession at all.

The desk clerk, an immaculately made-up and well-spoken young woman, checked the reservation and looked up at Black apologetically. 'My apologies, sir. We no longer have any SUVs available. Only compacts.'

Black glanced at the others. A compact was out of the question. 'Then perhaps you'd be good enough to cancel the booking and direct me to somewhere where we can get one.'

'No one has an SUV, sir. Compacts only.'

'We made this reservation forty-eight hours ago.'

'Again, my apologies. Unfortunately, I have no control over what is advertised on the website. Would you like the compact?'

'Hold on.' Fallon went over to the plate-glass window and looked out to the car park. Identical rental vehicles were parked side by side in order of size. Compacts, intermediates, sedans and SUVs. He strolled back. 'They've got ten of them out there.'

Black turned back to the girl. 'Would you call your manager? I'd like to speak to whoever is in charge.'

Her pleasant expression faded and her eyes hardened. 'He will ask you for five hundred dollars. I will take three hundred. Cash.'

'And if I don't want to pay you three hundred?'

'Is this your first time in Caracas?' Black didn't answer. He didn't have to. She already knew. 'We all have to eat. On the plus side gasoline is cheaper than water. Five cents a gallon.' She shrugged. 'My country.'

Black reached into his jacket and brought out his wallet. He peeled off six $50 bills and pushed them across the desk.

The girl tucked them into a drawer and found her smile again. 'Automatic or stick shift?'

They stepped out from the cool of the airport's air-conditioned interior into a humid wall of heat and sunlight so sharp it hurt their eyes. By the time they had walked thirty yards to the car Black's shirt was already glued to his back by a thick film of perspiration. The black Hilux had a four-door cab in the front and a covered pick-up bed in which they stowed their rucksacks. Riley was the appointed driver and Fallon the navigator. Black had the privilege of being the back-seat passenger. They headed out of the airport and on to the Avenida La Armada, then navigated the junction that filtered them on to the Autopista Caracas, the main road to the capital, which sat in a steep-sided valley fifteen miles inland.

The modern highway, paid for by the petro-boom of the previous decade, was identical to any in the richest countries, but that was where all similarity with the First World ended. Cars clung on to each other's tails, swerved in and out of lanes without warning, horns honking and all at terrifying speed. It reminded Black of the lawless frenzy of Libya or Nigeria, where to be caught in a jam or marooned at the side of the highway was a sure invitation to robbery or kidnap. If the neurosis of a country could be judged by its traffic, Venezuela was on the edge of a breakdown.

Riley stuck to the inside lane, his eyes flicking by professional instinct between the mirrors, while Fallon called out every landmark and bend in the road in advance. He was a good advertisement for his training: he had studied the maps and committed every detail of the route to memory. Leaving them to their tasks, Black began the process of making contact with their local fixer, whom Towers had assured him was primed and ready to assist with their two necessities. He took out his phone and dialled his number.

After several rings the call connected to a generic voice-mail message. He waited for the tone. 'Good morning, Mr Cordero. Leo Black speaking. I look forward to meeting you later today. Perhaps you would be kind enough to call me back on this number?'

It was a message calculated to send the signal that Black was neither nervous nor skittish. He intended to give Cordero all the confidence he needed to complete his side of the bargain.

Black's phone rang less than two minutes later, Cordero's number flashing up on the screen.

'Mr Cordero?'

'I will send you an SMS. You will erase it. Please, no more phone calls. Goodbye.' He rang off.

Cordero had sounded distinctly tense, which Black took as a good sign of a man who had placed himself out on a limb for financial gain. If he had greeted him with grace and geniality, Black's alarm bells would have rung instantly. The duplicitous were always charming.

As promised, a text message promptly arrived: *Catedral de Caracas, Plaza Bolívar 19.00.* An unusual choice for a black-market arms deal but better than a back alley. Black allowed himself to feel hopeful.

The highway swept around the base of the mountain and the skyline of Caracas came into view. Skyscrapers and high-rise apartment buildings thrust up from the valley floor and chaotically stacked, brightly painted slum dwellings covered the surrounding hillsides. Even from a distance the simmering energy of the cauldron-like city that was home to three million souls was palpable.

They entered the outlying barrios where the traffic began

to mount but without slowing down. The lane swapping grew to a level of insanity. Riley was repeatedly forced to jam on the brakes as the taxis and motorbikes, which had joined the fray in large numbers, cut in front of him at will.

'These fuckers must have a death wish,' was all Riley had to say, and slowly shook his head in the way most Englishmen do when confronted with inexplicable foreign madness.

The city had started to close in around them when Black noticed Fallon staring hard into the wing mirror.

'What have you seen?'

'Black Lexus, two cars back. It's been with us for the last five k. Two male occupants.'

Black glanced over his shoulder and caught sight of the Lexus tucked in behind an elderly rust-coloured Ford. 'Leave at the next exit.'

Riley nodded.

Fallon glanced up at the overhead signs. 'Exit approaching, four hundred metres.'

Riley kept up a steady fifty miles per hour, approached the slip road and at the last moment turned the wheel sharply to the right. A chorus of car horns erupted. Black glanced back and saw the Lexus one hundred yards behind them.

'They're still following,' Fallon said. 'They're not bad.'

'What's it to be, boss?' Riley said.

Black made a swift calculation. If they were being tailed by cops hoping to squeeze out a bribe, they could deal with them, but if they were already under surveillance, they were in trouble. Descriptions of them and their vehicle would already be circulating.

'Act like we're lost. Pretend not to have seen them.'

Riley pulled up at the next junction and prevaricated, indicating one way, then the other, making a good job of appearing like a clueless tourist. He turned left and then right, then suddenly right again. The Lexus clung on, although now there were three vehicles separating them. Black issued instructions, leading Riley through a maze of poor, narrow streets. Groups of idle, bare-chested men stood smoking on corners, women hung out washing on lines attached by pulleys to either side of the street and in every gutter there were skinny barefoot children.

'I've think we've lost them, boss,' Riley said.

Black glanced behind. He could see for two clear blocks and there was no sign of the Lexus. They emerged on to a busy market street. Beaten-up scooters and pick-ups moved at a crawl through a swarm of people picking over stalls heaped with fruit, plantain and bunches of green beans.

'Plan B. We need to split up. Park the vehicle under cover and find somewhere else to stay. Message me the address. I'll catch up with you after I've met Cordero.'

'Roger.'

'See you later.'

Riley slowed. Black jumped out and melted into the crowd with a feeling that things were destined not to run smoothly.

He had no idea just how accurate his instincts would prove to be.

41

If you want to survive, act more native than the natives. It was advice from basic training that had saved his skin many times from Luanda to Kabul. Wearing a fake Dodgers baseball cap bought from a market stall, Black walked quickly through the slow-moving crowds, shaking off the emaciated beggars with a gruff *'¡Lárgate!'* – get lost – and ignoring the dead-eyed gazes of the young men he took to be lookouts for the local street gangs stationed on the corners of each block. Harder to ignore were the beckoning smiles of the beautiful bare-legged prostitutes who were never far from them. He quickly realized that the outward impression of a feral free-for-all was an illusion. This was a neighbourhood carved up into small, strictly controlled territories watched over by eyes both visible and invisible.

Black's intention had been to book a room in a small out-of-the-way *pensión* where he could hole up while he made his deal with Cordero, leaving Riley and Fallon to concentrate on keeping out of sight, but after only a few minutes on the teeming streets he concluded that nowhere outside the centre of the city would be safe. A stranger stood no less chance of passing unnoticed here than in the remotest upland village. Aside from its unrivalled homicide rate, Caracas was also a world leader in kidnappings for ransom and now he understood why. He needed to head west but to turn down the side streets that would take him in that direction would mean leaving himself exposed and isolated. For the present he was best sticking with the crowds. Safety in numbers.

He continued to move confidently with the flow, pausing here and there to look at the stalls, playing the part of a shopper hoping to find something in particular. He had made it almost to the end of the street and could see a wider thoroughfare up ahead where he might stand a chance of catching a bus or a taxi, when a slightly built young man, little more than a teenager, fell into step behind him.

Black pretended he hadn't noticed and pressed on, manoeuvring between the shoppers and through a small crowd that had stopped to listen to a pair of street musicians playing samba. Forty yards to the main road. He saw a taxi go by and resolved to hail the first one he could find.

He was almost at the junction when a beaten-up white Chevrolet, a gas-guzzling relic from a previous era, pulled across the end of the market street. The two shaven-headed figures who climbed out of it were no corner boys. Black altered course to pass the rear end of the car. They stepped in front of him.

The shorter of the two greeted him with a gap-toothed smile. His sunburned scalp was covered with a sheen of sweat as if he'd been in a hurry to get here. Black realized that he must have been spotted and claimed as booty the moment he got out of the Hilux. The boy who had tipped off these two had been marking him all the way along the street.

'American?'

'No. *Perdóneme* –'

Black stepped to the side and immediately felt a hand placed firmly to his chest.

'Uh-uh. *Billetera*.'

The man wanted his wallet.

The smile evaporated. His companion stepped up close behind his left shoulder. His face was lined and scarred and his thick neck decorated with a badly inked spider's web. A thug. Passers-by quickened their pace and averted their eyes. It was more than their lives were worth to challenge these petty tyrants.

Black had no option. Number two was already reaching around to the back of his jeans. He stepped forward, spun on his right foot and swung his full weight behind his left elbow, which he slammed into the gap-toothed gangster's throat. It was a clean hit straight to the larynx. Enough to crush it. A fatal injury unless a paramedic arrived in time to cut open his windpipe. The man dropped to his knees. Black caught Spider's right arm as it came up with a hand-gun and drove the heel of his right palm upwards into his already flattened nose. His head jerked back, rocking him off balance. Black rammed a knee hard into his groin. The double shock caused the gun to drop from his fingers and he folded at the waist. Black took a half-step back and chopped hard into the back of his neck, midway between his skull and shoulders. His legs splayed. He staggered forward in the comical way of a baby giraffe taking its first steps, then, as all nervous activity ceased, toppled face first into the tarmac.

Under the stares of the astonished onlookers Black grabbed the gun from between the two prone bodies and jumped behind the wheel of the Chevrolet. He fumbled the ignition, selected drive and stamped on the throttle, leaving behind the smell of scorched rubber to mingle with the street's aroma of rotting fruit and roasting coffee beans.

Black drove several blocks on the busy road, checking his mirrors for pursuers. None came. He cut left through side streets, found another main road and followed a sign to CENTRO URBO.

Block by block, the pervading sense of poverty diminished. After several miles he had left the ramshackle tenements and apartment buildings behind and found himself in a leafy neighbourhood that could have been a suburb of a Mediterranean city. There were bars and cafés and shops with goods in the window. The traffic was of a better class, too; most of the vehicles were less than twenty years old. The Chevrolet began to stand out. Time to dump it. He turned into a quiet street of low-rise villas and pulled over. He left the keys in the ignition as a small act of charity for whoever found it, crammed the pistol into the money belt he wore under his shirt and made his way back to the main road, where he joined the huddle waiting at the nearest bus stop.

Half an hour later Black was sipping a cold beer and eating a swordfish steak with a side of mango and pomegranate salad in the air-conditioned comfort of a downtown restaurant. He had chosen one a short walk from the National Assembly building, working on the assumption that it was likely to be the safest part of town and the last place anyone who might be searching for a desperado would be likely to look. The surrounding tables were occupied by suited professionals engaged in animated discussions over working lunches. He counted two other pale-skinned foreigners in the room, which meant that for the first time since setting foot on Venezuelan soil he passed unnoticed. Here he was just another member of the small privileged caste insulated from the harshness of the streets beyond. Relishing his welcome anonymity, he blanked the memory of his unfortunate encounter at the market and savoured his meal.

Dessert or just a coffee? A WhatsApp message from Fallon interrupted his dilemma: *Hotel Ávila. Avenida Este 3. $s talk. Cocktails by the pool. Missing you already.*

He messaged back: *No problems?*

All good.

Enjoy it while it lasts. ETA 20.00.

The waitress reappeared and greeted him with a smile. *'Señor?'*

'Espresso, por favor. Y un gran cônac.'

What the hell? He had more than three hours to kill before meeting Cordero. He would linger over his digestif, then maybe take in a sight or two.

Black emerged from the National Museum of Architecture on to the Avenida Bolívar to find that darkness had descended. The short tropical days always took him by surprise. In Caracas the sun vanished from the sky at roughly six p.m. and rose precisely twelve hours later from January through to December. There was no winter, spring or autumn. Just one long sweat interrupted by the occasional deluge.

To the steady drumbeat of cicadas he made his way two blocks north and four to the west through the government district, towards the Plaza Bolívar. There, in the tree-lined square, families had gathered to enjoy the relative cool of the evening. Children scampered and fat old women sat gossiping on benches while the men played cards and dominoes at fold-up tables, smoking bitter-smelling cigars.

Black checked his phone. There was no message from Cordero.

He proceeded across the square with caution, appearing casual but alive to every possibility. He could only guess at Cordero's appearance, whereas he was sure that Towers would not have left his contact at the same disadvantage. He stood back in the shadows and scanned the square in search of a likely candidate. Seven o'clock came and went. Several minutes passed. Still no sign. There was nothing for it but to place himself in view. He approached the white façade of the colonial-style cathedral that stood at the head of the square and waited to the side of the large central door.

Three more minutes elapsed. Black began to fear that their tail from the airport had sparked a bigger search and that Cordero had got wind of the fact that they were already wanted fugitives. A police officer armed with a semi-automatic rifle wandered past. Black tensed in anticipation of being spotted. The cop glanced vaguely in his direction and moved on.

Cordero was now fifteen minutes late. Black brought out his phone, ready to take the initiative and risk a text to his number.

'Mr Black?'

He looked up from his screen to see an earnest-looking man in his late fifties. He was respectably attired and was clutching a small hardback book.

'Mr Cordero?'

He gave a sideways flick of his head, gesturing Black to follow him inside.

They entered the cathedral where mass was underway. The congregation, concentrated mostly in the front pews, was singing responses while a priest prepared the host at the high altar. The air was thick with incense that hung in ghostly layers around chandeliers suspended from the vaulted ceiling of the nave. Black noticed that otherwise it was strikingly devoid of ornamentation for a Roman Catholic church. A pared-down building that belonged to the New World.

Cordero led the way to a pew at the rear of the right-hand aisle. A few worshippers, absorbed in their devotions, were scattered throughout the rows in front of them. Once installed, Cordero stooped briefly to his knees and crossed himself in what Black took to be a genuine act of piety, or perhaps a plea in advance for absolution.

'I have spoken to Colonel Towers,' Cordero said in the excellent English of an educated man. 'I am assured of your credentials and I trust he is assured of mine.'

'You were recommended by impeccable sources,' Black said, engaging in what he felt was a necessary dance.

Cordero nodded and pensively fingered the corner of his book, the cover of which Black could now see bore an embossed gold cross. 'You must understand that this is not my normal line of business. Until recently I was a respected economist in the Ministry of Finance. I hasten to add that I saw it all coming – oil could not hold its price for ever. That was my sin – to challenge the orthodoxy. Sadly, this was not considered a virtue in my country.' He let out a regretful sigh. 'So I am forced to find other means to support my family, although, I assure you, I am not without principles.'

Black felt like a priest hearing the confession of a sinner. 'And I can assure you, Mr Cordero, nor am I. I'm not at liberty to discuss details, but this is not a matter that need trouble your conscience.'

'My country is vulnerable, Mr Black. It has many problems, but its ideals, however misguided, are at least proof of its soul.'

'What can I say, except that I'm here on the side of the angels?'

A smile broke through Cordero's expression of unease. Then he fell quiet, as if he were wrestling with a dilemma. 'I have two names and two numbers for you. The first is that of the man who will provide your hardware. He is an old acquaintance and no friend of our government. You can trust him absolutely. The second is that of a pilot. In other times one of my duties was to arrange shipments of American dollars to foreign territories on behalf of our esteemed politicians. Alas, like all good Marxists, their true love was what they professed to despise. I used this man because he could not help but give the impression of being a criminal. No one would believe him to be in the employment of a government, not even one as disreputable as ours.'

'Did he make his deliveries?'

'He did. But I cannot vouch for any other aspect of his character.'

'Then that's good enough for me. Has Mr Towers wired your payment?'

'Yes. I am much obliged.'

Black waited for Cordero to deliver, but his attention seemed to have been caught by proceedings at the altar.

'Are we ready to conclude business?'

'Of course.' He snapped back from his reverie and handed Black his prayer book. 'Goodbye, my friend.' He stood up from the pew and made his way forward to join the queue for communion.

Black opened the book at a page that had been marked with a folded square of paper. He opened it out to see two names with accompanying mobile phone numbers: Colonel Emmanuel Silva and Gregori Buganov.

A Russian.

As if he needed any more excitement.

42

The Hotel Ávila stood on a busy corner next to a row of abandoned shops, their drawn shutters plastered with vibrant graffiti. Riley was waiting inside the entrance, where he handed Black a key card and delivered the news that he had been kidding: there was no pool, and no restaurant or cocktail bar either. A quick glance around the starkly lit lobby confirmed that the only nod in the direction of hospitality were three defunct vending machines. Hyper-inflation had had many bizarre consequences and the need for a bucket of loose change to purchase a packet of chewing gum had been one of them. Fortunately, the Ávila's machines had found a second life – their dispensing trays were filled to the brim with cigarette butts.

A man with a swollen drinker's face and sweat stains beneath his arms was watching TV behind a reception clad in faded plastic bamboo. He glanced over at Riley as they passed through, acknowledging him with an uptick of the head that suggested that they were on familiar terms.

'Joachim,' Riley said under his breath. 'Speaks good English. Told me he was a structural engineer until the country went bust.'

'What did you tell him about us?'

'That we were in town for a couple of days before heading south. He thinks we're mad to be in Caracas.'

He swiped his card through a reader at the side of a door that led from the lobby to the accommodation. It was faced with wood-effect plastic but as it clicked open it revealed itself to be constructed of three-inch-thick steel plate.

'Joachim told me they put this in after the fifth kidnap,' Riley said.

'Reassuring.'

They went through into a small windowless tiled area. An out-of-service lift was sealed shut with hazard tape.

'The good news is we're only on the second floor,' Riley said, starting up the stairs.

'I feel at home already.'

'Wait till you see your room.'

They walked up the four flights to the second floor. The air in the stairwell was damp and stale. Flies circled lazily beneath the dim fluorescent lights. The building was strangely silent. Not even the hum of an air conditioner.

'Are we the only ones staying here?' Black asked.

'I've a feeling it's the sort of place that might liven up a bit as the night wears on.'

'Great.'

They had two rooms on opposite sides of a tiled corridor. Riley and Fallon were on the right, Black on the left.

'We scraped some rations together,' Riley said. 'See you in ten?'

'Sure.'

Black slotted his card into the lock and entered a darkened room. He switched on the light, sending several large cockroaches skittering beneath the rickety furniture. The room's only saving grace was its plainness. A bed with greying sheets, a desk, chair and an open-fronted wardrobe. All decades old, scuffed and scarred, but functional. There was no carpet, no curtains. The room was lit by a solitary unshaded bulb. Black tugged on the cord of a ceiling fan positioned above the bed. It started to turn and chop through the air.

He nudged open the door to the en suite. A limp towel of a similar colour to the bedsheets hung from a chrome rail. A mirror, cracked across one corner, was screwed to the wall above the basin. Black had stayed in worse. In Gambia he had once been confronted with an entire bathroom wall crawling with colourful insects, some the size of his palm.

He stripped naked, fetched his wash kit from his rucksack and stepped into the shower. His face was scratchy from a day's growth of beard but he resisted shaving, both in the interests of disguising his appearance and of hygiene. Where he was going, even the smallest shaving nick could quickly become an infected and debilitating wound that could make the difference between life and death. The water was hot, at least, and plentiful. He stood underneath the powerful stream, letting it massage the muscles in his back and shoulders.

He felt good. Loose, supple and focused. Better than he had in years. It was the effect of mind and body combining for a single purpose. To those who had never had to risk their lives in action it was an almost indescribable sensation. There was no drug that could emulate it. It wasn't a high – there was no euphoria – nor was there any sense of separation from reality. He could only describe it as a state of attunement. Mental peace married with raw physicality. The elemental condition. And there was a purity to it that left no room for misgivings or self-doubt, which was why, Black presumed, he felt no guilt.

He was glad to be in Caracas.

Showered and refreshed, Black made his way across the corridor to Riley and Fallon's room. It was virtually identical to his except more cramped due to the presence of an extra bed. They dragged the desk into the centre of the room and used it as a table. Needing to hold back their rations for the jungle, dinner comprised the few items they had been able to pick up in the local store – canned beans, hunks of rough bread and strips of dried meat washed down with cans of the local Zulia brand beer. Better than starving, but not by much.

While they ate Riley explained that after dropping Black off at the market, they had driven towards the centre of town and parked in an underground car park beneath an apartment building. It had an armed guard at the entrance and remotely controlled bollards that rose out of the ground. There were BMWs, Mercedes and Cadillacs down there gathering dust, their owners too frightened to drive them for fear of kidnap or a bullet in the head. The fee was twenty dollars per night but they had tipped the guard an extra fifty as an insurance policy. They were as sure as they could be that the vehicle would be there if they needed it.

After checking into the Ávila they had scoured the neighbourhood and found a hole-in-the-wall kiosk where they had picked up a couple of burner phones. They had passed several police in the street but hadn't been stopped. The cops had seemed edgy, as if they had more important things on their minds than bothering a couple of foreigners. Chatting with Joachim on their return, Riley had learned that police were among the most common murder victims in the city. The better armed criminal gangs would shoot them, steal their weapons and disappear into the lawless warren of barrios that lined the hillsides.

Desperate times made for desperate men.

Black kept his encounter with the thugs at the market to himself. His job was to remain in control, not to brag about his exploits. Instead, he told them about his meeting with Cordero and the two names he'd given him.

'I propose that we try to make contact tonight. Any objections?'

It was important to include them all in essential decisions. It left no room for blame.

'Not from me,' Riley said.

'I don't believe anything will be straightforward in this country,' Fallon said, 'but yeah. No point waiting.'

Black used one of the new phones to call Colonel Emmanuel Silva's number. There were four long continuous rings, then a fifth, before a male voice answered abruptly. *'Dígame.'* Speak to me.

'Colonel Silva? I was given your number by Mr Cordero,' Black said in English. 'I think you may be expecting my call.'

'Yes, of course,' the Colonel answered in a refined accent that suggested a Sandhurst education. 'He informed me of your requirements several days ago and I am happy to be able to meet them. The fee is fifty thousand dollars, payable in advance of delivery.'

'Wouldn't fifty per cent in advance be more conventional?'

'Not in Venezuela, Mr Black. Not in times such as these. Please write down these account details. When the money is transferred I will call you back.'

Black placed a hand over the receiver. 'Get me a pen.' He returned to the conversation. 'We're on a tight schedule, Colonel. When might that be?'

'I was hoping tomorrow at dawn.'

'That soon?'

'I would prefer to be relieved of my burden as soon as possible. I'm sure you understand.'

'I'll do my best.'

Fallon retrieved a ballpoint from the pocket of his rucksack. Black grabbed a paper napkin and wrote down the details of an account he presumed was held a long way from Caracas.

'The transfer will be from a London bank?'

'Yes,' Black confirmed.

'Good. These days they are the best kind. I am afraid the Swiss have squandered their reputation for discretion. I hope to speak to you soon, Mr Black.' He rang off.

'So far, so good,' Black reported.

He fetched out the phone he had brought with him from the UK and dialled Towers' number.

He answered instantly. 'Leo? What progress?'

'I've made contact with Cordero's man. He wants fifty thousand dollars up front for a delivery first thing tomorrow. I'll message you his details. He's expecting a transfer tonight.'

'Can we trust him?'

'We have no choice.'

'What about a plane?'

'That's next on the agenda. I have a name and number.'

'You haven't fixed anything?'

'I left Cordero less than two hours ago.'

'Well, hurry up, man.'

Black was suspicious. 'Is there a problem?'

He was met with ominous silence.

'Freddy?'

'Potentially.'

'Meaning?'

Another pause.

'What is it?'

'My contact in '6 had word from the British Embassy in Caracas. They've had contact from the local intelligence service asking if they are aware of any British commercial interests carrying out unauthorized exploratory activities in the interior. The Embassy asked the reason for the enquiry and was told that three English citizens they suspect of being prospectors entered the country this morning. They had your names.'

'We were tailed into Caracas. We must have been picked out at the airport. We lost them.'

'If they're on to you, they're bound to be on to the airlines. All the small operators depend on government contracts. You might have to think about heading south by road.'

'Road? Then what – travel the last three hundred miles by canoe?'

'You'll find some local pilot out in the sticks. They'll be easier to bribe.'

'Freddy, look at the map. It's a big country but there's precious little room to hide. There's only one road in the direction we're heading. I'd rather take my chances with a Russian pilot.'

'Russian?'

'Yes. Cordero gave me a Russian. Probably out of the same mould as some of those pirates we encountered in Africa. Old Soviets who decamped to the few countries with rules slack enough to let them land their ancient Ilyushins.'

'Consider alternatives.'

'Wire the money. We'll be fine.'

Towers was silent.

'Wire it. Goodbye.'

Black ended the call. Riley and Fallon were looking at him expectantly.

'The local intelligence service is looking for us. They think we might be illegal prospectors.'

Fallon shrugged as if it were a minor inconvenient detail.

'It rules out the SUV for picking up the weapons,' Riley said. 'We'll need another vehicle. Can't risk hiring one. We'll have to help ourselves.'

'No hold-ups. I don't want witnesses.'

Riley and Fallon traded a smile.

'We'll be discreet,' Fallon said.

Black nodded and picked up one of the burner phones. He dialled the Russian's number.

Six rings. No answer. Black stayed on the line, waiting. Another six, then another. Then, finally, it connected. A low snarling voice uttered a few incoherent syllables.

'Mr Buganov? My name is Black. I'm a friend of Mr Cordero. I understand you have an aircraft.'

There was a grunt followed by a long inhalation as if Buganov were drawing on a cigarette.

'I would like to charter your plane. Tomorrow if possible.'

'Where you want to go?' His voice was thick and rasping.

'To the south. Platanal. You know it?'

Another grunt. 'Tomorrow not possible.'

'I'll pay your rate plus two thousand dollars, cash. And the same again on return.'

'Day after tomorrow. Wednesday. Tomorrow I work on the plane. Maintenance.'

'Can't it wait?'

'No. Wednesday.'

'All right, Wednesday it is – as long as I have your guarantee there'll be no change of plan.'

'Three thousand dollars. Each way.'

'Two and a half.'

'Forget it.'

Black sighed. 'All right, Mr Buganov. Three thousand dollars each way. You'll have three passengers and two hundred kilos of cargo. Where and when are we to meet you?'

'What cargo?'

'Not the kind you can pass through security.'

'This is a problem.'

'And I'm paying you to solve it.'

Buganov murmured and grumbled under his breath.

'Do we have a deal?'

There was a brief pause during which Black could sense the Russian's resistance weaken and give way.

'Wednesday morning. Ten o'clock.' He gave an address in Charallave, a town fifty kilometres to the south of Caracas where, Black recalled, there was a small internal airport.

'I'll look forward to it.'

Black ended the call. 'He sounds old, drunk and unreliable, but he's all we've got. Unless anyone's got a better idea?'

'Old's good,' Fallon said, reaching for the last remaining piece of dried meat. 'Pilots are like soldiers – the best ones live to tell the tale.' He tossed the scrap into his mouth and chewed, his eyes bright and alive with the anticipation of adventure.

Black sensed that the comment was partially aimed at him – a compliment, perhaps, but it also carried a sting. He was more than aware that in Fallon and Riley's eyes his age made him a potential liability. They needed to know that he still had what it took. They were entrusting their lives to a man with whom they had never stood side by side when bullets were flying. For the sake of morale he would have to prove himself at the first opportunity.

They drank the last of the beers and waited for Silva's return call. It came twenty minutes later. The money had arrived. He gave details of a location on the eastern outskirts of the city where he promised he would be waiting at six a.m. He ended the brief exchange with words from which Black drew a crumb of comfort. 'I think you will be very pleased with the inventory, Mr Black. Very pleased indeed.'

'We're in business,' Black said. 'We'll leave at four thirty, find a vehicle and make our way to the rendezvous. Then we lie low until the following morning. I suggest we camp up somewhere in the hills between here and Charallave.'

His suggestion met with smiles and nods of agreement. They had a plan.

He swept up the few remaining breadcrumbs into an empty beer bottle to use as a cockroach trap and left his two companions to get their heads down.

Black lay awake in the near-darkness, listening to the dull thump-thump-thump from the prostitute's bed in the room above and the sounds of the city leaking through the open window: the rumble of traffic combined with the excitable voices of late-night revellers, church bells that struck every quarter-hour, a crying baby in a nearby apartment, and the distant, sporadic pop-pop of gunshots that to the innocent ear would sound like firecrackers. It was a city that refused to sleep. A city of midwives, gravediggers and thieves.

The bells struck midnight and Black continued to stew in his own sweat. Then he heard them – one, two, three, four – the roaches climbed the paper gangplank and dropped into the empty bottle. For a short while they scrabbled frantically against the glass, then, as if suddenly exhausted, fell still.

Something seemed to settle inside him. He sank into a dreamless sleep.

43

Black woke abruptly to the alarm on his wristwatch. The illuminated display read three thirty a.m. He swung out of bed and felt the welcome cool of the tiles on his bare soles. Only once he was upright did he remember the purpose for getting up in the middle of the night. He was going to steal a car, alone. Unseen. He couldn't afford for the three of them to be seen together. Not by anyone.

He stood under a cold shower and stepped out feeling sharp and alert. He dressed in hiking shorts, desert boots and T-shirt and fetched a small LCD torch and his Leatherman multi-tool from the pocket of his rucksack. Using the tool's wire-cutting jaws, he snipped the hook from the solitary coat hanger in the wardrobe, wound the remaining length small enough to fit in his hip pocket and silently exited the room.

He descended the stairs and opened the door to the lobby, prepared to make small talk with Joachim and play the dumb tourist who couldn't sleep. He needn't have worried. The TV was off, the lights were dimmed and Joachim was slumped in a chair behind the desk snoring like a sow. Black padded across the floor, turned the handle on the inside of the door, secured the latch so that he could let himself back in and stepped outside. He glanced back through the glass to see Joachim still dead to the world.

The hotel stood on a wide street that would once have been a prosperous commercial area on the edge of the central business district. The traffic had thinned to no more than the odd car and delivery truck. Save for several sleeping bodies in nearby doorways there was no one to be seen. Sticking to the shadows, Black walked a block to the east, then turned north into narrower streets lined with apartment buildings.

In the still of the pre-dawn the city seemed almost content. The only clue to its troubled soul was the odd daub of graffiti and the state of the cars. The crashed economy and cheap fuel had made Caracas into a museum of large and ancient American models that reminded him of old movies. In among the battered compacts and pick-ups were Fords, Lincolns, Chevrolets and Pontiacs, with bonnets that stretched six feet in front of their windshields and with boots to match.

He pressed on for three more blocks and spotted the car he wanted on the far side of the street: a mid-brown Pontiac Parisienne. An '85 or thereabouts. Dented, scratched and with missing hubcaps, it was suitably anonymous and big enough to carry three men and their kit. The windows in the surrounding five-storey buildings were unlit. The coast was clear. He stepped out of the shadows and crossed the road.

Arriving at the driver's window, he reached the coil of wire from his pocket, bent the end into a small hook and forced it between the rubber seal and the glass. He worked it up and down, fishing for the lever mechanism that would spring the locks. It was trickier than he remembered. Precious seconds ticked by without any joy. He tried to remain patient. Slowly, the vibrations transferring to his fingertips began to form a picture of what lay inside the door. He isolated the horizontal rod he was aiming for and twisted the hook inwards to catch it underneath. It snagged, then with another twist, flicked into place. He pulled sharply upwards and was rewarded with a satisfying click. He tugged the wire free and let himself in.

Now the difficult part. He fetched out the Leatherman and unfolded the cross-head screwdriver. He ran his fingers over the plastic trim beneath the steering column and found the four screws that held it in place. Working in the dark beneath the dash, he removed each of the screws in turn and pulled the trim free, exposing the steering column and the multi-coloured clusters of cables leading from the ignition and headlight and wiper controls. He switched on his torch and examined the ignition barrel. There were six wires leading to it. One green, one black, two red and two brown. Using the Leatherman's wire strippers, he snipped and stripped the two reds – the live circuit – then, using the tips of the pliers, twisted them together. The lights lit up on the dash. Next, he did the same to the two browns – the starter circuit – and touched them one against the other, causing a spark. The engine coughed and turned over. Black pumped the gas pedal. It sputtered, then roared into life, the sound of its barely muffled engine resounding down the sleeping street.

He shifted into drive and moved off smoothly, switching on the lights only after he had travelled several blocks. He checked the mirrors. All was quiet.

Joachim was still asleep when Black eased back into the lobby. He took fifteen seconds closing the door inch by inch, then padded noiselessly across the floor. He swiped his key pass. The security door clicked open and he slipped quietly through. Joachim stirred but didn't wake. There was a full ten minutes before Black was due to meet with the others.

He knocked at Riley and Fallon's room at exactly half past. They were ready and waiting for him.

'We were thinking, boss – maybe the two of us should shoot off and get a car first. Shave the odds of all three of us being seen.'

'I had the same idea. It's waiting outside.'

They exchanged a look of surprise.

'Let's go.'

He slung his rucksack over his shoulder and headed for the stairs.

Joachim stirred as they entered the lobby.

'Checking out. Early bus,' Riley said. 'Might see you again in a couple of weeks.' He crossed to the desk and handed over their key cards, together with a twenty-dollar bill.

Joachim took the money gratefully but looked at them with concern. 'Have you got a taxi? You need one you can trust. Some of these guys are criminals.' He reached for the phone. 'Let me call my friend.'

Black smiled. 'I appreciate the thought but we're fine. We like to walk.'

'Walk? But it's dangerous.'

'We like a little danger, too. It's what we're here for. Goodbye.'

They headed out, leaving Joachim folding the note into his shirt pocket and shaking his head at the crazy Englishmen.

Black had parked the Pontiac several spaces along from the hotel. He popped the trunk allowing himself a moment of pride as they stowed their rucksacks. Riley took the passenger seat, Fallon the back. Black touched the bare wires and the already warm motor started without complaint. He pulled out into the sparse pre-dawn traffic.

'What do you think?' Black asked, hoping for at least a word of acknowledgement. 'Will she do?'

'Perfect,' Riley said, poking through the contents of the glovebox. 'Just a pity it belongs to a cop.'

'What?' Black failed to hide the note of alarm in his voice.

Riley grinned back between the seats at Fallon, who laughed.

They'd got him.

Black nodded, tight-lipped, taking it on the chin. It would take a lot more than stealing a car to impress this pair of bastards.

Riley navigated using his hand-held GPS. The location Silva had given them looked only a short distance away on the map but in reality involved a tortuous route to the south-east of the city, followed by a series of switchback climbs over steep hillsides. Here poor outer suburbs – no more than clusters of single-storey houses built from whatever materials were to hand – clung precariously to the slopes among increasingly dense forest.

The buildings were spread more thinly the further they travelled from the city until they petered out entirely. They crested the top of a hill and started down the far side. The road gradually narrowed and heavy tropical vegetation pressed in from both sides. Black guided the unwieldy Pontiac through several winding miles of steep descent until the sense that they were heading nowhere in particular was confirmed by a sign announcing that they were approaching a dead end. After a short distance the tarmac turned to dirt and the headlights picked out a length of steel crash barrier marking the end of the road. They came to a halt at the head of a deep ravine.

Black turned the car to face the way they had come and switched off the engine.

'Nice quiet spot,' Riley said. 'How many are we expecting?'

'He's got his money. I can't see why he would involve any-one else.'

'Best not take the risk.' He glanced back at Fallon. 'Shall we?'

The two of them climbed out of the car and headed in opposite directions to keep watch from the cover of the sur-rounding trees.

There were thirty minutes to go until their scheduled rendezvous. Black waited in the car with the windows down, watching and listening, aware of how blunted his senses had become in civilian life. It took a soldier on extended jungle exercise anything between a month to six weeks to hear, see and smell with anything like the acuity necessary for extended, unarmed survival. There had been a time when Black had been at maximum sensitivity permanently. He could enter an apparently empty building and from the smell alone tell if there was anyone inside. It was an ability that had saved his life on more than one occasion.

The clock on the dash crept slowly towards six a.m. Dawn started to break and the landscape appeared in monochrome that slowly rose to colour. They were in a narrow, steep-sided valley with a view over forested hilltops beyond. Here and there accessible parcels of land had been terraced and planted with banana palms, but for the most part the surrounding country remained in its natural state. After the dirt and squalor that lay only a few miles to the north, it should have made for an attractive scene, yet something in its atmosphere felt oppressive. Then Black put his finger on it: territory this untamed so close to a violent city told him that inevitably it would serve as a dumping ground for the bodies of the murdered. Root around at the foot of the ravine and he'd put money on reaping a grim harvest of white bones.

Two minutes ahead of time a single pair of headlights flickered in the near distance. Black stepped out on to the dirt road as a Ford Ranger painted in military green approached. Its windows and windshield were heavily tinted, obscuring the face of what appeared to be a single occupant. It turned in a tight arc in front of the Pontiac, spewing up dust from its tyres, eased forward, then backed up until its rear end drew level with Black's boot.

Black waited for the driver to show himself but the doors remained shut and the engine idling. Whoever was inside was determined to remain anonymous. He doubted it was the Colonel. He had most probably sent an underling. Someone anxious to make the drop and disappear.

There was a green tarpaulin stretched tight over the pick-up bed. Black went to the tailgate, slid the pins from the hasp that secured it and lowered it to ninety degrees. He peered under the tarp and made out three black nylon hold-alls. The driver revved the engine as if urging him to hurry. Black ignored the prompt and took his time. He dragged the nearest holdall forward and unzipped it on the tailgate. It contained three AK-47s with separate bayonets, three Smith and Wesson M&P 9 pistols fitted with suppressors and three shoulder holsters. An interesting mix – Russian assault rifles and one of the FBI's preferred sidearms. In among them were three Aselsan intercom units with headsets and mics, each one smaller and sleeker than a phone.

He dumped the bag on the ground and reached for the next. It was a dead weight. He opened it to find thirty-round magazines for the rifles, boxes of 7.62 x 39-millimetre ammunition and more boxes of 9-millimetre slugs for the pistols.

The third and final bag was heaviest. It contained a wooden crate two feet long. Printed on its top: 30 x M67 FRAGMENTATION GRENADE. NATO's favourite since 1968. Light, effective and reliable. Jammed in alongside the crate was a further package: a two-and-a-half-kilo lump of plastic explosive, four detonators and a remote-control unit. The Colonel had been true to his word – the inventory was better than he could have hoped for. He slapped the side of the truck twice and the driver took off in a cloud of red dust.

Black remained on his guard, wanting to be sure he was alone before he turned his back on the road. He waited for the sound of the engine to die away until all he could hear was the throbbing chorus of waking cicadas. No tricks. A straightforward drop and run.

'All clear.'

Riley and Fallon emerged from their hiding places.

'Looks like Colonel Silva delivered,' Black said.

Riley and Fallon stooped to examine the contents of the holdalls, making approving noises as they checked the weapons.

'Hate to say it, boss, but I'd take an AK over our carbines every time. These babies look brand new.'

'Straight out of the stores,' Fallon said, peering down the barrel of a Smith and Wesson. 'Still got grease in the barrels.'

Riley brought out a rifle and turned it deftly in his hands. 'Nice. Very nice.'

He handed it to Black, who held the butt to his shoulder and stared down the scope. He felt a pulse of excitement. It was as familiar to his touch as an old lover.

'Where to now?' Fallon said, hauling the load of ammunition into the Pontiac's boot.

'We'll take back roads down towards Charallave, pick up a few provisions and tuck ourselves away till morning. Conserve our energy. We're going to need it.'

They hefted the holdalls into the Pontiac's boot and set off in high spirits. Craftsmen reunited with their tools.

In the space of minutes the sky lifted from flat grey to brilliant blue. The air was warm and sweet. Riley and Fallon laughed and joked as Black nursed the car's battleship bulk back up the hill.

As they neared the summit they turned a sharp corner to be met with a sight that caused the laughter to stop in their throats. The Ford Ranger that had delivered the weapons was half buried nose first in dense bushes at the side of the road as if it had swerved to avoid a collision. A young soldier was standing, legs splayed, with his hands pressed up against the passenger door and a gun aimed at his back. It was wielded by a man in a similar uniform wearing a blue helmet with white letters printed on its front. A third figure, also in a blue helmet, was standing in front of a military Toyota SUV parked in the centre of the road. He raised his rifle and aimed it at the Pontiac's windshield as his colleague held up a hand, ordering them to stop.

Black stepped on the brakes. 'Hands up where they can see them. Sit tight.'

He came to a stop a short distance from the Toyota. Close enough to be able to make out the letters on the blue helmets: P.M. Policía Militar. Black looked over at the driver the two military police had run off the road and saw that he was no more than eighteen years old. A kid. Colonel Silva had screwed up badly.

Black, Riley and Fallon held their hands above their shoulders and remained casual, looking puzzled, as if they had no idea what the problem could possibly be. The two blue-helmets exchanged words in Spanish then the one who had been aiming his weapon at the young soldier ordered him to lie face down on the ground before cuffing his hands behind his back. Both men then approached the Pontiac with their rifles raised, one covering the left flank of the car, the other the right. They were also young. Twenty-three or twenty-four at the most. Tense and scared, their fingers were twitchy on their triggers.

Black smiled at the MP who was coming alongside the driver's window, letting him get a good look at his face, trying to let him know that there was no need for drama. He guessed that their plan was for the one on their right to continue providing cover while his partner would order each of them out in turn and have them lie on the ground before cuffing them.

The options were limited.

The MP on their left motioned Black to step out first.

'No problem,' Black said, keeping up the friendly pretence. He reached for the door handle. 'I got this,' Black whispered to his passengers.

Riley and Fallon met each other's eyes in the rear-view mirror.

Black stepped out, hands raised, still smiling. *'Habla inglés?'* Do you speak English?

'¡Al suelo!' Down! The MP pointed to the ground at the side of the road.

Black nodded and walked three steps away from the car. On the third he looked sharply to his right as if something had startled him. It was an old trick but worked every time. The MP's head turned instinctively in the same direction. In his split-second of distraction Black sprang to his right and caught the muzzle of his rifle in his left hand. Turning on his left foot he swung his right elbow into the man's jaw and hit the sweet spot. The shock of the impact caused the soldier to loosen his grip. Black tore the rifle from his hands and continued through an anticlockwise arc, spiralling to the ground to face the Pontiac as the second MP opened fire over its roof. Black found the trigger and fired a return burst beneath it, cutting the shooter off at the ankles. He cried out in a mixture of surprise and pain as his legs folded beneath him. As he hit the deck, Black loosed a second fatal burst into his head and torso, rolled twice, then came up into a crouch to see the first MP scrambling to his hands and knees, groping for the pistol holstered on his belt. Black took aim at his chest and fired again. Six rounds ripped through his tunic, exploding his heart and lungs. His limbs flailed. He jerked and twisted and came to rest on his back with his knees bent awkwardly under his body.

Black spotted movement to his right. The young soldier, the one who had delivered the arms, had made it to his feet and had started to run, his hands cuffed behind him.

Black shouted after him. 'Halt!'

He kept going.

Shit. A witness.

The greater good.

He had no choice.

Black took aim and made sure to do it cleanly. A single round to the back of the skull.

The fleeing boy's legs stopped moving but his momentum kept propelling him forward. He pitched face first into the road.

And then there was silence.

'All clear.'

Riley and Fallon's heads appeared above the tops of the doors. They surveyed the scene and climbed out with the look of men trying hard to disguise the fact that they felt lucky to be alive.

Black saw them trade a glance. 'What's the problem?'

'No problem,' Fallon said.

Black spat a bad taste out of his mouth. 'Let's clean up and get out of here.'

It was a crude job by normal standards but it would have to do. When the dead men's colleagues finally got a fix on them they would arrive to find two vehicles having narrowly avoided a head-on collision. The teenage driver of the Ranger was lying naked and handcuffed next to his truck, apparently having been executed by a single bullet to the back of the head. The Ranger's tyres were slashed and its seats torn open, their stuffing ripped out as if during a search for drugs or other contraband. The two MPs were lying on opposite sides of the road with their weapons at their sides, seemingly having turned their fire on each other, most probably during a dispute over the blood-stained US twenty-dollar bills that were scattered around the scene.

Just another day in Venezuela.

44

Sarah Bellman picked at her breakfast while Holst held forth from the position he had recently assumed at the head of their table in the corner of the compound's mess hall. In a small concession to their dignity the four scientists were allowed to eat together, away from the Sabre officers and NCOs who shared the same mealtimes. Kennedy, sitting opposite her, and Sphyris to her right, were feeling equally queasy. Oblivious to the effect he was having on his three colleagues, Holst tucked into his sausages with gusto, gesticulating with his fork between mouthfuls.

'Everything is ready for the next trials. I can assure you no harm will be done.' He smiled at Bellman. 'When can I expect you to deliver the first batch of usable particles?'

She glanced at Kennedy. He had grown thinner and frailer even in the last two days and hadn't said a word since they had sat down.

'Professor?' she prompted.

'In a day or two,' Kennedy said.

'Excellent. If we are anything like as successful as you have been in your primate trials, the end will soon be in sight.' Holst smiled, his eyes bright and alive above his glowing cheeks.

Holst noticed, as if for the first time, that the others weren't sharing his enthusiasm.

'Are you quite all right, Professor?' he said to Kennedy. 'I hope it's not rude of me to say that you've not been looking yourself lately.' He appealed to the others for confirmation.

Sarah stared into her cup. Sphyris pretended to be absorbed in removing the peel from an orange.

'I've felt better,' Kennedy said sourly. 'You, on the other hand, Dr Holst, seem to be positively thriving. This work seems to be suiting you.'

Holst's smile faded.

Sphyris, who had scarcely uttered a word, stepped in to defuse the tension. 'We all have different ways of coping with stress, I'm sure.' He offered Holst a conciliatory smile.

'Nevertheless, I think perhaps you ought to see a doctor, Professor. Just to be on the safe side.'

Kennedy put down his fork and placed his yellowing hands either side of his plate. 'You have no need to worry about my ability to complete this project, Dr Holst. I will do it just for the pleasure of telling everyone who cares to know exactly what you have done. Perhaps you would be well advised to spend the next forty-eight hours finding some obscure corner of the planet on which to live out your days, because no decent human being will ever want to consort with you again.'

'Good morning, everybody.' Dr Razia appeared with his breakfast tray. 'May I join you?'

Kennedy pushed up from the table. Abandoning his food, he marched unsteadily towards the door.

'Is everything all right?' Razia said, detecting the frigid atmosphere.

'He's not well,' Sarah said. 'I'd better go.'

Leaving the others at the table, she went after him.

Bellman caught up with Kennedy halfway across the parade ground that separated the mess hall from the block that housed their quarters and laboratory.

'I told them you were ill. You shouldn't work today. You need to rest.'

'I've made up my mind, Sarah. My involvement with this project is over . . . You must do as you wish.'

'What will you do? They're not going to let you –' She stopped mid-sentence as Kennedy came to a sudden halt. His breathing was laboured. He staggered as if about to faint. Bellman caught and steadied him. She called out to the guard standing outside their quarters, who jogged over to help.

Bellman entered the laboratory alone. Kennedy was sleeping, having received a large dose of intravenous antibiotics for a suspected infection. She had been able to tell Holst that he was delirious and to take no notice of his outburst. She would handle the remainder of the work. The first batch of nanoparticles was nearly complete. They would be ready for their first human trials in forty-eight hours.

She sat at her computer and brought up the lines of genetic code that would be programmed into the targeting mechanism. This sequence of several thousand letters would be chemically translated into the biological equivalent of a weapons guidance system that could distinguish and lock on to a handful of cells amidst the billions that made up the human body.

But what if the code didn't work? What if she could jam a spanner in the wheel that would slow their progress and buy them time to find a way out?

Dare she try?

Bellman glanced over her shoulder. There was no one at the door. She was alone with her conscience. For the first time in her life she decided to be brave.

45

On either side of the road people were emerging from their shacks to go to work on the land or to catch one of the over-crowded minivans that shuttled from these outlying parts into the city. Riley and Fallon ducked down beneath the Pontiac's windows and Black drove with a cap pulled low over his eyes, but the car was being noticed. The shots would have been heard. Questions would be asked. By seven a.m. the police and army would have learned about the brown Pontiac that had driven by earlier. The new reality was that they were anonymous no longer.

The immediate dilemma was how best to use their brief window of opportunity, the hour or two before the bodies were found and the dots were joined. The first option was to stick to the original plan of holing up in the bush in the hope of being able to drive in to Charallave unnoticed in the early hours of the following morning. The second was to steal another vehicle, transfer their gear, then hide. Despite the risk involved in committing yet another crime, Black was inclining towards the second course of action when one of their two burner phones rang.

Riley fished it out of his pocket and handed it forward between the seats.

'Hello.'

'Good morning, Mr Black.' It was Colonel Silva. He couldn't have sounded more cheerful. 'I trust you received your goods?'

'Yes, we have them. Then your driver received a bullet

from a pair of Policía Militar who ran him off the road at the top of the hill. We understood you were a reliable man, Colonel.'

There was no reply.

'Hello?'

'He's dead?' the Colonel said, a rising note of panic in his voice.

'Afraid so.'

'They were waiting for him?'

'Looked that way. So either they're on to you, or your man made an elementary mistake, like making the drop-off in a vehicle he borrowed without permission. One with a tracker. Send a boy to do a man's job . . .'

'The Military Police? You're sure?'

'Two of them. The good news is they'll no longer be a burden on the Venezuelan taxpayer.'

Colonel Silva didn't appreciate the joke. 'This is not good news, Mr Black. Our country may be broken but our military is not. If those arms are seized, I need your assurance that my name will not be mentioned.'

'That's a big ask –'

Their conversation was interrupted by a sudden commotion: a woman's voice calling out in panic accompanied by the sound of violent banging, like fists pounding on a door.

The call ended with no further exchange.

Black checked the time. It was six forty-seven a.m. He handed the phone back to Riley. 'Sounds like Colonel Silva just got paid a visit by what passes for the law around here,' he said with measured understatement. 'I had a feeling he was pushing his luck.'

'He'll talk,' Fallon said.

'No doubt. So, do we take our chances on the road or persuade Buganov to fly today? My vote's for the Russian.'

'Fuck it. If I'm going to get shot at, I'd rather do it in style,' Riley said. 'I'm with you.'

'Roger that,' Fallon said with less enthusiasm.

Black leaned back in his seat and pushed his foot to the floor. The old Pontiac responded with a pleasing growl. He couldn't help but smile. Finn would have enjoyed this. He would have called it a perfect day.

Instead of turning west to pick up Highway 1, which would have taken them due south to Charallave, Black chose instead to head east, looping round to come at his destination from a counter-intuitive angle. Anything to stay a step ahead. He crossed the hills on minor roads carved out of the rock, some of them little more than glorified cart tracks, making his way towards the small town of Santa Teresa del Tuy. There they stopped for fuel at a one-pump gas station and bought pine-apple juice and cheese-filled corn breads the locals called *arepas* from a toothless old woman trading from a handcart. Her eyes lit up at the sight of American dollar bills. She snatched them in bony fingers and tucked them into the folds of her clothes.

Black continued on his circuitous route, skirting the centre of town and heading south-west to the larger settlement of San Francisco de Yare, from where he turned north on to the Autopista Charallave–Ocumare. A few miles from the edge of the city of Charallave itself, they pulled over into a truck stop. Riley and Fallon climbed out to smoke and stretch their legs. Black visited a foul-smelling urinal before returning to the car and dialling Buganov's number. Waiting for the call to connect, he glanced across to the trucker's diner. A row of customers were sitting on high stools facing out of the window. They were eating sausage and drinking coffee chased down with shots of brandy, racing each other to a heart attack.

Buganov answered with a Russian '*Da?*' He sounded as if he'd been woken from a coma.

'Buganov, it's Black. There's been a change of plan. We need to fly today.'

'Not possible. I told you. Plane not fixed until tomorrow.'

'I have money. How long will it take?'

'Parts. Hoses. Hydraulic hoses. They arrive today. I have to fit them.'

'How many hoses?'

'What does it matter how many hoses?'

'How many?'

'Two.'

'And how many hoses on your plane? I'm guessing a lot more than two. So improvise. How soon can you be ready?'

'You're a crazy man. Forget it. *Zavtra.*' Tomorrow.

He rang off.

Fallon wandered over with Riley. 'Problem?'

'Two worn hoses. He's waiting for replacements.'

'What kind of pussy is he?' Riley said.

Black stared out at the highway with the feeling that he was at a crossroads at which he couldn't afford to take a wrong turn. He was tempted to change his mind and head south, as far away from people and trouble as they could get. The furthest they could travel by road was Buena Vista, some 1,200 miles away, but that still left a huge distance across largely uninhabited country to Platanal. That meant they would have to find a plane to hire at one of the small airstrips serving the southern settlements. It was possible, but in order to risk a long highway journey they would need to steal another vehicle as a matter of urgency and in broad daylight. Success would then depend on making it to Buena Vista without a breakdown or being stopped by a bored cop in search of a bribe. The odds were against them.

Riley and Fallon finished their cigarettes and climbed back into their seats.

'Second thoughts?' Riley said.

Black's phone interrupted. He checked the screen. It was Towers.

'Hold on.' He took the call. 'Freddy?'

'Where are you?'

'I doubt you'd know it.'

'Did you get your equipment?'

'Yes. I'll spare you the details.'

'Bad news, I'm afraid.'

Black felt an unpleasant sensation in his stomach.

'Just had a call from my pal in '6. Apparently Cordero called him about thirty minutes ago in a blind panic. He was en route to our Embassy in Caracas. He'd been tipped off by a mutual friend that his colleague, Colonel Silva, has been detained on suspicion of theft of military ordnance.'

'I suspected as much.'

'Well, now Cordero's threatening to rat us out unless he's granted asylum and safe passage. He'll be given a fair hearing, but we'll have to deny everything, of course. What you'd call a right royal fuck-up.'

'Quite,' Black said, resisting the temptation to add his own description.

'What about your transport south?'

'We're working on it.'

'I thought Cordero had given you a pilot?'

'There's been a delay.'

'The fact is, Leo, I can buy you an hour. Two at the most. My man will make sure the Embassy staff go through the motions, take a statement, give every impression of playing along with a harmless lunatic. But beyond that, I think we may be in difficulties.'

'Delicately put. I appreciate it.'

'Get out of there, Leo. As quickly as you can.'

'Understood. Keep me posted.' Black signed off and turned to the others.

'We heard,' Riley said. 'Guess we'd better drop in on Buganov.'

Charallave was a small city of 129,000 souls named after the Charavares indigenous people who had been the area's unfortunate inhabitants when the conquistadors arrived. Of those that weren't slaughtered, most of the remainder had died of either smallpox or influenza. Little evidence of them or their ancient culture remained. The city was crammed into a flat plain between surrounding hills and consisted mostly of tightly packed concrete apartment buildings encircled by a highway of grand, hubristic proportions. According to the GPS, Buganov's address was on its north-east rim, a short distance from the Autopista Francisco de Miranda and no more than two kilometres from the airport.

The traffic was light and spread thinly along the vast sweep of the Avenida Perimetral. The cars and vans were of an even older vintage than those in Caracas and looked incongruous on a highway built for the twenty-first century. Black imagined that somewhere gathering dust in a government office there were fifteen-year-old plans for a modern city, five times the size, spreading out across the surrounding countryside. Plans that had not only come to nothing but which were fast going into reverse. The signs of decay were everywhere to see. The road was breaking up at the edges and giving way to encroaching weeds. They passed an abandoned fast-food restaurant and gas station, the buildings stripped of their cladding and the windows staved in. Bored, emaciated children were kicking around in the rubble.

The scene reminded Black of just how fragile a thing civilization was. It needed money to sustain itself. Lots of money.

Turn off the supply, even for a short time, and it crumbled into ruin.

They bypassed the centre of the city, continued north, then took an exit off the highway that led them into an area of scattered low-rise housing punctuated with dead areas of rubbish-strewn scrub. After a further mile they arrived outside a single-storey property set on its own and surrounded by a ten-foot wire fence. Inside the quarter-acre compound there was a storage shed constructed of rusted tin, stacks of empty wooden crates and a beaten-up white panel van painted with the words *Bug Air.*

They pulled up and climbed out on to the unmade road.

The gates were padlocked and metal security grilles were drawn down over the two windows at the front of the house. There was no bell or intercom. Black reached through the open driver's window and leaned on the horn twice.

'Plan B,' Riley said. He clasped his hands in front of his waist. Fallon used them as a step, placed his hands on top of the locked gates and vaulted over.

Black followed suit, landing rather more heavily than the younger, lighter man.

'I'll keep an eye on the wagon,' Riley said.

Black led the way to the front door and knocked loudly.

'Mr Buganov? It's Leo Black.'

Getting no response, he crossed to the window to the left of the door and peered through the dense mesh of the grille. Cupping his hands around his eyes to block out the peripheral light, he made out a bed and a prone figure beneath rumpled sheets.

'Good morning, Mr Buganov. Would you be kind enough to open the door? We have business to transact.'

'You're a bastard,' Buganov uttered from the darkness.

'Surely even you would get out of bed for three thousand dollars.'

Buganov refused to stir.

'Two minutes, or I'll take my money elsewhere.'

He stepped back to the front door and waited.

Several minutes later, grumbling and cursing, Buganov drew back multiple bolts and opened the door. He was a man of around sixty, dressed in crumpled grey boxer shorts and a stained vest. He was bald, fat and unshaven with devilish eyes the colour of coal.

Black liked him at once.

'Pleased to meet you.' He offered his hand.

'Fuck your mother.'

Buganov turned and plodded back into the darkened interior. Black and Fallon exchanged a glance and followed him inside.

They entered a room which was both kitchen and general living space. There was a table and chairs, an old sofa, an antique television bracketed to the wall, a desk spilling untended papers and a shelf filled with assorted bottles. Buganov grabbed one and slumped into a seat at the table. Black and Fallon sat opposite as the Russian poured himself a shot of Pampero rum, tossed it down and reached for a packet of cigarettes. Only when both the alcohol and nicotine had reached his bloodstream did he raise his gaze and speak. Black used the intervening moments to cast his eyes around the room. Propped up on the shelf above the desk he noticed a small framed photograph of a slim, handsome young man dressed in the uniform of the Soviet Air Force.

'Have you ever flown a plane, Mr Black?' Buganov said.

'No. Although I have jumped out of a few.'

'You cannot land a plane without brakes. The consequences would be unfortunate.'

'We can fix hoses well enough for a couple of landings,' Fallon said. 'Heard of duct tape?'

'You're a funny guy.'

'Five thousand dollars if we take off today,' Black said. 'The same on our return in a week or so's time.'

He reached under his shirt and unclipped a money belt he had retrieved from his rucksack at their last stop. He brought it out on to the table and pulled back the zipper. Buganov's eyes fixed on the fat green wad of notes.

'What is the nature of your business?'

'Never mind that,' Black said.

'Cargo?'

'Something that mustn't be seen. Nor must we. Can you arrange it?'

Buganov sighed. 'Five thousand dollars for the risk of jail? I was in jail once – in Yakutsk. Another crazy adventure just like this one. I would rather freeze to death in a cell in Siberia than boil to death in Caracas.'

'Ten thousand for a return trip, Mr Buganov. Are you really going to turn me down?'

Buganov stared at the money and blew out a thick cloud of blue smoke.

'Platanal. I've never been there.'

'There's an airstrip that will easily accommodate your plane.'

'They have police. Even way out in the jungle.'

'You've nothing to fear from the police,' Fallon said. 'We're just three adventurous tourists off for a hike in the Amazon.'

Buganov looked at his visitors with an expression of contempt tinged with reluctant admiration.

Black took out the money and pressed it into his hand. 'Do we have a deal?'

'You sons of whores.' Buganov clutched it in an ape-like fist. 'You'll kill us all.'

46

Buganov unlocked the front gates and slid back the door on the corrugated shed. It was stacked with more empty crates, oil drums, boxes of dry goods awaiting transport, old aircraft parts and several decades' worth of assorted junk.

'We need to store our car in there out of sight,' Black said.

'You want to make a space, fine,' Buganov said. 'And if you want to get into the airport without being seen, you'd better find some place to hide.' He tossed Black the keys to his panel van and shuffled back into the house, lighting another cigarette. 'I need something to eat.'

Black lifted the roller shutter at the van's rear to reveal a space approximately twelve feet long by eight wide. It smelled of rotting fruit and was hot as an oven. There were no obvious voids in which to hide their weapons and little scope for concealing three men in any way that would defeat even a cursory search. It left them little choice but to load the van with empty crates and hide behind them in the hope that Buganov could bluff his way through airport security.

'Unless either of you has a better solution?' Black said.

They shook their heads. Sometimes the obvious risk was the one to take.

From the markings on the crates Black deduced that Buganov's regular trade was in foodstuffs and essential goods. He evidently brought fresh fruit and vegetables north from the remote plantations in the south and returned with staples and farm supplies. The mundane nature of this business was all to their advantage. They transferred their rucksacks and holdalls to several crates and, leaving a void two feet deep at the front of the van, filled the rest to the ceiling with more empty crates and boxes of rice, flour and salt. It was crude but it would have to do. Lastly, they manoeuvred the Pontiac into the empty shed, covered it with a tarpaulin, stacked boxes and aircraft parts on its roof and more crates in front of it.

'That'll fool them,' Fallon joked.

Black shrugged. 'Best we can do.' He checked his watch. It was ten forty-five a.m. Time they were in the air. 'Someone get Buganov.'

Fallon did the honours and Riley went with him to find the bathroom, leaving Black a moment alone. Bracing himself for bad news, he took the opportunity to call Towers.

'Leo, I was about to call you. Still on the ground?'

'Give it thirty minutes and we should be in the air. Any more on Cordero?'

'Nothing. He didn't make it to the Embassy, which I'm reading as a bad sign. If they've caught him, it won't be long before they have your name and your pilot's. You can't file a flight plan, Leo. Not under these circumstances. There's a military base at La Esmeralda less than a hundred miles from Platanal. They'll be waiting for you on the runway if they don't shoot you down first.' Towers paused. The usual gung-ho spirit was completely absent from his voice. 'You know, I wouldn't normally say this, but I'm not sure you've got the resources to see this through.'

'Any more men and equipment would only make us more conspicuous.'

'I don't mean those kind, Leo . . . Perhaps you ought to withdraw? Head for Guyana and think again.'

'Isn't it a bit late for second thoughts?' There was no answer. 'Are you instructing me to abort, Freddy?'

After a further pause Towers said, 'Only you can make that call. I need you to weigh the risks. Carefully.'

'Consider them weighed. See you in a week or two.'

He ended the call and switched off the phone. Towers could keep any more bad news to himself.

Fallon emerged from the house with Riley and Buganov, who had dressed in a worn pair of blue slacks and a crumpled white shirt with short sleeves and matching blue epaulettes. He had made an attempt to shave but had cut himself in two places. Bloody scraps of tissue paper clung to his upper lip and neck. In his right hand he was holding a carrier bag containing clinking bottles.

Buganov stopped at the open rear of the van and waited, muttering profanities under his breath while Black and the others climbed in and worked their way round to their hiding place behind the crates.

'OK,' Black called out, signalling they were ready to move.

'*Sukiny deti.*' Sons of bitches. Buganov pulled down the shutter, belched up the gas from his breakfast and made his way to the cab.

Black, Riley and Fallon were jammed into a twelve-inch gap between crates stacked floor to ceiling and the front wall of the van. Buganov drove with no thought to their comfort, slewing round corners and lurching violently each time he came to a stop or pulled away.

'He's driving like he's drunk already,' Riley said from somewhere to Black's left.

'Don't suppose he's ever sober,' Fallon said. 'And I doubt you'd want him any other way.'

It was a thankfully short distance from Buganov's home to the nearby airport. Black pictured the satellite map he'd studied on his phone. An access road led around the side of the passenger terminal to an entrance several hundred yards further along, which served both a flying school and a number of airfreight businesses. He had found details of several reputable cargo operators on the internet but Buganov had no website or even directory listing. Black guessed that all his work came by word of mouth or was subcontracted by the other firms. Sorties out into the bush paid for in cash or in kind.

They had been moving for less than ten minutes when the van slowed.

'We're coming to the gate,' Buganov called out, his voice travelling through the thin aluminium panel separating them from the cab.

They came to a stop. There were footsteps outside on the tarmac. Buganov exchanged greetings in Spanish with a security guard and they chatted good-naturedly, like two guys at the bar. In the midst of the conversation Black heard Buganov mention 'Puerto Carreño', which he knew to be a port town on the Orinoco River, just inside the Colombian border. The two men continued to talk. Black felt his muscles start to cramp. The corners of the crates were digging into his flesh. He was aware that nearly twenty minutes had passed since he had spoken with Towers, every one of them another opportunity for Cordero to disclose Buganov's name to whichever official might now be confronting him in a locked interrogation room. A simple phone call and Buganov would be grounded. And even if he did make it into the air, Venezuela had a very efficient air force.

That was the next problem on the agenda.

Finally, Buganov and his friend at the gate parted company. The van jerked forward and proceeded straight ahead for a short while before turning right, then right again.

'You wait,' Buganov said.

He left them sweltering for a full fifteen minutes. They

endured the ordeal in silence, each retreating by instinct into the inner space in which they could detach from the discomfort of their physical bodies and step outside time.

The now familiar sound of Buganov's feet dragging heavily across the ground signalled his eventual return. He stopped at the rear of the van and threw up the shutter, flooding the interior with light and a welcome draught of air.

'Two of you into the plane. The other one is maintenance crew. You help me fix the hoses.'

'That had better be me,' Riley said. 'My old man was a mechanic. Grew up balls-deep in engine oil.'

They inched out from around the crates and saw that the rear of the van was backed up towards a midsize twin-prop aircraft, which was parked at the side of a large hangar out of sight from the airport's entrance. Black dimly recognized it as a De Havilland Caribou. He was no aviation expert but he had a pretty good idea that the Caribou had ceased production in the 1960s although he recalled having flown in one in East Timor back in '99.

'Beautiful, isn't she?' Buganov said, reading Black's unease. He was holding a toolbox and a high-vis waistcoat. 'I bought her in '98, when my old Antonov was grounded. Do you know how I got the Antonov?'

'I have no idea,' Black said, jumping down on to the tarmac.

'Every month I was flying supplies to Cuba from Vladivostok. That traitorous dog Yeltsin gave the order to stop. I made my final flight and never returned. I threw myself on the mercy of true comrades and they welcomed me like a brother. They gave me a regular route from Havana to Caracas, then I was invited to work here. Venezuela is a proud country, Mr Black. Faithful to the cause. Loyal to its friends.'

Black could smell the rum on Buganov's breath. 'I'm glad to hear it.' He climbed through the open cargo-bay door into the back of the Caribou, Fallon coming after him.

'Jesus. What a wreck.' Fallon joined him on the worn flip-down seats bolted to the aircraft's hull.

The interior of the Caribou was like a window into the past. The hull's inner frame was constructed from aluminium struts that had begun to fur with age. Heavy canvas drapes were stretched between them and secured with lengths of fraying rope. The cargo-bay floor was decked with pitted and scarred sheets of plywood. The cockpit, which was open to the rest of the aircraft, had no modern instruments, just two control columns whose handles were worn to the bare metal, and a basic radio, the handset of which was dangling from the overhead unit by a length of cloth-covered cable.

'All right, girls?' Riley's grinning face appeared through the cargo-bay door. He was wearing the fluorescent waist-coat Buganov had given him bearing the words *EQUIPO DE MANTENIMIENTO*. Maintenance crew.

Buganov followed him up the steps lugging the toolbox. He pointed to some crudely drilled finger holes in a section of the plywood floor. 'There. Take it up.'

Riley raised the inspection hatch and set it aside, exposing an unpromising tangle of wires and hydraulic hoses. Buganov sank stiffly to his knees and began, bad-temperedly, to sort through them.

Fallon looked away, shaking his head.

Black watched with morbid fascination as Riley and Buganov sifted through the aircraft's guts. Eventually they located the leaking hoses and with the aid of a torch Riley crawled into the space beneath the floor armed with Jubilee clips and rolls of silver duct tape. Buganov barked unhelpful instructions from above while he made the crude repair:

'Make sure to wrap them tight, but don't strangle with the clips. You split the hoses we all die. Not good.'

Black checked his watch. Another hour had slipped past. If only they could get into the air, he could manage the situation. Every second they remained on the ground they were vulnerable.

'That's it, boys. Let's load her up.' Riley re-emerged from the hatch, his hands and cheeks smeared with filthy hydraulic fluid.

'Will they hold?' Fallon said.

'I wouldn't bet your house on it.' Riley smirked, sensing that he had found Fallon's weak spot.

They loaded quickly and in silence, forming a three-man human chain while Buganov went through his preflight checks and started the engines. All the while, Black kept his eyes on him, ready to step in the second he reached for the radio. When the moment arrived, Black slipped into the co-pilot's seat and caught hold of Buganov's wrist as he brought the handset to his mouth.

'It's important you don't log a flight plan to Platanal. Puerto Carreño is fine.'

Buganov's black eyes slanted towards him.

'You can't fly incognito, Mr Black. The Colombian drug runners try that – the air force shoots them down.'

'I understand. Puerto Carreño. OK?'

'And then?'

'We have a technical issue. An electrical failure.'

'This was not part of our arrangement.'

'What are you going to do – turn us over to the authorities?' Buganov glared at him with fresh hatred.

'Would it help if I told you we are here in a noble cause?'

Buganov jerked his wrist free and spoke into the handset. Black listened carefully. The Russian did as he was told.

Riley called out from the back. 'All set, boss.' They had loaded the crates containing their kit and had stacked a further dozen empty ones on top. All were roped tight against the hull. He pulled the cargo-bay door shut and fastened it.

'One more thing before we go, Gregori – may I call you that?' Black said, buckling into the co-pilot's seat.

Buganov dipped his chin in Black's direction, his features set in a hostile scowl.

'Any chance of an upgrade?'

'*Mudak!*' Asshole.

Buganov released the brakes and started to taxi towards the head of the runway, where they came to a halt. He exchanged messages with the tower and was cleared for takeoff. He pulled back on the throttle. The Caribou's twin engines stuttered, caught, then picked up revs and rose to a deafening pitch. They lurched forward and accelerated into a heat haze that turned the runway ahead of them into a blur. The airframe rattled and shook like an old-fashioned train carriage careering to its doom. For several anxious seconds it seemed they had reached peak velocity yet still lacked the power to make it off the ground.

The end of the runway raced towards them.

Buganov glanced at his airspeed indicator and gently eased back the stick. The nose lifted, the plane's wings bit into the thick tropical air and they started to climb. They continued upwards in a straight line to 1,000 feet, then banked sharply to the right, turning through ninety degrees to head due south.

Black looked right out of the cockpit window at his side and saw a white vehicle with strobing blue lights heading at speed along the airport approach road. It continued on to the entrance through which they had passed little more than an hour before.

He assumed that Cordero had run out of luck.

Which meant that so had they.

47

They had been airborne for a little under ten minutes when the call came over the radio. Black saw Buganov's forehead crease with concern as he spoke in Spanish to the control tower. He heard him repeat his destination, Puerto Carreño, several times, then insist, '*No, no, sólo. Sólo yo. Como siempre.*' No, no, alone. Only me. As usual.

Black shot him a glance, warning him to stay cool. Buganov glowered back at him.

Another voice came over the radio. This one more insistent. A police officer, no doubt, or worse. Buganov repeated his claim to be alone with an admirable air of exasperation, adding words to the effect – as far as Black could glean – that the chance of some paid passengers would be a fine thing; he hadn't even had any offers from criminals wanting him to fly over the Colombian border lately.

'*Informe a la policía en Puerto Carreño.*'

'*No hay problema. Como desee.*' He hung the handset back on its hook, his jaw set in anger. 'The police are looking for three Englishmen. They've ordered me to report to the police at Puerto Carreño.' He reached into the carrier bag at the side of his seat, brought out a bottle, uncorked it with his teeth and took a large mouthful.

Black glanced over his shoulder at the others. Fallon's face was pale. He was eyeing Buganov as if he might just knock his lights out.

Black snatched the bottle from his hand and tossed it over

his shoulder. It smashed into fragments on the cargo-bay floor. 'Enough.'

Buganov gripped the control stick with white knuckles, his face hardened into an expression of defiance. 'Fuck you.'

'Your friend, Mr Cordero,' Black said. 'Does he send you other customers?'

Buganov gave a dismissive shrug of his shoulders.

'Or is it another kind of cargo? Do you fly up to the Virgin Islands, Panama perhaps, offload a few crates of pineapples and hand over a bag to a man in a suit?'

Buganov continued to sulk.

'It's a shame for men like you,' Black said, 'people who believed in something, only for men like Cordero to sell you out. Not what you'd call very fraternal.'

'You watch your mouth, Mr Black. Maybe we'll have an accident.'

'He's betrayed you, Gregori. I'm sorry about that. But we have a plan for this contingency. An expensive one, but for us, not for you.'

Buganov's eyes slid right at the mention of money.

'I'm afraid it's rather drastic – it involves you not returning home. After we put down in Platanal you fly on north-east to Georgetown, Guyana. I'll give you the address of the British Embassy and a phone number to call right away. You'll speak to my colleague in London, Colonel Towers. He'll arrange a regular payment, enough for you to live comfortably. A pension courtesy of the British government.'

'Pension?'

'It probably won't be more than forty thousand dollars a year, I'm afraid.'

'US dollars?'

'Whatever currency you choose.'

'US dollars is fine . . . Forty thousand . . . ? Every year?'

'Yes, for life. Can you live with that?'

Buganov gave another shrug, making an admirable job of hiding his elation.

'I'm grateful, Gregori. And sorry to put you to this trouble.' Black sat back in his seat, resisting the temptation to glance back at the others to gauge their reactions. He felt a small measure of remorse at having fed their pilot such an appealing lie, but survival came first. It left them with the problem of their return trip but whatever way you cut it Buganov would be out of the picture. They would just have to find a way.

Move forward. Don't look back. Stay alive.

It was what they had been trained to do.

They headed almost due south towards Puerto Carreño, which lay 300 miles distant. Platanal was a further 570 miles and three hours' flying time to the south-east. Buganov made his move after 150 miles when they were skirting the Aguaro-Guariquito National Park. Slowly, he began to lose height, then veered to the right, then to the left, then right again, laying down an erratic track on any radar that was recording his movements. Steep, wooded hills came into view. Buganov continued on a downwards trajectory that, if he were to have continued on it, would have seen them smashing into the ground in approximately two minutes' time.

He reached for his radio and made contact with the nearest airfield at the provincial city of San Fernando de Apure. He communicated with the tower, evidently telling them he was having problems with his electrical and navigation systems. He requested a bearing that would send them in the direction of the airfield. A female voice responded with details of his position and the correct course.

Buganov thanked her but remained on the same course.

Seconds later the voice returned. *Was he OK? What was the problem?*

Buganov said something about his *'Presión hidráulica'* and added an accumulating list of other faults in a tone of mounting alarm.

The local air traffic controller fired back with an urgent instruction to *'Ganar altitud!'*

'Mierda! Mierda!' Buganov responded. *Shit! Shit!*

He reached up to the radio unit and switched it off.

Black braced himself. The mountainside was coming up fast. 'It has to look convincing,' Buganov said.

The wall of green increased in size until it was filling the entire windshield. Black swallowed, fighting the urge to grab hold of the co-pilot's control column.

Buganov wore a big yellow-toothed grin, enjoying his passengers' discomfort. 'Hold tight.'

He stamped on the rudder pedal and at the same time turned his control column sharply to the left. Black felt his stomach being hurled towards his boots as Buganov threw the groaning plane through a steep, banking turn. Now it was the ground confronting them. Black heard what sounded like a moan coming from the seats behind as Buganov maintained his rapid descent to below 1,000 feet. Just as Black began to consider the possibility that their pilot had no intention of pulling up, Buganov yanked hard on the stick, causing Black's stomach to hurtle in the opposite direction.

Buganov laughed as he levelled out at what felt like only tens of feet above the forest canopy. 'Rest in peace, gentlemen. According to the radar screen, we are all officially dead men.'

Black turned around in his seat and gave the others a weary thumbs up. Riley responded with his usual irrepressible grin. Fallon unclipped his belt, hauled himself to his feet and walked unsteadily to the back of the aircraft, where he dropped to his knees and retched.

Buganov maintained a steady altitude of 500 feet, which, he claimed, would keep him under both the civilian and military radar. He continued due east for a further 100 miles before heading south to make his way through the mountains. Holding the aircraft well below the ridgeline, he navigated through a network of deep valleys, ensuring his passengers' hearts stayed in their mouths as his wing tips threatened to graze the rocky cliff edges each time he made another turn.

At last they emerged from between the peaks and breathed easily again at the sight of the wide, glinting expanse of the Orinoco River stretching from the eastern horizon to the west. And, beyond it, an uninterrupted expanse of rainforest, smothering the contours of an unending, gently undulating plane.

'That's your jungle, Mr Black,' Buganov said. 'You like it? Nowhere to put down between here and Platanal. Five hundred kilometres.'

Black looked out at the green ocean spread out in all directions. Even from inside the aircraft, he could smell it. Its scent was heavy and humid, perfumed and dank like the inside of the glasshouse in Oxford's botanical gardens magnified a hundred times.

Oxford. It was the first time he had thought of it in days. His existence there seemed so remote as to belong to another life. From his seat in a rickety plane skimming the Amazon, the very thought of lecturing and theorizing seemed absurd. He couldn't begin to conceive that he might find himself resuming such a cosseted, irrelevant existence.

This was where he belonged.

There was no sensation that could begin to match it: the thrill of the hunt.

*

Fifty miles out from Platanal, Buganov switched on the radio and listened. There was nothing but the crackle of static. He flicked through all the channels with the same result. There was no chatter at all. Nothing except an occasional exchange of Portuguese-speaking voices from across the border in northern Brazil. They had now travelled several hundred miles having seen not a single road and only the occasional clearing. They truly were at the back end of beyond.

Buganov waited until they were thirty miles out from their destination before ascending to 4,000 feet and sending a message over the radio. '*Platanal, soy Bravo Alpha 954. Se puede escucharme?*' He repeated the same call three times before the voice of a man woken from his siesta replied drowsily in the affirmative.

Buganov gabbled excitedly back at him. Now attuning to Buganov's brand of Spanish, or at least to the words that vaguely resembled English, Black caught the essence: *Thank God. Thank God. I've had electrical and mechanical problems. Lost all my instruments. I've been flying blind for hours. Am I free to land?*

'*Sí. Claro. Libre de aterrizar.*' Yes. All clear. You're free to land.

Buganov continued to communicate with the ground as they closed in on the runway. Once again, the silver streak of the Orinico appeared ahead of them. The jungle settlement of Platanal lay in a clearing on its banks, not far from the river's source in the jungle to the east. The river travelled in a great semicircle that embraced much of the country and within it, beneath the rainforest canopy, lay the untapped minerals and precious metals that the government was now so eager to exploit.

A long, rectangular patch of brown appeared ahead of them: Platanal's unpaved airstrip. Beyond it Black made out a disorderly collection of buildings, some roofed with tin, others thatched in the traditional manner with dried vegetation. It was closer in size to a small village or hamlet than a town.

Buganov took the plane in a sweeping curve, first out to the right, then turning back left to line up with the runway. They were now three or four miles out, descending from 4,000 feet at a steady rate. The tension inside the aircraft rose. Through the windows in the cargo bay Riley and Fallon could see the ground drawing closer. Black glanced behind to warn them they were no more than a minute from landing. He saw that Riley's grin had faded to a fatalistic smile. Fallon's face was corpse white.

Buganov eased off the throttle. The noise of the engine faded. They entered their final approach.

'You sons of bitches,' Buganov muttered beneath his breath, his eyes locked on to the runway, which was surrounded on all sides by thick, unforgiving forest.

200 feet. 100. They skimmed the tops of the trees. Buganov pushed the throttle forward and raised the wing flaps. The wheels thumped heavily on to the uneven ground. Buganov pushed down on the brake pedals, willing them to hold. The treeline at the end of the runway bore down on them.

Black shot their pilot a look – they weren't going to stop in time. Buganov pressed down harder. Black felt the brakes engage. He was thrown forward against his seat belt but still their rate of deceleration was too slow – they were heading straight for the trees.

Taking matters into his own hands, Black stamped down as hard as he could on the co-pilot's brake pedals. The brakes bit and held. The Caribou juddered to a stop thirty yards short of tree trunks that would have crushed them to pulp.

Black looked over at Buganov to see him staring out through the windshield in a daze. 'What were you doing?'

'I was afraid to burst the hose.' He shook his head and

reached into the carrier bag at the side of his seat and brought out the remaining bottle.

Leaving him to his drink, Black unbuckled his seat belt and issued orders to Riley and Fallon. 'Kit out. Packs on. We're going to hit the bush without being seen.' He addressed Buganov: 'Taxi slowly back round to the left. Keep tight to the trees and stop on my order.'

Buganov took several more mouthfuls of Palmero and wiped his wet lips with the length of his forearm. 'The number.'

'Of course.'

Buganov reached into his pocket and handed over his phone.

'I'll log the details under Towers,' Black said. 'Colonel Freddy Towers. Call him as soon as you get to Georgetown and tell him you've delivered us safely to Platanal.' He keyed the number of Towers' personal mobile phone into the directory of contacts, pleased to see that the phone's screen was reporting 'no service'. For good measure he added an invented address for the British Embassy. He had no doubt Towers would be able to string him along for a few days while they completed their business. After that Buganov faced an uncertain and unhappy fate.

Black handed over the phone. 'Thank you, my friend.'

The Russian took another pull on the rum and belched from the depths of his belly.

Riley and Fallon moved quickly to extract their packs and three holdalls from their crates. Black joined them in the back, pulled on his pack, pulled the waist belt tight and grabbed the heaviest holdall containing the ammunition. He called out to Buganov to start taxiing, then opened the cargo-bay door. He waited until the wing tip was grazing the undergrowth at the runway's edge and gave the order to stop.

They jumped out with a second between them. Black went last. He landed heavily but his ankles held. Following the others, he plunged into the forest. They had made it to the ground and their fate was back in their own hands. Just the three of them, the jungle and their objective.

48

Black led them north-eastwards for half a mile, before calling a halt in a small puddle of light let in by a fallen barrigona tree. Unprompted, all three paused to listen out for any sound to indicate that they were being followed. They heard nothing except the hypnotic insect drone of the forest overlaid with a cacophony of bird calls. There were approximately two hours of daylight left before nightfall. If they moved quickly, they could cover four or five miles and be safely buried deep in the jungle before they made camp. It was a little over fifty miles to their objective, which if they made steady progress from sunrise to sunset, meant a further two days' solid hike.

Barely exchanging a word, the three of them reverted to the drills that in their early training had been so firmly cemented that they had become second nature. The first task was to change into their hiking gear. Tough cotton combat trousers tucked into lightweight, calf-length boots and cotton khaki T-shirts to wick the sweat away from their skin. They smeared their faces, necks, arms and the backs of their hands with camouflage cream, tied khaki bandanas around their heads to stop their sweat from trickling into their eyes and sprayed themselves from head to toe with DEET. Next, they assembled the three AK-47s, fitting them with bayonets and thirty-round magazines, then loaded each of the Smith and Wesson pistols to their full capacity of nine rounds. The pistols were secured in shoulder holsters worn outside their shirts and the rifles were strapped to the sides of their packs.

Lastly, they distributed the remaining ammunition equally between them and took ten grenades each, storing them in webbing pouches fastened across their chests. Black then hid the three empty holdalls beneath a carpet of dried leaves. Packs on and armed with razor-sharp machetes, they were ready to move.

The Sabre facility lay on a bearing of eighty-five degrees, taking them almost due east towards the Brazilian border. From their examination of satellite photographs they had detected signs of a dirt track connecting it to Platanal but had decided not to risk using it. Instead, they planned to follow a route running parallel to the road, approximately two miles to its north. Using a compass in order to preserve the precious battery life of his GPS, Black set a course and took first shift in the lead.

The deeper they pressed into the forest, the hotter and more humid it became, so that they soon found themselves gasping for air. The ground was covered with several inches of slippery mud that made the going harder still and, despite the DEET, Black experienced regular sharp stabs, like jabs from a needle, as fat mosquitos attacked his neck.

Physical discomfort, the extreme variety, could be tolerated. The body could anaesthetize itself to pain with the help of a determined will, but the pervading claustrophobia of the jungle was far harder to master. Without trails, waymarks or lookout points, the mind's natural demand to orientate itself was frustrated. It had only a needle on a compass on which to focus. Pressed in on all sides and with no recognizable change in the landscape, it was easy to believe that you were travelling in endless circles and would never see open country again. Black was aware that this was his weak point, that his chief enemy was a restless desire to push on faster, risking draining previous reserves of energy. He made a conscious effort to hold himself in check and attempted to settle into a steady rhythm – walking, slashing, walking, slashing – reminding himself that the jungle was not something you could ever overcome. The most you could achieve was to adjust yourself to its laws and assimilate. Anything less would be fatal.

After thirty minutes at the front Black ceded the lead to Fallon, who seemed to make easy progress. He cleared their path with slow, lazy strokes of his machete that absorbed minimum effort. His body was young and agile and slow to tire. Bringing up the rear, Riley was noisy and bull-like in comparison. Black had fought alongside both kinds of men and appreciated their relative strengths and weaknesses. The Fallons of this world were stealthy and clinical, at their most useful in operations in which patience and invisibility were paramount. In face-to-face combat, you wanted a Riley at your side. Finn had been one of those: a man who would have been at home wielding a broadsword in a medieval pitched battle. Black's skills lay somewhere in between. He was neither the strongest nor the stealthiest, but Finn used to joke that he had a sixth sense, an awareness of danger that at times bordered on witchcraft. Black thought of it as a simple will to live. He had known soldiers who were reckless and some who were infected with romantic ideas of noble sacrifice. Both were equally alien to him. So long as he drew breath, he was certain of one thing: he would do whatever it took to keep doing so.

The light began to fade. They arrived at a stream with thick ferns growing along its banks. On the far side was a small clearing. Black stopped to switch on and check his GPS. It confirmed that they had covered a little over four miles and had remained on course.

'Pitch up for the night?' Riley said.

'As good a place as any.' Black peered into the gathering shadows. It was impossible not to imagine unseen figures hiding in the gloom.

Fallon arrived alongside him and shrugged off his pack. 'I don't know about you boys, I could eat my own mother.'

In the few remaining minutes of daylight they suspended their hammocks and fly sheets from trees on three sides of the clearing and filled their canteens – all fitted with integral filters – from the stream. They quenched their thirst, then, using a simple hexamine-tablet stove, brewed the best coffee Black had tasted since the last time he had spent a night in the open. Dinner was foil-packed, self-heating portions of beef and vegetable stew with mashed potatoes. Despite the state-of-the-art packaging, the contents were the same old army rations Black remembered – all tasting identical, regardless of the contents. They followed them with hand-fuls of small tart fruits called camu camu, which Fallon had spotted growing on a shrub beside the stream.

By eight p.m. they had changed into their dry sets of clothes and were lying in their hammocks listening to the pulsing throb of the jungle night. Black's limbs were heavy and aching and his mind flooded with images from their long and eventful day.

'Good to be back, boss?' Riley said.

'Feels like I never left.'

'Finny would've loved this,' Riley said. 'Never known a bloke so keen to get stuck in.'

'One of a kind.'

'That's what he said about you,' Fallon said in a voice half-way to sleep.

'Don't tell me anything more.'

Riley didn't give him any choice: 'He said God made man and the Devil made Black.'

Black said nothing.

'I think it was a compliment, boss.'

'From Finn? Never.'

Black woke from a deep sleep in the darkness. He pressed the button that illuminated the face of his watch. Five thirty a.m. Thirty minutes before sunrise. He swung silently out of his hammock, found his upturned boots, carefully shook them out to dislodge any unwanted intruders, and pulled them on.

With his eyes adjusting to the tiny amount of ambient light he walked a few yards away from camp to relieve himself against a tree. Unable to see more than a few feet, he was alive to every sound and smell. The surrounding vegetation rustled and cracked with the movements of insects. His nostrils flooded with the scent of decomposing leaves which formed a carpet on the forest floor. He finished and zipped up, then on turning back to camp, felt a sensation through the soles of his feet. The faintest of vibrations that gradually intensified until, over the course of a full minute it became an audible thump-thump. At first he mistook it for something or someone running towards them, but then another faster sound in a higher register accompanied it and became the familiar rapid chop-chop-chop of a large heli moving steadily in their direction. It grew louder, coming from the east, then slowly tracked away west in the direction of Platanal, no doubt following the line of the road.

Black walked back into camp to find the others on their feet.

'Sabre?' Riley said.

'Can't see who else it could be.'

'I'm going to enjoy blowing that little baby up,' Fallon said.

In the semi-darkness Black saw him smile broadly for the first time since they had boarded the plane, invigorated by their first sniff of the enemy.

They washed in the stream, breakfasted on porridge and struck camp by six thirty. Half an hour later the heli passed by again, making its return journey. This time it seemed to come closer. Black felt the beat of its rotors in his chest. He pictured the crew inside. Relaxed and chatting. Another well-paid day in the jungle.

And with no idea what was coming to them.

They marched silently throughout the morning with renewed purpose, each taking turns in the lead. They moved neither quickly nor slowly but at an even pace agreed unconsciously between them. When not at the front, Black stroked a whetstone along the length of his machete – one stroke for every two footsteps – the rhythm of the motion rendering him into a semi trance. At midday they paused briefly to eat – fallen cacao fruit and cereal and protein bars that tasted foul but refuelled their tiring muscles. Then they pressed on, matching their previous speed of a steady two and a half miles per hour.

As the afternoon wore on, fatigue set in. Rubbing straps and aching feet conspired to deny Black the comfortable, somnambulant state in which he had spent the first part of the day. The deeper he dug into his physical reserves, the more his mind roved restlessly. Images of Finn on the mortuary slab, his empty boots among his children's shoes, the smiling picture on the kitchen wall and Kathleen's pale and tragic face. Domestic, wrenching, weakening thoughts that began to merge with dim ghosts of memories from distant childhood. Stripped of all distractions, Black was plunged into the dark pool of his subconscious mind, the silt at its very bottom stirring up so thickly he could taste it. He tried in vain to retreat from it, to contain his thoughts to the business of putting one foot in front of another, but the inner world became as vivid as the outer. Was he trying to tell himself something? Was he afraid? Unsure of his abilities? Or was he searching for a motive powerful enough to steel his resolve?

The power of this final thought sent a chill sensation the length of his spine. With it came the realization that in all his years of soldiering he had scarcely thought of motive, only of objective. Identify, isolate and destroy. Nothing more was needed. He had operated at the level of instinct and reflex, no more self-questioning than a snake poised for the kill. Self-consciousness and doubt were the enemies of action, more dangerous than any bullet.

He was suddenly envious of his two younger colleagues, confident and comfortable in their own skins. This was just another job to them. The kind of excitement they couldn't live without. An adventure to recount to their mates in Credenhill. That had been him and Finn once. Forces of nature. No more complicated than a pair of wolves. Kill, eat and howl at the moon.

Fallon checked his GPS. 'That's twenty miles.' He glanced back at Black, sensing that he had started to flag. 'It's five o'clock. Do you want to stop?'

'I'm good for one more shift.'

Fallon and Riley glanced at one another, as if about to object. Black strode to the front and picked up the pace, determined that they wouldn't see him weaken. To admit tiredness, even to himself, was too dangerous to contemplate. He pushed on, head down, leaning into the straps of his Bergen and feeling the burn in his thighs on every stride. After fifteen minutes his left calf started to tighten. He fought against the pain, aware that at the first signs of a limp Riley and Fallon would start to see him as a liability and with that his authority would drain away.

He stopped suddenly and held up a hand. In a puddle of mud in front of him were two sets of boot prints. They were fresh. A large bubble of air squashed into the ground by a heel remained unburst. Riley and Fallon came alongside him and followed his gaze.

'I'll go ahead,' Black mouthed, giving them no opportunity to protest. He pressed a finger to his lips, indicating that he was demanding absolute silence, then slid off his Bergen. The others did the same. Ignoring their concerned glances, he moved off, holding his machete in his right hand and ready to reach for his pistol with his left. Several yards behind, Riley and Fallon came after him, silently easing off their rifles' safety catches.

Black tracked the line of footprints that seemed to follow a game trail heading north-west. He continued for several minutes, the light beginning to fade.

He heard them before he saw them. Two male voices, talking in a Spanish dialect. He inched towards a dense thicket, staying out of their sight. Just visible through the interwoven stems were two men in their thirties, both dressed in jungle combats without insignia. They had taken off their packs, one of which had a radio aerial protruding from it, and were making ready to camp for the night at the foot of a large tree. Black assumed they were a foot patrol, probably one of several that at any one time circled the forests outlying the Sabre compound. He was forced to a decision – retreat and risk being heard or seen or eliminate the danger before it presented itself. The answer was obvious. He turned and gestured to Riley and Fallon to fan out either side of the thicket to cover him.

The three of them waited, silent and still, ready at any

moment to seize their opportunity. It came as the taller and younger of the two men headed off into the bush on the far side of their campsite to urinate, leaving the other to set up a cooking stove. He lit the gas with a match and the flame roared noisily into life. Black used the moment to make his move, his footsteps disguised by the sound of the stove. The crouching man glanced up as if sensing a presence, but in the opposite direction from which Black was approaching.

It was perfect. Black stooped forward and in a fraction of a second drew the blade of his machete across the kneeling man's throat. There was hardly a sound, except that of the blood that fountained out from the severed neck hitting the ground in a single spot several feet ahead of the already limp body. Black caught the dead man's collar in his left hand and lowered him so that his forehead was resting on the ground in front of his knees, inches from the stove, giving him the appearance of having leaned down to inspect it.

Black crept sideways to the trunk of the tree and waited for the sound of footsteps. Moments later he heard the second man returning. He started talking, picking up the conversation he had been having with his companion. With his back pressed to the rough bark and facing the slumped body, Black sensed the second man approaching from his right. A shaft of moving shadow was his cue to step left around to the far side of the trunk as his target passed by on the other side.

The machete blade sliced the air. Some instinct caused his victim to raise his right hand and make a quarter turn in Black's direction, giving him a glimpse of his astonished eyes as the blade sliced through his raised fingers and sank at a downwards angle into his neck. It was a deflected blow and not fatal. The man stumbled, pouring blood, kicking over the stove as he fell. Black struck again – once, twice.

A detached head rolled away from its body and came to rest, rocking slightly, in a thick pool of blood. Black turned away and wiped the blade of his machete on the fabric of one of the packs. Already, a swarm of flies was descending and a small army of ants crawling out of the earth. Black stooped to turn off the stove, confirmed that neither of the dead mercenaries was wearing a dog tag or carrying identification and rejoined the others.

'Probably Sabre,' Black said. 'We'll have to be careful. There may be more.'

They nodded, neither saying a word.

Black strode back along the game trail in the fast fading light to find their Bergens.

He had made his point.

49

Kennedy had been roused from his sickbed for the occasion. Dr Razia had been insistent. They would all be present to witness the coming together of their work.

Sarah Bellman stood at the far left of the row of scientists who had been joined by Brennan and Drecker. She, Kennedy and Sphyris now found themselves for the first time in the laboratory in which Razia and Holst had been working alongside each other for weeks. They were looking through a window of one-way glass at a slightly built young man of twenty or so dressed in a plain, khaki T-shirt, who was seated at a white-topped table on which there was a pair of speakers and a silver crucifix: a gesture, designed by Holst no doubt, to make the experience as digestible as possible.

Razia and Holst were thoroughly enjoying themselves, smiling and laughing with one another as they carried out the last checks on the equipment that would control the strength of the signal to be transmitted to the subject. Even Brennan and Drecker seemed infected by their optimism. They sat, relaxed, on stools, like investors confident that their big gamble was about to pay off.

Razia called the room to order. 'Ladies and gentlemen, before we begin, I would like to thank you all for your incredible efforts. In the space of weeks we have married your expertise to create a result – we hope – that will be as momentous as any we have seen in the field of neuroscience, or, indeed, the whole of medicine. The human condition is determined by the mind. What you have given us is no less than the ability to *improve* that condition immeasurably. In fact, if properly applied, suffering in the sense of mental pain and anguish need no longer exist.' He nodded to Holst. 'I shall allow my colleague to lead the demonstration.'

Bellman felt trickles of sweat run down her back. She glanced to her right. Kennedy and Sphyris were staring impassively at the glass. Should she have told them? No, she was clear in her own mind. She had done the right thing. This was her responsibility. She held the cards and was the only one to be trusted with them. Sphyris was too timid to negotiate his way out and in his current state of mind Kennedy was too angry. Behind their military uniforms Drecker and Brennan were business people who spoke the language of deals. The terms she would strike were simple: they could have the correctly ordered code in exchange for their immediate release, safe passage and the balance of their money, but they wouldn't receive the code until they had arrived safely home. If there was to be haggling, Bellman would negotiate over the cash, nothing else.

Holst leaned forward to a small microphone connected to the speakers on the other side of the glass: '*Cuando oye el sonido, recoja el crucifijo, por favor.*' When you hear the sound, please pick up the crucifix.

He pressed a key on his laptop. The same white noise they had played to the macaque was played to the young man.

No doubt glad of something to break the boredom, the young man picked up the crucifix and held it in his palm.

What happened next was not what Sarah was expecting. He pressed the crucifix to his chest, then to his lips and then to his forehead. Holst played another short burst of encoded sound. The subject sank to his knees, proclaiming in Spanish, '*¡Alabado sea el Señor!*' Praise God!

Sarah felt eyes on her. She glanced to her right and saw the smiling face of Dr Razia.

50

They made camp, cooked and ate in silence, tuned in to the jungle, alive to the tiniest sign of human approach. Since dealing with the two mercenaries, Black had felt his equilibrium return. His mind was clear and focused. The balance of power between the three of them had shifted. The bond between Riley and Fallon seemed to have loosened and he detected a renewed respect from both of them. Their muted reactions suggested to him that while they might have seen action in Syria, it was of the kind conducted at arm's length, through the scope of a rifle. Killing up close with a blade was a large step up in every way. If it overwhelmed you, if afterwards you shook and trembled and had nightmares, you were the kind of soldier who was likely to be killed very soon. Survival required a cool head and a cold heart.

The colder the better.

Sometimes, in order to stay alive, you needed to be more dead than death.

Throughout the night they took turns on watch, crouching, alert, rifles cocked, until again the heli passed overhead on its pre-dawn run to Platanal. At first light Black skirted the circumference of their camp, checking the tripwires he had tied across the access points. There were no alien footprints. No signs of disturbance. It was good news. They were still ahead of the game.

In the absence of a stream or overnight rain to fill their canteens from the palm-leaf funnels they had placed in their necks, Black chopped down lengths of thick bamboo, cut nicks in the stems and tipped out the water trapped inside. It had a bitter, pithy taste but was fresh and clean. They used it to brew coffee, topped up their supplies from more stems and set out, aiming to reach their objective by nightfall.

Black marched without pain or stiffness. He was just another animal in the jungle, observing, anticipating, ready on a hair trigger to react. To counter the danger of meeting more patrols he imposed a new drill. Every ten minutes they would stop for thirty seconds to listen, watch and sniff the air.

They continued in this way for more than three hours. Marching, stopping, listening, marching, then, during one of their silent pauses, Black caught a faint change of scent.

'Smell that?' he whispered.

Riley and Fallon shook their heads.

At first he believed it might be human sweat. The smell of a man who hadn't seen soap for a week. He sniffed again and changed his mind. 'Woodsmoke. Could be wrong.'

The others couldn't detect it.

They pressed on for another half hour, Black occasionally catching the same scent and wondering whether his mind was playing tricks. He was bringing up the rear of the party when Fallon held up a hand. He pointed to a rubber tree a short distance in front of them. A flash had been cut in its trunk with a machete. Black stepped up for a closer look.

The scars in the bark were far from fresh and showed the early signs of healing. They had been made months rather than days or weeks before. The symbol that had been carved consisted of two parallel lines bisected with a slanting vertical: $\neq$. Black felt an unsettling sensation in his stomach. It was a symbol he had seen before, many times. Every experienced bushwhacker had his own distinctive sign he used to mark his way or to signal his route to others who may be searching for him.

'Boss?' Riley said.

'That flash . . . It's the one Finn always used.'

Riley and Fallon exchanged a glance as if doubting Black's sanity.

Black quickly assembled the evidence in his mind: the mention of Brennan in Finn's diary, the cover story to Kathleen about a job in Africa, his shame when going cap in hand to Towers and the distinctive flash. Its presence could be purely coincidental, but the fact that it was here, on the precise bearing between the airstrip and the Sabre compound, lent weight to his theory: that its maker was navigating by compass rather than GPS. Its position on the trunk, at ninety degrees to their current course, suggested that if it were Finn who had left it, he was heading to their left.

There was only one logical explanation. If Finn had been following a straight compass bearing, the flash would have marked a point of deviation from his route. A point to which he would have had to return in order to resume his previous course.

Finn had been here. He was following the same trail. Somehow, for reasons he had yet to explain, their destinies had contrived to combine.

He smelled it again.

This time there was no doubt. The others smelled it, too: smoke from a cooking fire. It was being carried on the gentlest of breezes from his left, from the direction in which Finn – if that's who it had been – had been travelling.

'We should take a look,' Black said.

'What if it's trouble we could do without?' Fallon said.

'We need to know what we're up against – what we might run into on the way back.'

The argument was unanswerable. They brought out their GPS units, got a fix on their current position and marked it as a waypoint. They could now head out in any direction and be guided back.

The smoke was coming from the north. Black followed his nose and after a hundred yards found another similar flash. After another hundred there was a third, and a short way beyond it they picked up the meander of a small stream that wandered between the rubber trees. One by one the signs started to add up. The ground began to rise ahead of them. A gentle slope became a steeper one. They arrived at yet another flash and up ahead, saw an unusual glimpse of sky – a break in the trees.

They crept upwards to the top of the rise where they remained in cover behind a dense clump of leafy palms. On the far side was a sight Black hadn't expected to see: a clearing no more than fifty yards in diameter, in which there were a number of circular huts and a single traditionally built longhouse thatched with palms. On top of the building was a wooden cross, signalling that it was a Christian mission. A number of semi-naked children were playing football on an area of dirt shared with chickens and goats. A few older ones were crouching at the margins. Black noticed that several of these teenagers had lifeless, glazed expressions of the kind he had seen on the faces of the young in conflict zones across the globe.

'Sorry, boss. Not sure we can handle them,' Riley said.

Black ignored the remark and continued to watch. A short while later, a woman of about thirty-five wearing a blue smock dress and sandals, her hair tied back from her face, came out of the longhouse carrying a small child. She set it down with two young girls and went to talk to a teenage boy who was sitting by himself. He watched her place a hand on his shoulder and talk to him gently.

'Seen enough?' Fallon said.

'Stay here. I'm going to talk to her.'

'You're *what*?'

'I want to know where all these kids are coming from.'

'What does it matter?' Fallon said.

'Personal reasons. Take a break. Relax.'

Ignoring their objections, he sloughed off his pack and tried the best he could to scrub the greasy camouflage cream from his face and arms with water from his canteen. Then, leaving behind his rifle, pistol and machete, he circled around to the far side of the clearing where he arrived at a narrow but well-trodden trail that led northwards from the settlement into the forest. Just outside the margins, he took up position behind the knotted roots of a large 'walking palm' – a wigwam-like structure of roots, on top of which a full grown tree was improbably balanced. From this angle he could see inside the various buildings in the encampment. In total there were perhaps forty or fifty children and teenagers and one more adult woman moving about inside the longhouse. The smoke they had smelled was coming from a fire burning inside a crude cooking range built from mud bricks, situated in an open-sided structure that served as a cookhouse.

Black paused to question his motives. Was he taking an unnecessary risk in exposing himself? Of course he was. There was no logical answer but some instinct told him that it was something he had to do. He decided to trust it.

'*Hola. Buenos días. Habla inglés?*'

The woman in the blue dress spun around, her hand pressed to her chest in alarm. She was younger than he had at first thought, perhaps not yet thirty.

He held out his hands in a gesture of openness and smiled. Some of the footballing children, who, at first sight of the stranger had frozen in curiosity, ran towards him. They swarmed around his legs and tugged excitedly at his clothes.

'I'm English,' Black said, noticing the second woman coming to the longhouse door. She was identically dressed and of a similar age. She exchanged an anxious glance with her colleague but overcame her fear and stepped forward. 'I'm trying to find out what happened to a friend of mine.' It was hard to make himself heard above the babble of the children's voices. He 'may have passed this way last year. His name was Finn. Ryan Finn.'

The woman nodded and called out to her colleague, translating what Black had just told her. A look of understanding, though not quite one of relief, spread across the other woman's face.

'Yes, Mr Finn was here,' the woman closest to him said guardedly, in good but heavily accented English. Her features were plain and her hair scraped back, but her deep brown eyes had the arresting quality of one motivated by a higher purpose. 'You look like a soldier.'

'I'm sorry. I didn't mean to frighten you. I'm an old friend. We were soldiers together – in the past.' He paused to consider the significance of this revelation. Finn had come halfway across the world to work for Sabre and upped and left before he got paid. 'You said he was here?'

She nodded. 'Just a moment.' She came forward and called the children away, clapping her hands and sending them back to their game.

They obeyed without question, letting go of his clothes and straggling back to the open area at the side of the longhouse.

'I'm sorry. This is unusual,' the woman said. 'We don't have many visitors.'

'I understand. My name's Leo. Leo Black.'

She swept him cautiously with her eyes. 'Isabel. My colleague is María Luisa.'

'Is this an orphanage?'

'Not all of them are orphans, but most.'

'May I ask what happened?'

'Their parents were miners. Illegal miners. They were here for years, since the 1990s. Our mission tended to them. Just north of here there's a trail that leads down to the river that will take you across the border to Brazil. That's where we're from, my order – Boa Vista.'

'The families were cleared out?'

Isabel nodded. 'Two years ago there was a government ultimatum. The mineral rights were sold to a private company. The miners who refused to go were hunted down and killed. Men and women. The lucky ones were taken to work elsewhere. The children were left to fend for themselves. In a bankrupt country there is nowhere for them to go. Brazil doesn't want them either. So –' she shrugged – 'that is why we're here.'

'Was it Sabre who killed them?'

She hesitated before giving a guarded nod. He admired her courage, coming out unarmed to meet a strange man who had emerged from the forest.

'I think my friend, Mr Finn, had been working for Sabre. I believe he may have disliked what he saw there.'

His words seemed to register. She looked at him squarely as if deciding to trust him.

'Would you like some coffee?'

'Yes, please.'

She led him to the open-sided hut, gesturing to María Luisa to leave the visitor to her. María Luisa smiled uncertainly at Black, then turned back to the sullen teenager she had been tending to.

They entered the shade of the hut. Black sat on one of the wooden stools arranged around a rough-hewn table while Isabel poured coffee from a pot on the stove. She set down two tin mugs and took a seat opposite. Black thanked her, noticing her tough, practical hands as they lifted their cups to their lips.

'So, tell me – what do you want to know?' Isabel said.

'What were the children's parents mining?'

'Coltan. Also gold. Believe me, none of them got rich.'

'And the company that bought the rights, is that Sabre?'

'Yes. They have a mine twenty kilometres from here.' She nodded towards the east. 'Some of these children have parents who are employed there.'

'Does the company give you money?'

'No. But they leave us alone.'

She held him in a level gaze which was neither friendly nor hostile but which asked him to get to the point.

'My friend, Mr Finn, is dead,' Black said. He noticed a flicker of emotion register on Isabel's face. 'He was killed last month – in Paris, France, as a matter of fact. He was working on something unconnected but I fear his death had something to do with his time with Sabre. You said he was here –'

Isabel took another sip of coffee, her eyes softening a little. 'Almost one year ago, he arrived here one morning. He was sick with fever, delirious. He had nothing, no possessions, just the clothes he was wearing. We thought he might die . . . he didn't. After a week or so he started to recover. He stayed for another week doing some repairs on the mission house. Then we told him how he could travel over the border into Brazil. He was a good man . . .' Her voice carried a hint of sadness. She glanced over to María Luisa, who was still talking gently to the boy. 'That's Rafael. He doesn't speak. He's fifteen years old. He's been with us for two years. He sits all day by himself. Your friend, Mr Finn, he got Rafael to help with his work. Taught him how to use a saw and a hammer. He was good to him.'

'He had children of his own. Three.'

'Yes, he told us.'

'Did he tell you anything else – what he'd seen at the mine, perhaps?'

'Only that he didn't like the way it was run. He had a disagreement with the people there and decided to leave, even though he was sick. He thought we should leave here, too. He was worried we might be in danger.'

'In danger of what?'

'These children are all witnesses. One day they might give their testimony.'

'He had a point. What's stopping you?'

'Their lives have been disturbed enough. If we have to leave, we will know.'

'God will tell you?'

Isabel gave a hint of a smile. 'I thank you for your concern, Mr Black. You don't have to worry about us. We will be looked after.'

Black looked into her dark, determined eyes and hoped that she was right. Eyes that Finn must also have gazed into as she told him the exact same thing. *We will be looked after.* What would Finn have done? The man he knew would not simply have left them to their fate without any prospect of help.

The sound of a child's cry carried over the sound of the football game. They looked over to see María Luisa picking a sobbing boy off the ground. He was bleeding from a cut on his knee.

'I should let you get back to them,' Black said. He finished his coffee and stood up from the table. 'Goodbye. And good luck.'

He waited for a moment in order to give her the opportunity to ask him what exactly he was doing here at her mission in the middle of the rainforest. She was wise enough not to take it.

'Goodbye, Mr Black,' Isabel said. 'I am sorry to hear about Mr Finn. We liked him very much.'

She gathered up the empty cups then went to help María Luisa with the crying child.

Black headed back the way he had come.

The silent boy, Rafael, rose up from his haunches and watched him until he disappeared from view.

51

Riley and Fallon were waiting impatiently, Bergens on, ready to march out.

'Finn was here. Almost a year ago exactly. He deserted. Arrived sick. They nursed him. There's a trail around the far side that leads to the Brazilian border. I think we may have found our way out.'

'They're sure it was him?' Riley said.

'They knew his name.'

'And Fireballs didn't know he'd been here?'

'Not that he told me.'

'Does he make a habit of withholding information?'

The question came from Fallon.

Black thought carefully before answering. 'Not usually without good reason.'

Riley and Fallon exchanged a glance.

'What's the reason?' Riley said.

'Best guess – Finn took dirty money working for Sabre. Crossed one of my red lines.'

'And you wouldn't have come if you'd known?'

'It's not a question worth asking. We're here.'

'What did you tell the woman?' Fallon said.

'That I was a friend of Finn's trying to find out what happened to him.'

'Do you trust her?'

'They're two nuns looking after the orphaned kids of miners murdered by Sabre thugs – no doubt the kind Finn was employed to train.' He pulled on his Bergen. 'Are we ready?'

'We need to be clear what the objective is, boss,' Riley said. 'Is this purely a sabotage and rescue or are you and Towers looking to settle a score?'

'I had no idea Finn had been here. Yes, the fact that he was gives me a keener edge but the objective remains the same.'

His answer was met with silence.

'Is there a problem?'

'The way you dealt with those two last night,' Fallon said. 'The three of us could have done it with bayonets. Clean. No risk.'

'What was the risk? You were ten feet away ready to shoot.'

Neither answered.

'My objective was to neutralize them as silently as possible. That's what I did.'

Still no response.

Black looked from one to the other, straining to keep his rising anger in check. 'Would one of you be kind enough to tell me what's going on?'

'There was no need for it,' Fallon said, prompting a glance from Riley. 'And no need to risk talking to those women.'

His patience snapped. 'If either of you wants out, you know the way.' He pointed to the far side of the clearing. 'You have my permission to leave.'

He turned and headed back down the slope, following the footprints they had made on their way up. He continued on alone, picked up the first flash, then made his way to the second. He was nearly at the third when he heard footsteps jogging behind him. He glanced round to see Riley.

'Boss.'

They walked on in silence. They had covered more than a mile and were back on their easterly bearing when Fallon caught up with them. An exchange of nods was enough to bury the hatchet. It was twelve miles to the Sabre compound and they had four hours of daylight in which to get there. Black took the lead and upped the pace.

They marched for two solid hours through dense, unyielding understorey, before the ground started to rise up a gentle gradient that led them to higher, rockier terrain where the trees were sparser and light shot down through the canopy in golden shafts.

It was like an omen.

But whether it was one of life or death, Black had no idea.

The low rumble of diesel engines, at first almost indistinguishable from the background hubbub of the jungle, was the first indication that they were drawing close. It rose steadily in volume as they drew nearer, reverberating through the trees until they could hear the sounds of individual engines shifting gears. And beneath them, like a steady bass rhythm, the chug of an industrial generator.

The light was fading. Black brought them to a halt and proposed they camp, eat and sleep before commencing their recce at three a.m. They could use tomorrow's daylight hours to plan their attack and rest before making their move the following night. Tired at the end of their relentless march, Riley and Fallon agreed without objection.

Black estimated that they were within 400 yards of the perimeter fence. The satellite images had shown that a hill rose steeply from this northern end of the compound where the mine workings were sited. He led off in that direction. Several minutes later they hit the base of a steep slope and tacked upwards, their boots slipping on damp rocks that were criss-crossed by knuckles of roots. It was as inaccessible and inhospitable as Black had hoped. No regular patrol would bother coming this way.

They climbed for several hundred feet and, as darkness enveloped them, found a thicket of bamboo flourishing along the line of a small spring that trickled out from the rocks above them. Wearing their night-vision goggles, they cut down stems as thick as their arms until they had carved out three individual spaces in which to hang their hammocks. Dinner was more self-heating rations, tepid and bland, but after a day's march as good as a feast . . .

Black took first turn on watch. The air was unnaturally still with no breath of breeze and in the suffocating heat the animals were restless. Monkeys quarrelled high in the branches overhead and mice and rats, drawn towards their camp by the lingering smell of food, skittered over the rocks. Peering into the night through the green-tinged lens of his goggles, Black watched a tree snake drop noiselessly from a thick, hanging drape of creeper to the ground. Sensing his presence, it lay still, then cautiously craned its head to peer at him through curious slits of eyes. Not liking what it saw, it raised its body back towards the foliage from which it had descended, and, as if drawn by an invisible cord, slowly wound its way back upwards to its nest.

They moved out at three a.m. with rifles cocked, full canteens and webbing pouches crammed with GPS units, ammunition and grenades.

The distance they had to cover before reaching the compound was even shorter than Black had estimated. After approximately one third of a mile they arrived at its edge. The forest was cut back to a distance of ten yards from a sturdy fence, which stood twelve feet high and was topped with coiled razor wire. From cover Black scanned the fence from left to right. Tall metal poles were spaced at twenty-yard intervals, each of them fitted with what appeared to be motion-activated cameras. It was primitive security of the sort that wouldn't pass muster at a facility in the US or Europe, but was sufficient to deter the unlikely incursion of any chancers or bandits in this out-of-the-way corner of the Amazon.

From their elevated position at the compound's north-west tip they had an uninterrupted view through the trees over its full length. It was almost exactly as they had seen it from satellite photographs but with the addition of several new prefabricated buildings, and with a bigger chunk quarried out of the hill to their left. It was an impressive sight. An opencast mine with a military encampment attached. Two outsize excavators, each with shark-toothed buckets, stood close to the exposed hillside. Behind them were a number of JCB earth movers which transferred the spoil torn from the earth on to a conveyor. This led to a separation plant: a building in which grading machinery sorted the valuable coltan ore from the rest. The waste emerged on a further conveyor angled upwards at forty-five degrees, which deposited it in a large mound. Two outsize bulldozers spread this out across a large flat area that over months and years would rise up into a vast spoil heap.

The mine workings took up two-thirds of the entire site. The remaining third, separated by a large drainage ditch and a further secure fence, housed Sabre's less conventional venture. Four long, single-storey buildings were arranged in rows at right angles to a roadway, which led from a gate at the compound's entrance at its south-eastern corner. This was guarded by a sentry post. The furthest building was distinguished from the others by an array of satellite dishes attached to its roof. A fifth building, which was double the width of the others, stood between the other four and what looked to be a parade square and training area, complete with a military assault course.

A sixth substantial structure, and the one of most interest to Black, stood by itself on the far side of the square. Unlike the others, which were prefabricated metal structures, it was built from concrete breeze blocks and had metal grilles bolted across the windows. It was approximately 150 feet long and 25 wide and was the only building on site with air-conditioning units attached at regular intervals to the outer walls. From this Black concluded that it must be where the four scientists were being held.

Several much smaller buildings were arranged in the south-west corner of the compound, close to a grassed area on which a single heli – the same Super Puma they had identified from the images at Credenhill – was parked. Black guessed that these sheds housed the compound's vital plant – the generator and water and sewage pumps. Next to these was an area protected by an earth bund, which, it was safe to assume, had been built around large tanks storing aviation fuel and far larger supplies of diesel oil to power the generator and mining machinery. Black counted six identical Toyota pick-up trucks parked close to the helipad, two of them with heavy machine guns mounted on their beds. Water was stored in a large cylindrical tank supported on steel legs that held it fifteen feet from the ground to generate a head of pressure. The whole inhabited area was dimly lit and, viewed without goggles, glowed a flickering orange.

'Not much sign of life,' Fallon whispered.

'There's a couple of guards – walking this way from behind that building,' Riley said.

Black adjusted the focus on his goggles and zoomed in. A pair of sentries, dressed in identical uniform to those worn by the two men they had encountered thirty hours before, had emerged from behind the breeze-block building, rifles slung over their shoulders. They continued to circle it and even at this distance gave the impression of being tired and listless, as if the last thing they were expecting was any trouble.

'Where's the water coming from?' Black said. 'See any pipes?'

'There's one coming from that building at the mine,' Riley said.

Black spotted it. A large pipe, perhaps two, emerged from the building, travelled across the ground as far as the drainage ditch, then turned ninety degrees to follow it to the compound's far edge, where the ground fell away into a shallow valley. The compound, it seemed, sat on a large flat shelf, slightly raised above the floor of the valley, along which, he suspected, ran one of the many thousands of tributaries of the Orinoco.

'That'll be the barracks,' Fallon said. He indicated the double-width building. 'You could house two hundred men in there. You really think we can take all of this down with three of us?'

'Sometimes being outnumbered is an advantage,' Black said.

Fallon gave a dismissive grunt.

'A rat runs through a crowded room and then down an empty alleyway. Where is he most in danger?' He waited for Riley and Fallon to give it some thought. 'Think like a rat. The lowest, filthiest kind. OK, I want to check out their plumbing before first light.'

Staying under the cover of the trees they circled the north end of the compound, navigating the steep side of the unexcavated hillside before descending its eastern side and continuing along its flank until they were level with the drainage ditch. Here a muddy swathe, some 30 yards wide, was cut through the forest and sloped steeply downwards for around 200 yards, where, as Black had suspected, it met a small river. Two plastic pipes, one twice the bore of the other, ran above ground from the compound down towards the water. It was reasonable to suppose that the narrower of the two was the supply and the other discharge. He motioned the others to follow.

They picked their way down the slope, treading silently, aware that a single slip or a tumbling stone might be sufficient to give them away. Eventually they arrived at the bottom, close to the banks of the river. The sound of running water was a relief from the monotonous hum of the jungle. Creeping tentatively through dense, fleshy clumps of vegetation, they spotted a light off to their left. Crouching low, Black made his way to the water's edge and saw that it was coming from a pump house, approximately twenty yards up ahead, sited on their side of the river. A dam ten feet high, constructed from wire gabion baskets filled with rocks, created a pool behind it, from which the compound's water was being extracted.

The building was little more than a shed made of corrugated tin and through its window Black could see the outlines of two figures, one of them smoking a cigarette and gesturing with his hands as he spoke to his companion. They were young men, fit and physically honed. Trained mercenaries ready to be deployed wherever Sabre found their next customer. The kind of men Black had been obliged to fight and kill in more countries than he could remember.

Black returned to the others. 'I think we've found the start of our rat run.'

52

By five a.m. they were back in their original position, watching the compound come to life. The main generator had kicked into life and bright floodlights had been switched on. Personnel in military fatigues were moving busily about the camp. Twenty or so men dressed in civilian clothes emerged from one of the buildings, filtered into another that appeared to be the mess hall and emerged again ten minutes later. Most made their way towards the mine workings, while two of them went to collect pick-up trucks which they drove to the separation plant. Once there, half a dozen men loaded the truck's beds with heavy sacks of coltan ore, then, balancing precariously on top of their loads, they travelled across the compound to the heli, where they transferred the sacks to its cargo bay.

At five thirty a.m. a flight crew emerged from the mess and started the Puma's engines. With the aid of the floodlights Black could now see that the heli was equipped with forward guns and rocket launchers that protruded from its hull like two sets of fangs. It was a deadly weapon that would have to be disabled. It rose slowly into the air, switched on powerful dual searchlights, dipped its nose and headed west across the canopy towards Platanal.

As the sun rose above the treetops, activity intensified and then mining machinery got to work. Excavators took hungry bites out of the hillside while the JCBs trundled up and down behind them under the watchful gaze of a permanent guard detail. At the other end of the camp, Black counted approximately 120 men form up on parade. They appeared to be a mixture of nationalities, as many white faces as Hispanic and black. A sergeant major put them through their morning drill before three officers arrived to deliver the day's orders.

Using his night-vision goggles as binoculars, Black adjusted them to full magnification. He watched patiently, waiting for a clear view of the officers' faces. He was rewarded with a glimpse of one that belonged to a tall, lean man with pale, tightly drawn skin and eyes set in deep sockets that gave him the appearance of an animated skull. It wasn't a face one could easily forget. It belonged to Mitch Brennan, formerly of the Australian Special Air Service Regiment. The man who had tempted Finn – no doubt with many false promises – to lend his expertise to this dubious operation.

The men divided into four platoons. Two of them dispersed, then arrived promptly back on the parade ground carrying full packs and weapons. They jogged off out of the camp and along the road with a five-minute interval between them. The morning run. If Finn had had anything to do with establishing the training regime, they would be gone for between three and four hours. The other two platoons meanwhile started into a round of rigorous circuit training. Push-ups, sit-ups, sprints, log hauling. The usual routine that armies used to keep men fit and occupied while waiting for proper work to begin. Black was encouraged by the sight. If, as he suspected, the men currently working their muscles to exhaustion on the parade ground would spend the afternoon yomping, by nightfall they would be spent.

There was no activity at the breeze-block building until shortly after seven a.m., when a detachment of six armed guards arrived at its entrance. A door was unlocked and, shortly afterwards, Black counted eight figures emerge dressed in identical shorts and T-shirts. They were of assorted ages and seven of the eight were male. The single female was in her late twenties and had dark hair. They had to be the four abducted British scientists plus four others Sabre had snatched from elsewhere. Flanked by their guards, they made their way across the road to the mess hut. There was little communication between them. Their stooped shoulders and downcast gazes reminded Black of the many hostages he had viewed from a distance over the decades. They made a pathetic sight. He could almost feel their helplessness.

'That must be Bellman,' Fallon said. 'She's our number-one priority, right?'

'If we get to them,' Black said. 'We concentrate on destroying as much as we can and worry about her afterwards.'

'Even if we razed the whole place, I don't see how we could extract them,' Riley said.

'You've got a choice of six trucks,' Black answered. 'Did you watch the mine workers first thing? They left keys in the ignition overnight.'

'And how do you plan on getting in?'

'Through the gate,' Black said.

He saw his two companions exchange another of their sceptical glances.

'Do you boys have a problem with that?'

Riley shrugged. 'Your gig, boss.'

'Keep watching.'

They remained in place, closely observing and noting the routines of the camp. The Puma returned shortly after eight a.m., bringing barrels of fuel, crates of food and numerous other boxes which were distributed to the various sheds. Hoping to determine the function of each one, Black tracked the food supplies being carried to the building standing closest to the mess and boxes of other supplies and hardware being divided into the two adjacent buildings. A man in uniform clutching a clipboard, and with the unmistakable, bureaucratic demeanour of a quartermaster, appeared. He shuttled between his three stores, ordering a pair of young soldiers to move incorrectly stowed boxes to their correct locations. Assuming that the generator was housed in the building closest to the fuel tanks, Black made an educated guess that the one standing next to it, which had been left undisturbed, was the armoury.

After their breakfast the hostages were returned to their quarters and the door locked behind them. Three sealed wooden crates unloaded from the heli were later delivered to the entrance and carried inside. There was one further visitor to the building who arrived several minutes later. Black spotted him as he crossed the parade square smoking a cigarette. He was of Middle Eastern appearance and in his mid to late fifties. He was distinguished from the Sabre personnel by his civilian dress and the fact that nothing in his gait or demeanour suggested any background in the military. He was an anomaly, which told Black that he had to be of significance. Focusing in as tightly as his goggles would allow, Black followed him to the door of the breeze-block building where he turned to stub out and discard his cigarette. The action afforded Black a window of nearly three seconds in which to register his face.

He had last seen it fifteen years before. It belonged to Ammal Razia, a neurosurgeon who had worked alongside the infamous Dr Rihab Taha, otherwise known as Dr Germ, the architect of Iraq's chemical and biological warfare programme. Taha had masterminded the gassing of Iranian troops during the Iran–Iraq war of the 1980s and the genocide of the Marsh Arabs. He had experimented on human subjects and Razia had been a willing student and disciple, devising surgical techniques to 'cure' religious fanaticism and political non-conformity. The unwilling victims had been inmates of Saddam's many prisons. Their only crimes had been to offend the tyrant.

Unencumbered by ethical restraints, Taha, Razia and their colleagues had made great strides in their fields. Razia, in particular, by surgically nullifying distinct areas of the brain over the course of thousands of procedures, had contributed an inestimable amount to the understanding of evolution's most complex creation. Though not published officially, his findings had been widely disseminated throughout the global scientific community.

Black knew all this because he had read MI6's detailed dossier on Razia and several of his colleagues in Saddam's secret weapons programme. Having established their likely whereabouts he had personally led the snatch operations that had resulted in their arrests and transfer to Camp Cropper. He recalled the arrest of Razia in minute detail. He had been hiding in a house on the outskirts of Baghdad belonging to a cousin. He claimed to be a schoolteacher and had documents to back up his claim, but there had been no doubting the match with the multiple photographs that both US and UK military intelligence had on file.

Black remembered a charming and sophisticated character who had kept up the pretence of being the innocent victim of mistaken identity throughout his transfer to military prison. There had been no doubt in Black's mind that he was a psychopath and a committed and unrepentant member of Saddam's scientific cadre.

Spotting Black's intense focus on this individual, Riley asked, 'Any idea who he is?'

'No,' Black lied. 'You?'

Riley shook his head. 'I think he wants putting to bed, though.'

'Agreed.'

Razia drew keys from his pocket and let himself into the building.

By midday Black had seen enough. Razia was still inside with the hostages, which confirmed any lingering doubts over his identity. The silent hours of observation had also given Black some time to think. To piece together fragments of memory and set them into an order which led him to a set of dark conclusions.

He had delivered Razia and his colleagues to interrogators from the British intelligence services who were operating alongside American counterparts in Camp Cropper. He had assumed that, like other high-value detainees, Razia would be interrogated at length before either being released or more likely charged with serious offences. Some three or four months after his arrest, Black recalled asking Towers whether his interrogation had yielded any further leads to aid in their ongoing sweep-up operation of senior members of the Ba'ath regime and its cronies. Towers had told him that unfortunately Razia had not survived the interrogation process. At the time Black had interpreted this euphemism as meaning that he had either drowned while being waterboarded or suffocated. It had seemed perfectly logical: if Razia had admitted to his crimes, the Iraqi authorities would have hanged him. Remaining silent presented his only chance of staying alive.

Towers had lied. Somehow, Razia had fallen into the hands of Sabre, as had Brennan and Drecker, and all three had been there in Baghdad. Towers had had ultimate responsibility for Razia's arrest and detention and would have known if he had been released. If the reason had been legitimate, he would have had no reason to withhold the truth from Black, his right-hand man. Why lie? Why pretend he was dead? Black could come to only one conclusion: Razia was an asset. He was young, fiercely intelligent and possessed knowledge with huge commercial value; he was a leading expert in the field of neuroscience. The USA had scooped up 1,600 German scientists in Operation Paperclip after the Second World War. Could they have done the same in Iraq? Or could Sabre have stolen a march and got their hands on him first?

Finn had been on the mission to arrest Razia. Like Black, he wasn't a man to forget a face. He would have recognized him and when on his return he connected with Towers he would surely have told him. Towers could have dodged or disowned the situation but for one fact: he had lied to Black about Razia's fate. And if the day came when Towers found himself hauled to the Hague to account for his actions in the chaos of post-invasion Baghdad, Towers was afraid that Black would mention Razia.

Black tried every mental convolution to avoid it, but arrived at the same conclusion every time: he had been sent here by Towers to die. To be tidied up along with all the other problems of his past.

53

The knock on the door came shortly after Sarah Bellman returned from breakfast. She was greeted by two uniformed men and marched across the compound to Dr Razia's office. Shortly afterwards, she was joined by Professor Kennedy, who had also been forcibly escorted from his quarters. They were instrcuted to wait in silence. Eventually, Razia made an appearance, smelling of cologne and cigarette smoke. He bade them a friendly good morning and relaxed into the reclining chair behind his desk.

'I apologize for the unscheduled nature of this meeting but we have a busy day ahead. You are looking much better, Professor. I trust the medication has done the trick?'

'It would appear so,' Kennedy said, avoiding Razia's gaze.

'Good. I'm glad to hear it.' He turned his attention to Bellman. 'And you are keeping well?'

'Yes . . . Thank you.'

Razia rocked back in his chair and clasped his hands over the comfortable dome of his stomach. 'No doubt you are aware of the matter we are here to discuss?'

He let the question hang.

Neither Bellman nor Kennedy replied.

'Allow me to prompt you. For reasons that are too obvious to need explanation, with the help of Dr Holst I conduct a regular review of your work. The data you enter on your computers is not of course private to yourselves. It's the property of our employers. Therefore, in my position of oversight, I have unfettered access.'

Another pause. He looked from one to the other, like a schoolteacher waiting for the thief to confess.

Bellman felt her heartbeat quicken. A sensation of panic simultaneously rose up from the pit of her stomach and pressed in on the sides of her skull. All the while, Kennedy remained still and poker-faced, his level gaze fixed on Razia.

'Yes, Dr Bellman, you have every reason to feel anxious. I know that it was you who attempted to sabotage the code. Thankfully, Dr Holst has a keen eye for these things and was able to repair the damage.'

Kennedy turned to her with a look of disbelief. 'There's been a mistake,' he said.

Bellman tried to speak but her tongue refused to respond.

'I'm afraid not, Professor. All the evidence points to your protégée being determined to undermine our work.' He let out a regretful sigh. 'Which leaves me with a very difficult and unpleasant decision.'

'No. Please –' Bellman found her voice. 'I was angry . . . It was a misjudgement –'

'Indeed. Your work until then had been excellent. Faultless, in fact.'

Professor Kennedy leaned forward. 'Whatever you're contemplating, Razia, don't do it. We didn't ask to come here, so if either of us gave in to frustration, you've only yourselves to blame.'

'I should hate to lose Dr Bellman. I really would. She has such a unique and promising mind. You, on the other hand, Professor, have already done your best work. And singularly failed in your responsibility to manage your junior colleague.' He turned to Bellman. 'Let this be a lesson to you.' He nodded to the two men who had been standing silently at the door.

In an instant they had hoisted Professor Kennedy from his chair and were marching him to the door.

'No! What are you doing?' Bellman said. 'Please, don't hurt him. He's got a family —'

The single gunshot silenced her protest. She heard the sound of a body slumping in the anteroom to the office, followed by the grunts of the two men as they hoisted it from the floor and carried it from the building.

'Next time there will be no chance to explain yourself, Dr Bellman. We will shoot you in your sleep.' Razia gave a dismissive wave of his hand. 'Please remove yourself from my sight.'

54

They returned to camp shortly after midday. Black let the others eat and brew coffee before laying out his plan of attack. It was simple and direct: create maximum chaos and confusion and move unseen among it. The risks were considerable but no higher, he assured them, than those on many other similar operations he and Finn had nailed, like the time they rescued five British and US hostages from an al-Shabaab enclosure in the Somali desert, leaving more than one hundred dead and as many wounded.

He was expecting resistance but Riley and Fallon listened with the impassive yet resolute expressions of men about to take their fight to the enemy. When he had finished talking, he looked into their eyes for signs of doubt. They stared straight back at him with almost unnerving calm.

'Are we agreed?'

They nodded.

Then Fallon smiled, breaking the sombre mood. 'What did you expect, boss? It's not like we signed up for the Girl Guides.'

They laughed harder than the joke deserved.

They agreed to make their move at midnight when the Sabre mercenaries would be at their most tired and ineffectual. The early afternoon was spent checking and preparing kit. Everything they needed would be carried in four webbing pouches worn across their bodies: ammunition, grenades, plastic explosives and detonators, goggles, radios and GPS units. Before launching their assault, they would make their way around to the south of the camp and stow their packs and machetes at a position set back from the road half a mile out from the gates. This would also serve as their default rendezvous point. If all went as they hoped, they would be making their escape driving the only functioning vehicle remaining in the compound. If not, they would be forced to improvise. In combat, spontaneity and instinct were every bit as important as meticulous preparation.

From four o'clock onwards they rested. Black took the first watch and was relieved by Riley two hours later.

Six hours to go.

Black lay silent in his hammock as darkness fell. Several feet behind him, separated by a thicket of bamboo, Fallon lay in his own hammock breathing with the slow and steady rhythm of a man who had fallen deeply asleep. When the last of the light had vanished, Black pulled on his goggles and scanned the surrounding area. He saw Riley standing ten yards away, facing out, composed and still. For a moment Black doubted himself. Was he imagining things? Had Finn's death cast him into a state of irrationality and paranoia? Perhaps Freddy Towers had had nothing to do with the transfer of a genocidal criminal in his custody into the hands of a private army? Perhaps it had been a freak, unfortunate coincidence that Towers had arranged for Finn to act as bodyguard for Dr Sarah Bellman only to be killed by the same people he had fled from months before?

He turned the possibilities over and over in his mind and each time came back to the same conclusion: the only coincidence, if it could be called that, was that Kathleen had turned to him to identify Finn's body. For Towers it had proved an unbelievable stroke of luck, a gift that he had grasped with both hands.

There was another explanation, of course, offered in the words of the young Classics student, Sam Wright, who had spoken to him in the hours before Kathleen's phone call: *Events unfold only because they're heading towards an inevitable conclusion.*

Black thought of the bullets he had dodged, the explosions he had avoided by seconds, the two dozen times he should have returned home in a box. By any objective measure he had far outlived anything that chance could explain. He was the flipped coin that had come to rest on its edge.

It was a consolation of sorts. If his fate was sealed and his destiny set, nothing barring the collapse of the eternal laws of the universe would alter the fact.

Keep going and take what comes.

Try to survive.

It was all he knew.

He slipped silently from his hammock.

Black watched from dense cover twenty yards out from their camp as Riley made his way back towards Fallon. It was a minute before eight. Even at this short distance the beat of the jungle night drowned out the sound of his footsteps and the brief exchange of words between the two men. Through his goggles Black watched Fallon climb out from his hammock and reach for his own goggles and rifle only to find that neither were where he had left them. He said something to Riley, who turned, his body language betraying alarm.

Black spoke into the headset mic of the intercom stowed in his webbing. His voice was transmitted to Riley's unit, which Black had placed in the undergrowth next to Fallon's hammock.

'Listen up.' He watched both of them turn to the source of his voice. 'Do exactly as I say or I shoot, understood? Stay where you are. Chris, take off your goggles, drop your rifle. I won't tell you twice.'

Black waited. Riley stiffened but did as he was told. The

two of them were now standing by Fallon's hammock, staring out blindly into the night.

'Pistols on the deck.'

This time there was a longer pause as they weighed the risks, then decided to comply.

'Thank you. I apologize for the circumstances of this conversation, but I'm afraid I've no choice. These are the rules: lie to me and I shoot, tell the truth and you live.' He watched them straining to see through the darkness, hoping against hope they could locate him and scatter. But there was only the faintest moonlight. Barely enough to see a hand at arm's length.

'Ed. You first. You'll answer clearly, directly and fully. Understood?'

'Boss.'

'State the full extent of your orders from Colonel Towers.'

Fallon took a breath. A moment to collect his thoughts. 'To accompany you on the mission. To sabotage and disable the Sabre base. To eliminate as many Sabre personnel as possible, especially senior officers and staff. And if circumstances allow, to extract hostages.'

'Nothing else?'

'No, boss.'

'Why did you agree to accompany an ex-officer you had never worked with before?'

'Just obeying orders, boss.'

'I thought you volunteered.'

'We were asked, boss. You don't say no.'

'How much is Colonel Towers paying you?'

'Nothing, boss.'

'How much?'

Fallon hesitated. One second. Two.

Black lined the sights of his M&P with his forehead and fired. The suppressor reduced the noise of the shot to a click no louder than a door catch. Fallon dropped – his knees folding beneath him – and lay still.

Riley froze, his body rigid and paralysed with fear.

'You've got a wife and child at home, Chris. I'd like you to see them again. That's why I didn't want to tempt you to lie. How much is Colonel Towers paying you to be here?'

'Thirty thousand, boss.'

'In exchange for what?'

'To achieve the objectives Ed stated –' he paused to swallow – 'and to make sure you didn't come home.'

'Were you given a reason for killing me?'

'He said you were a dirty soldier, boss. That you were heading for court and would smear the Regiment.'

'Did he specify my alleged crimes?'

'He said you killed women and children. Tortured prisoners. Cut off their fingers and raped them. He said there was a dossier that the Iraqis had compiled. Your name was top of the list. He wasn't going to give them the satisfaction of putting you on trial.'

'When were you planning to kill me?'

There was a short pause.

'After the op.'

Black took a moment to weigh his options and hoped Riley was doing the same.

'OK. We have a challenge. I want you to think very carefully before you answer, Chris. Can we find a way to work together, to get the job done and both get home alive?'

'Yes, boss.'

Black pulled the trigger.

It was a lie.

Whatever. However.

It was binary.

Live or die.

55

Black dragged the two bodies away from the camp and returned to his hammock. Sleep came easily. He fell under in seconds and woke, refreshed, at midnight. He ate quickly, like an animal, raided Riley and Fallon's packs for extra ammunition and rations and moved out by twelve thirty. Navigating with the aid of his GPS unit and night-vision goggles, he plotted a course that took him west past the Sabre compound and half a mile beyond it, parallel to the access road.

He made rapid progress, feeling strong and sharp, his senses melding with the jungle, until in his bones and sinews and in every ganglion of his brain he felt a sensation like the subtle, harmonious vibrations of a plucked string.

He arrived at his destination and logged its position on his GPS unit. It was a spot fifty yards back from the road, half a mile from the compound's entrance, where a dense clump of palms provided a spot in which to conceal his pack along with his machete. All that he needed he transferred to the array of webbing pouches strapped across his chest. Armed with his rifle, pistol and Bowie knife, he set off towards the road, zig-zagging from the cover of one tree to the next, until he arrived at the edge of what turned out to be little more than a dirt track, barely wide enough for a truck to pass along it. He waited several minutes, checking both ways, before flitting across and disappearing into the forest on the far side.

Navigating by GPS, he cut back in the direction of the compound, gradually descending the gradient towards the valley floor. On arriving at the river's edge he made his way along the bank until he glimpsed the light from the pump house. The sight of it sent a shot of adrenalin coursing through his veins. He paused, took a breath and waited for his racing heart to settle before pushing on to within ten yards of his objective.

Through an opening in the leaves he saw two men sitting on chairs on either side of a small table inside the pump house. The door to the outside was open to the night with a bug screen pulled across. They were drinking cans of cola and had rested their rifles up against the wall. To the left of the building was a small area of level ground on which a Toyota pick-up, identical to those Black had observed inside the compound, was parked.

He waited, hidden from sight, watching and listening. Fifteen minutes passed, more than long enough for a man on foot patrol to walk to the compound and back. Once satisfied there was no third guard, he crept closer, the sound of the water tipping over the dam masking the sound of his approach. He sniffed the air and detected the ammonia scent of stale urine. He traced it to a thick-stemmed palm that stood no more than fifteen feet from the building's door. He tracked left, finding cover midway between the pick-up and the tree. There he crouched low, waiting for the inevitable moment when one of the two emerged.

Ten minutes later his patience was rewarded. One of the two, a tall, thin-limbed man, stepped outside without his rifle and made his way casually towards the tree, unzipping himself as he went. Black waited until he was midstream before he pounced. He drove the blade of the Bowie knife in hard to the right of the spine, at the same time cupping his left hand over the man's mouth to stifle his momentary gasp of surprise. Black pushed down hard on the knife's handle and twisted. Blood from the severed aorta gushed out of the wound and drenched his fingers as he extracted the blade and lowered the body to the ground. He quickly dried his hand on the shoulder of the dead man's shirt, his eyes fixed on the open door of the pump house. There was no movement inside.

Black sheathed his knife, picked up his rifle and walked towards the pump house. He yanked open the bug screen and stepped inside without breaking stride. The second soldier, a stocky white man with a thick neck and biceps to match, looked up from his chair with a look of alarm. He reached instinctively for his rifle and swung it by the muzzle, deflecting Black's oncoming bayonet and throwing him momentarily off balance. The soldier used the precious second of advantage to flip his weapon and come up for a shot as Black regained his footing and hurled the bayonet at his face.

Black felt the impact of steel on bone and saw the lights go out in his victim's eyes as the rifle dropped from his slackening fingers. Black yanked back on the butt of his rifle, extracting the blade from the dead man's open mouth. He caught the body as it slumped forward, grabbed the shirt collar and hauled the lifeless bulk backwards across the table so that the head was hanging over the far side. This time he wanted to keep the shirt clean. He succeeded. The blood brimming out of the wound spilled out of the corpse's mouth and over its stubbled scalp to the floor.

Black stripped the dead man of his Sabre fatigues and swapped them for his own. They were a size too large and stank of sweat but they would have to do. He turned his attention to the pumps, currently idle, that filled the water tank and supplied the separation plant. He found the master stopcocks and closed them, then isolated the incoming power supply and ripped out the cables. There would be no more water to the compound.

Behind the door he found the keys to the pick-up hanging from a hook. He took them and went down to the water's edge, where he took his time meticulously washing his face and arms clean of blood and scrubbing the stubborn camouflage cream from his face and neck. Once clean, he approached the truck, stowed his goggles, webbing and weapons in the passenger footwell and started the engine. Before pulling away, he flicked on the interior light, placed a sand-coloured Sabre beret on his head and checked his reflection in the mirror. Aside from four days' growth of beard, he looked almost respectable. The whites of his eyes shone back at him with arctic brilliance.

The four-wheel-drive Toyota took the steep, rutted track that led up the side of the valley to the compound in its stride. Black drove slowly, wanting the sentries at the gate to hear only an unhurried, routine sound. The track snaked to the right, turned through 180 degrees and joined the main road leading to the compound's entrance. Remaining in second gear, Black approached the floodlit area in front of the sentry post and came to a stop. There were two men inside the small, insect-proof guard hut and two TV screens, each relaying multiple images from the perimeter security cameras. One of the two sentries stepped out, peered through the glare of the headlights and caught sight of Black's hand as he gave a friendly wave. He reached for a switch and the barrier rose. Black drove through unchallenged. He glanced in the mirror and saw the sentry step back inside.

As he had anticipated, getting inside the compound was the easy part.

Black followed the road a short distance, then took the left fork towards the area where the storage and plant sheds and fuel tanks were housed. Shielded from the sentry post by the bund protecting the fuel tanks, he pulled up alongside the other pick-ups, switched off the headlights and killed the engine. He climbed out, pocketed the keys and pulled on his night-vision goggles, pleased to hear the reassuringly loud chug of the diesel generator. He scanned the surrounding area and confirmed that the security cameras were trained along the line of the perimeter fence. He had a view the length of the camp and detected no sign of movement. Nevertheless, he was aware from what he had observed in the early hours of the previous day that somewhere a pair of guards would be patrolling. Counting the two sentries at the gate, that meant four men to be avoided.

There was an art to sabotage. It was more than merely causing damage, it was doing so in a way that caused maximum panic, bewilderment and terror. SAS recruits spent weeks studying the discipline but it had always come naturally to Black: running through his plans for slaughter and destruction he felt entirely at ease, like a painter preparing his palette.

Satisfied that he had settled on a running order, he placed the goggles back in the pick-up and put on his beret. He strapped on his shoulder holster and webbing, left his rifle in the cab and locked it.

There was no going back.

Black walked calmly through the shadows towards the centre of the semicircular earth bund, which enclosed two above-ground tanks. The area in front of them was concreted and two large fuel pumps were set against a retaining wall. There was a diesel pump similar to one found on any filling station forecourt and a second, larger one, which pumped aviation fuel through a hose reel to the heli which stood twenty yards off to the right. A storm drain covered by metal grating ran through the centre of the concrete apron and connected with a network of similar drains criss-crossing the compound, all of which conjoined to empty into the drainage ditch that separated the inhabited area from the mine.

Black lifted the grating and took the diesel pump from its holster. He inserted the nozzle into the storm drain, pulled the trigger and clicked the catch that held it in the *on* position. The pump's motor whirred into life at a higher pitch than the generator but after a few seconds the initially discordant notes seemed to blend into a single sound. He replaced the grating so that the weight of it held the nozzle in position. The diesel poured into the drain, giving off only a light odour, many times less powerful than petrol or the even higher-octane aviation fuel, which made it the arsonist's perfect choice.

Leaving the pump to do its work, Black moved on to stage two. He returned to the row of pick-ups and ducked down low beneath the windows of the furthest vehicle. He opened the driver's door, removed the keys that the mine workers had left in the ignition, tossed them away, then pressed the tip of his Bowie knife into each of the tyres in turn. Air hissed from the slits and the truck sank until the wheels were resting on their rims. He moved to the next truck, then the next, repeating the procedure until only the vehicle he had driven from the pump house remained in a usable condition.

Now they could no longer be driven, it just left the problem of the pair of heavy machine guns mounted on two of them. The weapons themselves were unloaded but their ammunition belts were stored in metal boxes which were firmly bolted to the pick-up beds. The only way to disable them was to destroy the whole vehicle. He unclipped a jerrycan from the rear of one of the trucks and carried it to the diesel pump. He lifted the nozzle from the drain, filled the can, then replaced it again before lugging the full can back and emptying the contents through the vehicles' open windows.

Retreating to the shadows at the side of the bund, he took a large lump of yellow Semtex from his webbing pouches and divided it into five separate portions: two of approximately two pounds each, and three of roughly half that size. Into each of them he pressed a detonator the size of a large rifle round. These contained battery-activated explosive charges which he had programmed to ignite when he simultaneously pressed the two red buttons on the phone-sized control unit.

He replaced the bombs in his pouches, double-checked to ensure that the control unit was switched to *off* and moved out.

There was no other route to the heli other than across a stretch of open ground and no way to approach it other than by acting as if he had every right. He strolled across the scrubby grass to the helipad, looking out for the two patrolling guards and arrived at the Puma's hull without being seen. It was a big, solid hulk of metal that seemed far too large and heavy to be capable of flight. Adding to its bulk was armour plating strong enough to repel machine-gun fire from the ground. It would have been a grave error to fix a pound of explosive to its hull and expect to ground it. Even two pounds of Semtex, incorrectly positioned, would cause little more than a slight dent in the bodywork.

Black ducked under the mid-section to the starboard side of the machine, where he was hidden from view. He tried the doors. They were locked. There was nothing for it but to climb. He put his right foot on the mounting step, reached up to the casing above the door which housed the external winch unit, placed his right foot on the door handle and scrambled on top of the winch, grabbing the lip of the wide exhaust port above to steady himself. He was now within touching distance of the main rotor mechanism and engine air intakes. It was a toss-up, but he chose to attack the potentially more vulnerable rotor rather than the engines. He pressed a pound of explosive in around the main shaft, moulding it like plasticine, hoping the shock waves would be enough to blow apart the bearings and render it immobile.

He dropped to the ground, more noisily than he would have liked, and walked back towards the cover of the bunds, resisting the urge to hurry and make himself conspicuous. His progress had been good but he was on borrowed time: the smell of diesel was starting to spread through the humid air.

Time to up the pace.

Black pulled out the second one-pound lump of Semtex and pressed it against the side of the aviation fuel tank. He took hold of the hose and ran it across to the nearest building – a rectangular box of reinforced concrete – which, he had deduced, was the armoury. He set the nozzle down on the ground close to its steel-plated door, returned to the pump and pressed the button that switched it on. The second pump struck a louder, more conspicuous note than the first. Black hesitated for a moment over whether to kill it, but decided to risk it.

The overpowering smell of evaporating aviation fuel reached his nostrils. His carefully plotted curve of risk was rapidly getting steeper. Soon it would be close to vertical.

He gave himself three minutes.

A taunting voice told him they might be his last.

56

Black pressed hard against the side of the building covered with satellite dishes, which he had termed the admin block, and peered around its edge. He could see them on the opposite side of the road that ran through the centre of the compound: two soldiers walking past the entrance to the double-width barrack house towards the parade ground. They were moving smartly towards the block on its far side where the hostages were held, rifles strapped tightly over their shoulders, taking their duties more seriously than the pair he had observed from a distance the previous morning. Black caught the pungent smell of diesel. It had reached the central drainage channels and was making its way steadily across the camp towards the ditch on the far side. When the two guards looped around the building and came back they would smell it and head straight to the tanks.

It was now or never.

Black darted out from cover and crossed the road, alternating his gaze between the two men walking away from him to his left and the sentry box at the gate, which stood fifty yards away in the opposite direction. He trod lightly and made it across unheard and unseen. On the far side he disappeared between the two adjacent buildings, one of which was the mess hall and the other accommodation for the mine workers. When he reached their far end, he turned right and crossed a short stretch of bare ground that separated them from the larger, wider, barrack block.

Ducking low, he jogged to the centre of the building, where

he stopped at a midpoint between two of the evenly spaced windows. He pressed one of the larger lumps of Semtex into the corrugated ridges of the metal siding, then retraced his steps, making his way around the rear of the building to its far end from where he had a clear view across the parade ground. The two guards had almost made it across and were only yards from the long structure in which the hostages were quartered. Black calculated that at most he had thirty seconds while they were behind it and out of sight to plant his remaining two charges.

He waited, filling his lungs with several long, slow, deep breaths while he brought out the second two-pound bomb.

The patrolling guards turned the corner and disappeared behind the single-storey structure.

Black ran a short distance along the wall of the barracks exposed to the parade ground, jammed the explosive against it, then set off at a sprint across the open space towards the hostages' building. The seconds ticked down in his head – twelve, eleven, ten. He made it across on five, his chest heaving and his shirt wringing with sweat. Tucked tight into the shadows, he heard the voices of the two soldiers as they re-emerged from behind the building and set off back across the square. They spoke in Spanish. He couldn't understand the words but the pattern of their speech was clear: a question from one to the other, an uncertain response, a pause, then the first man spoke again as if to confirm a suspicion. They picked up their pace.

They had smelled the diesel.

The clock had run down.

Black moved quickly to the back of the building, ran along its length and turned the far corner, from where he could now see the two soldiers breaking into a run as they headed in the direction of the fuel tanks. He squashed the last remaining lump of explosive against the jamb of the building's heavy triple-locked door, then ran out from cover into the centre of the parade ground.

Now was the time.

He counted out twenty-five seconds – long enough for the guards to arrive at the fuel tanks – brought out the detonator control unit and pressed both buttons at once.

There was a one-second delay as the capacitors in the detonators charged up before firing. Black used the moment's grace to cover his ears to protect them from the shock waves. The five explosions were simultaneous and deafening. Ten thousand gallons of aviation fuel and many thousands more of diesel spontaneously ignited, lighting up the night with a billowing mushroom cloud of flame. Moments later the compound's lights flickered and died as the generator standing next to the tanks failed under the intense heat. Tongues of head-high flame ripped along the central drainage channels at lightning speed and within seconds grew into towering walls of fire.

Black ran towards the barrack block that now had a large, jagged hole in its metal side. Shouts, screams and hellish wails of agony were coming from inside. He took out a grenade, pulled the pin and tossed it through. It exploded with a violence that even outside the walls sent shock waves through his internal organs. He followed up with a second and a third, then ran the length of the building, tossing more grenades through the blown-out windows.

Like shooting fish in a barrel.

After the eighth explosion he paused to listen – the screaming had all but stopped – then threw in a ninth for good measure.

He glanced back across the parade square. There was no sign of anyone leaving the hostages' block. A flame flickered behind the window closest to the door and thick grey smoke was curling up from under the eaves.

He had a minute or two in which to escape through the chaos unnoticed. He had killed more than enough men to avenge Finn and many more besides.

And he wasn't ready to die. Especially not to please Freddy Towers.

Choose to live.

Whatever it takes.

He ran towards the perimeter fence and hidden in the darkness made his way back towards the truck. He looked left and saw dazed and disorientated figures spilling out of two of the four unharmed buildings. Some were civilian mine workers, barefoot and dressed in their underwear, and others were Sabre officers, shouting to each other through the confusion.

Black approached a scorching wall of heat as he made for his truck. Boiling waves of fire, fifty feet high, were rolling upwards from the burning fuel tanks and lashing furiously against the sky. The unearthly light illuminated the burned, inert bodies of two men lying with their limbs jutting at obscene angles. Close to where they lay, the armoury building was invisible behind a white-hot wall of burning aviation fuel. Over to his right, the heli's rotor was tilting at an almost vertical angle. The explosives had done their work: the Puma was a dead hunk of metal with mocking flames reflected in its windshield. He sprinted for the pick-up, his lungs burning on every breath. The furiously hot handle scalded his fingers as he unlocked the door and threw himself inside. Shielded momentarily from the infernal heat, he reached for the ignition. The engine burst into life.

He stamped on the clutch and rammed the stick into first. Then as he made to press hard on the throttle, he was seized by a sudden paralysis, like ice-cold hands around his throat. He should be aiming straight for the gates and the road to Platanal. Mission accomplished. Sabre was degraded. A triple strike from Predator drones couldn't have inflicted more damage. As if to emphasize the point, the two pick-ups mounted with heavy machine guns erupted into flame as the evaporated diesel inside their cabs spontaneously ignited.

Something was holding him back.

What would Finn have done?

An image flashed before Black's eyes: his old comrade running through flames and a hail of bullets into a burning, bombed-out house. Black outside providing cover, down to his last magazine, waiting for the lights to go out – *stupid bastard!* – when Finn lumbered through the smoke, face black with soot and a kid under each arm.

Go! Go! Go! The big man's voice sounded in his head as clearly as if he were sitting next to him.

Black's foot hit the floor. He accelerated across the rough ground, heading for the perimeter fence, where he swung the wheel to the right and gunned down the outer flank of the compound past the blown-out barrack house. He snatched a glance to his right and saw that the people who had spilled out of the buildings were mostly gathered in the road on either side of the flaming drainage channels, responding to their instinct to shelter from the unknown that lay in the darkness beyond the fence.

He sped across the parade ground and careered around to the rear of the building on the far side, dirt and stones rattling the underside of the truck as he skidded to a stop. He grabbed his rifle and jumped out.

He was met with the sound of several desperate voices and in the dim light the sight of hands beating against the barred windows. He ran to the doorway and found the door blown off its hinges. A dead Sabre mercenary was sprawled on the concrete floor inside the entrance, his left arm blown clean off his mangled torso, which lay in a foul pool of liquid. The interior of the building beyond was filled with thick, toxic smoke that was circling down from burning ceiling panels.

A prison-style steel gate separated the entrance from the rest of the building beyond. From the little light cast by the flames Black gained the impression of a long corridor with locked doors either side that were being pummelled from the inside. He stooped to unhook a bunch of four keys from the guard's belt, shook them off and tried several in the lock of the gate. The voices from within called out in desperation. People running for their lives did so in silence; the trapped and dying screamed until their last breath.

He turned the key as he heard the first spray of gunfire coming from somewhere in the midst of the compound. Panicked men firing at phantoms, he hoped. The smoke in the corridor was thick and choking and stung his eyes so that they streamed. Holding his breath, Black went to the first door and attempted to find the key to fit the lock. He tried two without success, his lungs screaming out in pain. Giving up on the keys, he stepped back, raised his knee and stamped hard against the door. It held fast. Solid timber with heavy-duty locks and concrete frames. No match for a boot.

Coughing and retching, Black ran back to the entrance and grabbed a lungful of air. He heard voices and glanced right to see three armed figures running towards the building across the parade ground. One of them raised a rifle. Black stepped back as he loosed off a burst of fire. Shots bounced off the masonry and spattered the ground outside the door. Black poked the barrel of his AK-47 around the jamb and let off a burst of his own. He glanced out and fired again, this time accurately, sweeping low and cutting the three down.

They fell. He fired again at their horizontal bodies, then raised his gaze to the road beyond and saw more figures running in his direction through the flames.

The odds had narrowed. He had seconds. The element of choice was gone. Now it was a numbers game.

He ducked back inside and yelled at the top of his lungs. 'Everybody down.'

No one heard. Their cries grew louder.

He ripped open the Velcro flap of his webbing and reached out two of his remaining eight grenades. He pulled the pins and threw them through the smoke into the black pit of the corridor beyond. Two seconds. He brought out two more, pulled the pins and threw them with less force. He ran for the door and dived to the ground outside, as four evenly spaced explosions ricocheted along the corridor, the shock waves bursting open doors.

Black scrambled to his feet. A haggard, wild-eyed figure emerged, coughing and half blind through the thick haze.

'Outside! Turn left! On to the truck!'

He ran back into the corridor and ducked through the first door to his right. The smoke-filled room beyond was the source of the unearthly screams. He made out the outline of several large cages. Monkeys the size of small children were rattling the bars.

Too bad.

'Everybody down.'

Two more grenades, then another. He threw them around the door and along the corridor, then swung back behind the frame, covering his ears as four more explosions rocked the building on its foundations.

The monkeys fell silent.

Another bewildered figure emerged from the smoke and dust: a young man Black recognized from a photograph he had seen at Credenhill. It was Sphyris, the computer genius who had modelled the human brain.

'Sarah Bellman. Where is she?' Black shouted.

'At the end. On the right.'

'Outside. On the truck.'

Black plunged into the wall of smoke. Burning, molten gobs of tile dripped down from above, speckling the floor with flames. He made it to the end of the corridor, his chest bursting with the effort of holding his breath. The door on the right had failed to blow.

Multiple rapid bursts of gunfire sounded outside the building.

There was no way out.

Black had no breath left to shout with. He raised his rifle and aimed the muzzle down at the lock at an angle close to vertical. He fired, the recoil causing the weapon to bounce crazily in his hands. Spent, red-hot cases sprayed out of the breach. Fifteen rounds ripped through the thick timber. Black stepped back and kicked hard. The weakened door split down its length and swung open.

A female figure was cowering face down in the far corner of the room. She was dressed in shorts and a T-shirt and had a towel over her head. Her body was still. She was either in shock or unconscious. Either way, it didn't matter.

Gunshots ripped down the corridor and ricocheted off the walls. They were at the entrance to the building.

Fish in a barrel.

Suffocating fish in a burning barrel.

Black grabbed the young woman by the ankles and dragged her back towards the door. She kicked out, resisting him.

He couldn't speak. His lungs were on fire. He felt himself swoon, as if he might collapse and choke to death with her.

There was no air to breathe. Nothing. He reached out a hand to steady himself, feeling his knees start to give way beneath him. He staggered. Pinpricks of white light danced in front of his eyes.

He was dying.

57

From somewhere deep in the core of his being Black felt a surge of energy, like erupting lava spewing out from his core.

The death rush.

He reached for his rifle and emptied the rest of the magazine into the breeze-block wall beneath the window. Fragments of exploding concrete flew around the room like shrapnel. He fetched another magazine, locked, loaded and fired. More stinging shards hurtled in all directions. Black ran at the wall with his bayonet and thrust repeatedly. The shattered breeze blocks crumbled. He punched out a hole two blocks wide, stepped back, reloaded and fired again, blowing the two blocks above it to smithereens. He kicked with the heel of his boot. Kicked for his life. The two shattered blocks crumbled away and with his last ounce of strength he kicked out the two above.

He dropped to his hands, stuck his head to the hole and gasped like a man who had sprinted a mile. More gunshots rang out behind him. There were voices: an order to advance.

Black's hand went unconsciously to his webbing where his fingers closed around his final grenade. He pulled the pin, stepped over Bellman and tossed it along the corridor, following up with a sharp burst of fire.

He turned, grabbed Bellman's now limp body and was feeding it head first through the opening in the wall when the grenade blew. There were no more gunshots. He clambered out after her, rifle first. He lay inert and insensible for a moment as his lungs returned oxygen to his starving brain. The stars swimming in front of his eyes cleared and he became aware that Bellman was lying next to him, coughing her guts out. And ten yards to his right Sphyris was struggling to lift the body of his wounded companion on to the truck.

Black hauled himself to his feet, seized his rifle and rammed in his last magazine.

'Leave him! Fetch her!' he shouted to Sphyris, and ran past the pick-up to the corner of the building.

He poked his head around the edge. Two injured men were lying either side of the door, one of them struggling to his knees and reaching for his rifle. Black put him down with a single shot only to spot three armed figures hurling themselves to the ground on the far side of the parade ground. He took aim, fired a sweeping burst, then ran back to the truck as another flurry of fire rattled through the air behind him.

Sphyris had hauled Bellman on to the Toyota's tailgate and was still struggling to raise the other casualty – a hefty, middle-aged man – from the ground. He was conscious but bleeding freely from an ugly wound in the left side of the stomach and groaning in a way only the dying can. He had been shot through the liver. It was only a matter of time.

'It's Dr Holst,' Sphyris said.

'Get in the cab.' Black drew his pistol. 'You're driving.'

Sphyris looked at the gun in Black's hand and ran to the driver's door.

Black glanced down at Holst and made an executive decision. Two rounds between the eyes. In the army they had called it 'offing'.

Holst's lips moved as if in a plea.

Black delivered the mercy shots.

It was a kindness.

He ran to the cab and shouted through the door. 'Straight

422

down the road and out of the gate, fast as you can. Don't stop for anything. I'll be up top.'

Sphyris shook his head as if it were beyond his powers.

'Do it!'

Black jumped on to the pick-up bed and ordered Bellman to stay down. She pressed herself on to the metal floor. He slapped the roof of the cab. Sphyris started the engine and lurched forward.

'Faster! Like you fucking mean it!'

Sphyris stepped on the throttle and aimed towards the end of the building where he turned sharp right. Black set his AK to single shot to save ammo and fired off single rounds in rapid succession – pop-pop-pop – as the truck's wheels bumped over the bodies of the dead hostages. He could see one active shooter and two bodies on the far side of the parade ground. He ducked as a flurry of rounds screamed over his head.

'Faster!'

Pop-pop. Two more shots. The truck was closing in on the shooter, who scrambled to his feet to avoid being run down. Black recognized him as one of the officers he had spotted during their recce. Black took aim as well as he could from the moving truck and caught him in the thigh. He fell on all fours and tried to drag himself along by his hands.

'Over him.'

Sphyris swerved to the right. The injured man raised his hand in a hopeless attempt to ward off the oncoming vehicle. Black felt the moment of his death as the broken parts of his body thudded against the undercarriage.

'Faster!'

The truck cleared the parade ground and gunned along the road through flames, scattering the few who hadn't already fled for cover. All along one verge were the injured and bloody survivors who had dragged themselves out of the barracks. The lame and dismembered. A vision from hell.

They closed on the gate. From the corner of his eye Black caught sight of two figures running for cover between buildings. He swung round to take aim but was a fraction late. They had disappeared from view. He swung his attention back to the sentry post. The single remaining man on guard took aim. This time Black was on point: three shots, three hits. The target jerked, flailed and fell, leaving the way ahead clear.

They sped through the gate and out of the other side into the dark embrace of the jungle.

Black turned to Bellman, who had welded herself to the truck floor. 'We're out. You're OK. You're going to be OK.' He called through to Sphyris. 'Keep going till I tell you to stop.'

Sphyris switched up into fourth gear. The headlights lit up a clear road ahead.

Peace. The cool air licked through Black's hair. He leaned back against the cab and felt a surge of elation.

He had done it.

The bullet caught him beneath the left collarbone. For a second it felt like nothing, then came a sharp pain like a stab from a hot poker. Almost at the same moment the truck bounced over a rut, throwing Black off balance. He reached out for a handhold but the momentum had carried him too far. He pitched over the edge and landed heavily on his back in the scrub at the edge of the road.

The last he saw of the truck were two red tail lights fading into the night.

Black lay winded and gasping, feeling blood dribble from somewhere to the right of his shoulder into the crook of his armpit. His whole body was trembling as intensely as if he had been plunged into icy water. It was as much as he could do to snatch tiny gulps of air. He listened for footsteps, waiting for whoever had shot him to arrive and deliver the coup de grâce.

Seconds passed. No one came. But it didn't mean they wouldn't. It meant they wouldn't come alone and without the ability to see. His own goggles were still in the pick-up. He was as good as blind.

Little by little, the ring of steel around his chest loosened, until at last he could force out his ribs and fill his lungs again like a skin diver returning from the depths. The trembling subsided. He rolled on to his side and, clenching his jaw against the tearing pain, reached his right hand over his left shoulder to feel for an exit wound. There was none. The bullet was still lodged in his body – a small mercy. A rifle round would have blown his shoulder apart and bled him to death. The slug must have come from a pistol. A lucky shot at distance.

The officers had pistols. He had seen them during his observations. Brennan and Drecker had been wearing side-arms on their belts. An image of Brennan formed in his mind and froze in vivid profile: tall, lean and cadaverous. Then he realized the reason why. Brennan had been one of the two figures he had glimpsed vanishing between buildings as the truck had sped towards the exit. Long spider-like legs and a thin neck jutting out at an angle from sharp-bladed shoulders. And the one behind him: shorter, but quick and agile like a rat.

Black locked his left arm tight against his side, rocked over on to his right elbow, drew up his knees and managed to kneel. He paused for breath, then forced himself to his feet. His head swam but his legs held steady. He glanced back at the sentry post that stood a little over a hundred yards away. It was lit up by the flames still billowing from the fuel tanks. The body of the dead sentry lay across the roadway, and, from beyond it, came the sounds of panic and confusion. He groped in his webbing and found the single self-adhesive field dressing he had brought. He tore the wrapper with his teeth and reached under his shirt to press it to the raw flesh.

A series of sudden explosions issued from the compound. They came one after another with increasing frequency until they climaxed in a single earth-shaking boom that echoed off the sides of the valley. A jet of flame shot high into the sky above the compound. The armoury had gone up. Tens of thousands of rounds of ammunition as well as mortars, RPGs and explosives. Black watched an inverted avalanche of burning gases spiral upwards and extinguish into nothingness. Despite the pain, he smiled. Finn couldn't have done it any better.

His moment of satisfaction was short-lived. Two figures armed with rifles and night-vision goggles approached the sentry post. Black tossed the wrapper from the dressing into the road and stepped back into the trees.

The only light he could muster was the dim glow cast by the screen of his GPS unit. He held it like a candle out in front of him and staggered into the jungle. The ground was soft and muddy. There was no way to proceed without leaving a trail of deep footprints. He increased his pace in the hope of finding firmer going but encountered only thicker and thicker clumps of palm and tangled webs of vine and creeper. He thrashed and barged his way through them. Several minutes had passed since he had left the road. They wouldn't be far behind. Finally, his boots hit solid ground. He pushed on quickly, stumbling over roots and fighting the stabbing pain in his chest that felt as if it might tear him open on every breath. He covered thirty yards, then came to a halt. He reached under his shirt, peeled off the blood-soaked dressing and placed it on the ground. Then he struck left for another ten paces. With his visibility limited to no more than a few feet he couldn't afford to be choosy.

Through the gloom he made out a thick, grizzled tree trunk. He stepped behind it, switched off his GPS and drew his pistol.

He waited in the near pitch darkness. Slowly, by tiny degrees, his eyes adjusted as best a human's could to the minimal light. Solid objects became dark shadow against a vaguely lighter backcloth, but the moment he strained to discern their detail they bled into one another again. Without eyes and with his ears filled with the sound of cicadas he was forced back on his animal sense.

It told him they were drawing closer.

Further minutes passed. He imagined them picking their way, step by step, drawn deeper into the bush against their better instincts by an irresistible need to kill and dismember him. They would be angry and excitable. Emotions that led to quick and bad decisions. It was all he had in his favour.

The first indication of their approach was an almost imperceptible crawling of the skin at the back of his neck that spread down his spine and slowly out along his arms to the tips of his fingers. Black held this sensation in his body, as if by maintaining the wavelength he might detect subtle movements beyond the range of his lesser senses. He was rewarded soon after with the sound of a foot landing gently on damp leaves.

The footsteps grew louder. He strained his ears and made out two sets. He willed them closer, picturing them sweeping the ground through their goggles, then alighting on the strange object on the forest floor. They would come to inspect it. They wouldn't be able to resist. And that would be his moment. His best shot.

The anticipation was electric. Black felt its erotic drug seep into his blood and dissolve away his pain.

Kill or be killed.

What could be simpler?

The footsteps stopped.

Whispered voices.

They had seen it.

Now they would be scanning, searching for signs.

Black drew in a slow, deep breath, kissed his pistol to his forehead and stepped out. He let go six rapid shots sweeping left to right, covering an angle of thirty degrees. There was a high-pitched cry and a lower grunt. Two bodies hit the ground as they fell or dived for cover. Black ducked back behind the tree. A long burst of rifle fire cut through the air off to his right. The shooter had misread his position.

Silence.

And then a moan.

A female. She was hit. Irma Stein. The woman they called Susan Drecker. It had to be.

Black stepped out and loosed off another two shots.

Mistake.

The shooter fired back, running straight at him, screaming like a demon. Pieces of bark exploded off the trunk, stinging Black's body and face. He poked a hand around the outside and let off another shot, his eighth. He had only one round left.

The shooter pitched forward and hit the ground to his right. Black holstered his pistol, drew his Bowie knife and threw himself at the dark shadow on the ground. His target rolled. Black's blade hit the dirt.

A fist slammed into Black's temple. A shock of stars exploded in front of his eyes. He lost his grip on the knife and was knocked sideways, landing on his back. A wiry body squirmed over him, clamping a single hand over his throat. It was Brennan. The bitter, acid odour of his sweat filled Black's nostrils.

Black lashed out with his right hand and ripped the goggles from Brennan's head. The fingers tightened, digging into the flesh either side of his neck, searching for the jugular. Black forced his shoulders tight up against his jaw, balled his fist and punched Brennan's bullet of a head. The fingers dug and twisted. Black punched again, then again, and with each blow he heard the sound of more air sucking and gurgling into a punctured lung. Brennan had taken a shot in the chest.

Black punched once more, smashing the cartilage of Brennan's nose. An angry, strangled cry escaped the other man's mouth but his grip refused to slacken. Black felt his windpipe slowly collapsing and the strength draining from his limbs. He tried to raise his left arm but it was a useless appendage at his side. He groped with his right hand to find Brennan's throat, but was outreached, his fingertips barely grazing Brennan's bloody chin.

Black felt the paralysis creeping through his body as his life receded to its last vital parts. Brennan coughed with the effort of strangling him. His regurgitated blood spewed over Black's face and into his mouth and spurred him into a dying rage. He thrust his hand at Brennan's chest and found the weeping bullet hole. He jammed the ends of his fingers into the open wound and twisted them left and right, forcing his knuckles between the ribs and driving for the heart. He felt its pulse just beyond his fingertips. Brennan let out a scream. His fingers spasmed and slackened for a split second in which Black drew a breath and thrust harder until he was wrist-deep in Brennan's chest. He clasped his fist around the hot, beating muscle and squeezed the life from it.

Brennan's body jerked and twitched. Black ripped his fingers from the open wound and swept Brennan's hand from around his neck. Brennan slumped, blood flooding from his chest and spilling over Black's body. Black threw him off in disgust and scrambled free on to his knees. He groped in the darkness and found the tip of his blade. He reached for the handle and closed his fingers around it. He turned and heard Brennan drowning in his own gore. He decided to show him mercy he didn't deserve. He sheathed his knife and drew his pistol. He aimed at the source of the sounds and fired.

Silence.

He replaced the pistol and reached out again with the sensitized tips of his fingers, sweeping in wider and wider arcs until they brushed the strap of Brennan's goggles. He put them on and saw the dead man's body lying four feet in front of him. He was spread-eagled on his front, his right cheek pressed to the ground. His deep-set eyes were wide open either side of an exit wound the size of a fist. A short distance away, lying on her back, was a female figure, who was pumping blood from wounds to her legs and upper chest. An AK lay at her side and she wore a pistol on her belt. Black picked up Brennan's rifle and approached cautiously.

Her eyes were obscured by her goggles. She appeared to be playing dead but the rise and fall of her chest betrayed her. Black saw her problem: a bullet had entered a fraction beneath her collarbone as she had turned at the sound of his shots. It had travelled through her body and most probably hit her spine.

He poked the muzzle of the rifle under her goggles and flipped them off.

It was Stein.

She stared up into the face of the man she couldn't see. There were many questions he would like to have asked her but she was way beyond speech.

Black stroked the rifle along her cheek and brought the tip of the muzzle gently to rest on her forehead.

'Your choice. Yes or no?'

Her breathing quickened.

He waited.

Eventually, she tilted her chin a fraction.

The thought of killing her turned his stomach, but so did the thought of leaving her to the creatures of the night.

He squeezed the trigger.

It was done. He unfastened her belt and, using his knife, cut a strip from the leg of her combat trousers. He folded the fabric into a thick pad, pressed it against his wound and wrapped the belt twice over his shoulder and under his armpit, before pulling it tight to hold the makeshift dressing in place.

He retrieved his GPS, intending to plot a course through the jungle, but familiar words sounded once again in his head: *events unfold only because they're heading towards an inevitable conclusion.*

The job wasn't finished.

Black made his way on foot towards the compound's entrance. As he drew closer the flames still burning from the fuel tanks and along the drainage channels illuminated a scene of carnage that outdid anything he had ever witnessed. The ground was littered with bodies, limbs and entrails. Anyone within a hundred yards of the exploding armoury had been torn apart and hurled in a thousand directions by the force of the blast. All the buildings this side of the parade ground had been flattened.

He made his way past the blown-out sentry post, stepped over the maimed body of a civilian worker and made his way along the main roadway, passing the remains of the admin block, mess hall and barracks. Here and there he spotted signs of life. The occasional disorientated figure huddled in the darkness. Mercenaries and civilians lying groaning and wounded beyond all help. Anyone capable of moving, it seemed, had fled into the jungle to take cover wherever they could.

Black pulled on his night-vision goggles and continued towards the parade ground, following an instinct that was leading him back to the building where the hostages had been housed. He passed the mangled remains of the officer they had run over in the pick-up, his features crushed into a bloody pulp and his neck snapped so that his head lay fully to the side of his shoulder like a broken puppet.

He continued on for several paces and beyond the smoking, bullet-scarred building detected a solitary figure, exhausted and limping, dragging a jerry can towards it. He moved slowly, every step a great effort. He had evidently brought the can from one of the large machines in the mine and dragged it back into the compound. Black adjusted his focus and zoomed in. His instinct had been correct. It was Ammal Razia.

Without either goggles or torch Razia could see only by the light of the fires at the far end of the compound. Nevertheless, he was determined in his task, a man driven by a need that overcame pain. Black circled left and came around the back of the building. He stayed in shadow, observing Razia dragging the heavy can the last yards to its entrance. The purpose of his mission became clear when Black spotted a feature that had escaped his notice in the earlier confusion: an air-conditioning duct that emerged from the ground tight to the rear of the building.

There was a basement.

Razia dragged the can through the blown-out entrance, grunting with the exertion.

Black drew the pistol he had retrieved from Brennan's body and followed.

He came silently to the doorway. Several bodies lay on the concrete floor. Bitter, acrid smoke from the burned-out ceiling hung in the air. Beyond them, to the left, Razia was unlocking a door. He hauled it open. Through his goggles Black saw that beyond it there were stairs going down, but Razia made no effort to descend. He stooped to unscrew the lid of the can. Black took careful aim and fired a single shot into the back of his knee. Razia let out a scream of equal pain and surprise as he dropped to the floor where he squirmed and thrashed and cried out in terror as Black moved towards him.

'Dr Razia.'

Clutching his shattered joint, Razia breathed in short, terrified fits.

'Leo Black. We met in Baghdad. I had the dubious pleasure of accompanying you to Camp Cropper.'

Razia found his voice. 'Please . . . I didn't want to be here. I had no choice.'

Black scanned the interior of the room and stepped back over the bodies to the doorway. Hanging from a hook inside it was a torch. He retrieved it, lifted his goggles to his forehead and switched it on.

He was leaking blood from his wounded shoulder and losing strength. His limbs were leaden. Time and energy were running short.

He turned to Razia and trained the beam into his frightened eyes. 'Who let you go from Cropper?'

Razia shielded his eyes with a hand. 'I-I don't know –'

With his spare hand Black drew out his Bowie knife and brought the tip to the soft underside of Razia's chin. Razia flinched and recoiled.

'If your tongue's no use to you, Razia, I'll cut it out. Now try again.'

'I think it was Brennan.'

'You *think*?'

'It was him.'

'Where did he take you?'

'Into the city. Stein was there, with Daladier and others. I was traded . . . Many of us were. Sabre bought me.'

'I've watched you, Razia; you're no prisoner. You've got a stake in this enterprise.'

'No . . . No. I swear.'

'Like you swore to me that you were just a schoolteacher.' Black shone the torch into the stairwell. 'What's down there?'

Razia swallowed. 'I've got money. I can get you a million dollars. Two million.'

Black gestured with the muzzle of his pistol. 'Down the stairs. Go.'

'I can't –'

Black kicked him hard in his wounded leg. He let out a scream and in response, from somewhere in the darkness beneath them, came sounds of alarm. Human sounds without words, male and female.

'Down.'

Whimpering and sobbing Razia dragged himself on his belly down a flight of concrete steps.

Black followed him, detecting the stench of unwashed bodies mixed with disinfectant as they descended.

They arrived in a tiled room that had the oppressive feel of a laboratory. While Razia groaned at his feet, Black aimed the beam of his torch into the room's centre. Behind the bars of a steel cage the size of a prison cell, four emaciated human figures crouched on their haunches, covering their faces with their hands. They were barefoot and naked. Two males, two females. In the corner of their cage was a steel toilet bowl and a basin and in its centre a steel sphere, mounted on a pole, that rose some three feet from the ground.

Black briefly shut his eyes and looked again to ensure that what he was witnessing was real.

'Are these experimental subjects?'

Razia didn't answer.

Black shone the torch around along the margins of the

room. There were workbenches, computers, monitors, cameras, all of them rendered redundant by the lack of power.

'Please, I'm bleeding –'

'What's wrong with them? Why are they behaving this way?'

'They are not suffering . . . If anything, they are more content than they have ever been. This existence is simple and rewarding for them.'

'You believe that?'

'I do.'

Black saw that he was serious and not for the first time in his life struggled to comprehend how such an intelligent mind could be so devoid of feeling.

'And your goal is what, exactly? To programme us like machines?'

'There is no morality in knowledge . . . what can be known will be known . . . by whatever means. If not by me, then by someone else.'

'That much is true,' Black said.

A spark of hope ignited in Razia's eyes, as if he thought that at last they had found common ground.

'Where's the key?' Black said.

'Really. It's no good –'

'Where?'

The sight of the pistol trained at his forehead prompted Razia to raise a trembling finger and point to a shelf at the far end of the room.

Black retrieved it from the hook on which it hung, unlocked the cage door and stood back. The four figures inside remained hunched and squatting, refusing to move.

Black cajoled them. 'Come on. Out. Go.'

His urgings fell on deaf ears. Black realized for the first time that their eyes were all focused on the sphere in the centre of the cage.

'Why are they doing this?'

'They would rather die than leave this room,' Razia said. 'The sphere – it's all they live for.'

'Go. Get out!' Black kicked the bars, hoping to frighten them into quitting their prison, but Razia's victims recoiled and curled into themselves even more tightly.

'Even if you dragged them out, they would scream to be let back in . . . Three million dollars, Mr Black.'

Black turned the beam of light back on Razia's face. Was this what evil looked like – a pleading child in a man's body? The pathetic shells in the cage were easier to fathom than he was.

Razia blinked and cocked his head slightly as if he might yet charm his way out of his predicament.

Black had seen enough. He stooped down to grab Razia by the collar and with his remaining strength dragged him across the floor, screaming and protesting, and hauled him into the cage. He slammed the door and tossed the key into the far recesses of the room.

'Goodbye, Razia. I trust you'll be as happy as they are.'

58

They found him the following afternoon quite by accident. One of the younger boys had kicked the football far off into the trees. Isabel sent some of the older ones to look for it and made Rafael, the silent one, go with them. A short while later, Rafael came running back, breathless and frightened.

'What's the matter?' Isabel asked, not because she expected an answer but because she made it her habit to speak to him like any of the other children.

'*El hombre* . . . *el hombre está muerto.*' The man. The man is dead.

Isabel and María Luisa exchanged a look of alarm.

'Rafael? Which man?'

'*El amigo de señor Finn.*' The friend of Mr Finn.

He led them to a spot some distance down the slope beyond the far edge of the clearing. The prone figure was almost hidden in a clump of ferns. Unconscious but not dead, he was bleeding, badly dehydrated and running a high fever. Five boys, including Rafael, helped carry him back to the mission house, where Isabel made up a bed in the corner of the large and spacious room. Together with María Luisa, she sponged him with damp cloths, dressed and disinfected his wound and rigged up a saline drip which they retrieved from their emergency medical supplies.

Their efforts seemed in vain. The fever grew worse. During the early evening Black fitted, before collapsing into an even deeper torpor, from which they were certain he wouldn't recover. By the early hours his pulse was barely detectable.

The two missionaries prayed over him and commended his soul to God.

Black dreamed that he was swimming across a dark and bottomless lake with no shoreline in sight. Somehow, he knew there was a monster of unspeakable size and horror lurking far beneath its surface. He was caught between an instinct to lie still and float in the hope of becoming invisible and an equal urge to swim as fast as he could away from danger.

Night was falling.

Live or die.

He swam for his life.

He saw the outline of what he took to be a spit of shingle and made for it, only to find himself among a clutter of debris that frustrated his progress. At first he took the obstructions for pieces of wood and a sign that they must have drifted out from a human settlement on nearby land, but then he realized that they were the bloated, drowned bodies of men. And the harder he swam, the more he encountered, until there were so many bobbing corpses pressing in on him from every side that he could make no progress in any direction.

And then he felt a stirring beneath his bare feet and the sense of something vast and cold coiling upwards towards him from the bottomless depths.

He opened his mouth to scream and it flooded with freezing water.

Black woke with a violent shudder. The startled eyes of a boy stared back at him.

'¡Está vivo! ¡Está vivo!' He's alive! He's alive!

The boy ran away, calling out the same words over and over.

Black blinked, still partially trapped in his nightmare, unsure if he was awake, asleep, alive or dead. His mind searched for anchors in this unknown place. He was beneath a roof thatched with palm leaves, in a room with walls made from rough-hewn planks. At the far end was a table covered with a blue cloth, a wooden crucifix sitting in its centre. Bright sunlight flooded through an open window behind it. He became aware of voices – children's voices – and of the smell of cooking.

Children . . . The mission.

A wave of relief swept through his body. And as he realized where he was, fractured images of his agonizing slog through the jungle returned to him.

A woman wiping her hands on her apron hurried through the door and came to his bedside. It was Isabel. She crossed herself and picked up a water bottle with a drinking spout like an outsized child's beaker.

'Mr Black. You're awake.' She seemed astounded, as if she had witnessed a miracle. 'How are you feeling? Does your shoulder hurt?'

'A little.'

'You need to drink.'

She bent over him and lifted the spout to his lips. He drank deeply. Mouthful after hungry mouthful. When he could drink no more, he saw that the boy had reappeared and was standing at Isabel's side holding a long wooden object. It was a bat. A cricket bat carved from a single piece of wood, with a flat front and curved back. He held it up for Black to see, as if searching for his approval.

'Your friend made it for him,' Isabel said. 'Actually, they made it together.'

'Señor Finn,' Rafael said.

Black smiled.

The boy smiled uncertainly back at him.

'It was Rafael who found you. You were very lucky. You

would have died otherwise. Maybe when you're feeling better, you can play with him.'

'Yes. Tell him I'd like that.'

'*Cuando se siente mejor, Rafael.*' When he's better, Rafael. She turned to Black. 'You must be hungry.' She didn't wait for an answer. 'I'll get you some breakfast.'

She bustled out as quickly as she had entered.

Black eased his legs over the edge of the bed and tried to sit up. A tearing pain in his shoulder forced him back on to the pillow. Rafael put down the bat and extended his hands in an offer to help. His expression was so eager that Black couldn't refuse him.

'*Gracias.*'

The boy hooked his hands under Black's good shoulder and helped him up.

Black planted his feet on the floor and caught his breath.

'*Bueno,*' the boy said, screwing up his nose and taking a step backwards.

'Oh . . . I see. I stink.' Black sniffed an armpit. 'My God, I do.' He waved a hand in front of his face, mimicking Rafael's pained expression.

The boy laughed like it was the funniest thing he had ever seen. And Black laughed with him. They laughed until tears streamed down their cheeks.

Six days of convalescence, followed by eight more trekking across the Brazilian border to the Mucajaí River, where he traded his pistol for a canoe, gave Black all the time he needed to think through the events that had begun with Kathleen Finn's phone call. He paddled for four more days and made his way, ragged and unshaven, into the small provincial city of Boa Vista with few doubts left in his mind. It brought a peace of sorts. Mostly it allowed him to make peace with himself, to move beyond anger and accept that he must have been acting for reasons of his own. Reasons he hadn't dared form into words.

Such are the forces that drive us. Unconscious. Unknowable. Overwhelming.

He roamed like a tramp along the broad, straight boulevards until eventually he chanced on a street market where he found a trader willing to exchange his GPS unit for a mobile phone and a few reals, the local currency. He made for a cheap café and filled his empty belly with steak, beans and cold beer. Sated, he sat back in his chair, smoked a cigarette and listened to the old men gossip as they played cards.

It was a fine afternoon to be alive.

59

The city sat beneath a pall of cloud and fine drizzle. Typical British August weather. Black stared out from the shuttle bus from Heathrow Airport at the familiar sights of west London. The office buildings alongside the elevated section of the M4 motorway and the slate roofs of a multitude of terraced houses spreading out in all directions combined, as they always did in the mind of the returning traveller, to create a sense of deflation at the dullness of it all. Excitement and unpredictability belonged on foreign shores, this drab vista seemed to say. This was a land where orderly lives were lived quietly, behind closed doors.

Black was at once depressed and vaguely comforted by the scene. Part of him longed to melt anonymously into the grey suburban streets.

The bus rumbled on through Hammersmith to Cromwell Road and finally to Knightsbridge where he disembarked with nothing but a nylon rucksack and the cheap set of clothes – picked up from a Brazilian market stall – that he was wearing. He headed north on foot, angling west across Hyde Park and Kensington Gardens to emerge at Queensway. Here he made his way along the parade of tatty souvenir shops and restaurants and found a café that provided assorted services to tourists, including passport photographs, cheap international calls and internet time. He handed over five pounds for an hour at a well-used terminal, brought out the notebook he had filled during the long flight across the Pacific and began to type.

His statement ran to five full pages. When he had finished he emailed a copy to his solicitor, which he followed up with a call from one of the café's payphones. The bewildered man at the other end of the line was Ian Watkin, a lawyer who occupied a small office in the Welsh border town of Hay-on-Wye and whose work seldom strayed beyond the settling of wills and the buying and selling of properties in the surrounding countryside. Nevertheless, he knew Black's history and represented many other past and present members of the Regiment.

Watkin took careful notes and in an anxious voice read them back: 'I am to forward your statement immediately to as many of the following as I am able to contact: the Director, Special Forces, the Chair of the Joint Intelligence Committee, the Permanent Secretary to the Ministry of Defence, and the Clerk to the International Criminal Court. And if anything should happen to you, I am to publish the statement online and alert all media outlets.'

'Correct.'

'I'll do my best . . . If you don't mind my asking, are you in trouble, Leo?'

'I'll let you know later. How are Jane and the girls?'

'Very well, thank you.'

'Glad to hear it. Speak soon.'

Black glanced over the banister from the floor above and saw Towers step out of the lift. He made his way noiselessly down the carpeted stairs and along the short length of corridor. Towers was turning the key in the lock when the sound of approaching footsteps caused him to glance to his right. A momentary look of alarm crossed his face and just as quickly vanished again.

'Leo! How the devil are you?'

'Not too bad, all things considered.'

'Excellent. Ha. I wondered what had become of you. Thought you'd gone native.' He hesitated, holding the door partially open as if uncertain whether to go inside.

'I could murder a cup of tea,' Black said.

'Of course.'

Towers entered the flat. Black followed.

They passed through the short hallway and into the sitting room, Towers shrugging off his jacket as they went.

'I keep getting calls from some Russian drunk who claims we owe him a pension.'

'That would be Buganov. Our pilot.'

'Well, I told him he can buggerov.' Towers laughed and hung the jacket over a chair. 'Been back long?'

'Flew in this morning. Alone, I'm afraid.'

'Oh. I am sorry to hear that . . . What happened?'

'Not entirely sure. It was very confused. You know how it is.'

'Of course. I did manage to see some satellite images of the aftermath . . . Well, at least you're back in one piece.'

'Any news of Colonel Silva or Cordero?'

'None at all, I'm afraid.' He smiled regretfully. 'But, overall, I think you can count your efforts a success.'

Black nodded. 'Any chance of that brew?'

'Coming up. Make yourself at home.'

Towers bustled through to the kitchen. Black listened to him filling the kettle and slid open the drawer beneath his desk.

'You'll be glad to know that Drs Bellman and Sphyris are extremely grateful for your assistance,' Towers called through. 'And they've been most helpful. Most helpful indeed.'

'We were separated.'

'So they said. They called the Embassy from the airstrip at

Platanal. We sent in a plane from Guyana to pick them up. A few cuts and bruises, nothing major . . . They thought you were shot.'

'Caught a round in the shoulder. A kind missionary helped me fish it out.'

'Well, they were most apologetic for leaving you. Apparently they didn't have much choice.'

'Apologies accepted.'

Towers returned with two mugs of tea and handed one to Black. 'There we are. Just like mother made it.'

'Thank you.' Black took a seat on the sofa while Towers perched on the hard-backed chair at his desk.

They looked at each other in silence. Finally, Towers shook his head with an expression somewhere between exasperation and relief. 'I don't know what to say, Leo. I admit, I feared the worst.'

'No such luck.'

'I should have known better. It's a shame about Holst but, in any event, I hear his work is rapidly being replicated by others.'

'I'm sure.'

Towers became suddenly earnest. He started to speak at high speed as if desperate to unload his thoughts as rapidly as possible. 'This is dangerous technology and we need to be abreast of it. I've spent the last three days debriefing Bellman and Sphyris at a safe house and what they've had to say is chilling. Holst had perfected a neurochemical reaction powerful enough to overcome the human survival instinct itself. Bellman suspects Sabre had been bankrolling him for several years. He planned to use her research to industrialize the means of delivery and Sphyris was supposed to model future applications. The aim was to programme human behaviour, just like you'd programme a damn computer.'

Black observed Towers' eyes lose their focus as he was swept up in the intensity of his monologue. 'Bellman's nano-particles would have delivered Holst's chemicals to neurons isolated by Sphyris. Things minute enough to be absorbed through the pores of your skin. It could have been applied to almost any product or ideology you care to mention. Imagine, Leo – opening a packet of washing powder, swiping the screen of a new phone or going to a political meeting and being delivered a dopamine hit powerful enough to ensure your lifelong loyalty. And then there are the military and industrial applications: soldiers and workers unwittingly pro-grammed to operate like machines. Can you even begin to comprehend? That much power in the hands of an outfit like that?' He paused and smiled. 'The Committee are delighted, by the way. Over the moon.'

'Do we have control of this technology now?'

'Rest assured, Leo. Rest assured.'

'And Mathis and Daladier?'

'Already in detention. The only question is whether they're extradited here or whether our American friends find grounds to indict them in the US. Either way, a suitably dis-mal future awaits. Good news on Pirot, too, and the young woman we suspect helped hook Bellman in the George V. The French picked them up attempting to board a flight to Cayenne. They're currently in the tender embrace of the Directorate General for External Security in Paris.'

Black took a cautious sip of tea that was predictably foul. He had never known Towers make it any other way. It was oddly reassuring. Further confirmation of who he was dealing with: a man incapable of appreciating the experience of others.

'I can only thank you, Leo.' Towers tapped his fingers abstractedly on the desk. 'I suppose now might be an appro-priate moment for us both to turn the page ... We've delivered all that was asked of us. I think we can consider ourselves home free.'

Black was briefly tempted by the idea to get up and walk away. To leave it all behind and let Towers be quietly put out to grass. But there was another voice aside from his demanding to be heard.

He gave it voice. 'Finn trusted you, Freddy . . . So did I.'

Towers looked at him quizzically.

'How much did you make – from selling Razia to Sabre?'

Black waited, watching his mind whirring and calculating, searching for an exit that no longer existed.

'Was it just him or were there others?'

'Are you all right, Leo? You look a little pale –'

'It takes its toll – killing and remaining sane.'

Towers' eyes flitted towards the door.

Black held him in his gaze. 'I've made a statement. It's gone to the Committee and the International Criminal Court. I've copied you in. I'll be happy to testify against you.'

Silence.

'You wouldn't –'

'It would be my pleasure. You were going to have me killed, Freddy, just as you arranged for Finn to be murdered. You served him up to Sabre on a silver platter. We were the witnesses who could have put you behind bars. The ones who could have exposed you as the grubbiest of dealers in human misery. Would you like me to spell out for you exactly what Razia was doing?'

'I didn't intend any of this, Leo. It was a mistake. A single moment of weakness in a long career. You've known me long enough to –'

Towers stopped mid-sentence as his eyes fell to the Glock that Black had drawn from his pocket.

'You should lock that desk of yours. Or maybe part of

you wanted me to find it . . . ? The court or a bullet. What's it to be?'

They were disturbed by the shrill ring of Towers' phone. Black motioned him to answer.

Towers picked it up and glanced at the screen. The remaining colour bled from his face. He braced himself and answered. 'Duncan, hello. What can I do for you . . . ? No, I wasn't aware of that . . . Really . . . ? Yes, well, let me have a read and I'll get back to you directly. Of course.' He rang off and lowered the phone slowly to the desk.

Black waited, the gun trained at Towers' head.

'Would you mind if I took a moment?'

'Be my guest.'

Towers stood up from his chair and crossed to the French doors that opened on to the balcony. He stepped outside, pulled the doors behind him and turned his face to the cooling breeze. He stood perfectly still for a short while, then glanced in at Black and placed a hand on the railing.

Black looked away and studied a mark on the wall while he counted to ten. When he looked back Freddy was gone.

The bastard had left as he had lived.

On his own terms.

60

The college clock struck ten. Black looked up and rolled his aching neck. After twelve hours of rewriting and proofreading, the words had started to swim in front of his eyes. Only two more pages and he would have reached the end. Three straight days handcuffed to his desk and he had finally wrestled his paper into something approaching order. He forced himself back to the task.

He had made it only to the end of the first paragraph when there was a knock at the door. He ignored it. The caller knocked again. Black continued to pretend he hadn't heard. Whoever it was seemed to give up. He refocused on a troublesome sentence with too many subclauses and attempted to rephrase it.

A tap at the window behind the drawn blind prevented him.

'Leo? I know you're there. I can see you. You've been there since seven this morning when I went out for a run. But you didn't see me, did you? Just like you haven't seen anyone or anything since you came back. I could have left you alone but I thought perhaps you ought to make contact with another human being for the sake of your mental health . . . Oh, and I've got wine. Decent stuff. Eight pounds a bottle decent . . . Leo?'

He opened the door to see Karen wearing a damp anorak, clutching a bottle of Rioja.

'Got caught in the rain,' she said, as if any explanation were needed. 'I think summer gave up the ghost this year.' She smiled, waiting for a cue that didn't come. 'Can I come in?'

'Of course –'

He stepped aside, aware that he had been staring at her like an idiot, and helped her off with her coat.

'Sure you don't mind?'

'It's good to see you. I was about to call it a night anyway.'

'It feels like ages. Six weeks?'

'Seven. My fault. I've been hunkered down in the country, then holed up in here.'

He brought her inside and realized that every surface, including the chairs, sofa and much of the floor, was littered with papers. 'Sorry. It's got a bit out of hand.' He started to clear a space, feeling suddenly clumsy and self-conscious.

'Corkscrew?'

'In the kitchen.'

She went through to the back while Black hurried around the room gathering up bunches of handwritten notes.

'God, Leo. When did you last wash up?' Her voice travelled along the short connecting passageway.

'I've been preoccupied.'

'These dishes are going to get up by themselves and crawl away if you leave them any longer.'

'I wish they would.'

There were sounds of rummaging and a tap running and moments later she reappeared armed with a corkscrew and two clean glasses. She surveyed the heroic levels of mess from the doorway with a look of pity.

'Finished the paper yet?'

'Give or take the odd comma. I'm supposed to be delivering it in three days' time.'

'I suppose you're excused, then.' She smiled and pushed her hair back from her face. Her cheeks were flushed from running through the rain. Or perhaps they had pinked in embarrassment? Black couldn't tell. 'Leo, I owe you an apology – for how we left things. Or didn't.'

'I've forgotten all about it,' he lied.

'I haven't. I was short with you. I had no reason to be. I know what happened to me wasn't your fault. I was scared, that's all.'

He nodded, wishing he could tell her the truth. 'How are things?'

'Getting better. Joel's even started to be reasonable. Our lawyers are due to meet to discuss a settlement.'

'Good news.'

'More like a miracle.' She handed him the corkscrew and held up the glasses.

He drew the cork and filled them.

'I did try to call but your phone was never on.'

Black sensed that this was less an observation than a question.

'Patchy signal.' The outright lie caused him a painful stab of guilt. He took a large mouthful of wine.

Karen seemed to sense his discomfort. Black suspected that she saw straight through him. She nodded to the sofa. 'May I?'

'Of course.'

They sat at opposite ends, nervous of invading the other's space.

'Were you working hard the whole time?'

'Did my best.'

'I'd get lonely spending that much time by myself.'

'Guess I'm used to it.'

He glanced away. The deception and half-truths that used to be second nature were demanding an effort he could no longer maintain.

'You never did let me read anything you've written. The

offer's still open. For what it's worth I'd be happy to give you my opinion.'

'Thank you. I just need to work a few things out first . . . And how about you? Have you been busy?'

'Only with the usual. Running my experiments, doing battle with the bureaucrats. We'll get there in the end. One interesting thing happened, though –' She met his gaze and held it. 'Sarah Bellman – the missing biologist – she turned up. About a week ago. No official explanation, so of course the rumours have been flying around like crazy.'

Black gave a non-committal shrug.

'You haven't heard anything?'

'No.'

Karen held his gaze. 'The reason I ask is because all the fellows had a message from the Provost. About you. Apparently the leaks and rumours have been confirmed as malicious. You had an exemplary military record and were decorated numerous times. A shining example to us all.'

Black glanced down at his feet. 'My former CO. He was indignant on my behalf. Wanted to set the record straight.'

'Leo, you disappeared all summer and came back twenty pounds lighter with a suntan you couldn't get on a Welsh hillside if you were staked to the ground from May to October.' Still she stared into his eyes and wouldn't let them go. 'I'm going to ask you again. Who are you, Leo Black?'

'I suppose . . . I'm just a man who's trying to move on.'

'And can you?'

A strange and unexpected feeling stirred inside him, as if her question had roused some delicate and previously undiscovered emotion. 'I intend to try.'

She nodded, seemingly satisfied that she had at last glimpsed into his soul.

She placed a hand on top of his.

Their fingers meshed.

Black felt a deep warmth spread throughout his body.

'Would you like to come with me to America?' he asked.

'If you'll come with me to Canada.'

'Deal.'

Then Karen kissed him with lips like velvet.

Black waited at the side of the stage as Colonel McIvor delivered a glowing introduction to the three hundred delegates assembled in the lecture hall; they were about to hear from the former soldier reputedly responsible for neutralizing and capturing more enemy insurgents in Iraq and Afghanistan than any other. In the audience there were four-star generals, admirals and diplomats from thirty-five countries, along with assorted senior officials from the US State Department, the UK Foreign Office, NATO, and the governments of France, Russia, Turkey and China. And mingled in among them were some of the biggest hitters in the academic field of international relations and security. They had all come to the Third International Symposium on Military Strategic Planning at West Point, New York, to hear what their friends and enemies were thinking, with the sole aim of gaining an advantage, the slightest edge that might advance their respective country's position in the world.

The Colonel led the applause as Black climbed the steps to the stage. Approaching the lectern, he felt like a junior infantryman caught in the open under enemy fire. He looked up at the imposing bank of braided uniforms and picked out Karen's face at the end of a row. She smiled and gave him a thumbs up. He was certain he couldn't have done this without her.

He looked down at his notes. It was his moment to speak truth to power but his tongue sat like a dry stone in his mouth.

He read and reread his opening remarks feeling as if the floor might give way beneath his feet. An expectant hush descended, one that became an increasingly uncomfortable and protracted silence as Black wrestled with his conscience and came to a dreadful realization.

He had got it wrong.

But what to say?

He had to tell them something.

He cleared his throat. 'Ladies and gentlemen . . . I was going to begin my address to you with these words –' he paused to swallow, then forced himself on – '"*I am a soldier who as a result of long and regrettable experience has largely ceased to believe in the ability of war to deliver peace*" . . . Looking at those remarks now, I'm afraid I realize that I was being too much of an idealist, trying to escape my own nature perhaps, or at least part of it.' He paused again and looked up from the lectern, deciding to abandon his text altogether. It felt like a millstone that was pulling him under. 'I fear I was writing what I wanted to believe – that inside every man of war there lies a far better man of peace. But more truthful and very different words might be those attributed to George Orwell: *People sleep peaceably in their beds at night only because rough men stand ready to do violence on their behalf.* I have been one of those rough men. One who in a long career perfected the art of killing – whoever, whenever I was told. People like me have always existed and will probably need to exist so long as human beings walk this earth. But we must never abandon the hope that this need not be so.

'So my opening message to you should perhaps be this: each one of us in this room is, at least in part, a savage intent on domination who also happens to be capable of love for his fellow man or of being transported by a Beethoven symphony. And for every educated, civilized one of us who denies this fact, somewhere there is a young soldier who can barely write his name, defending our ideals and our delusions equally, at the end of a rifle. Life, my friends, is something that is fought for, and killing to preserve the best of it is an ugly but a necessary business. Acknowledge this horror that lies at the heart of our very existence, accept both the good and the evil in our nature, and we have taken the first step on a long path to truth.'

The room was silent.

They were listening.

He was on his way.

While Black's audience was rising in applause, Kathleen Finn was driving home from a half-day shift at the hospital, which in reality meant six hours straight without a break. It was good to be back among friends and colleagues but it was hard, exhausting work and meant the kids spending all day in the school's summer club. They had managed, just. In a week's time the autumn term would be underway and they stood a chance of getting into a steady routine. Normality was what they needed most. Predictability, regular meals on the table and plenty of time with her in the evenings to share their worries.

It was tough doing everything alone, but it wasn't as if she hadn't got used to it as an army wife. She'd cope. The kids were all that mattered. They were young enough to recover and move on. They'd remember the good bits of their dad and gradually the pain would fade. She'd dig in until Sarah-Jane was eighteen and then see what life had left to offer her.

She arrived home with fifteen minutes to spare before she would have to dash out again for pick-up. Just enough time to shower, change and get her head straight. Coming through the front door, she found a letter on the mat. She stooped to collect it and noticed the Oxford postmark. Inside was a photograph of her grinning husband standing next to a skinny teenage boy who was proudly holding up a cricket bat. They were in a small jungle village with young children and animals milling in the background. In a short accompanying note Leo Black wrote that it had been given to him in Venezuela and that he would come to see her the following week when he was back from the USA to explain.

Kathleen didn't cry. Once you started down that road you would never stop. She tucked the picture back into the envelope and took it through to the kitchen. She would put it away for now, along with Ryan's other things, and bring it out again when she was ready.

Acknowledgements

Leo Black was originally a character conceived for television. I pitched a version of his story a few times and was met with the smiles and rejections that us screenwriters never get used to. But had I somehow smuggled him through to production, I have no doubt he would have emerged as a neutered and tamed or at least as a troubled and conflicted version of his true self. When you talk to the men and now women who have served in the Special Forces you soon become aware that they are a race apart: people who switch from combat to tucking up their children at night without missing a beat. They're also intelligent, civilized, measured and unassuming. People with nothing to prove and sure of their place in the world. Now that's interesting.

So, thank you to the executives who said no. For once, you were right. Leo Black belongs in print.

Far greater thanks are due to Rowland White, my very patient editor at Penguin, and to Ariel Pakier for all her input on the story. Thanks also to my agent, Zoe Waldie; my wife, Patricia, for her incisive observations; and to Tony for giving me so much valuable inside information.